AN
AMISH
PICNIC

ALSO BY THE AUTHORS

A Kauffman Amish Bakery YA Story
Reckless Heart

Story Collections
Amish Sweethearts
Seasons of an Amish Garden

Stories
A Plain and Simple Christmas
Naomi's Gift included in *An Amish Christmas Gift*
A Spoonful of Love included in *An Amish Kitchen*
Love Birds included in *An Amish Market*
Love and Buggy Rides included in *An Amish Harvest*
Summer Storms included in *An Amish Summer*
The Christmas Cat included in *An Amish Christmas Love*
Home Sweet Home included in *An Amish Winter*
A Son for Always included in *An Amish Spring*
A Legacy of Love included in *An Amish Heirloom*
No Place Like Home included in *An Amish Homecoming*
Their True Home included in *An Amish Reunion*
Cookies and Cheer included in *An Amish Christmas Bakery*

Nonfiction
The Gift of Love

Roadside Assistance YA Series
Roadside Assistance
Destination Unknown
Miles from Nowhere

• KATHLEEN FULLER •

The Amish Brides of Birch Creek Novels
The Teacher's Bride
The Farmer's Bride
The Innkeeper's Bride

The Amish Letters Novels
Written in Love
The Promise of a Letter
Words from the Heart

The Amish of Birch Creek Novels
A Reluctant Bride
An Unbroken Heart
A Love Made New

The Middlefield Amish Novels
A Faith of Her Own

The Middlefield Family Novels
Treasuring Emma
Faithful to Laura
Letters to Katie

The Hearts of Middlefield Novels
A Man of His Word
An Honest Love
A Hand to Hold

Story Collection
An Amish Family
Amish Generations (available June 2020)

Stories

A Miracle for Miriam included in *An Amish Christmas*
A Place of His Own included in *An Amish Gathering*
What the Heart Sees included in *An Amish Love*
A Perfect Match included in *An Amish Wedding*
Flowers for Rachael included in *An Amish Garden*
A Gift for Anne Marie included in *An Amish Second Christmas*
A Heart Full of Love included in *An Amish Cradle*
A Bid for Love included in *An Amish Market*
A Quiet Love included in *An Amish Harvest*
Building Faith included in *An Amish Home*
Lakeside Love included in *An Amish Summer*
The Treasured Book included in *An Amish Heirloom*
What Love Built included in *An Amish Homecoming*
A Chance to Remember included in *An Amish Reunion*
Melted Hearts included in *An Amish Christmas Bakery*

• VANNETTA CHAPMAN •

The Shipshewana Amish Mystery Series

Falling to Pieces
A Perfect Square
Material Witness

The Amish Village Mystery Series

Murder Simply Brewed
Murder Tightly Knit
Murder Freshly Baked

Stories

Where Healing Blooms included in *An Amish Garden*
An Unexpected Blessing included in *An Amish Cradle*
Love in Store included in *An Amish Market*
Mischief in the Autumn Air included in *An Amish Harvest*

AN AMISH PICNIC

FOUR STORIES

AMY CLIPSTON

KELLY IRVIN

KATHLEEN FULLER

VANNETTA CHAPMAN

ZONDERVAN

An Amish Picnic

Baskets of Sunshine Copyright © 2020 by Amy Clipston
Candlelight Sweethearts Copyright © 2020 by Kelly Irvin
Reeling in Love Copyright © 2020 by Kathleen Fuller
Picnics and Prospects Copyright © 2020 by Vannetta Chapman

This title is also available as a Zondervan e-book.
This title is also available as a Zondervan audio book.

Requests for information should be addressed to:

Zondervan, *3900 Sparks Dr. SE, Grand Rapids, Michigan 49546*

ISBN 978-0-310-35788-9 (trade paper)
ISBN 978-0-310-35789-6 (e-book)
ISBN 978-0-310-36195-4 (downloadable audio)

Library of Congress Cataloging-in-Publication Data
CIP data is available upon request.

Printed in the United States of America

20 21 22 23 24 LSC 10 9 8 7 6 5 4 3 2 1

CONTENTS

GLOSSARY

ab im kopp: off in the head; crazy

ach: oh

aenti: aunt

appeditlich: delicious

bedauerlich: sad

boppli: baby/babies

brot: bread

bruder: brother

bruders: brothers

bruderskinner: nieces/nephews

bu: boy

buwe: boys

daadi/daddi: grandfather

daddi's haus: grandparents' house

daed: father

danki: thank you

dat: dad

dochder: daughter

dochdern: daughters

dummkopf: stupid

dummle: hurry

Englisch/Englischer: English or non-Amish

fra/fraa: wife

freind: friend

freinden: friends

froh: happy

gegisch: silly

geh: go

gern gschehne: you're welcome

Gmay: church district

Gott/Gotte: God

Gotte's wille: God's will

grandkinner: grandchildren

groossdaadi/grossvatter: grandpa

grossmutter: grandmother

guder daag: good-bye

gude mariye: good morning

gut: good

gut nacht: good night

haus: house

Ich liebe dich: I love you

in lieb: in love

jah: yes

kaffee/kaffi: coffee

kapp: prayer covering or cap

kichli: cookie

kichlin: cookies

kinner: children

krank: ill

kuche: cake

kuchen: cakes

kumm: come

liewe: love, a term of endearment

maed: young women, girls

maedel: young woman

mamm: mom

mammi: grandmother

mann: husband

mei: my

mudder: mother

naerfich: nervous

narrisch: crazy

nee/nein: no

nix: nothing

onkel: uncle

Ordnung: unwritten rules for Amish living

rumspringa: running-around period when a teenager turns sixteen years old

schee: pretty

schmaert: smart

schtupp: family room

schweschder/schwester: sister

schweschdere/schwesters: sisters

seltsam: weird

sohn/suh: son

was iss letz: what's wrong

Wie geht's: How do you do? or Good day!

wunderbaar/wunderbarr: wonderful

ya: yes

yer: your

yerselves: yourselves

yung: young

youngie: teen to young adult

*The German dialect spoken by the Amish is not a written language and varies depending on the location and origin of the settlement. These spellings are approximations. Most Amish children learn English after they start school. They also learn high German, which is used in their Sunday services.

BASKETS OF SUNSHINE

·

AMY CLIPSTON

With love and hugs for my super-cool sons, Zac and Matt

CHAPTER 1

· · ·

A shout sounded from the lake, followed by a thunderous splash and a burst of laughter.

Kevin Weaver raised his head at the sound, but then he took a potato chip from a bag in the center of the picnic table and ate it. He nodded at Phoebe Kurtz, who was sitting across from him. "*Danki* for inviting me to join your youth group this afternoon."

"I'm so glad you could come." Phoebe's pretty face lit up with a smile as her bright-blue eyes sparkled in the June sunlight. She popped a chip into her mouth and then lifted a bottle of cold water to her lips.

Members of Phoebe's group were scattered all around the park. Some played volleyball, others swam in the lake, and the rest sat at picnic tables, snacking and talking. As he took in all the activity, Kevin thought about how he'd hesitated when Phoebe invited him.

Last Wednesday, she'd come to his job site with lemonade for him and the rest of her father's brick mason crew. That was the first time he'd ever seen her, and she was difficult to miss with her gorgeous smile, contagious laugh, and striking, powder-blue eyes. Then she introduced herself and asked questions about the foundation they were building for the large house. He was immediately drawn to her friendliness and sweet demeanor.

When Phoebe came to the site again on Friday, she invited him to join this group for a picnic after church today, at a park convenient to both her church district and his. Wondering if she thought they might be more than friends, his first reaction was to say no. He wasn't interested in being more than friends with anyone. Not after . . .

Besides, he was too old for her. One of the other workers mentioned she was nineteen like the man's daughter was, and Kevin was twenty-four. He didn't even attend his own youth group anymore.

She was also his boss's daughter, and that could cause problems.

But then he focused on her captivating smile, and he heard himself agreeing to meet her there. Just being her friend should be okay. And if she was interested in more than friendship, she'd soon realize he was interested only in being on his own. At least until he was ready for a wife and family.

Kevin snatched another handful of chips and dropped one into his mouth just as Suzanna Byler turned to Phoebe. The two young women were sitting side by side, and Kevin gathered they were best friends.

"Hey, Pheebs." Suzanna bumped her shoulder against Phoebe's. "Are we going to swim? Or are we going to sit at this picnic table and stuff ourselves with snacks all day?"

"You can go swim." Phoebe gestured toward the lake behind them. "I'm going to talk to Kevin for a while."

"Okay." Suzanna removed the blue headscarf from her dark-brown hair. Then she jumped up and rushed to the edge of the lake, where she dove in from the short drop on the shoreline.

"So." Phoebe leaned forward and tilted her head. "How do you like working for *mei dat*?"

"I really enjoy it." Kevin bit into a cracker with cheese on top.

"Did you work for another brick mason before *mei dat* hired you?"

"No." He shifted his weight on the bench. "I worked on *mei bruder*'s dairy farm."

Phoebe's light-brown eyebrows rose as she rested her arms on the table. "What inspired you to change professions?"

Kevin rubbed his chin as he crafted his response. "I want to be more independent, not keep relying on *mei bruder*. So when my best *freind* Ben told me he heard your *dat* had an opening for an apprentice, I applied. I'm grateful he was willing to train me since I had no experience."

She seemed to study him. "Is your *dat* a dairy farmer?"

"He was before he passed away."

She tilted her head, and the sympathy in her eyes sent heat curling through his chest. "I'm so sorry you lost your *dat*."

"*Danki*. I was fourteen when he died in a traffic accident. *Mei bruder*, Dathan, is eight years older than I am, and he took over the farm. I still live there, but I already know it will go to his *sohn*."

"Oh, wow. *Mei schweschder* is seven years older than I am. Do you have your own *haus* on the farm?"

"No, I don't, but I plan to build one."

She seemed to hesitate for a moment. "Does your *mamm* live there?"

Kevin shook his head. "She died when I was four. Cancer."

"*Ach*. I'm so sorry."

"It's all right. It was a long time ago." He needed to change the subject before the sadness in her expression broke his heart. "Tell me about your family and what you do. You've had some time to visit the job site, but I assume you help your *mamm* with chores at home?"

Phoebe sat up a little taller as her smile returned. "*Ya*, I do. You know"—she counted a list on her fingers—"sewing, cooking, cleaning, laundry. All the things we women do. But I also help at *mei schweschder*'s business sometimes. She has a booth at the Bird-in-Hand market called the Bake Shop. I help her bake for it at home, and then I help her at the booth on busy days." She smiled again, and he was mesmerized for a moment.

She's your boss's dochder!

She's too young for you.

And you don't want a girlfriend. Not yet.

The voice in his head snapped him out of his reverie.

"Phoebe!"

She spun when Suzanna called her name. *"Ya?"*

"Come in!" Suzanna beckoned her as she stood on the bank of the lake, her blue, one-piece swimsuit soaked. "The water is perfect!"

Phoebe gnawed her lower lip as she turned back to Kevin. "Do you want to swim?"

"Not really." Kevin picked up another cracker. "I'll stay here and guard the snacks."

"I'll stay with you." She picked up a cookie.

"No. You go." He waved her off. "Don't sit here just because I don't want to swim."

"Are you sure? You're my guest, and I don't want to be rude."

He held up a hand. "I promise I'll be fine."

"Phoebe! Kevin!" Suzanna called again. "Come on!"

"You should go. I'll wait for you here." Kevin leaned across the table and nudged her arm.

"Okay." She stood and turned away from him before slipping off her purple dress to reveal a blue-and-white, polka-dotted, modest one-piece swimsuit with a skirt that fell to her mid-thigh.

She gave him a sheepish smile as she removed her purple headscarf and set it on the bench beside her dress. Her light-brown hair was fixed in a tight bun, and for a moment, he wondered how long her hair would be if she let it flow freely down her back. Would her locks reach her small waist? Was her hair as soft as it looked? Did it have any wave? Or was it straight?

He mentally slapped himself and forced his eyes to focus on the bag of chips instead of her.

"Let me know if you change your mind, Kevin." Phoebe gave him a nod and then hurried off to where Suzanna stood laughing with a group of their friends. Ray Fisher, whom he'd met earlier, said something to Phoebe, and she grinned. Then she stuck out her tongue and laughed before pushing him off the short drop, sending him careening into the lake.

Kevin gasped. He stood and walked closer to the water's edge as Phoebe and the rest of the group laughed. Thank goodness Ray came up splashing. The group clapped for him.

"That wasn't much of a dive, Ray!" one of the other young men teased, and they all laughed again.

"Phoebe didn't give me a chance to dive." Ray pushed his dark hair out of his eyes as he focused on Phoebe. "Why don't you jump in now?"

"Okay!" Phoebe leaped off the drop and slipped into the water with the grace of a swan.

Kevin walked back to the picnic table and sank onto the bench. He drummed his fingers on the wood top as Phoebe frolicked in the water with her friends. The urge to go home consumed him, but it would be impolite to leave without saying good-bye to her. He didn't want to hurt her feelings, but he also longed to escape. He didn't belong here with these kids.

After several minutes, Phoebe returned and wrapped a large,

blue beach towel around her soaked swimsuit. "Have you changed your mind yet?" she asked.

"No, I—" Kevin's response was interrupted as Suzanna and a young man he'd heard someone call Benji approached the table.

"Hey, Phoebe!" Suzanna said. "Do we have any snacks left?"

"*Ya*." Phoebe pointed to the table as she sat down across from Kevin again and then grabbed her bottle of water.

Benji sat down beside Kevin. "Here you go, Suzanna." He grabbed a few crackers and threw them at her. "Take that!"

"What was that for?" Suzanna sat down beside Phoebe and threw a cracker at Benji.

"You don't do that to my bestie and get away with it." Phoebe laughed as she tossed a cracker at Benji too.

Soon all three were laughing as snacks flew all around the table.

Kevin dodged a flying potato chip, and his nostrils flared. Seriously, what was he doing here? He scanned the area, taking in the clusters of young men and women. Were any of them older than nineteen? If he was going to spend time with anyone, it should be with people his age, not these kids who thought it was perfectly fine to push an unsuspecting friend off a drop and into a lake. What if Ray couldn't swim or had hit his head? Would it be just as hilarious if he had started to drown?

And the food fight made their antics even more ridiculous.

The "fun" over, Benji and Suzanna sauntered back to the lake.

Phoebe looked at Kevin with a squint. "Are you okay?"

"Not really." He shook his head, frustration tingeing his response.

She seemed to wince at his harsh tone, and he felt guilty. It wasn't her fault that she was immature. She just had more growing up to do.

"Are you angry about something?" she asked.

"No." He worked to keep his tone even as he stood. "I just need to get going."

"Why?" She blinked twice. "You just barely got here."

Kevin gathered his bag containing his beach towel and a snack he would have been happy to contribute—if he were staying. "I need to help Dathan with the animals."

"Oh. Well, could I get a ride home with you in your buggy?"

Leaving early—with him? Well, why not? No matter what she had in mind, he wouldn't be spending time with her after today. They'd be friends whenever she visited her father's job site, and that was all they'd be. She'd realize that soon enough.

"Sure."

"Let me just dry off and then let Suzanna know I'm leaving." She moved the towel over her suit, pulled on her dress, and shrouded her hair with her headscarf before jogging over to the lake. Kevin watched her. When she said something to Suzanna, her friend glanced at Kevin, her brow furrowed, before responding.

Phoebe made her way back to Kevin and retrieved her bag and picnic basket. "I'm ready."

As they walked toward his buggy, a hot jolt of regret hit Kevin. Agreeing to attend this gathering today had been a mistake. He just hoped negotiating even a simple friendship with Phoebe wouldn't cause any problems with her father.

• • •

Phoebe glanced at Kevin, taking in his stiff posture as he gripped the reins. His gaze focused on the road ahead, and irritation seemed to come off him in waves, mixing with her swelling confusion.

He'd been so warm and friendly when they chatted before she went swimming in the lake. What happened to change his demeanor so drastically? Now he acted as though he were traveling alone instead of with a new friend, and the silence was suffocating. The *clip-clop* of the horse, whirr of the buggy wheels, and roar of passing cars were the only sounds she heard.

Her mind raced with questions. How was she going to find out what had broken between them? Her shoulders slumped and her brow pinched as she hugged her bag to her chest and leaned back in the seat.

Phoebe turned toward Kevin again, this time taking in his handsome profile. She'd noticed him immediately while visiting her father's job site last week. Her mother had suggested she take snacks to the men since the site was just down the street from their house. Phoebe was acquainted with most of her father's workers, but she'd never met Kevin.

Her father had hired a few *Englischers* to work for him, but most of his employees were Amish, like Kevin. He wore the traditional broadfall trousers, plain shirt, and suspenders, yet she didn't think of him as an ordinary Amish man. Something about him drew her interest, and she'd walked over to him to get a closer look.

She guessed he was in his mid-twenties, and he was clean-shaven, indicating he was single. When he stood to wipe the back of his hand over his forehead, she took in his height, guessing he was close to six feet tall. His medium-brown hair complemented his eyes, which reminded her of milk chocolate.

She couldn't explain the sudden urge to get to know him better, but she struck up a conversation with him about the foundation. Kevin was friendly and kind, and when he smiled, her heart took on wings—something she'd never felt with any of the young men she knew. It was as if Kevin had awakened something deep inside her heart.

Phoebe couldn't get him out of her thoughts after their first meeting. When she told Suzanna about him, her friend encouraged her to invite Kevin to join them at the lake. Phoebe was thrilled when he agreed to go, and she imagined a day full of fellowship and fun as they got to know each other better.

But instead, she found herself riding beside him in this heavy silence. How could their time together have gone so wrong?

But Phoebe was no quitter. She wasn't going to allow her hope of being Kevin's friend evaporate after one trip to the lake. A surge of confidence ripped through her, and she sat up straight.

"So . . . did you like *mei freinden?*"

He looked at her. "Sure."

Then he turned his gaze back toward the road, and with no further comment, he guided the horse through an intersection and onto the road that led to her home.

When they moved past the job site she'd visited, she angled her body toward him once again.

"*Was iss letz?*" she asked. "Did you not have a *gut* time today?"

"It was fine."

"Oh. Well, would you like to stay for supper?"

He looked at her again, but she couldn't decipher what she saw in his eyes. "Like I said, I need to get home to take care of the animals, but *danki* for the invitation."

"*Gern gschehne.*"

The two-story brick home where she'd been born and raised came into view. Their ride was coming to a close, and she still hadn't remedied their fallout. She needed to think fast.

"It looks like you have company." Kevin nodded toward a horse and buggy at the top of the driveway.

"Jeff must be here."

"Who's Jeff?" Kevin halted the horse by her back door.

"*Mei schweschder*'s boyfriend." Phoebe's hope deflated like a balloon as she gathered her belongings. "Well, *danki* for the ride, Kevin. I-I was ready to go home too."

"Have a *gut* night." Kevin's expression remained solemn, and discouragement settled heavily on her shoulders.

"You too." She climbed out of the buggy and started up the porch steps.

When she saw movement out of the corner of her eye, she turned toward the pasture and found *Dat* and Jeff leaning on one section of fence, talking. They met her gaze and waved, and she returned the gesture before turning toward the driveway in time to see Kevin's buggy disappear out of sight.

Was their friendship officially over? Her heart sank.

"Phoebe!"

She spun toward her sister, who was standing on the porch. "Hi, Christiana."

"How was your youth gathering?" Christiana walked down the steps, and the late afternoon sun hit the red hair peeking out from under her prayer covering. It reminded Phoebe of fire. While Phoebe had inherited their mother's coloring, Christiana had gorgeous, bright-red hair and dazzling, blue-green eyes. Phoebe had always been envious of her older sister's beauty, but she kept those thoughts to herself.

"It was okay." Phoebe hoped she seemed nonchalant as she climbed the steps.

"Just okay?" Christiana matched her pace. "You were so excited when Kevin agreed to join you today. I thought you'd be doing cart-wheels when you got home."

Phoebe swallowed an annoyed sigh. Why had she told Christiana and *Mamm* about inviting Kevin? If she had kept that information a secret, she could have avoided this conversation. At least they promised not to mention her interest to *Dat* yet. He was protective of his daughters!

"Wait." Christiana took Phoebe's arm and gently spun her to-ward her. *"Was iss letz?"*

Mamm pushed open the screen door. "I *thought* I heard a horse and buggy. You're home early." She looked beyond the porch. "Who brought you home?"

Phoebe bit back a groan. Well, at least she could tell them both at the same time so she wouldn't have to repeat her disappointing story. "Kevin did."

"Oh! Didn't you invite him to stay for supper?"

"Ya. But he declined. He said he had to get home to help with the animals."

Concern clouded *Mamm*'s pretty face. "Is something wrong?"

"Our time together didn't go as well as I'd hoped." Phoebe gave a little laugh that sounded more like a squeak. "It's no big deal." She tried to move past her mother, but she blocked the door.

Mamm's expression warmed. "What happened?"

Phoebe took a deep breath. "One minute, Kevin and I were talking, and everything was great. The next minute, he said he was ready to leave. He told me then that he had to get home to care for the animals, but he seemed upset about something. At least he gave me a ride home, but he barely said a word to me on the way. Then when I invited him to stay for supper, he used the animals as an excuse again. At least he sounded like he was making an excuse."

Mamm clucked her tongue and touched Phoebe's hand. "*Ach, mei liewe.* I'm sure you didn't do anything wrong."

"*Mamm*'s right," Christiana chimed in. "I'm sure it wasn't you. You're always so sweet and thoughtful."

"Exactly." *Mamm* smiled. "If he didn't like you, he wouldn't have showed up today."

"Maybe he just agreed because he works for *Dat* and felt obligated." Phoebe longed to erase the anguish that overcame her. Why was she so sad over a man she hardly knew?

Christiana looped her arm over Phoebe's shoulders as they all stepped from the mudroom into the kitchen. "I seriously doubt that."

"Why don't you go shower and get ready for supper?" *Mamm* gestured toward the stairs that led to her daughters' rooms.

"Okay." Phoebe nodded as she headed out of the kitchen.

Christiana caught up to her. "Wait." She stopped Phoebe at the bottom of the stairs. "Did something else happen?"

Phoebe heaved a deep sigh that seemed to bubble up from her toes. "No. I'm just so disappointed. I really like him."

Christiana's eyes brightened. "Then invite him to another youth gathering."

"I don't think he'd come, but *danki* for your optimism." Phoebe spun and started up the stairs.

Christiana's footsteps echoed behind her. "Wait! Surely we can come up with another plan."

Phoebe rolled her eyes. Why couldn't her sister just leave this alone? She longed to take a hot shower to wash away the disappointment. "I appreciate your encouragement, but I think if I invited him again, he'd turn me down, and it would make me feel worse. It's better if I just forget it. I tried, and it didn't work out."

She reached the top step and headed down the hallway to her bedroom.

Christiana marched in behind her and slammed her hands on her small hips. "When have you ever given up so easily, Phoebe?"

Phoebe pursed her lips. "Really, Christiana. I—"

"Don't you remember how Jeff and I had a huge misunderstanding when we first met?"

Phoebe sank onto her desk chair. "Of course I do."

"Jeff and I had our problems, but we worked it out. You never know. Kevin could be the one God has chosen for you." Christiana wagged a finger at Phoebe. "Give him another chance. Invite him again and see what happens."

"If I agree to do that, will you let me take a shower?"

Christiana smiled. "*Ya*—if you not only agree but promise."

"I agree, and I promise."

"*Gut.*" Christiana started for the door. "Now, don't take too long. We're having *Mamm*'s amazing chicken salad for supper."

"Christy." Phoebe called her older sister by the nickname Jeff had given her, and her sister pivoted toward her. "*Danki* for believing in me."

"That's what *schweschders* are for."

Phoebe sighed as her sister left the room. She wanted to spend more time with Kevin. She just hoped he'd give her another chance.

CHAPTER 2

Rachelle smiled as Kevin stepped into the kitchen from the mudroom. "You're home early. I wasn't expecting you before ten."

"*Onkel* Kevin!" Hannalyn, his four-year-old niece, jumped up from the table. She'd been coloring, but now she rushed over, wrapping herself around his legs with a tight hug. "I missed you." She grinned up at him. With her hazel eyes and honey-blond hair, she was the spitting image of her mother.

Kevin laughed and touched her nose. "I bet you didn't even notice I was gone."

"Of course I did! You're my favorite *onkel*!" Hannalyn giggled, and Kevin's smile widened. How he loved that sound!

"I'm your *only onkel*," he said, correcting her.

"*Onkel! Onkel!*" Tommy, Hannalyn's two-year-old brother, called from his booster seat as he waved a green crayon in the air.

"Hey, buddy." Kevin mussed Tommy's honey-blond hair as he sat down at the table. Although Tommy, like his sister, had Rachelle's hair, he was blessed with his father's dark-brown eyes.

"What's this?" Kevin rubbed his chin as he examined the haphazard green scratch marks on Tommy's paper. "Let me guess. A waterfall? A horse and buggy?"

"Nooo!" Tommy belly laughed as he swatted Kevin's arm.

Kevin snapped his fingers. "I've got it. It's a drawing of your *dat*."

Tommy laughed louder as he held the piece of paper up in the air. "No. A doggie!"

"Oh!" Kevin pointed. "I see it now." He took the paper from Tommy and turned it sideways before setting it back down on the table. "It *is* a green dog. In fact, it looks just like Spike, the neighbors' dog."

Tommy hooted, and Rachelle joined their laughter.

Hannalyn sat down beside Kevin. "You're so *gegisch*, *Onkel* Kevin."

Kevin grinned at his niece and then looked at Rachelle. "Is Dathan in the barn?"

"*Ya*. He's feeding the animals." Rachelle crossed to the refrigerator and began sifting through it.

"I'll go help him." Kevin pushed back his chair and took the snack out of his bag. After he placed it on the counter, he said to the children, "Would you please draw me a picture of the *haus* and barn?"

"*Ya!*" they responded in unison. Then they each reached for their own box of crayons. Thank goodness they wouldn't have to struggle with who got the right color crayons first.

Kevin snickered to himself as he headed for the stairs. He cherished his time with those kids. He made his way to his room on the second floor, just across the hallway from Tommy's room and beside Hannalyn's.

As he set his bag on his bed, he glanced around the space that had been his since he'd been born. His life had changed drastically over the years—especially when his mother died and then his father. But through all the grief and upheaval, Kevin's room had remained the same.

The dresser that had been a hand-me-down from his brother sat in the corner next to the desk his grandfather had given him. The shelves clogged with his favorite books stood at the far wall. And the quilt his grandmother made for him when he was ten still covered his bed.

While Kevin enjoyed the privacy and sanctuary of his room, he still longed for his own home. It would be his, all his. He'd finally be on his own, and his brother and sister-in-law would no longer feel the need to take care of his needs as though he were one of their children.

Kevin's thoughts turned to the youth gathering as he changed into his work clothes, and he pressed his lips into a frown. Why had he ever thought he and Phoebe could be good friends? Today had proved that their five-year age difference was more than just a number. His life experiences also made him feel much older than he was, including his failed relationship with Mary.

Mary.

She had never understood his need to have his own career and home before contemplating marriage. Instead, she'd broken his heart with her attitude, and he'd had no choice but to break off their relationship. The whole experience had also left him leery of dating at all. Phoebe was attractive, but if he dated her and she adopted the same attitude Mary had, he'd be hurt again.

He headed back downstairs to the kitchen. Hannalyn and Tommy were still busy drawing, and Rachelle was putting together their Sunday supper.

"How are those pictures coming along?" he asked the kids as he crossed to the mudroom.

"*Gut!*" Tommy called.

"I'm almost done with mine," Hannalyn announced.

"Great. I look forward to seeing them when I come back." Kevin sat on the bench in the mudroom and pulled on his work boots and straw hat before walking out to the horse barn. Once there, he found Dathan leaning against one of the horse stalls. Rachelle had once remarked that the family resemblance between the brothers was obvious, and sometimes Kevin realized that more than others. They both had inherited their father's dark hair and eyes as well as his six-foot height.

"I thought you were feeding the horses," Kevin told his brother. "But it looks like you're just hiding from your *fraa* in here." He ensured his teasing was evident in his eyes.

"Ha-ha," Dathan said, deadpanning. But then he grinned. "I thought you'd be at that lake well into the evening. Why are you back so soon?"

"I just decided to come home early." Kevin leaned back against the barn wall and shoved his hands into his pockets.

"Why?" Dathan lowered himself onto an overturned bucket. "A day of swimming sounds like some much-needed relaxation and fun after laying bricks all week."

"It was all right." Kevin shrugged and looked around the barn. "Have you fed all the animals?"

"I've practically raised you, Kev, so I can tell when you're avoiding a subject. What are you not telling me?"

Kevin blew out a puff of air. "I guess I'm disappointed. Phoebe isn't who I thought she was."

"What do you mean?"

"She's just, well . . ." Kevin kicked a stone with the toe of his work boot. "She just seems so immature, and so do her *freinden*. I guess I expected too much. I felt like a fish out of water today. I don't belong with that group. Phoebe is only nineteen. I think they all are."

To his surprise, Dathan guffawed. "That's only a five-year difference. You're twenty-four, not forty-four. You've been working hard, and you don't spend enough time with *freinden*. You need to get out more and meet new people, especially since you stopped going to your own youth group last year, after Mary."

Dathan hesitated before going on. "I know you don't want to spend the rest of your life as a bachelor, and you're not going to meet any *maed* if you work all day and stay home every night."

"I go to church," Kevin said, challenging him.

"It's not the same, and you know that. You don't have time to socialize at church. Give it another try. And maybe you're more ready for another girlfriend than you realize. You said Phoebe was *schee* and sweet. So what if she's younger? Rachelle is younger than I am."

"But you and Rachelle married when you were older."

"We started dating when I was about your age, and Rachelle was younger than Phoebe."

"But you had the farm. I want to be independent and on my own before I get serious with anyone again. I also thought maybe Phoebe could just be a *freind*."

"Well, you have a new job, but you don't need to be so focused on a *haus*. You have a place to live. You can build your *haus* later. In the meantime, let God lead you to the right *maedel* in his own time."

Dathan stood. "Did you come out here to help me or just talk?" He started for the door leading to the dairy barn.

As Kevin followed his brother, he let his words roll through his mind. Who was he kidding? He was attracted to Phoebe despite her apparent immaturity. But he still couldn't imagine fitting in with her group of friends. And she was still his boss's daughter. He also couldn't risk dating her if he wasn't sure she'd understand that marriage was a long way off for him.

. . .

Phoebe's heart pounded as she squared her shoulders and walked up the rock driveway toward the job site, pulling a rolling cooler. The hot, mid-morning sun beat down, warming her back as the cooler bumped along behind her.

"Would anyone like a bottle of cold water?" she announced as she approached the group of men working on the exterior of the house. She parked the cooler and pulled out the bottles, condensation dripping as she distributed them.

Dat approached her with a wide smile. "You're a blessing on this hot and humid Tuesday! The water I brought already ran out."

"Is that why I'm your favorite *dochder*?" she said, teasing him.

Dat grinned. "I didn't say you're my favorite. *Danki* for bringing these over." He took a bottle of water and walked back to several of his workers.

"Hi, Phoebe."

She spun and faced Kevin. He wore dark trousers and a dark-blue shirt that complemented his handsome face. He lifted his hat and pushed his hand through his thick, dark hair, and his tentative smile sent her senses spinning. Why did this man she hardly knew have such an effect on her—especially when he'd acted as though he didn't even like her, as though he'd changed his mind about getting to know her?

"Hi, Kevin." Her throat felt so thick she could barely say his name.

He pointed to the cooler at her feet. "You're an answer to prayer today."

"Help yourself." She fingered her black apron as he chose a bottle and then opened it and took a long drink.

23

"How are you?" he asked.

"I'm fine. You?"

"*Gut.* And grateful for water this cold." He took another drink.

Phoebe lifted her chin and reached inside herself to find some confidence. "My youth group is getting together to play games this Sunday. Would you like to join us again?"

"Ah. Well . . ." He swiped the back of his hand over his chin. "I'll have to see what *mei bruder*'s family is doing."

"Oh." She felt her smile wobble.

"But *danki* for the invitation." He pointed to the cooler. "May I have another one?"

"Take as many as you'd like."

"*Danki.*" Kevin took two more bottles and then winked at her. "I need to get back to work before your *dat* calls me a slacker. See you later."

"Bye," Phoebe called as he walked away. A heavy defeat pressed down on her shoulders. He hadn't readily accepted her invitation, but then again, he'd winked at her. Would he have done that just because she brought the water?

She distributed the remaining bottles and then returned home.

After stowing the empty cooler, she stepped into the kitchen, where the aroma of peanut butter cookies caused her stomach to gurgle with delight. Christiana had spent all day baking items to sell at her booth at the market. The oven made a hot day even hotter, but the whole house smelled heavenly. Christiana pulled a sheet of cookies out of the oven before sliding the next batch into it.

Mamm looked up from where she sat at the table packing cooled cookies in cling wrap. "How did it go with Kevin today?" *Mamm* knew about the promise she'd made.

"Fine." Phoebe moved to the sink to wash her hands.

Christiana used a spatula to slip the warm cookies onto a cooling rack. "That didn't sound like a very *froh* response. Did you invite him to the youth gathering on Sunday?"

"I did." Phoebe slipped into a seat across from *Mamm* and began pricing packages as her mother handed them to her.

"And . . ." Christiana moved to the counter to mix more batter.

"He said he'll see what his *bruder*'s family is doing." The words tasted sour in Phoebe's mouth. Wink or no wink, the more she thought about it, it was obvious Kevin didn't want to spend time with her, and there was nothing she could do about it.

Mamm's smile was as bright as the sunlight spilling through the kitchen windows. "Maybe after talking to his *bruder*, he'll let you know he's free to join you."

Phoebe kept her eyes focused on her task. "He hesitated as if he was trying to find an excuse to say no."

"Don't be so hard on yourself." Christiana tossed the words over her shoulder. "Maybe he honestly isn't certain what his *bruder* has planned for Sunday afternoon."

"I doubt it," Phoebe grumbled as she priced another package of cookies.

Mamm reached across the table and touched Phoebe's wrist, forcing her to look up. "You always go out of your way to make sure your *freinden* are *froh* and included. I've seen you walk over to someone standing alone and invite that person to join the group. It's your nature to be kind and thoughtful. I think you're imagining Kevin's hesitation."

"*Ya*, maybe you're both right." Phoebe tried her best to sound positive, but she knew deep in her heart that Kevin wasn't interested. Her efforts had been in vain.

• • •

CHAPTER 3

anki for helping me load up." Freeman set the last of the tools in the bed of his driver's pickup truck. Kevin knew the job site was close to his boss's home, of course, but the crew had too many tools and supplies to transport in a buggy.

Kevin shook his boss's extended hand. *"Gern gschehne."*

"Will your driver be here soon?" Freeman asked.

Kevin jammed his thumb toward the road. "He should be here in a while. He told me he would be late today, but that's okay. I'll see you tomorrow."

"Why don't you call and tell him to come later?"

"Why?"

"Help me unload all this at *mei haus*, and then you can join my family for supper." Although Freeman Kurtz was a few inches shorter than Kevin, with graying, light-brown hair, a matching beard, and powder-blue eyes that mirrored Phoebe's, he was an imposing man. His stern demeanor commanded respect from both his employees and his customers, but he was also fair and caring with his employees and offered them guidance and assistance when needed.

In some ways, Freeman reminded Kevin of his own father, who

had been stern but also caring and kind beneath his cool exterior. The thought tugged at Kevin's heart.

"Oh." Kevin studied his boss, a little stunned. "*Danki*, but that's not necessary. I can—"

"I insist." Freeman patted Kevin's shoulder. "My older *dochder* is home, and her boyfriend might even be there since he frequently joins us for supper. You're a *gut* worker, and I'd like my whole family to meet you. So far, you've only met Phoebe, right?" He steered Kevin toward the truck.

Why was Freeman so determined to introduce him to the rest of his family? Did this have anything to do with Phoebe? Did he *want* something to develop between them? Or did he suspect something was going on and wanted to size him up away from the job site?

When they arrived, they unloaded everything in a large barn that had been converted to a workshop. Then Kevin went into Freeman's office in the back to use the phone. He left a voice mail message for his brother, explaining he wouldn't be home for supper. Then he dialed his driver's cell phone number and told him he'd call when he needed to go home.

"You ready?" Freeman asked as Kevin stepped out of the office.

"*Ya. Danki.*" Kevin walked with Freeman out of the barn and toward the sweeping back porch of the large, two-story brick house. His heartrate ticked up when he imagined Phoebe in the kitchen. Clad in a light-blue dress that brought out the blue in her eyes, she'd looked radiant this morning.

He swallowed a groan and shoved that image out of his head. He couldn't allow himself or anyone else to think she could ever be more than a friend to him. He'd been tempted to say yes when she invited him to her next youth gathering, but then he recalled how out of place he'd felt with her friends. He'd never fit in with her or any of them. Their age and immaturity would always force a wedge between them.

"We're both dirty from working all day." Freeman gestured toward his soiled blue shirt. "We can wash up out here by the yard pump, and I can loan you a fresh shirt from my office. I always keep a couple out there."

"*Danki*," Kevin said.

After washing his hands and face by the yard pump, Kevin changed into a fresh gray shirt.

Then Kevin followed Freeman up the porch steps and into a mudroom, where they removed their hats and work boots. The aroma of beef filled his nostrils, reminding him that lunch had been nearly six hours earlier.

The three Kurtz women were scurrying around as he and Freeman entered the large kitchen. Phoebe reached into the oven while a pretty redhead placed drinking glasses on the table, set for four.

Freeman's wife set a basket of bread on the table and then turned toward them. She smiled when she saw Kevin. "Hi, there." Then she said to Freeman, "Do we have a guest tonight?"

"*Ya*," Freeman said. "Kevin, I'd like you to meet Lynn, *mei fraa*. Lynn, I invited Kevin to join us for supper."

"*Wunderbaar!*" Lynn announced as she opened a cabinet and pulled out another dinner plate.

Freeman moved to the sink to wash his hands.

The redhead approached Kevin as she wiped her hands down the front of her apron. "So, you're Kevin. I'm Christiana. I've heard quite a bit about you."

"It's nice to meet you." Kevin glanced at Phoebe, who now leaned against the kitchen counter, holding a large casserole dish.

Her cheeks were stained bright pink, and she looked adorable. "Hi, Phoebe."

"Hello." Phoebe nodded and then turned to her sister. "Would you please put the big trivet on the table?"

"*Ya.*" Christiana grinned at Phoebe as if she were having a silent conversation with her.

Phoebe's eyes rounded and then went back to normal size. Her sister set the trivet in the center of the table, and Phoebe carried the dish over and set it down.

Kevin walked to the table and peered down at the casserole. It looked like a version of beef and noodles. "That smells *appeditlich*. What is it?"

Christiana's grin widened. "It's called Yumazuti. Phoebe made it. She's a great cook."

"Not really." Phoebe shook her head and crossed the floor to the counter. She seemed embarrassed by her sister's compliment.

"She *is* a great cook," Lynn chimed in.

Phoebe shot her mother a look that seemed to ask her to be quiet. Why was she so nervous and sheepish? She'd always seemed so confident and comfortable in her own skin when they talked at the job site. She'd even been that way the day they were at the lake—until he'd clammed up without explanation. He felt sorry about that.

"Why don't you wash up, Kevin?" Freeman dried his hands with a paper towel as Kevin moved to the sink.

"I'm so glad you could join us tonight," Lynn said as she set utensils and a drinking glass by the additional place setting.

Kevin looked over his shoulder. "*Danki.*"

"Jeff isn't here tonight?" Freeman asked Christiana.

"He had to help his *dat* and *bruder* with a project at the farm. He said he might come for supper tomorrow night, though."

"Everything is ready," Lynn announced. "Let's eat."

"Kevin, you can sit by Phoebe," Christiana told him.

He grabbed a paper towel and turned toward the table, where Phoebe was glaring at her sister. Then she turned toward Kevin, and her glare melted into a tentative smile. Something was wrong, and he longed to read her thoughts. Was she upset because he was there? Maybe she caught his hesitation when she asked him to join her youth group again and wasn't too thrilled to see him. He probably should have gone home as originally planned.

Well, he didn't want to upset his boss. He would just have to make the best of it. At least supper smelled delicious.

. . .

As Phoebe sank into the chair beside Kevin, she longed to crawl under the table and hide from him.

When he'd appeared in the kitchen, she thought she was dreaming. After all, he'd hovered at the back of her thoughts ever since she'd been at the job site earlier. But it wasn't a dream. He was standing there, staring at her. And he looked just as handsome as he had then.

Now he was sitting right next to her, and she was aware that he smelled of moist earth, soap, and just a hint of sweat as his leg brushed hers when he pulled in his chair. Her heart did a strange flip-flop, and she tried in vain to ignore it.

When her father lowered his head for silent prayer, she didn't join in. Instead she looked down at her lap and tried to slow her pulse to a normal pace. But her mind raced with questions. Why had *Dat* invited Kevin for supper? Would this become a regular occurrence? But why? And if so, how would she ever grow accustomed to sitting next to him?

Her father shifted in his seat and began spooning casserole onto his plate. Then Phoebe sat up straight and took a roll from the basket before passing it to Kevin.

"Danki." His smile was warm, and her pulse jumped once again.

"So, Kevin, how do you like working as a brick mason?" *Mamm* asked.

"I like it a lot. It's been a great opportunity," Kevin responded as he buttered his roll.

"He's doing a great job," *Dat* chimed in.

Phoebe sensed someone was looking at her, and she glanced across the table at Christiana, who gave her another big grin. When would her sister stop making such a big deal about Kevin's presence? Phoebe was nervous enough without Christiana's adding fuel to the fire!

Turning her attention to the meal, Phoebe dropped a scoop of casserole onto her plate and focused on eating without making eye contact with anyone.

Mamm continued peppering Kevin with questions. "I understand your *bruder* runs a dairy farm and you live there. Is that right?"

"Ya. The farm has been in my family for a few generations. When *mei dat* died, *mei bruder* took it over. He told me I could keep working there, but he has a *sohn* to continue the business. When I heard about the apprentice position with Freeman's company, I thought it would be a good opportunity to start my own career."

Kevin shifted in his seat, and his leg brushed against Phoebe's again. She tried to breathe evenly and keep her eyes focused on her plate.

"I'm sorry you lost your *dat*," Christiana said.

"Danki. Mei bruder pretty much raised me." While Kevin

31

explained how he had lost his parents and when, Phoebe lost herself in thoughts of the youth group event on Sunday.

"Phoebe?"

"What?" Phoebe's head popped up, and she found all the eyes in the room focused on her. Her cheeks ignited as she glanced around the table. "What did you say?"

Christiana gave her a knowing smile. "Kevin said the casserole is *appeditlich*."

"Oh." Phoebe looked at Kevin, who was studying her. *"Danki."*

"Gern gschehne." His gaze lingered on her, and she felt itchy in her own skin. If only she could hear his thoughts.

Mamm spent the remainder of the meal asking Kevin about his family, and he shared stories about his niece's and nephew's antics, making everyone laugh.

At the end of the meal, Phoebe helped *Mamm* and her sister clear away the dishes. Then after they all ate some of Christiana's carrot cakes, Kevin followed her father out to the porch with coffee in hand.

Phoebe carried the dessert dishes to the sink.

"He seems nice," *Mamm* said as she wiped down the table.

Christiana set a pile of utensils on the counter. "And he's handsome. I can see why you like him."

"Shh," Phoebe hissed as she pointed to the open window that faced the porch. "He'll hear you."

Her sister waved off her worry. "They aren't paying any attention. They're probably talking about bricks."

Phoebe pressed her lips together and began filling the sink with water. Frustration tightened the muscles in her back.

"Was iss letz?" Mamm asked.

Phoebe spun to face her. "He doesn't *like* me." She worked to keep her voice low. "He sat here and had a nice meal with my family, but he doesn't think of me as a possible girlfriend. Maybe not even as a *gut freind*. I don't know why, and it's driving me *narrisch*."

"Doesn't like you?" Christiana said as she and *Mamm* shared a look. "I think he *does* like you."

Mamm nodded. "He kept looking at you during supper, and if you had looked up, you would have seen him. I think your *dat* even noticed."

"If that's true, why won't he go to another youth gathering with me?"

Mamm and Christiana shared another look, and Phoebe turned back to the sink. Hopelessness washed over her, causing her eyes to sting with threatening tears. She had a crush on a man who wasn't interested in her, and pain sliced through her soul.

No wonder it was called a "crush."

* * *

Freeman rocked back and forth in his chair beside Kevin while the cicadas serenaded them. "I think you have a *gut* future with my company. You're a quick learner and a hard worker."

"Danki." Kevin stared out toward the lush, green pasture and row of red barns behind Freeman's house and breathed in the aroma of coffee mixed with grass. Above them, the setting sun sent streaks of orange across the sky. It was a beautiful night, and his belly was full of delicious food.

Kevin smiled to himself as he swallowed the last sip of coffee in his mug. Behind him, he heard Phoebe talking with her mother and sister through an open window, but he couldn't make out what they were saying. His curiosity piqued.

Phoebe had been so quiet during supper. She'd spent most of the meal studying her plate as if it held all the answers to her worries. He longed to get her alone and ask if she was upset with him. Or maybe she was upset about something else.

But it wasn't any of his business if something was bothering her, and he couldn't help it if he'd upset her. He didn't know her well, he didn't have the right to ask her personal questions, and he couldn't risk getting involved with her. She wasn't his close friend, and she never would be.

The screen door clicked open, and Phoebe appeared on the porch.

"Phoebe! Join us." Freeman gestured toward the glider beside him.

"No, *danki*." She pointed to his coffee mug. "I'm just here to collect your mugs so we can finish up in the kitchen."

Freeman sighed. "I suppose it is time to check on the animals and then get ready for bed."

Phoebe nodded, and when her gaze met Kevin's, he felt a stirring in his chest. Something in her eyes drew him to her. What was wrong with him?

Freeman stood and handed her his mug. "I'm going to head to the barn." He turned to Kevin. "Would you like to come call your driver?"

"*Ya, danki*." But Kevin couldn't seem to make himself move, and Freeman stared at him for a moment before looking at his daughter and then back at him again.

"All right, then. Be sure to grab a lantern before you come." Freeman picked up one of the two lanterns sitting on the table between the rocking chairs and then started down the porch steps.

Kevin turned to Phoebe. "Supper was amazing."

"I'm glad you liked it." She held out her hand for the mug.

When he handed it to her, his fingers brushed hers, and an explosion of heat seared his nerves and zipped up his arm. He studied Phoebe's face to see if she'd felt it, too, but she continued to stare up at him, her expression unreadable. Yet nothing there seemed . . . immature.

"Have a *gut* night," she said, her voice soft.

"You too."

Then she turned and entered the house, the screen door clicking again behind her.

Kevin grabbed the lantern and made his way toward the barn with the phone, confusion bogging his steps. He'd never felt a spark like that with any other woman—not even Mary. The notion both thrilled and terrified him. His heart longed to get to know Phoebe better. But Freeman had looked like he was suspicious, and he couldn't afford to let his feelings be so obvious to him or to his daughter.

If only growing close to Phoebe wouldn't lead to all kinds of trouble.

The solution hit him as he walked into the barn. He would ignore his attraction to her and do his best to remain distant if she visited the job sites. That way, he wouldn't risk causing problems with his job or involvement with a woman too young for him. For now, his goal of independence had to come first.

But as simple as that solution seemed, Kevin still wondered if Phoebe had felt that spark too.

• • •

CHAPTER 4

• • •

Phoebe slipped the customer's baked goods into a bag and then handed her a few bills and a couple of coins in change. "Thank you for coming to the Bake Shop today. Please come see us again."

"Oh, I will, honey," the woman said as she slipped the money into her purse. "You have the best whoopie pies in all of Lancaster County. I'll be back before you know it."

Phoebe leaned on the counter after the woman disappeared and then turned to Christiana, who was placing a cookie sampler on a nearby shelf. "I can't believe how busy it's been, and we just opened an hour ago."

"Tomorrow is the Fourth of July, so the tourists are here in full force for the holiday weekend. I'm so glad you're here to help me." Christiana set another sampler box on the shelf.

"I am too."

Phoebe plastered a smile on her face as three *Englischer* women stepped into the booth. "Good morning. Welcome to the Bake Shop. May I help you?"

One of the women gave Phoebe a little wave. "Hi there. We heard you have fantastic cookies. Do you have oatmeal raisin and macadamia nut?"

"Absolutely. Follow me." Phoebe led her to the cookie display and helped her find what she wanted.

Soon she was back at the register, taking the customers' money and packing up their goods. She was handing the last woman her change when she heard a familiar voice. She glanced up, and her heart seemed to leap into her throat. Christiana was talking to *Dat* and Kevin, who both held coffee cups from her cousin Bethany's coffee and donut booth. It had been more than two weeks since she'd seen Kevin, and she had tried her best to convince herself she was over her attraction to him.

But now as she took in his handsome face and enticing smile, the familiar longing skittered through her.

"Miss?"

"Ya?" Phoebe looked at the customer. "I'm sorry. What did you say?"

The woman grinned and pointed to the bag in Phoebe's hand. "I asked if you would please hand me my bag."

"I'm so sorry." Phoebe handed her the bag, and then she gripped the edge of the counter with both hands as the women exited the booth. While she longed to join Christiana's conversation with *Dat* and Kevin, she also had no idea what she would say.

"Phoebe! *Kumm!*" Christiana waved her over. "I was just telling *Dat* and Kevin about the brilliant idea you had earlier."

Phoebe crossed the floor to where they all stood, another smile plastered on her face, and then nodded at Kevin.

"Wie geht's?" he asked as he smiled back.

"I'm fine. You?"

"I'm great." He held up the cup. "Your *dat* insisted I have some of Bethany's *kaffi*. He says it's the best in town, and he's right."

Dat chuckled. "Bethany won't share her secret, but it's amazing."

Kevin took a sip and nodded. "It sure is. We were on our way to our new job site after getting supplies when your *dat* decided to stop by."

"What is this brilliant idea?" *Dat* asked.

"It's nothing." Phoebe looked at her father, but she could tell Kevin's eyes were focused on her. Her nerve endings pricked under his gaze.

"No, it was great." Christiana gestured with her hands as she spoke. "We were talking about how customers ask for certain *kuchen* for birthdays or anniversaries. Phoebe suggested I start a sign-up sheet for custom *kuchen*. If I got the orders about a week or so in advance, I would have plenty of time to bake them. I could even personalize them with icing. This would really help the business, especially when we're waiting for the tourist season to start up."

Christiana looped her arm around Phoebe's shoulders. Usually Phoebe didn't mind, but today she wondered what her sister was up to.

"It's really a *wunderbaar* idea," Christiana said. "I was a little concerned about making booth rent during slow times, but this could fill in the gaps and make us more of a community destination. My little *schweschder* is a genius."

Phoebe bit her lower lip and shrugged. "Not really."

"I think that sounds fantastic," *Dat* said.

Phoebe allowed her gaze to move to Kevin's, and she found his eyebrow raised as he grinned at her. He seemed . . . impressed? But why would he care about her sister's bake shop—or any idea that came from her?

"Well, we'd better get going," *Dat* said. "Our new job site is a little bit of a drive, but I'm glad the market was on our way."

"Wait." Christiana stepped to one of the shelves and picked up a box with two apple fritters inside. "You have to try these, Kevin. They'll go great with your *kaffi*."

Kevin pulled his wallet from his back pocket. "How much?"

"Stop." Christiana waved off his offer and handed him the treat. "Just enjoy them."

"*Danki.*" Kevin took the box.

"*Gern gschehne.*" Christiana glanced at Phoebe, and her sister's devious-looking smile sent a tremor of worry through her. "Are you busy on Sunday afternoon, Kevin?"

Phoebe held her breath. What was her sister doing now?

"I'm not sure. Why?" Kevin's gaze bounced between Phoebe and Christiana.

"Phoebe's youth group is going to a park to play volleyball. It should be a lot of fun, and the weather is supposed to be perfect. They'd love to have you." Then she shared all the information he'd need.

Phoebe rubbed her temple as irritation throbbed like a bad headache. Why did Christiana have to embarrass her like this?

"I'll see if I can make it. *Danki* again for the apple fritters." His eyes moved to Phoebe once again. "It was *gut* to see you."

"You too." Phoebe said good-bye to her father and then rested her hands on her hips as she watched the two men leave. Once they were gone, she spun to face her sister. "Why did you invite Kevin to the youth gathering? Why can't you just mind your own business instead of meddling in mine?"

"Whoa!" Christiana held up her hands. "I was just trying to help."

"Don't do me any favors." Phoebe moved to the desk in the back of the booth. She stepped behind it and began arranging paperwork to keep her hands busy.

Christiana had followed, but Phoebe wouldn't look at her.

"I'm sorry," her sister said. "But you've been moping around for two weeks, ever since Kevin had supper at our *haus*. I thought I might be able to encourage him to get to know you better, at least in a group. I hate seeing you so *bedauerlich*."

Phoebe blew out a deep sigh, and then she took in her sister's caring expression. "I know you're trying to help, but he doesn't like me. If he did, he wouldn't have stayed away ever since that supper."

"I disagree. Just wait. He'll show up on Sunday, and everything will be fine. He's had two weeks to miss you."

"I don't think he's missed me at all."

"I think he has. I saw the way he looked at you just now. You shouldn't give up on him so easily. Jeff and I struggled in the beginning, but now we're going strong. If relationships were easy, we wouldn't appreciate them as much."

"That's where you're still wrong." Phoebe gestured widely as frustration simmered in her veins. "I'm tired of trying to figure out what I did or said wrong with Kevin. I deserve someone who wants to hang out with *mei freinden* and me and jumps at the opportunity to do so. Kevin's acting wishy-washy, and he keeps sending mixed signals. Sometimes he's grinning at me or winking or thanking me for something, and other times . . . nothing. So please stop pressuring me to try to make it work with someone who does that."

Her sister blinked and then nodded. "Okay." Then she turned toward the entrance of the booth as another customer entered. "Good morning! Welcome to the Bake Shop."

As Phoebe stepped from behind the desk, she wondered if Kevin might show up on Sunday. She still doubted it. But even if he did, she'd have to shield her heart from him unless he indicated any interest in developing a relationship with her.

. . .

Kevin moaned his appreciation for the delicious apple fritter as he sat in the back seat of the pickup behind Freeman. Christiana had been right; apple fritter was the perfect companion to Bethany's delicious coffee.

He smiled as his thoughts moved to Phoebe. He'd seen a different side of her today. She looked professional as she interacted with customers, and he'd been impressed by the way she contributed to the business with her idea for making Christiana's bake stand more profitable. Maybe he really had misjudged her. Maybe she was more mature than he'd assumed after what he'd seen at the picnic.

Phoebe had also looked so pretty today in a pink dress and black apron. He'd thought about her for the past two weeks, wondering how she was and if she'd stop by the job site again. As the days wore on, he realized he even missed her, but finding a way to see her was not the plan!

Then today his heart seemed to jolt a little when he saw her. Still, he couldn't tell if she'd been happy to see him. She'd barely spoken to him. She'd also seemed mortified when Christiana suggested he go to another youth group gathering—an odd invitation coming from her sister.

Maybe he'd been way off base to think Phoebe might want to be more than friends.

"Are you interested in my Phoebe?"

Kevin was startled by the question. He looked up and found Freeman had turned around to face him. Had the man read his thoughts? "Why would you ask that?"

"I just have a feeling, just like I did the night you ate supper at our *haus.*" Freeman seemed to study him. "Don't think I didn't notice you staring at her or that you seemed to want to talk to her alone before you went home. And I could tell you were happy to see her today. Just remember, she's young. I know she invited you to her youth group, but I wouldn't want you to break her heart. If you aren't interested in a girlfriend right now, in exploring a future with Phoebe, I'd prefer you stay away from her. Do you understand what I mean?"

"I understand. I don't want to jeopardize your trust. I respect you too much, Freeman."

"Gut." His boss gave him a curt nod and turned around.

Freeman began talking to their driver, and Kevin stared out his window. Freeman was right when he said he shouldn't show interest in Phoebe if he wasn't ready for a future with someone. How could he even consider marriage when he was still trying to establish the career he wanted and finance a home?

It was for the best if Phoebe wasn't interested in their getting to know each other after all.

* * *

The following afternoon, Kevin pushed a shopping cart down a Lancaster Hardware aisle in search of chicken feed. Dathan had given him a list for this run to the store, and Kevin was grateful Ben Zook had stopped by and offered to ride along with him. They were best friends.

"I'm glad my tip worked out," Ben said as he followed him. "You seem a lot happier since you started working your new job."

"I think I'm a lot more satisfied with my work." Kevin found a large bag of feed and dropped it into the cart, followed by a second bag. "I feel as if I finally have something of my own."

"Is Dathan really okay with your working for Freeman?" Ben leaned on the cart handle.

"Why wouldn't he be?" Kevin turned to face him.

"I don't know. I was worried he might want you to help him at the farm no matter what he said."

"He did want me to stay, but he understands that I need to have my own life, to not be chained to the farm. He hired a farmhand to help him until Tommy gets older."

"*Gut.*"

"Kevin?"

Kevin turned and found Ray, Phoebe's friend from her youth group, walking toward him. "Ray. *Wie geht's?*" He shook Ray's hand and then made a sweeping gesture toward Ben. "Ray Fisher, this is Ben Zook."

"Nice to meet you," Ray said as Ben shook his hand.

"How have you been?" Kevin asked. He wasn't just being polite. He still wondered about that unplanned plunge Ray had taken into the lake.

"Great. It's been super busy at *mei dat*'s construction firm. We're working on a huge *haus* in Strasburg."

"That's great. Hey, were you okay when you left the lake that day I was out there with Phoebe?"

"*Ya.* Why?" Ray's brow knitted.

"I saw Phoebe push you into the water. You came up sputtering and acted like you were okay, but I thought maybe you got hurt."

Ray chuckled. "Are you serious? One reason that swimming hole is the best place for diving is that there's nothing to hit on the way down. And it's plenty deep. Besides, Phoebe knows I'm an excellent swimmer. She was just joking around. We were having fun."

Kevin paused. Had he overreacted that day?

Ray smiled. "Did you really think I was hurt?"

Kevin swallowed as he contemplated what to say.

"You should join us tomorrow," Ray said, thankfully changing the subject. "We're going to a park to play volleyball." He looked at Ben. "You both should come." Then he gave them directions and told them about what time to be there.

"I already have plans tomorrow," Ben said. "But *danki*."

"Okay." He turned back to Kevin. "It was great seeing you again. Hopefully, I'll see you tomorrow too." Ray gave them a wave and then headed down the aisle.

Kevin considered Ray's invitation as he gathered the rest of the items on the list and then paid for them before he and Ben loaded everything into his buggy.

"Tell me the story about Ray and the swimming hole—and Phoebe," Ben said as Kevin guided the horse toward his house. "You haven't told me about any Phoebe."

"I haven't had that much to tell." He'd also had a feeling Ben would have the same advice Dathan had, and he didn't want to get into it. But he'd have to tell him the whole story now. At least he could do it on the way home and get it over with.

When Kevin was finished, he said, "Phoebe is sweet and all, but she just seemed as immature as her *freinden* that day. They even had a food fight at the picnic table."

"And that's why you don't want to go back to her youth group?"

"From your tone, it sounds like you disagree with me."

"I don't think that's a reason to avoid meeting new *freinden*." Ben seemed to be looking into his soul. "Does any of this have to do with what happened between you and Mary? You stopped coming to our youth group after you broke up with her—even though she's in a whole different district from ours—and I've never really understood why."

Kevin swallowed a groan at the mention of his ex-girlfriend's name. "You know she was pressuring me to get engaged. She didn't understand that I wanted my own career and *haus* first. After that, I just didn't see any point in going to gatherings—especially if anyone was going to pressure me to pair up with someone."

"But you need to get out more. You *can* have a little fun, you know."

"You do sound like *mei bruder*," Kevin grumbled.

"I do? Well, that's because he's right. You should go tomorrow. From what you've told me, all you do is work, work, work. You don't have to be looking for a girlfriend to enjoy yourself."

Maybe Ben and Dathan were right. Maybe he should take this opportunity to have some fun and give Phoebe's friends another chance.

"Why don't you come with me?" Kevin gave Ben a sideways glance.

"I promised my parents I would go to *mei daadi*'s *haus* tomorrow, but you'll be okay. You're a big *bu*, and Ray will be there if you get scared." Ben gave Kevin's arm a playful punch.

"Ha-ha." Kevin rolled his eyes at his friend's teasing.

"Seriously, you should go. It sounds like fun."

"Maybe I will."

What made Kevin smile, though, was the thought of seeing Phoebe again. He'd just have to make sure they were only friends, no matter how attracted he was to her.

But he couldn't be sure she'd be happy to see him.

CHAPTER 5

Sitting on her large quilt, Phoebe leaned back on her palms, and then she heaved a heavy sigh as she looked at the three make-shift volleyball courts. Members of her youth group had broken up into teams, and the others laughed and cheered for the players.

"So, Pheebs," Suzanna began, again calling her by her child-hood nickname as she sat across from her, "are you going to tell me what's wrong? Or should I try to guess?"

"What makes you think something is wrong?" Phoebe asked. It was a lost cause to fib to her best friend, but she'd give it a try anyway.

"Let's see." Suzanna rubbed her chin and then pointed at her. "You're frowning on this glorious day the Lord has given us with our *freinden*." She gestured around the park. "The sun is shining, and we're healthy. But you look like someone just told you they've canceled your birthday party. Also, it's obvious you'd rather be somewhere else. Why is that?"

Phoebe sat up and brushed a few blades of grass off her black apron. "It's not that. I'd rather be here than at home."

"Please tell me what's bothering you. I don't like seeing you this way."

46

"I just have a lot on my mind." Phoebe looked out toward the volleyball games again, trying to focus on her friends instead of the disappointment that whipped through her.

"Go ahead." Suzanna crossed her legs and scooted closer before resting her chin on her palm. "I'm listening."

Phoebe looked at her best friend's eager smile and couldn't stifle a laugh. "You're never subtle."

"You've known that since we were seven." Suzanna tilted her head. "Come on. I'm worried about you. Let me know how I can help."

"I don't think you *can* help. I'm just *bedauerlich*. Jeff came for supper last night, and I was watching him with Christiana. They're so *froh* together. I'm not jealous. I'm happy for her. Honestly, I wish her the best. I just keep wondering when I'll meet someone. Someone who will love me and want a future with me."

"I promise you will—in God's time. You just have to be patient." Suzanna's smile was warm.

"I know, but what if I missed my time?"

Suzanna's brow pinched. "What do you mean?"

Phoebe pulled at a blade of grass as her thoughts turned to her brief encounter with Kevin at her sister's market booth. "I've tried so hard not to, but I keep wondering what I did wrong with Kevin. He seemed to like me when I first met him, but now I'm exhausted by his mixed signals. I know if he doesn't like me, I should move on. But I'm, well, confused. I can't stop thinking about him, and my thoughts and feelings are a jumbled mess."

Phoebe looked up, expecting Suzanna to lecture her about letting go of her worry and giving it to God. But instead, Suzanna glanced behind Phoebe, and then her lips turned up in a smile.

"Why are you grinning?" Phoebe asked.

"I think you're going to be really *froh* in about ten seconds."

"What do you mean?"

"Phoebe," a familiar voice said behind her.

Phoebe looked up and then gasped when she found Kevin looking down at her. Was that a sheepish smile?

"Kevin?" Her throat dried. He'd accepted Christiana's invitation to come today. She could hardly believe it.

"Hi." He glanced at Suzanna and nodded. "Hi, Suzanna."

"Hi, Kevin. How nice to see you again." Suzanna's grin widened as she divided a look between Phoebe and him.

"I didn't think you were coming today." Phoebe studied his eyes, looking for any signs of irritation or disappointment, but he seemed happy to be there. What changed?

"Kevin!" Ray jogged over and shook Kevin's hand. "It's *gut* to see you. I'm glad you could make it. You didn't seem sure you could when we talked yesterday."

"I was able to make it work. *Danki* for inviting me."

Phoebe's heart sank as she looked up at the two men. Kevin had come at Ray's invitation—*not* Christiana's. His presence had nothing to do with her.

"Ray!" a young man standing on one of the volleyball courts called. "Are you going to serve the ball? Or stand there and talk?"

Ray spun around and held up his hand. "I'll be right there, Phil." Then he turned back to Kevin. "I need to go, but we'll talk later. Join us when you're ready."

"Sounds *gut*." When Ray left, Kevin pointed to the quilt. "May I sit here?"

"*Ya*, of course." Phoebe sat up and brushed her hands down her apron as renewed excitement buzzed through her. Maybe Kevin did want to talk to her.

She glanced at Suzanna, who smiled as she stood. "I'm going to see if I can join a volleyball team. I'll talk to you two later." Then she winked at Phoebe before heading off.

As Kevin sank toward the quilt, she pulled her picnic basket over between them. She opened it and began pulling out snacks. "Are you hungry? I have lunchmeat, bread, macaroni salad, crackers, cheese, pretzels, potato chips, *kichlin*, and popcorn."

His eyes widened as he grinned. "Wow. You sure know how to pack a picnic basket."

"It's a little much, isn't it?"

"If we eat all that, we won't be hungry again for a week."

Phoebe smiled. "No, I suppose not. I always try to pack what my family calls a basket of sunshine, but I guess I overdid it. It's no wonder Ray complained it was heavy when he carried it for me."

"His arm must be sore."

Phoebe's eyes locked with Kevin's, and they both started to laugh. The awkwardness between them dissipated, and she felt as if they were friends. After all, he was sitting on the quilt with her, not playing volleyball with Ray.

"The cheese and crackers look *gut*. May I have a few?" he asked.

"Of course." She retrieved two bottles of water, a paper plate, and a few napkins from the basket before setting out the crackers, a cheese ball, and a knife. Soon they were spreading cheese on crackers and eating them.

"How was the rest of your day at the booth on Friday?" he asked.

"Busy. We were closed yesterday for the holiday, but we'd sold out of all our goods on Friday anyway."

"You said before that you work at the booth whenever it's busy. How often is that? Only around holidays? Christiana said you have downtimes."

"It just depends. But lately Christiana's booth has been busier in general, and I'm always committed to helping her when she needs me." She brushed some cracker crumbs from her apron. "I'm sorry *mei schweschder* pressured you to come today. I didn't put her up to that. In fact, I had no idea she was going to mention this gathering to you." She hoped her face wouldn't reveal her humiliation.

He swallowed another cracker, and then he wiped his fingers on a napkin. "I'm glad she mentioned it."

"You are?"

He nodded. "Then I ran into Ray at the hardware store yesterday, and he invited me too. *Mei freind* Ben was with me, and he told me I need to get out more. So here I am."

She smiled, but disappointment still nipped at her. He hadn't come specifically to see her. She pushed the thought away.

"Christiana is seven years older than you, right?"

"That's right."

"How do you like having only one sibling who's that much older than you?"

She tilted her head and contemplated the question. "No one has ever asked me that before."

"It's something we have in common." He crossed his legs and leaned back on his palms as he looked at her. "I think I told you Dathan is eight years older than me, and most of *mei freinden* have several siblings who range in age from two years to ten years older or younger. You're my first *freind* who has just one sibling who's several years older."

Joy blossomed inside her. *He considers me a* freind! She was so surprised that she couldn't respond for a moment.

"I suppose that was a dumb question. I'm sorry. Forget I asked it." He reached for another cracker.

"No, no. I was thinking about how to respond. I guess . . . Well, it's great at times, but it's also bad at times."

"What do you mean?" He sat up and looked eager for her to continue.

"Sometimes I feel like Christiana's my second *mamm*. It's helpful when I need advice, but it's annoying when she tries to discipline me."

"Exactly." He held up his bottle of water. "I've actually reminded Dathan he's *mei bruder* and not *mei dat*." He grimaced. "But then I feel bad when he reminds me that he pretty much raised me."

"Losing both your parents when you were so young had to be difficult."

"*Ya*, it was. I'm grateful Dathan was so patient with me. I don't know what I'd have done without him." He bent one of his knees and rested both arms on it.

"How are your niece and nephew?"

He grinned. "They're *narrisch*."

"Why are they crazy?" she asked with a laugh.

"They crack me up. This morning Tommy announced he wanted to hitch a cow to the buggy instead of a horse to see if it would go any faster."

Phoebe laughed, and Kevin joined in.

"Tommy sounds like he's a lot of fun."

"He is. We never know what he'll do next. And Hannalyn is a great helper. She's always helping her *mamm* with chores or playing with Tommy to keep him busy so Rachelle can finish up a project." He picked up another cracker, spread some cheese on it, and handed it to Phoebe. "You look hungry."

"Do I?" She laughed. "*Danki.*" Then she took a bite.

"*Gern gschehne.*" He made one for himself and then ate it while looking toward the volleyball courts.

"Do you like to play?" Phoebe asked.

He met her gaze and shrugged. "I guess so."

"Do you play often with your own youth group?"

"I haven't been to one of my youth group meetings in about a year."

"Why?"

"I guess I felt like I'd outgrown it," he said after a moment's hesitation. Then he looked around the park. "I bet I'm the oldest one here."

Phoebe blinked and leaned toward him. "Is that what was bothering you at the last youth gathering? You felt too old to be there?"

He gave a half-shrug and then picked up another cracker and began spreading cheese on it.

Relief flooded her. Maybe she hadn't done anything to push him away!

"Kevin, some members here are twenty, and a few are twenty-one. They just like to take a break after working hard all week. You're not too old to be here."

He seemed to consider her comment as he looked around the park again. Then he looked at her. "Would you like to play some volleyball to work off the cheese and crackers?"

"That sounds like fun." Phoebe packed up the food and stowed it in the picnic basket. Then as they walked toward the volleyball courts, she couldn't help wondering if Kevin would ever want to be more than friends.

. . .

Kevin sidled up to Phoebe when the last volleyball game came to a close. The cooling air filled his lungs as lightning bugs dotted the air around them like miniature fireworks. "Would you like a ride home?"

She looked up at him, and her blue eyes seemed to glitter in the light of the pink streaks stretching across the sky. "Isn't *mei haus* out of your way from here?"

"Not at all." In truth, her house was a little out of the way, and he'd had no intention of offering her a ride when he arrived. But neither had he intended to spend the whole afternoon in her company. First, he'd quickly succumbed to the temptation to join her on that quilt, and then he'd let himself enjoy laughing and joking beside her as they played volleyball all afternoon. Now he didn't want their time together to end. Sitting beside her in his buggy would give him more time to memorize the sound of her voice and take in the sweet scent of her shampoo.

He wasn't doing a good job of following through with his plan.

"*Gut* game." Ray came up beside Kevin and gave him a high five. "But I still serve better than you do."

Kevin laughed.

"Will you join us again?" Ray asked.

"I hope to." Kevin glanced at Phoebe, and she blessed him with one of her pretty smiles.

He helped her gather her basket and quilt, and then they loaded his buggy before saying good-bye to her friends.

Soon they were riding toward the main road. When he gave her a sideways glance, she was leaning back in the seat beside him and cupping her hand to her mouth to cover a yawn.

"Did the volleyball games wear you out today?" he asked.

"*Ya*, I think so." She let her head drop back on the seat. "I don't know how you're still standing. You're the one who was jumping up in the air to return the ball. You looked like a pro out there."

He sat up a little taller. "I just like to take advantage of my height."

"Is Dathan tall too?"

"*Ya.*" He nodded. "We're the same height. I've been told there's a strong family resemblance."

"You've met Christiana. We don't look anything alike. Most people find it hard to believe we're *schweschdere.*"

He halted the horse at a light and turned toward her. "I can see it in the shape of your faces and your smiles, but you're right that your hair and eyes are different." An image of Phoebe having supper with his family filled his mind and caused him to smile. "You'll have to meet my family. Then you can tell me if you think Dathan and I look alike."

"I'd like that."

Their gazes locked, and his heart raced.

What was he doing? Why was he allowing himself to get close to her? Freeman's words returned to him: *I'd prefer you stay away from her.*

A car horn beeped behind him, and he guided the horse through the intersection. They talked about games they liked to play other than volleyball until they turned onto the road leading to her house.

"I had a great time today," she said as the horse *clip-clopped* up her driveway.

"I did too." He halted the horse and then turned toward her. "*Danki* again for inviting me."

"I didn't invite you. Christiana did." Phoebe gave him a mischievous grin as she lifted her picnic basket and quilt. "Be safe going home."

"I will. *Gut nacht.*" Kevin waited for her to make her way to the porch steps, and then he steered the horse down the driveway.

A flash of lightning lit the sky, and the smell of rain filled the

54

buggy as Kevin guided the horse toward his brother's house. A sudden sense of foreboding rolled over him as he thought about how comfortable he felt with Phoebe. He was falling for her, and the realization sent a mixture of fear and worry crashing through him.

If he did pursue a relationship with Phoebe, what if it didn't work out? What if she turned out just like Mary and wanted to move too fast toward marriage? He didn't want to break her heart, and he didn't want her to break his.

He also didn't want to lose Freeman's trust. Wasn't his career worth more to him than taking a chance with Phoebe?

But he'd had a wonderful time.

• • •

CHAPTER 6

• • •

Phoebe hugged her quilt and picnic basket to her chest as she headed up the path toward the porch. Her face felt sore from smiling, and the scent of rain tickled her nose as a flash of lightning skittered above her. She didn't care if it rained. Nothing could ruin this perfect day spent with Kevin and her friends.

Kevin.

She sighed as she recalled his attractive smile and boisterous laugh as they talked, played volleyball, and teased each other all afternoon. He was funny, thoughtful, sweet, handsome, and courteous. He would be the perfect boyfriend, if only he would ask her to—

"Phoebe Kate."

Phoebe's head snapped up to the porch, toward her father's voice. Her stomach lurched when she spotted both her parents sitting on the rocking chairs, watching her intently. She licked her lips and stood up straight as a mist of rain kissed her cheeks.

"I didn't see you." She picked up her pace and climbed the steps.

"Who brought you home?" *Dat*'s voice was stern as if she'd just been caught stealing from a store in town.

"Kevin did."

"Kevin Weaver?"

56

"*Ya, Dat,*" she said as the drizzle picked up and rain began to tap on the porch roof.

"Why was he the one to bring you home?"

"He came to the youth gathering. Remember? Christiana invited him? We played volleyball, and then he offered me a ride."

Dat's expression seemed to fill with concern. "I doubted he would come. For one thing, he's a bit older than you. Just be careful with your heart. I'd hate to see you get hurt. I'm not sure he's serious about dating, so it might be best for you to stay away from him."

"We're not dating." Phoebe worked to keep her tone even despite the anxiety pulsing through her veins. "We're just *freinden.*" *I'm not even sure he wants to date me!*

Dat nodded, apparently with relief. "That's much safer."

Phoebe nodded back, but with disappointment and doubt. Should she heed her father's warning? Would Kevin hurt her? "I'm going to take a shower."

"*Gut nacht,*" *Dat* said. *Mamm* had said nothing, but that didn't mean she hadn't come to believe the same thing about Kevin. Maybe she had.

Phoebe stepped into the house and stowed her snacks and picnic basket in the pantry before depositing her quilt in the laundry room. Her eyes burned as hope began to crumble. Maybe Kevin was too old for her. Maybe she was pinning her hope on the wrong man, a man who wasn't ready for a commitment to a woman.

Confusion filled her as she made her way up the stairs to her room. Earlier today, she'd been almost certain she and Kevin would be a couple, but now *Dat*'s concern had burst her happy bubble.

She needed advice. She needed someone to listen while she poured out the confusion that had seeped into her heart. She needed her sister.

She slowed to a stop in front of Christiana's closed door and raised her hand to knock. Then she let her hand fall to her side. She didn't want to burden Christiana with her problems. She had to figure this out for herself.

Phoebe stepped into her room and sank onto the edge of her bed. Then she hugged her arms to her waist and opened her heart to God.

God, I care for Kevin, and I think he cares for me too. But Dat *seems to think Kevin is wrong for me. Only you can help us find a way to make it work if you choose for us to be together. Please lead our hearts to a solution.*

She flopped back onto the bed and listened to the rain pound the roof, confusion still swirling through her like a tornado.

．．．

"You must have had a *gut* time if you stayed out this late."

Kevin jumped with a start as he turned away from the horse stall and found Dathan standing by the entrance to the barn. Rain beat a steady cadence on the roof above them. "I didn't hear you come in."

Dathan joined him. "Sorry. I didn't mean to startle you. How was the youth gathering?"

"It was great." Kevin couldn't stop a smile, making it impossible to hide his true feelings. "I had a *wunderbaar* time."

Dathan's eyebrow shot up. "What's her name?"

Kevin leaned back against the horse stall. "It's Phoebe."

"The *maedel* you said is too young for you?"

"*Ya.* I think I was wrong. We had a great talk today, and then we had a lot of fun with her *freinden.*" His shoulders slumped. "But she's still my boss's *dochder,* and that's the real problem."

"Why?"

"He warned me not to hurt her."

Dathan's eyes rounded. "When?"

Kevin told him. "He made it clear I shouldn't get close to her if I'm not ready for a commitment." His chest tightened as he recalled Phoebe's sweet laugh and gorgeous smile. "She's amazing, Dathan. I really like her. I could see myself falling for her. In fact, I think I already am."

"That means you have an important decision to make. You need to decide if dating Phoebe is worth risking your new career with Freeman's company."

Kevin cupped his hand to the back of his neck as his mind spun. Dathan was echoing what Kevin had come to realize on his way home. Freeman told him he had a future with the company, and that future meant the financial freedom he craved. But again, what if he and Phoebe started dating and then broke up? He'd be left working on the dairy farm and with no home of his own, and that wasn't his dream. Dread wrapped around his chest, pushing his breath out in a rush.

Dathan snorted. "Kev, talk to me. You look like you're either trying to solve a puzzle or going to be sick."

"I think it's a little of both." Kevin rubbed at the tension in his neck. "How do I know if I'm making the right decision? I don't want to risk losing my future with Freeman's business, but I also want to see where this friendship with Phoebe could lead."

"You said you enjoy brick work and that the pay is *gut*."

"That's true. I can pay you rent, and I have money in savings. I should be able to build a *haus* in a year or two."

"And building that *haus* is what you've talked about ever since you were sixteen years old. You've always said you wanted to build it on the other side of the pasture." Dathan pointed in that direction. "I think you know in your heart that you don't want to let that dream go."

Kevin's mouth dried as he shook his head. "I don't. I want my own place. Then you and Rachelle can enjoy the *haus* and raise your family without me in the way."

Dathan sighed and rolled his eyes. "I've told you more than a hundred times. You're not in our way. You're family, but that's beside the point. You just told me your answer. You want a *haus*. Everything else will work out as it should. Freeman has already warned you to stay away from his *dochder* if you can't commit to a relationship right now, so just concentrate on being the best employee you can be for him. Learn everything there is to know about being a brick mason, and don't think about Phoebe. Keep working hard and saving money to build that *haus*. Then if you're meant to be with Phoebe, God will find a way to work it out for you both—in his time."

Kevin nodded, but the knot under his ribs tightened into a hard rock. If the answer was so simple, why did it hurt so much to think about staying away from Phoebe?

"No matter what, trust God to lead you to the right path." Dathan patted his shoulder. "It's late. We should get inside."

As the two men walked into the pouring rain, Kevin couldn't help but feel he'd just made the decision he'd needed to make yet had left a piece of his heart with the sweet and kind Phoebe Kurtz.

* * *

Phoebe and Suzanna slipped into the Esh family's barn. It was an off Sunday without a service in their church district, and Phoebe's mother had suggested they visit the service in her cousin's district.

"I'm so glad your *mamm* asked my family to come here today too," Suzanna said.

Phoebe nodded, bouncing the ties on her prayer covering on her shoulders. "I'm *froh* you could all come."

Phoebe sat down between her sister and Suzanna in the back row of the unmarried women's section and then glanced at the unmarried men. She pressed her lips together. She hadn't seen Kevin for two weeks, and despite her father's advice to stay away from him, memories of their fun time at the picnic had teased her. She just couldn't erase that day's images from her mind.

She longed to spend more time with Kevin. But if he felt the same way about her, by now he would have made an effort to see her again. It was obvious that she'd misjudged his feelings for her—again. *Dat* was right. Kevin wasn't serious about dating, at least not about dating her. If only he had been clear about that. Now she had to ask God to help her move on. But as determined as she was to wait for someone who was forthright with his intentions, she couldn't stop thinking about Kevin Weaver.

Phoebe turned her attention to her lap and fingered her white apron as she waited for the service to begin.

"Phoebe. Phoebe." Christiana elbowed her in the ribs twice as she whispered in her ear.

"Stop that."

"Look over there." Christiana nodded across the barn.

Phoebe turned as instructed, and when she spotted Kevin sitting at the end of a row and staring at the floor, her breath hitched. Had he just arrived, or had she just missed seeing him? Her suddenly sweaty hands began to shake as she smoothed her apron.

"Did you know this was Kevin's church district?" Christiana's voice was close to Phoebe's ear.

"No," Phoebe whispered. It had never occurred to her to ask him what church district was his. She looked across the barn once again and found him still staring at the floor. Her mind whirled with questions.

Suzanna leaned over this time. "You okay?"

"*Ya.*" Phoebe forced her gaze away from Kevin and turned toward her friend.

The corners of Suzanna's lips turned up. "That means you can talk to him after the service, you know."

"If he wants to talk to me, he can," Phoebe murmured. "He hasn't made any effort to see me in two weeks, let alone show that he likes me. I'm tired of hanging on, waiting. If he's interested in me, he can tell me so."

Suzanna pressed her lips together and tilted her head as if in disbelief. "You've got to be kidding. He was just about glued to you at the last youth gathering." She lowered her voice even more. "Talk to him. Maybe he just needs to work up the courage to tell you how he feels."

Her pulse thudded as she considered that possibility. But if she did talk to him, would he want to talk to her?

A young man sitting across the barn had been chosen to serve as the song leader. He began the first syllable of the opening hymn, and Phoebe grabbed her hymnal and joined the rest of the congregation as they finished the verse. Then she did her best to focus her attention on worshipping God instead of on Kevin.

Throughout the service, though, she snuck glances in Kevin's direction, and he always seemed to be staring at his lap or the floor. Had he seen her and was trying to avoid her? Or was he deep in prayer about something troubling him? She ached to meet his gaze and see his eyes, but she also worried he would reject her with a cold stare.

Phoebe turned her focus back to the sermons, and relief flooded her when the fifteen-minute kneeling prayer ended. The congregation stood for the benediction and sang the closing hymn. While she sang, her eyes moved again to Kevin, and her breath caught in her throat when she found him watching her. His eyes were intense as their gazes locked, and a shiver danced up her spine. She tried to look away, but she was frozen in place.

His expression suddenly warmed, and then he smiled and nodded. She nodded in return, and when he looked down at his hymnal, she released the air trapped in her throat.

The service ended, and Christiana turned to Phoebe and Suzanna. "Let's go help serve the meal."

Phoebe followed the two women into the Eshes' kitchen, where she lifted a platter of lunchmeat and then carried it toward the barn. She slowed when she saw Kevin talking to a young couple. They looked to be in their early thirties. Or maybe the woman was a bit younger.

Although the man had a beard, he resembled Kevin with his dark hair and eyes and tall, muscular build. The woman held a toddler boy who had her same shade of blond hair. A little girl who resembled the woman and looked to be about four held the man's hand. This had to be Kevin's family.

Mustering her courage and squaring her shoulders, Phoebe approached them. *"Wie geht's?"*

"Phoebe." Kevin turned toward her. "It's *gut* to see you. This is my family." He made a sweeping gesture toward them. "This is my sister-in-law, Rachelle."

Balancing the tray in one hand, Phoebe shook Rachelle's hand. "It's so nice to meet you."

"You too." Rachelle's smile was bright.

"This is *mei bruder*, Dathan," Kevin said, and Phoebe shook his hand.

"Hello," Dathan said as he seemed to share a look with Kevin.

"And this is Tommy and Hannalyn," Kevin said.

"I've heard so much about you," Phoebe told the children.

"Did *Onkel* Kevin tell you I draw the best pictures?" Hannalyn asked with a grin.

"No, I do!" Tommy said, protesting his sister's assessment.

Phoebe held up her finger. "Actually, he said you both do."

"*Danki*," Kevin muttered under his breath, and Phoebe laughed.

Phoebe turned toward Kevin. "I need to help serve the meal, but it was nice seeing you again."

"*Ya.*" His expression grew serious. "It's been too long."

"Maybe I'll see you later." Phoebe fought the urge to stay as she forced her legs to move toward the barn. But surely if God had led her to this service today, he'd allow them more time to talk. And Kevin seemed . . . interested.

CHAPTER 7

Phoebe was the one in the pink dress sitting between the red-head and the brunette?" Ben asked as he sat across from Kevin. They were eating their lunch in the barn with the rest of the men in the congregation.

"*Ya.*" Kevin sipped from his coffee cup as his mind continued to spin with the fact that Phoebe had shown up at his church service today. How had that happened? Was Dathan right that God would find a way for them if it was part of his plan? But this soon?

"Who was the brunette?"

"What?" Kevin looked over at Ben.

"The brunette." Ben gestured with his hands. "She was wearing the yellow dress."

Kevin blinked. "You mean the *maedel* sitting beside Phoebe?"

Ben leaned forward and lowered his voice. "Are you all right?"

"*Ya,* I'm fine." Kevin mentally shook himself from distraction. "The redhead is her *schweschder,* Christiana, and the other *maedel* is her best *freind,* Suzanna Byler."

"Suzanna." Ben drew out her name as if enjoying the sound of it. "Is she single?"

Kevin almost dropped his cup. "You're interested in Suzanna?"

"Just answer my question. Is she single?"

65

"I think so."

Ben held up a pretzel and shook it at Kevin. "We should invite Suzanna and Phoebe to go to youth group with us today."

"*Our* youth group?"

"*Ya*, the one you haven't been to in a year. Let's invite them, and then we can spend the afternoon with both of them."

"But I told you. Freeman said I shouldn't get close to her unless I'm sure I'm ready for a commitment. He doesn't want me to risk breaking her—"

"Relax." Ben leaned forward and lowered his voice again. "I know what Freeman told you, but you've been moping for two weeks now. If we invite them to go *as a group*, you can spend some time with Phoebe without Freeman worrying about it, right? I know you want to."

Hope lit in Kevin's chest as he nodded. He couldn't turn down a chance to be with Phoebe. "You're brilliant."

"It's about time you acknowledged that." Ben tossed a pretzel at Kevin as they both laughed.

After the women had eaten as well, Kevin and Ben found Phoebe and Suzanna standing together near the barn. As they approached them, Phoebe's expression brightened, and she smiled.

"Hi, Kevin."

"Phoebe, this is *mei freind* Ben Zook." Kevin gestured between them. "Ben, meet Phoebe Kurtz and Suzanna Byler."

"Hi." Ben shook Suzanna's hand. "It's really nice to meet you. I noticed you during the service."

"You did?" Suzanna gave Phoebe a sideways look before meeting Ben's gaze again.

"We were wondering if you'd both like to join us at our youth gathering this afternoon," Ben said, his focus still on Suzanna.

Kevin squelched the urge to shake his head. Could Ben be a more blatant flirt?

"*Your* youth group?" Phoebe studied Kevin as if seeking a hidden meaning. "I thought you hadn't gone to that in a long time."

"He hasn't, but I convinced him to go today," Ben chimed in. "We'd both like you to come. We're going to play games at a nearby farm." He looked back at Suzanna. "You can ride with me, and then I'll take you home."

"That sounds like fun." Suzanna grabbed Phoebe's arm and gave it a tug. "Let's go ask our parents if we can go."

"Okay." Phoebe's gaze lingered on Kevin's, and then she allowed Suzanna to steer her toward the barn.

Kevin's heartrate launched into a gallop as excitement filled him. It was time to throw caution to the wind and get to know Phoebe. He was ready to open his heart to her. He rubbed his hands together as he imagined what it could be like to date her. Yes, he was ready, no matter the risk.

"This was a great idea," he said to Ben.

"You said it earlier—I'm brilliant, *mei freind*." Ben rested his arm on Kevin's shoulder.

"*Ya*, you are." Kevin took off his hat and spun it in his hands while he and Ben waited.

A few minutes later, Phoebe and Suzanna returned, both smiling.

Suzanna spoke first. "Phoebe's *mamm*'s cousin Sally is a member of this district, and she vouched for both of you!"

"When are we leaving?" Phoebe asked.

"Right now." Kevin's heart seemed to turn over.

. . .

Phoebe sat next to Kevin in his buggy after she and Suzanna changed into the everyday clothes they'd brought in case they made afternoon plans. She heaved a sigh of relief as she settled back into the seat.

The sun's rays streamed through the windshield, and she took in the lush, rolling patchwork of green pastures dotted with farmhouses, cows, and horses. It was the perfect day for an outdoor gathering, and it felt so good to be sitting next to Kevin again. But she had to caution herself not to get too attached. Not only had he not contacted her in more than two weeks, but her father's caution that Kevin might not be looking for a serious relationship lingered at the back of her thoughts.

"I was so surprised to see you at the service." Kevin's words broke through her thoughts. "How did you happen to choose my church district today?"

"It's our district's off Sunday, and *mei mamm* wanted to visit the service in her cousin Sally's district. *Mamm* is close with Suzanna's *mamm*, and she invited that family to come along."

She thought she heard Kevin mumble something about mysterious ways, but his words were soft, almost a whisper, and she wasn't sure.

"What?" she asked, leaning closer to him.

"Nothing." He gave her a sideways glance as he steered the horse down another road. "I think Ben likes Suzanna."

"I noticed that. And I think Suzanna likes Ben."

"Oh *ya*?" His dark eyebrows careened toward his hairline.

"*Ya.* When we went to ask our parents' permission to come with you and Ben, she told me she was already impressed."

"I was surprised when he asked me about her during lunch. He hasn't dated anyone in a while, so it seemed to just come out of nowhere. I have a feeling he'll ask her out." Kevin shook his head as he turned down another road.

Will you ask me out, Kevin?

Phoebe suppressed the words that threatened to leap from her lips.

"This is the farm." He pointed at a large, white farmhouse. Near it stood five red barns, and behind them she saw a white, split-rail fence surrounding a lush, green pasture. Dozens of buggies sat off to the right in an open, green field, reminding her of a herd of cows in her neighbor's pasture. Nearby, young Amish folks played volleyball while another group stood clustered around three Ping-Pong tables where several couples played.

Phoebe's stomach tumbled as she took in the unfamiliar faces. While she'd never had trouble making new friends, she always felt nervous visiting new youth groups.

Kevin halted the horse and then angled his body toward her. "Now, I have a serious question for you."

"Okay." Her body trembled as she looked into his eyes. This was it! He was going to ask her out!

"Do you want to play volleyball or Ping-Pong? Or do you want to just sit and talk?" He held up his hands. "Don't say it's up to me, because you're my guest. It's up to you."

"Oh." Phoebe scratched at her nose and tried to recover from the mental whiplash his questions had caused. "It really is up to—"

"Nope." He held up a finger. "You can't say it's up to me."

She glanced at the people playing volleyball and then the ones playing Ping-Pong. Playing games seemed to be the best choice since it would limit their alone time and stop her heart from craving more than friendship from him.

"Let's play Ping-Pong," she said.

"Great!"

Phoebe pushed open her door and climbed out of the buggy, and after Kevin settled his horse in the pasture, they walked toward the Ping-Pong tables. As they arrived, a pretty blonde squealed and rushed over to them.

"Kevin!" She waved her arms as she came to a stop in front of him, and then she wrapped her arms around his neck, giving him an awkward hug.

Kevin gave her back a half-hearted pat as his face clouded with a frown.

"Kevin Weaver! Oh my goodness! I haven't seen you for so long. How are you?"

Kevin might not look as though he was enjoying this attention, but jealousy still pricked at Phoebe as she stared at the beautiful young woman. Not only was she at least two inches taller than Phoebe, but she had flawless, ivory skin and stunning, dark-blue eyes. Her hair reminded Phoebe of yellow tulips, and her waist was so small.

Phoebe just stood there, feeling off balance as Kevin stared at his greeter.

"Mary. Hi." Kevin's voice sounded flat as he fingered his suspenders. "It has been a while."

"It sure has!" Mary smacked Kevin's bicep. "I heard you weren't working for Dathan anymore. Where have you been hiding, then?"

Kevin shifted his weight as his face remained stoic. "I'm working for a brick mason now."

"No kidding! And then you're going to finally build that *haus* you've always wanted, huh?"

"That's the plan."

"*Gut* for you." Mary turned to Phoebe and stuck out her hand. "Hi, I'm Mary Yoder. What's your name?"

Phoebe opened her mouth to respond, but Kevin cut her off. "This is *mei freind* Phoebe Kurtz. I invited her to come with me today."

Phoebe looked up at him. Had he meant to emphasize the words *mei freind*? Why had she agreed to come? She should have gone home or met her friends in her own youth group. Now she knew Kevin would never be interested in her, not if Mary was an indication of what he liked in women. Obviously, they had a history together, and she was certain they'd been more than friends.

"Hi, Phoebe." Mary's eyes scanned her from head to toe, prompting Phoebe to cross her arms in front of her chest. Then Mary turned back to Kevin. "My family asks about you all the time. You shouldn't be such a stranger."

Kevin gave her a half nod.

Mary pointed to the Ping-Pong tables. "I was just about to play Ping-Pong. Remember how we used to play? We had so much fun! Would you like to be my opponent for old times' sake?"

Kevin turned to Phoebe. "I'll play only if Phoebe plays."

Phoebe hesitated. Did she want to play a game with this woman?

Kevin looked back at Mary. "Give us a minute?"

"Okay." Mary turned and sauntered toward the tables.

Kevin faced Phoebe again, and his eyes seemed to plead with hers. "We don't have to play. We could go for a walk or just sit and talk for a while. How does that sound?"

Phoebe fingered the hem of her apron. If only she could just leave.

Kevin sighed. "I'm sorry. Mary's my ex-girlfriend, and I didn't know she would be here because her family is in a different district. We can leave, if you want. We can go spend time with your family. Or with mine."

Phoebe hugged her arms and swallowed, trying to keep her

threatening tears at bay. What was the point of spending time with Kevin? How could she compete with the Marys of the world? But she didn't want Kevin's ex-girlfriend to think she'd forced him to leave so soon.

"It's fine. Go play and have fun." Her voice was raspy, but she couldn't help it. Deep down, she was hurt.

"But you said you wanted to play." He nodded toward the far end of the pasture, where she'd spotted Ben and Suzanna just a few minutes ago. "Forget Ping-Pong. Let's go for a walk."

"No, it's fine." Phoebe fought against the thinness in her voice.

"Kevin!" Mary's whine carried across the breeze.

"Hey, Kevin's back!" someone yelled.

"Come play with us, Kevin," someone else called.

"We've missed you, buddy," a third chimed in.

Kevin kept his eyes focused on Phoebe despite his friends' request. "I don't have to play with them. Why don't we go do something else?"

"Really, I don't mind." Phoebe forced a smile on her lips. "Now that we're here, I'd rather watch everyone play than play myself."

Kevin reached for her, but then he pulled back his hand, his lips forming a thin line. "All right."

Phoebe sat on the grass near the Ping-Pong tables, wondering how much longer she'd have to endure this outing. She looked across the field toward the volleyball courts, where Suzanna and Ben now sat in the grass together. She thought about joining them, but she didn't want to interrupt them if Suzanna was enjoying getting to know Ben.

She considered again how hot and cold Kevin had been toward her. Sometimes he seemed to enjoy her company, but he hadn't exactly gone out of his way to seek her out. He probably asked her to the outing today just so Ben could spend time with Suzanna. And when he'd suggested they go somewhere else, he was no doubt using her to get away from the awkwardness of seeing Mary here. Whether or not that was true, they might be friends, but they'd never be boyfriend and girlfriend.

It was time to let go of her dreams about Kevin once and for all. Her father had been right all along. Her chance with this man had been doomed from the start, and she had to stop torturing herself. She couldn't wait to get home to the privacy of her room so she could unload her grief.

* * *

"I'm sorry about Mary," Kevin said as he guided the horse toward Phoebe's house later that afternoon. "If I had known she'd be there today, I wouldn't have suggested we go."

Phoebe kept her eyes focused out the window as if the passing traffic was the most interesting sight she'd ever seen. She hadn't said much to him since they'd walked to the buggy together, and the silence was deafening.

He'd hoped to play a few games of Ping-Pong with Phoebe and then walk over to the pasture fence and talk with her alone. He'd craved time with her for the past two weeks, and today gave him the opportunity. But once Phoebe met Mary, she'd shut him down.

Now, as they sat in the buggy together, Phoebe wouldn't even look at him. Mary had spoiled everything, but he had allowed it to happen when Phoebe wouldn't go along with changing their plans. Guilt and regret dug their sharp tentacles into his back.

"How long did you date Mary?" Phoebe's question came out in a strangled whisper.

Kevin's muscles tensed, and he kept his eyes focused on the road ahead. "Almost two years."

"When?"

He glanced at her, but she kept her focus on her lap. "We broke up last year."

"She seemed awfully *froh* to see you."

"That's Mary. She likes to put on a show and be the center of attention."

"I can see how she's easily the center of attention. She's so *schee* and outgoing." Phoebe turned back toward the window.

"I don't have feelings for her now." Kevin emphasized the words. "It's over between us."

"What happened between you two?"

He huffed out a breath as he gathered his words. "All she talked about was getting married."

"And that's not what you wanted?"

"First, I wanted to establish a career away from the dairy farm and build a *haus*, to support myself and stop depending on *mei bruder*. She didn't like that idea. She kept telling me I should be satisfied with working on the dairy farm so we wouldn't have to wait to get married. She didn't even care if we lived in *mei bruder*'s *haus*, at least in the beginning. She just wanted to get married."

When he glanced at her again, she was staring out the side window with her back to him. Guilt tightened the knots in his shoulders. "We should have just left. I'm sorry if she made you uncomfortable."

Phoebe remained silent, and the tension in the buggy was as thick as tar.

"Phoebe." He worked to keep his tone gentle. "I'm glad you went with me today."

74

Her house came into view, and she sat up in her seat and turned toward him. "We need more time to talk."

He guided the horse up her driveway and then halted it at the back-porch steps before facing her. "I'm listening."

He braced himself as her lips trembled.

"We shouldn't see each other anymore."

His stomach plummeted. "Why?"

"This friendship will never work." Her voice was thin and reedy.

He leaned over and gently took her arm. "I don't understand. I enjoy spending time with you, and I apologized for today. Tell me what else I can do to fix this."

She yanked her arm back and then brushed away the tears that had traced down her cheeks. "There's nothing to be done. *Gut nacht.*"

The pain in her eyes cut him to the bone. Before he could stop her, she climbed out of the buggy and hurried up the porch steps.

Kevin watched her disappear into the house, his heart shattering.

CHAPTER 8

A s Phoebe hung some freshly washed dishcloths on the line the following Thursday, the bright July sun and chirping birds' songs seemed to mock her miserable mood.

It had been days since Kevin invited her to the disastrous youth group gathering, and even though she'd told him their friendship would never work, she still couldn't fully convince her heart to let him go. She often found herself lost in a daydream where he had spent the afternoon laughing and talking with her and not his old friends.

But that wasn't what happened. He could have been more insistent that they leave, especially if he really didn't want to be around Mary.

Phoebe had to find a way to move on. But after all the pain Kevin had caused her—and not just at the youth gathering—why did he still have a hold on her heart?

She dismissed the thought and hung another cloth on the line that extended from the back porch to one of her father's barns.

"Hey, Pheebs! How are you?" Suzanna waved as she bounced up the porch steps.

"I'm fine. I didn't hear your horse and buggy. What are you doing here?"

"I was in the neighborhood." Suzanna sidled up to Phoebe. Why was her smile as wide as the pasture and as bright as a lantern in the middle of the night?

Phoebe studied her friend. "You look like you're about to explode if you don't tell me something."

"I am!" Suzanna clapped her hands. "Ben asked me to be his girlfriend." She squealed and then hugged Phoebe.

Phoebe gasped. "What? But you just met him on Sunday."

"I know. I need to tell you what happened." Suzanna took Phoebe's hand, guided her to the glider behind them, and then gestured for them to sit next to each other. "We've seen each other every night this week. After he gets off work at his *dat*'s furniture store, he comes to see me. He has supper with my family, and then we talk on the porch until it's dark." She rubbed her hands together. "I like him so much. It's as though we have this connection, you know?" She sank back in the glider with a silly grin. "I'm so *froh*."

"That's *wunderbaar*. I'm happy for you." Phoebe longed to escape the envy and sadness that overtook her. She was thrilled for her best friend, but she was distraught that Kevin had never made his intentions so clear.

"What about you and Kevin?" Suzanna asked.

Phoebe shook her head and looked out toward the pasture. "It's over between us."

"What do you mean?" Suzanna sat up straight.

Phoebe told her what happened when they were at the youth group gathering. "I don't think he ever cared much for me. I'm not his type. Besides, *mei dat* warned me to stay away from him because he doesn't think Kevin is serious about wanting a relationship. I don't know if that has anything to do with what happened between him and Mary, but *Dat* was right. I was just kidding myself when

I thought I had a chance with Kevin. It was all so confusing that I told him to stay away."

"But you're wrong. It's obvious that he cares about you."

"No, it's not."

"*Ya*, it is. And Ben told me Kevin likes you."

Phoebe turned toward Suzanna again. "He did?"

"*Ya*. Ben said Kevin has liked you since he met you."

"That's not true." Phoebe shook her head. "He ignores me for weeks at a time, and Mary . . . I can't compete with women like her."

Suzanna lifted her chin and pointed a finger at Phoebe. "You should talk to him again."

Phoebe shook her head. "If God had wanted us together, he would have made a way."

"You're giving up too easily."

"No, I'm not. God hasn't chosen Kevin for me. If he had, he wouldn't leave me confused all the time, would he? I just don't want to feel this way anymore." She wiped at her eyes with the heel of her hand and choked back tears.

"You still care about him."

"I do." Phoebe looked down at her lap. "But now I need to pray for God to heal my heart."

Suzanna sighed and pulled Phoebe into a hug. Phoebe buried her face in her friend's shoulder, and when she let her sadness break free, tears rolled down her cheeks.

. . .

Kevin walked up to the lunch counter at his favorite diner and picked up a menu. His stomach growled, and he was deep in thought about his choices when a hand squeezed his shoulder and a voice sounded next to his ear.

"Don't you have a job?" the voice said.

"Hey, Ben." Kevin turned and shook his best friend's hand. "What are you doing?"

"I'm having lunch with my *schee* girlfriend." Ben pulled Suzanna to his side as she smiled up at him. Then she grinned at Kevin. "Hi."

"Look at you two," Kevin said. "I knew you liked each other, but I didn't realize you were officially dating. You just met."

"We've been together for almost two weeks now." Ben looked down at Suzanna, and the affection in his eyes squeezed Kevin's heart.

"Wow. That was fast."

Ben shrugged. "Sometimes you just know."

"Huh." Kevin rubbed his chin as his mind turned to Phoebe and her beautiful smile. He'd thought he'd known about her, but then she'd rejected him for reasons he didn't really understand, leaving him with another broken heart.

"How have you been, Kevin?" Suzanna asked.

"Fine. Just busy." Kevin shrugged.

"Have you talked to Phoebe?"

"No." Wouldn't Phoebe have told her best friend about her decision? He folded his arms over his chest as if to shield his heart from the pain of losing her. He missed her every second of every day.

"You haven't talked to her at all?" Suzanna's question seemed to hold more meaning than her words conveyed.

Panic gripped Kevin. "No. Why? Is she okay?"

"She's fine, but she misses you."

Kevin snorted. "Right."

"What does that mean?" Ben asked.

Kevin stepped to the side and spilled it all. How Mary had interfered with their time at the youth gathering. How Phoebe had shut down and then told him they couldn't see each other anymore when he got her home. "It's over. Now I have to figure out how to move on."

"Do you care for her?" Suzanna asked.

"*Ya*, I do." Kevin shook his head. He was a lovesick dolt for clinging to the hope that Phoebe could care for him. He just didn't understand what happened to turn her away—not when he'd made it clear that he wanted to spend time with her, not with Mary or his friends.

"You need to tell her that," Suzanna said.

"Why would I bother? She told me our friendship would never work." Kevin fingered the hat in his hands.

"You need to make your feelings clear."

"How do you know?" Kevin said, challenging her.

"She spent a long time wondering if you liked her at all. Then when she saw Mary, thinking she's the kind of woman you'd want in your life, she told you it could never work between you. She *does* care for you, Kevin. She told me so."

Kevin tried to swallow against the lump that swelled in his throat, his emotion a dull throb.

"Is Mary the kind of woman you want?" Ben asked.

"No." Kevin shook his head. "I'm interested in Phoebe."

"You know what that means, right?"

"What?"

"You need to get her back."

Kevin gave him one palm up. "How am I supposed to do that if she's given up on me?"

"Come to our youth group picnic on Sunday and tell her how you feel," Suzanna said. "Then ask her to go for a walk and talk this out." Suzanna told him where they were meeting.

Kevin nodded. "I'll be there."

"Great." Suzanna grinned. "I can't wait to see Phoebe's face when you show up."

But he still doubted Phoebe would be glad to see him.

. . .

Kevin searched the sea of faces for Phoebe's. When he didn't see her, he scanned the youth group crowd until he found Suzanna and Ben sitting on a quilt by the pond. He rushed over to them, his heart pounding with anxiety.

"Where's Phoebe?" he asked.

Suzanna jumped up. "She wouldn't come. She said she wanted to just stay home and rest."

Kevin gritted his teeth. "I was ready to talk to her. I planned out everything I was going to say."

Ben waved him off. "Go to her *haus*."

"What if she won't talk to me?" Kevin lifted his straw hat and pushed his hand through his hair.

"She will!" Suzanna said. "Walk over there. Leave your horse and buggy, and then ask her to walk with you back here. That will give you plenty of time to talk."

"*Gut* idea."

Kevin's pulse thundered in his ears as he marched down the path to the main road. He was going to knock on Phoebe's door and refuse to leave her porch until she agreed to come with him. It was time to work things out between them and make his feelings known.

81

. . .

"Phoebe! You have company!" *Mamm* called from somewhere downstairs.

Phoebe placed her book on her nightstand. Then she straightened her prayer covering before heading downstairs to the kitchen, where her mother stood smiling. "Who is it?"

"Go see." *Mamm* nodded toward the back door. Then she touched her arm. "Take your time."

"Okay." Curiosity nipped at Phoebe as she walked to the back door. Her mouth fell open when she found Kevin standing on the porch, both hands gripping the brim of his straw hat. She stepped outside. "What are you doing here?"

"Please don't tell me to leave." He held out a hand. "We need to talk, and I have some important things to say."

She closed the door behind her, and then she folded her arms over her waist as she lifted her chin. "I'm listening. Talk."

"Can we walk to the park where your youth group is? My horse and buggy are there. I went there looking for you, and then I came here when Suzanna told me you'd stayed home."

She hesitated, shocked that he had gone to such lengths to see her. Her heart warmed, and she nodded. "Okay. Let me just tell *mei mamm*."

She hurried into the house and let her mother know where she was going. *Mamm* didn't seem concerned that she'd be with Kevin. She seemed . . . happy. Maybe she still believed in him, no matter what *Dat* thought.

Then she grabbed her quilt and the basket of snacks *Mamm* quickly put together. Soon she and Kevin were walking side by side down the road. She carried the quilt, and he carried the basket.

"I'm sorry for last Sunday," Kevin began, his voice sounding shaky. "I never imagined Mary would interfere in our time together. I just knew it was an opportunity to spend time with you."

"But even if you and Mary broke up, seeing her must have reminded you what you liked about her in the first place." She was embarrassed by the anguish in her voice.

"No, it didn't." His answer was forceful as he stopped and faced her. "I told you Mary wanted to get married when I wasn't ready, and that's why I broke up with her. But there's more to it. I realized she wasn't even the kind of *muedel* I wanted for a *fraa*. Mary is a show-off. Like I said, she was showing off for you and the rest of the crowd at the youth gathering. She's used to men fighting for her attention, and I'm sure she can't stand the fact that I never wanted her back."

Phoebe searched his face but couldn't find any sign of a lie. "But if you really wanted to spend time with me, why did you spend all afternoon playing Ping-Pong with your *freinden*?"

Kevin set the picnic basket on the ground. His face was stricken as if she'd smacked him with her words. "You insisted you didn't want to play anymore and that I should play without you, so I decided to go ahead and spend time with *mei freinden*, even if Mary was there too. I didn't want to, but that's what you said you wanted. I should have known better. And I should have told you what I wanted from the start."

"What did you want?"

"I already told you. I wanted to spend time with you. That's all I ever wanted."

Phoebe's lower lip trembled. "I'm so confused."

"I am too." Kevin gave a little laugh. "We're both a mess, aren't we?"

"*Ya.*" She smiled as warmth radiated in her chest.

"Phoebe, I like you." His voice grew husky, sending a shiver through her. "I like you a lot, and I'm sorry I didn't tell you that from the beginning. You're truly amazing. But I had to sort out some things."

Her pulse tripped over itself and then rushed ahead as he cupped his hand to her cheek.

"When I first met you," he began, "I was afraid you were too young to understand my need to stand on my own. That happened when you and your *freinden* were having fun at the lake that day. When I saw behavior like that food fight, I overreacted to what I perceived as immaturity. I even feared you'd treat my dreams the way Mary did if we ever dated. But now I realize you're an incredible woman who's *schmaert*, funny, and also brave and confident. You're everything I could ever want in a girlfriend, and I'm tired of pretending I don't care about you. The truth is I can't stand another minute without you in my life."

Phoebe sniffed as happy tears gathered in her eyes.

"I want to ask your *dat*'s permission to date you," he added.

She shook her head and wiped her eyes. "I don't know if he'll agree. He told me he's worried you might break my heart."

"He told me the same thing."

"When?"

"The day I saw you at your *schweschder*'s bake stand, he asked me if I was interested in you, and then he warned me to not hurt you. He told me to not pursue a relationship with you if I had no interest in a future with you. I wasn't sure how I felt then, and that's also why I was standoffish. But I've struggled to stay away from you for too long. I don't want to do that anymore. Even if he wants me to give up my apprenticeship with him while we're dating, I'll go back to working on *mei bruder*'s dairy farm and put my dream of being independent and owning a *haus* on hold. I care about you too much to just walk away from you."

A breathy laugh escaped her throat. "I never thought I'd hear you say you care."

"Do you care about me?"

"*Ya*. I have since the first time I saw you at *mei dat*'s job site."

He moved his thumb over her jaw, and she enjoyed his touch. "*Gut*."

Then he leaned down and brushed his lips against hers, sending a shiver of sparks soaring from her head to her toes.

When he broke the kiss, he leaned his forehead against hers. "I want to talk to your *dat* right now. I can't wait to ask you to be my girlfriend."

She smiled and took his hand in hers. "Then let's not waste another moment."

CHAPTER 9

Phoebe and Kevin found her parents sitting on the back porch in their favorite rocking chairs. A colorful butterfly flittered past as she and Kevin climbed the porch steps together.

"You two weren't gone long," *Mamm* said with a smile.

"We want to talk to you and Freeman," Kevin told *Mamm*. Then he smiled at Phoebe before looking at *Dat*. "Freeman, you warned me not to break your *dochder*'s heart. You said you were worried I'd hurt her if I wasn't interested in a future with her. Well, I am interested, and I want to commit to a future with her because I care so much about her. I respect her. I'm amazed by her grace, intelligence, and bravery. I've had feelings for her for a while now, and I believe God led me to her. I would be honored to date her. Please give me your permission."

Phoebe clenched her jaw as *Dat* and *Mamm* exchanged a long and meaningful look.

Finally, *Dat* turned back to Kevin. "I believe you're a kind and respectful man, and as long as you continue to treat *mei dochder* with respect, you have my permission to date her. And you don't have to quit your job." He chuckled. "I can't afford to lose a *gut* worker like you."

"Danki, Dat!" Phoebe leaned down and hugged him. *"Danki* so much."

Kevin shook his hand. *"Danki,* Freeman."

"Gern gschehne."

Phoebe squeezed Kevin's hand as she looked up at him. "Why don't we go to the picnic now?"

"Absolutely."

.   .   .

Later that evening, Phoebe and Kevin sat on her back porch, moving the glider back and forth and holding hands as the crickets' symphony sang the sun to sleep. A stunning sunset gave way to a midnight-blue sky dotted with bright stars that seemed to wink and smile.

After spending the afternoon with their friends at the park, Phoebe and Kevin had returned to her parents' house to have supper with them, Christiana, and Jeff. Then they enjoyed coffee and lemon cake before heading out to the porch to talk alone.

Happiness bubbled through Phoebe as she looked up at Kevin. "I'm sorry for jumping to conclusions about . . . everything. *Danki* for coming today and talking everything through with me."

Kevin ran a finger down her jaw. "God wouldn't let me give up. He kept leading me back to you, and I'm so grateful."

"I am too." She smiled at him. "I want you to know I'm in no rush. Let's just take our time getting to know each other. I fully support your dream of building a career and a *haus* before any talk of marriage. We'll take everything step by step and in God's time."

"That sounds perfect, *mei liewe.*" His voice sounded husky in her ear, sending shivers dancing along her spine. And as Kevin leaned in to kiss her, she closed her eyes and cherished the feel of his lips against hers.

When he pulled back, he touched her lips with his fingertip. "I've never felt this way about anyone before. *Ich liebe dich*, Phoebe."

Her eyes misted at his words. "I love you, too, Kevin."

As he pulled her in for a warm hug, she closed her eyes and savored her overwhelming happiness.

Thank you, God, for sending Kevin into my life.

ACKNOWLEDGMENTS

As always, I'm grateful for my loving family, including my mother, Lola Goebelbecker, my husband, Joe; and my sons, Zac and Matt.

Special thanks to my mother and my dear friends Becky Biddy and Susie Koenig, who graciously proofread the draft and corrected my hilarious typos.

I'm also grateful for my special Amish friend who patiently answers my endless stream of questions. You're a blessing in my life.

Thank you to my wonderful church family at Morning Star Lutheran in Matthews, North Carolina, for your encouragement, prayers, love, and friendship. You all mean so much to my family and me.

Thank you to Zac Weikal and the fabulous members of my Bakery Bunch! I'm so grateful for your friendship and your excitement about my books. You all are awesome!

To my agent, Natasha Kern—I can't thank you enough for your guidance, advice, and friendship. You are a tremendous blessing in my life.

Thank you to my amazing editor, Jocelyn Bailey, for your friendship and guidance. I'm grateful to each and every person at HarperCollins Christian Publishing who helped make this book a reality.

ACKNOWLEDGMENTS

I'm grateful to editor Jean Bloom, who helped me polish and refine the story. Jean, you are a master at connecting the dots and filling in the gaps. I'm so happy we can continue to work together!

Thank you most of all to God—for giving me the inspiration and the words to glorify you. I'm grateful and humbled you've chosen this path for me.

DISCUSSION QUESTIONS

1. At the beginning of the story, Kevin believes Phoebe is too young and immature for him. Do you think he misjudged her? Why or why not?

2. Even though Phoebe insists that Kevin spend most of the youth gathering with his friends, including his ex-girlfriend, she's hurt when he does. But Kevin never meant to hurt her. Have you ever inadvertently hurt someone's feelings? If so, did you apologize and make amends? How did that turn out?

3. Freeman warns Kevin not to date Phoebe if he isn't looking for a real relationship. Freeman also cautions Phoebe to stay away from Kevin. Do you think Freeman's concerns about Kevin's intentions are valid? Why or why not?

4. Which character can you identify with the most? Which character seemed to carry the most emotional stake in the story? Phoebe, Kevin, or someone else?

5. At the end of the story, Kevin decides pursuing a relationship with Phoebe is worth risking his job and his

dreams. What do you think made him change his mind throughout the story?

6. What role did the youth gatherings play in the relationships throughout the story?

CANDLELIGHT SWEETHEARTS

KELLY IRVIN

To my family, love always!

But he said to me, "My grace is sufficient for you, for my power is made perfect in weakness." Therefore I will boast all the more gladly about my weaknesses, so that Christ's power may rest on me. That is why, for Christ's sake, I delight in weaknesses, in insults, in hardships, in persecutions, in difficulties. For when I am weak, then I am strong.

2 Corinthians 12: 9–10 NIV

FEATURED FAMILIES

Fergie and Lucy Cotter
Children: Darcie (husband: Bart Detweiler), Jasper, Salome,
Kimberly, James, John

Isaiah and Nadine Shrock
Children: Esther Marie, Jonas, Nathan, Timothy, Lulu

David and Diane Hershberger (bishop)

Matthew Miller (deacon)

CHAPTER 1

• • •

Decisions, decisions.

Oblivious to the three people waiting in line behind her, the customer squinted at the enormous blackboard-style price list that hung on the wall behind Esther Marie Shrock. Most customers tended to do this. Esther Marie didn't mind. Considering the sixty-five kinds of cheese and forty varieties of meat available at St. Ignatius's Valley Grocery Store, customers usually hemmed and hawed. It didn't matter how much time they had to make their choices before they arrived at the front of the line.

The woman rocked the fussy baby in her arms and sighed. "I know. I know." She shifted the sweet bundle to her other arm. The smell of spit-up and a damp diaper wafted over to the deli, lifted into the air by the overhead ceiling fan with its pleasant *whirring* like background music. "You're tired and hungry. Just give me a minute to make up my mind."

Here it comes. Here it comes. Please Gott, *don't let it be ham.*

"Let me see. Okay, for starters, I'll take a pound of ham, sliced thin."

There it was. Esther Marie squelched a sigh. She took a long breath and inhaled the briny scent of garlic dill pickles. *I can do this. In* Gott, *all things are possible.* "Whi-ch-ch-ch one?"

The woman's forehead wrinkled. She fanned her damp face with a piece of notebook paper covered with a grocery list in cramped cursive handwriting. "What do you mean?"

This lady had been in the store before. She'd ordered from the deli before. Still, Esther Marie reached deep into her well of patience. The woman was tired. New moms always were. Not that Esther Marie would know. As much as she dreamed of being a wife and mother, she'd never been asked to take a ride in a Plain man's buggy after a singing, let alone heard those precious words, *Will you marry me?* So here she stood making sandwiches and selling bologna. And liking it.

"We have thir-t-t-een kinds." *Breathe. Slowly. No block. No block. See the words. Say the words.* "Black forest, brown sugar, Cajun, honey, maple." The block hit her. She searched for the words lost in a hinterland of anxiety. Her hands fluttered as if they had a life of their own. "Hmm, you know, c-c-c-c-ooked s-s-s-super trim 10 percent, coo-k-k-ked off the b-b-bone, c-c-c-c-ooked off the bone honey c-c-c-c-ured, reduced so-so-sodium, hmm, you know, s-s-smoked s-s-s-liced, smoked, s-s-s-s-outhern s-s-s-smoked, V-V-V-Vir-g-g-g-inia."

The little boy with no front teeth and a smudge of dirt on his face standing in line with his grandma snickered. Grandma smacked the back of his head. "We don't make fun of disabled people, child." Her voice carried to the far ends of the earth. "It's rude. They can't help it. It don't mean they're stupid."

She had that right, even if the way she treated her grandson left him with tears in his eyes and Esther Marie feeling responsible for his pain. Years of enduring snickers, taunts, and a million suggestions for correcting the "problem" came with the territory when a person stuttered as badly as she did. Plain kids didn't tease her.

Her family never made fun of her, but they did finish her sentences and had to hide their impatience while she worked to say a simple phrase.

No wonder no man wanted her for a wife. The husband yoked to her signed up for a lifetime of listening to her tortured attempts to speak not one but two languages.

Esther Marie eyed her stash of jelly beans on the shelf under the scale. Sweets were her secret vice. Her go-to treat when the world seemed tear streaked and grimy. Nope. Chewing her favorite purple and pink candies would only make it more difficult for customers to understand her.

She arranged her happy face. "T-T-ake your time. It's a big ch-ch-cho-oice."

The harried mom decided on maple ham along with a pound of lacy baby swiss. She also wanted provolone and muenster as well as a pound of deluxe bologna. "Good ch-ch-ch-choice." Ignoring the sweat dampening her dress under her armpits and the heat creeping over her face, Esther Marie went to work. This was the easy part. With quick, efficient movements she sliced the meats and the cheeses, weighed them, and added price stickers in a matter of minutes. "Enjoy."

"Thank you."

The customer turned away, but not before Esther Marie saw the look she hated most. The pity look.

It didn't matter. Nothing mattered but doing the best possible job. Esther Marie had done her best every day for the past four years at the grocery store, popular with locals and the tourists who went out of their way to find it on the road to St. Ignatius's airport before they went on to Glacier National Park. Here at the store, the way she talked didn't matter. Fergie Cotter told her that when he hired her, and he repeated it whenever he observed a scene like the one she'd just endured.

"Coming through, excuse me, coming through." Jasper Cotter's deep voice rang out over the chatter of her waiting customers who used the time to compare notes on the latest gossip about the tiny Montana town's less than nine hundred people. A basket of leaf lettuce and plump tomatoes from the Cotter garden balanced on one shoulder, the owner's son barged through the swinging gates into the deli. *"Guder mariye."*

Esther Marie ducked her head and nodded. Jasper's solid, round body, so like his father's, invaded her pristine space. His face mottled red from the July heat and exertion, he swiped at the sweat beading on his nose with his free arm. Biceps bulged against the faded-blue cotton sleeves of his shirt. His man smells mingled with the aroma of teriyaki beef jerky. She heaved a breath. "Gud-d-d-er mari-ye."

He slid the basket onto the back counter and dusted off his big paws. "The line is too long. You should call *Mudder* back to help you."

And so it began.

"Your *d-d-d-aed* is s-s-s-ick to-to-day. Your m-m-m-udd-d-d-er is busy up-p-p-p front." A wave of embarrassed shame swept over Esther Marie. Her worsening stutter betrayed her inability to control her feelings when this man she'd known since childhood came around. Jasper might look like Fergie, but he had none of his father's easy way with people. He tended to go about business in a forward manner that put people off. "I-I-I-I've got it."

To prove her point she nodded to the next customer in line, Dr. Seeley, a retired dentist who lived on a plot of land next to the Plain community's school. His wife liked the roast beef with

Havarti cheese. He yelled when he talked to Esther Marie as if stuttering somehow meant she couldn't hear.

"There's no harm in asking for help." Jasper took a few steps back to allow her to access the cooler that held the roast beef. He lifted his straw hat and swiped at his auburn hair beginning to recede from his deeply tanned forehead. He must be twenty-five like Esther Marie, but he would be without hair by the time he reached middle age. Still, it didn't make him any less pleasing to the eye. He had milk chocolate–brown eyes half hidden by his dark-rimmed glasses. His smiles were rare, but that made them seem like a gift—especially when directed at her.

"Daed has indigestion and a headache. He said he'll be along as soon as the baking soda-and-water brew he drank does the trick."

According to Lucy, Fergie had been feeling badly all weekend. He wanted to chalk it up to Lucy's cooking, but she was sure he had the flu. She didn't want her husband to bring his germs into the store. Esther Marie didn't want to argue with Jasper. Her mother would say a good Plain woman never argued with a man. Being a good Plain woman required a steel trap for a jaw. At least it did for Esther Marie.

She slapped a price sticker on the roast beef package and handed it to Dr. Seeley. He grinned and shouted, "Thank you."

"I brought fresh tomatoes and lettuce from the garden. Both need to be washed well before you use them."

As if a person didn't know that. Esther Marie nodded at Hazel Kent, who reeled off an order for a dozen sandwiches for the ladies' auxiliary meeting at noon. Chips and cookies to go with it. "Giv-v-ve me a few m-m-m-inutes."

"No problem. Take your time." Mrs. Kent's phone rang, and

immediately took the call. "I'm waiting for the order, June. That girl who stutters is working on it. It's so nice they hire people with special needs here."

The unctuous tone grated on every nerve. Esther Marie managed to smile as she grabbed two bags of homemade whole wheat bread from the shelf. Special needs? The English had phrases that tickled her funny bone sometimes. This wasn't one of them. She had no special needs. To be like everyone else, to do her job, to become a wife and mother, to be a good, obedient, humble follower of Jesus, those were her only needs.

Jasper frowned. "We don't do it as a favor. Esther Marie is a good, smart employee—"

"It's o-o-o-o-k-k-kay." Esther Marie offered him her best smile. That he wanted to defend her was sweet. Despite his brusque ways, he never hurried her when she spoke and he never finished her sentences. A feat of patience for a man impatient with most people. "She m-m-m-m-eans well."

Still frowning, Jasper pointed to the machine she'd used to slice the ham and then the bologna. "The slicer is dirty. Aren't you supposed to clean as you go?"

Pause. Breathe. Imagine the words you want to say. The speech therapist her parents had taken her to see as a child had many tips, tricks, and exercises to help Esther Marie conquer her speech impediment. Books from a good friend had helped too. But a cure for what ailed her didn't exist. After a while, they couldn't afford to keep seeing a therapist who couldn't offer a cure. Esther Marie could do the exercises on her own. "I-I-I will—"

"Why are there jelly beans on the floor?"

In her haste to sample her snack, she must've dropped some. "I ▪ jelly beans."

A funny look flitted across his face. He opened his mouth. "I like—"

"Jasper, Jasper!" Lucy sped down the sewing notions aisle as fast as her short legs and chubby middle-aged body would permit. "I have to go. Salome called. She says your daed keeled over in the kitchen. She took him to the clinic. You're in charge of the store."

"*Nee!*" Jasper shoved through the swinging gates and strode toward his mother. "I'm going with you."

"But who'll take charge of the store?"

They both turned to stare at Esther Marie.

Her heart beat in her ears. Her stomach flopped. In four years she'd worked in every part of the store. She did inventory. She ordered products. She packed bulk items, unpacked discounted banana boxes, and priced canned goods. She even worked the registers over the lunch hour. "I can do it."

Not even a tiny stutter.

She waited until they rushed out the door to toss a handful of jelly beans into her mouth. A store manager needed her strength.

CHAPTER 2

S *tents. Blockage. Blood thinners.* Jasper Cotter dug in his heels and studied the cardiologist's face. Maybe if he read his lips, Jasper could translate the man's hurried speech about Father's condition into something that could be understood by Jasper's pea brain. Mother nodded, but she surely understood no more than he did.

The pain in Father's shoulder had increased until he could take it no more. In his agony he sank to the kitchen floor, scaring the bejeebers out of Salome. Jasper's younger sister called their favorite English driver, who took them to the community clinic in St. Ignatius. After a brief examination, arguments ensued. Father wanted to go home. The doctor said no and sent him by ambulance to the heart hospital in Missoula, forty-five minutes away.

The decision had been made in the time it took Jasper and Mother to arrive at the clinic. The ambulance darted away just as they pulled up. Fortunately, Eileen Jones hadn't left yet. The driver kindly filled her dusty gray minivan with gas and took the three of them—Salome insisted on coming along—the forty-two miles along Highway 93 south to Missoula.

"We're taking him into surgery now. It'll take a few hours."

The bespectacled doctor with clear gray eyes in a pale face looked younger than Jasper. He gestured toward doors in the distance in the long hallway where they stood. "Visit the cafeteria. Have some coffee. Get some food. You won't miss anything. The waiting room will be here when you get back."

"We'll be right here waiting." Mother gathered her faded-blue canvas bag against her chest. Her lower lip trembled, but her words were firm. "Take your time and fix him up good. Don't worry about us. We know what to do."

Pray and then accept Gott's will.

"I'll get the coffee and find us some snacks." Eileen patted Mother's arm as she smiled at Jasper and Salome. "You three rest your weary bones. I did this a few times with my sweet Bill before he passed, and the time will drag. Make yourselves comfy."

Her sandals made a clacking sound on the tile as she marched away in the opposite direction from the doctor, leaving them to find seats in the waiting room with its rows of cushioned seats and the flat-screen TV hanging on the wall. The muted show on it appeared to be some people talking or arguing about something.

Gaze averted, Jasper collapsed into the seat next to his mother and heaved a breath. Salome, who'd been sniffing and wiping her eyes with her apron during the entire ride to Missoula, took a seat on the other side. She was only thirteen. So young to be thrust into a situation like this. Another hour and Jasper would've been at the house for lunch before he returned to the field to harvest the corn.

No sense in playing the if-only game.

It seemed Jasper had been holding his breath since that moment in the store. What had he been doing in the seconds before his mother's shriek? He couldn't remember. Something about Esther Marie.

Yes, she was busy and didn't want to ask for help. He understood that. He should've offered to help her. What did he know about the deli meats, cheeses, salads, puddings, and pickles? Nothing. Not the menu or the prices. The thought twisted his gut into knots. He preferred to work behind the scenes. The idea of talking to strangers made his shoulders tense. His jaw got tight, like somebody had wired it shut.

As much as he wanted to help, he couldn't.

Esther Marie didn't seem to like him. Not so he could tell, anyway. She was never rude about it. She was far too kind to show it. She often seemed flustered around him. Her face turned red and her cornflower-blue eyes were downcast. She kept fiddling with her prayer covering as if it might slide from her wheat-colored hair. She couldn't wait for him to leave. That was obvious.

He set the thought aside, as he always did. With all the other facts that saddened him. Not having a wife or even the possibility of one. Which meant not having children of his own. Being so uncomfortable inside his own skin.

This isn't about you.

The voice in his ear sounded like *Groossdaadi* Stan's, but he had been dead for five years. Grandpa Stan was always right.

This wasn't the time to think about himself or the thin woman with a sweet disposition and sad eyes who made his heart do a funny little hippity-hop when he saw her. He turned to his mother. "It's hard to believe, isn't it?"

"As long as I can remember he's told me he's the picture of health." Mother's pensive face was a rare sight for the cheery woman who liked to sing English hymns while she cooked. "He always tells me, '*Fraa*, I don't need to go to the doctor. I'm healthy as a horse.'"

She imitated his hearty laugh perfectly. "That's what he always tells me."

"'I have the body of a twenty-year-old.'" Salome mimicked the way Father struck a pose at the supper table after a hard day's work at the store. With her blonde hair and blue eyes, his sister looked more like Mother than Father, but she managed a fair picture of the antics that made them all laugh as they finished off another delicious meal of moose steaks, fried potatoes, and huckleberry cobbler. "'Extra portions of cobbler for me.'"

Mother chuckled. Jasper managed a smile. "He'll be fine."

"Gott's will be done."

Mother closed her eyes. Salome clutched her hands in her lap and bowed her head. Jasper did the same. Two men arguing about the president's immigration policy droned on. A woman blew her nose with a noisy honk.

Gott, I know we're just passing through here. You know the number of days Daed will be with us. I'm asking You to let us have him awhile longer, if that's not too much to ask. Thy will be done. "Amen."

Mother raised her head and smiled. "What were you jawing at Esther Marie about?"

"What?"

"When I came out to tell you about your daed, it looked like Esther Marie was upset with you."

Mother never missed anything, no matter what was going on. Eagle eyes and elephant ears—that's what she always told her children, from Darcie, the oldest, down to John, the youngest. Her eight children knew better than to underestimate her ability to ferret out their transgressions.

"Nee. I brought in the lettuce and tomatoes you wanted for the sandwiches and salads." He leaned forward, put his elbows on his knees, and studied the rust-and-green geometric patterns in the gold carpet. The adrenaline of the past two hours drained away, leaving him with the desire to put his head in his hands and close his eyes. "She needed help. I thought she should call you, but she said nee."

"Esther Marie is more than able to handle a crowd. She knows when to call for help."

"I know that, but she should ask for help so customers aren't kept waiting." He softened his voice. His frustration had nothing to do with her work. He wanted her to like him. They'd known each other since they were babies. He didn't know what to say to her then, and he didn't know now. "I should've helped."

"I would've loved to see that." Mother chuckled, but her tone was kind. "You must really like Esther Marie if you're thinking about helping out with customers."

"I don't like—"

"Don't bother to deny it, *suh*." She patted his back as if he were still her eight-year-old with a skinned knee. "I see how your gaze follows her at church and at get-togethers. What I don't understand is why you don't do something about it. Poor girl will be an old lady if you don't court her soon."

"It's not that easy."

Nothing was easy when it came to people.

"I was going to ride my bike over to the store to help after I finished the laundry." Salome's eyes had reddened. She sniffed and wiped at her nose. "I was hanging the last load on the line when Daed came to the back porch and told me he felt real bad. I went into the kitchen to see what I could do. He fell to the floor right there in front of me."

She'd told them the story in the van, but her need to tell them yet again spoke of the shock she couldn't shake. Bless her heart for taking the focus off him and Esther Marie. If he were the hugging type, he'd hug his sister.

"It's okay, *dochder*." Mother stuck her arm around the girl's skinny shoulders and tucked her close. "You did the right thing. You went to the phone shack. You called Eileen. You went to the clinic with him. You called us. You did everything a dochder could do for her daed."

"Why do I feel like this?" She stifled a sob behind her hands. "Like I should've done more?"

"Because you love your daed." Mother smoothed back Salome's mussed hair, but it wouldn't slip back behind the prayer covering where it belonged. "It's hard, but you have to leave this in Gott's hands. Tears don't help. Worrying doesn't help."

"But it is human." Jasper didn't mean to contradict his mother. It was a fact. Salome shouldn't be made to feel bad because she felt sad or worried. Everybody did. He surely did. "We pray that Gott makes us stronger in our faith. He forgives us for our failings, sinful though they are."

Mother's gray eyebrows rose and fell. "You're right, suh. I forget you are a grown man and not a child."

As the oldest son he would be in charge of the farm and the store while his father recuperated. Jasper ran the farm anyway. That didn't bother him. But the store. That was another gaggle of geese. He stood and paced.

Eileen returned with a cardboard container filled with Styrofoam cups of coffee and a bag of pastries. "Comfort food all around." Eileen offered a cup to Jasper. "It'll warm you up. They keep it way too cold in these hospitals. I added sugar and creamer so it won't bother

111

your tummy so much. I know how that is, all those gastric juices boiling in there."

Eileen talked a lot, but she was kind. Jasper took the coffee. His hand shook. She smiled. "That's okay. That's why I put a nice, snug lid on it."

Heat blistered his face. No amount of steely determination quieted the shaking. He set the cup on an end table and resumed pacing.

"Suh."

He glanced at his mother. She shook her head and nodded at the chair. "Sit."

"I can't."

"Have a muffin."

His stomach rocked, and his throat closed. "I'll be back."

"Where are you going?"

He let the question disappear into the void of icy refrigerator air, stinky smells of cleanser and sickness, and the anxiety of the room's occupants, all waiting for word, hoping for good news, fearing the worst.

The hallway offered the closest thing to the wide-open spaces he craved. The Mission Valley where he'd been born and grown up offered a man open land to farm, clean air to breathe, and mountain vistas in the distance that provided a feast for the eyes every single day. No more beautiful place existed in this world.

The windows in the hallway revealed a parking lot and a busy road and more buildings beyond. No succor there.

Gott, worry is sinful. I know better in my head, but my heart is giving me trouble. I want to be obedient. I am humble. But I tremble at the thought that Daed will die. He's young still and full of life. People like him because he is kind and generous and funny, all things I'm not. I can't be him or like him. If You could see Your way to keep him on this earth a little longer, I would be forever thankful.

"Excuse me."

He squeezed against a wall to allow a woman in scrubs pushing a cart to pass him. She smiled. "There's a chapel on the first floor, if you need a quiet place to pray."

How did she know he'd been praying?

"A person can pray anywhere." Not the right answer. If Darcie were here, she'd rebuke him. His oldest sister often tried to peel off his hard, crusty outsides to what she called his internal honeypot. "I mean, thank you."

"I recognize a praying person when I see one." The woman pulled out a gold cross on a chain from inside her scrubs. "I sometimes walk down the hall praying as I go too."

"Okay."

With another smile she continued on her trek. "I'll pray for you. God bless you."

Her kind words eased the tightness in his chest. The headache that battered his temples ratcheted back to a low throb. God put people where they were needed. A person couldn't help but notice. *Danki, Gott.*

"At this rate, you'll beat a trench in this hallway with all that pacing."

The familiar booming voice of Darcie's husband, Bart Detweiler, filled the space. Just like the oversized man. He seemed incapable of quiet. Bishop David Hershberger and Deacon Matthew Miller followed. Darcie brought up the rear. A caravan of concern.

"Esther Marie sent Rachel to the house with the news," David added. "What do you hear?"

Nothing. They've heard nothing. Jasper worked to steady his

voice. "They did something called a heart catheter and found blockage, so they're putting in stents to open up the vessels that carry blood to the heart."

David tugged at his brownish-blond beard, now beginning to show signs of fine silver threads. He'd been young, only thirty, when the lot fell to him. "You should go back. You're needed at the store. Chuck is waiting to take you."

Chuck Larson, another regular driver, had a twelve-passenger van favored for family trips and vacations. Jasper didn't need a big van for one. "Eileen is with Mudder and Salome." He jerked his head toward the waiting room. "In there. Waiting."

Because that's what people did in places like this. They waited.

"We'll call the store with word." Bart poured earnestness into the statement. "Darcie will be with Mudder. Kimberly is at the house taking care of the *kinner*. Get James and John to finish bailing the hay. When your daed awakes, he can be happy that the family took care of business."

Bart had a plan for the entire Cotter clan. James, John, Darcie, and Kimberly were Jasper's brothers and sisters. Not Bart's. Jasper cleared his throat. "I should be here for Mudder."

"We're here," David pointed out. "Darcie and Salome are here for Lucy."

They were right. Duty called. Jasper would take charge of the store.

His stomach lurched. His breakfast of sausage, eggs, biscuits with strawberry jam, and milk threatened to spill onto the slick pale-blue tile floor. *Do not do that. Puking now is a sign of weakness. A sign of fear and worry. An obedient follower doesn't fear or worry.*

He inhaled and breathed out through his nose. He fixed what

he prayed was a calm look on his face. "It's been an hour. The doctor said two total, if all goes well. I'll expect your call."

He said his good-byes and walked out into the sizzling heat with Eileen chattering like a yellow finch in spring.

A man who ran a farm could run a store.

Even if it meant talking to people.

People like Esther Marie. If a woman who stuttered could do it, so could he.

CHAPTER 3

Walking a mile in Lucy's shoes felt more like forty miles uphill through snow mixed with sleet and gale-force winds from the north. Esther Marie smiled to herself. Such a fanciful exaggeration. In the three hours since Lucy and Jasper's mad dash from the store, she'd been pulled in every direction a dozen times over, but nothing had happened she couldn't handle. Years of experience held her in good stead.

Years in which she'd longed to be a wife and a mother, but God gave her this instead. Even if potential suitors didn't see past her stutter, Fergie did and so did God.

A woman had to take blessings where she found them.

Esther Marie knelt and gingerly picked broken glass from the mess of cherry jam on the floor in front of the homemade jelly-and-jam display near the front of the store. The towheaded English girl who dropped the jar whimpered and hid her face against her mom's pink-and-purple-polka-dotted leggings.

"It's okay." Esther covered the remains with an old washrag and scooped them into a trash can. "Ac-c-c-i-dent-s-s-s hap-p-p-p-pen all the time. We mop every d-d-d-ay."

"Thank you for cleaning up the mess. I'm sorry." The mother, who looked in a family way, patted her child's mass of curls. "I'll pay for it, of course."

"No n-n-need." Esther rose. "Accidents happen."

Two lovely words with no stutter.

In fact, Rachel had just cleaned up a package of pretzels from the floor on the bulk aisle, the result of a fight between two pre-schoolers who wanted to be the ones to open their snack.

The mother nodded. "That's kind of you. Thanks again." She scooped up the child and plopped her in the basket, which produced squeals of protest. "That's what happens when you touch something after I told you not to."

Off they went. A squawk on Esther Marie's walkie-talkie indicated one of the girls was trying to speak to her. Rachel hadn't mastered this simple technology Fergie had instituted to allow them to handle business quickly instead of running through the aisles of the big store to discuss business while customers often waited for service or answers.

Fergie was all about customer service.

Please, Gott, heal his body.

"Esther Marie, are you there? It's Rachel."

She tugged the radio from its perch on her apron waistband. "What do you need?"

"The tape ran out on Sally's register."

"Do you know how to put in a new one?"

"Jah."

"Then you should probably do it."

"Right. Jah. I will."

It seemed Rachel simply liked talking on the radio. Esther Marie kept that observation to herself.

"Oh, and the deliveryman is here with the ice cream."

A much more important piece of news. A multitude of ice cream flavors kept folks coming back to the deli for a single serving on a cone, a dish of their favorite rocky road, or a gallon of chocolate fudge. Plus all the cartons they toted in their baskets to the registers to take home. Ice cream was one of their biggest sellers in the summer.

Esther stifled a sigh. "Tell him to start bringing in the order. I'll be right there to sign for it." To count boxes and compare them to the order before she signed. Lucy had taught her well.

"Mrs. Lowell is on the line. She wants to know if it's too late to put in an order for two dozen sandwiches for a meeting tonight." Cara was less excited about using the walkie-talkie than her sister Rachel. She only spoke on it when absolutely necessary. Her voice squeaked, but then it often squeaked. She was always excited and always happy. "She wants potato salad, chips, pickles, and cookies too."

Esther Marie keyed the radio a third time. "It's not t-t-t-oo late. T-T-T-take down exactly what she wants, especially on the s-s-s-s-andwich-ch-ches. Put the order on the incoming p-p-p-eg at the d-d-d-eli. As s-s-s-soon as I get done with the ice cr-cr-r-eam order—"

"Mrs. Kowalski is upset about a box of cereal she bought yesterday." Rachel skidded to a stop a few inches from Esther Marie. "She says it's only half full. She wants to talk to Lucy."

Customers came first, then deliverymen. The sandwiches weren't needed until the end of the day. Prioritizing, that's what Fergie called it. A regular complainer, Mrs. Kowalski frequently wanted her money back for something. Fergie said the customer was always right. "Where is sh-sh-sh-he?"

"Fuming by the front door."

Wiping her hands on the towel she had tucked in her apron, Esther Marie followed the other woman through the bulk aisle.

"Uh-oh." A funny look on her pretty face, Rachel glanced back and halted. Esther Marie nearly collided with her. The other woman hunched her shoulders. "Does he know who he's dealing with?"

Uh-oh was right. Jasper stood by the door talking to Mrs. Kowalski. Her pudgy cheeks were bright red, and her index finger jabbed precariously close to Jasper's smooth-shaven face. Esther Marie slipped around Rachel and raced to intercede.

"The cereal boxes are sealed." Despite Jasper's flat tone, a pulse throbbed in his jaw. "It says on the box that the contents settle."

"I paid good money for a full box of cereal." Her double chins quivering, Mrs. Kowalski shook the offending box of corn flakes so vigorously they likely could be used as panko for breading chicken or fish now. "I don't know how you did it, but you siphoned cereal out and you're selling it on the bulk aisle. You're cheating me. I want my money back."

"W-w-w-we c-c-c-an do that." Esther Marie reached for the box. "You c-c-c-ould buy on the b-b-b-ulk aisle s-s-s-o you can see what you're get-t-t-ting."

Jasper tugged the box from her hand. "Why would we give her the money back? We didn't cheat from her. We didn't steal."

"C-c-c-c-ustomer is always r-r-r-right-t-t." No time to breathe. No time to imagine the words in her head. Esther Marie stood between a furious woman and an implacable man. Mother said men were always right. They should be respected and their decisions were final. Especially a man like Jasper. Someday Fergie's oldest son would own the store. But not today. "Fergie s-s-s-says hap-p-p-p-p-y cust-t-t-tomers come b-b-b-b-back."

Heat toasted her body head to toe. Blood pounded in her ears.

Gott? She never stuttered in her prayers. She longed for healing, but it never came. "I-t-t-t'-s *gut* b-b-b-b-usi-n-n-n-ness."

"Fergie's right." Mrs. Kowalski uttered a curse word. She didn't seem to notice how Jasper's body stiffened and blotches of red consumed his neck and fair-skinned cheeks. "And he knows better than to call me a liar."

"No one called you a liar." Jasper looked truly perplexed. "Nor do Plain people lie."

Customers stopped to stare. Even Cara had given up any semblance of checking grocery items on the register.

"It's F-F-F-Fergie's p-p-p-p-p . . ." The word wouldn't come out. Esther Marie struggled for breath. *Please, Gott, please.* "M-M-M-oney b-b-b—"

"Money-back guarantee." The wattle under her arm swinging beyond her sleeveless blouse, Mrs. Kowalski stabbed at the air in triumph. Her bosom heaved, making her pearl necklace rise and fall. "It's store policy."

"I'm in charge of the store now." The splotches on his face darkened. Jasper paused and frowned. "You're welcome to exchange the box for another one of the same price. That is a good compromise, isn't it?"

"It is not! Give me my box of cereal." Mrs. Kowalski swiped it from his hand. She whirled and shoved open the door. At the last second she whirled and drilled them with fiery indignation. "You won't see me spending my husband's hard-earned money in this store anymore."

Chins high in the air, she flounced out, and the door shut behind her.

Disbelief written across his deeply tanned face, Jasper scratched his nose with callused, stubby fingers. "What was she so mad about?"

CHAPTER 4

All's well that ends well. The door swung shut. Quiet prevailed for a few seconds. Sweet, soothing quiet. Jasper heaved a breath. His first crisis in Father's absence had ended peacefully. Mrs. Kowalski might be peeved now, but after she thought it over, she would see that Jasper had offered a good solution.

Or had he?

Esther Marie's expression said otherwise. An exchange of equal value for a box of cereal seemed a fair solution for everyone involved. Maybe Esther Marie didn't like it that he had intervened. Plain women shouldn't question a man's decision. Sure Mother argued with Father frequently, but she accepted his decisions without sulking. Esther Marie didn't look sulky. She looked worried. She probably enjoyed being in charge, but she had to have known that would be a temporary situation.

He picked up his hat from his head, wiped sweat from his brow, and settled the hat in its rightful place. The girls at the registers went back to work. The customers' chatter resumed.

Esther Marie didn't move. Her perturbed expression didn't fade.

"What?"

"We j-j-j-just lo-s-s-t-t-t a gut cus-s-s-t-t-t-omer."

"Nee. After she thinks it over, she'll realize my solution was a gut one."

"You d-d-d-on't know M-M-Mrs. K-K-K-K . . ." She paused. Her mouth worked. It gaped and closed. Her hands fisted.

Esther Marie had acne scars, but they made her face more interesting. Her eyes were the color of flowers. Even as she fought to do something everyone else took for granted, she couldn't be ugly. She fought a valiant struggle. He learned that word in a book about kings and queens and knights. They fought with swords. Esther fought to have words. He waited. His mother said that was the best way to help Esther Marie.

Don't hurry her. We're always in such a hurry. Why? We're not going to a fire. We sell groceries.

Mother's pearls of wisdom strung together would make a necklace like the one worn by Mrs. Kowalski, only it would stretch the length of the state of Montana.

"Kowalski." A flash of triumph brightened Esther Marie's face. "Hard to p-p-p-lease."

Jasper shrugged. Many people were hard to please. That didn't mean they should get away with it. He started toward the back of the store. Receipts would have to be tallied and the deposit slip filled out. A trip to the bank would be necessary. That much he knew.

The real problem came in determining what he did *not* know. How could he take care of a business that remained mostly a mystery to him? On the other hand, how hard could it be? As Mother often pointed out, they sold groceries.

"I'll be in the office." He threw the statement out for the girls at the registers, mainly. "Esther Marie, who's in the deli?"

"M-M-M-artha. How is F-F-F-ergie?"

The turmoil with Mrs. Kowalski had taken his mind from his father for a few minutes. "It's his heart. He's in surgery. The doctor says he can fix it."

"Gut." Her hands fluttered. "You lef-t-t-t the hos-s-s-pital?"

"Bart was there. And David and Matthew." His brother-in-law liked to be in charge, too, but as bishop, David had the most to say about the situation. "I was told to come here. They'll call when the surgery is over. You should be running the deli. That's what you do."

At least that's where he typically found her when he brought in the produce needed to make sandwiches, salads, and such.

"Don't you want to sign for the load of ice cream that just came in?" Rachel had one hand on a package of butter and the other on the register. "I think the man is waiting, and it's going to start melting soon."

"Why didn't you tell me sooner?"

Rachel's eyebrows rose. She looked past him to Esther Marie.

Esther Marie had already veered to the right and the far aisle that housed the refrigerated cases that held the frozen foods.

He lengthened his stride and followed. Esther Marie stood dwarfed by a tall, muscle-bound deliveryman. A tiny wrinkle in the middle of her forehead, she studied an invoice on a clipboard. The deliveryman talked in a low tone on his cell phone while he waited.

"I can do that." Jasper held out his hand for the clipboard. "You were going to the deli."

"You have to c-c-c-ount every-th-th-th-ing. Some of the ord-d-d-der goes to the d-d-d-deli."

"I know." Now he did.

Chewing her lower lip, she ducked her head, gave him the clipboard, and walked away.

"Hey, Esther, I think you've got a problem." The cell phone still stuck to one ear, the deliveryman opened one of the refrigerated cases. "Yeppers, that's what I thought. Warm air. This case ain't working."

"Are you sure, Kevin?" Esther Marie spun around and darted back to the man's side. "*Ach*. Nee."

She knew this man's name? Jasper set that strange fact aside for later examination and planted himself next to her. Melting ice cream dripped from the cartons already in the case. Dribbles of vanilla, chocolate, and strawberry meandered until they crossed paths and made mud on the shelf. The supply of cartons was low, but not so low they could afford to have what remained in the case go to waste. "What do we do?"

Kevin and Esther Marie exchanged glances. "You need to move everything in this case to one that's working." Kevin's kind tone didn't mask the surprised look on his face. *Obviously*, his expression said. "We'll have to make room for the new load somewhere else too."

"An-d-d-d c-c-c-call an elec-t-t-t-trician." Esther Marie scooted down the aisle to a case that held frozen vegetables and fruits. "There's r-r-r-oom here."

Jasper knew nothing about electricity. An enormous store like this required electricity to keep food at proper temperatures. The Health Department inspectors made a big deal about it. Bits and pieces of Father's long-winded explanations at the supper table had lodged in Jasper's memory. The *Gmay* permitted electricity for businesses, which allowed the grocery store and the dairy down the road and other Plain-owned businesses to continue to stay open.

It gave them a way to earn a living because their small farms no longer did. Farming was hard work, but it kept Plain families together and off the electricity grid that connected them to the rest of the world. The fallen world. "It's not your job . . ." Jasper searched for the man's name. "Kevin. You brought in the new order. You should go."

"I don't mind helping." Kevin flexed big biceps. The green polo shirt stretched tight across his chest muscles. "I'll pitch in and we'll get everything situated ASAP."

Esther Marie scurried away. Where was she going? Why did she leave him with the ice cream man? Jasper scrambled for a response. "Don't you have other deliveries?"

"They'll wait." Kevin pushed his oversized dolly several feet to the next case. "We'll stick these in with the veggies."

"But they don't go there."

"Desperate times call for desperate measures." Kevin grinned. He really was a cheerful guy. A nice guy, which was why Esther Marie liked him. "Besides, people would rather buy ice cream than veggies any day."

Jasper forced a return smile even though his heart wasn't in it. Smiling was a muscle that needed regular workouts. That's what Darcie said. Maybe if he smiled more, Esther Marie would like him more. She would also like a man who could take charge of a situation. Jasper opened several doors. Kevin handed him the cartons, and he made stacks by flavor and size.

"That Esther Marie sure is a nice girl." Kevin flashed another smile as he handed a gallon carton of old-fashioned vanilla to Jasper. "Is she your girlfriend?"

"No." What kind of question was that? Did English men talk about their special friends with strangers? He handed Jasper three one-gallon containers of old-fashioned vanilla ice cream. His favorite. It went best with apple pie, also his favorite, especially on a hot July night. "Is there room for the rest of this box?"

"Yep. I just wonder why no one has snapped her up. She's sweeter than a sugar cookie." Kevin rearranged the cartons to make more room for a stack of cherry-berry ice cream. "I know she stutters and she isn't much to look at, but she's a hard worker and she's so nice. When you get to know her, she kind of starts to look pretty. She would make some guy a good wife."

Kevin was right about a lot of things. Esther Marie was nice, sweet, and hardworking. But he was wrong about one thing. A man didn't have to get to know her to see how pretty she was. It sounded like this English man might be interested in Esther Marie. Angst wrapped itself around Jasper's windpipe and sucked the air from his lungs. Sooner or later, some man would snap her up, and then where would he be?

Jasper usually saved these thoughts for when he was alone in his room. Alone and lonely. It was his fault. A person couldn't court if he didn't ask a woman to take a ride in his buggy. The thought made his hands sweat and his stomach curl up in a knot. He cleared his throat. "Plain people don't talk much about looks. Besides, courting is private."

Now the man would think Jasper and Esther Marie *were* courting.

If only it were true. What would it feel like to touch the soft skin on her cheek? It would be nice to hold her hand. She had nice lips. What would it be like to kiss them? A shiver tickled his spine. Surely the draft of cold air from the case and the ice cream carton in his hands were to blame. Not his thoughts. A Plain man shouldn't have thoughts like that.

How did a man know? His father never talked about it, and Jasper didn't have friends his own age growing up. He spent most of his time working, hunting, fishing, and camping with his family. He hadn't been lonely then.

"Sorry. I didn't mean to overstep my bounds." Kevin shoved his Colorado Grizzlies cap back on his head. "I'm just naturally curious, and it gives me something to think about when I'm driving my route. That and whether climate change is real and who really started the internet and did extraterrestrials actually land in Roswell. I know you don't mix with outsiders, so what's a poor girl like Esther Marie to do?"

"Don't worry about it."

"Don't w-w-w-w-orry about w-w-w-what-t-t-t?" A basket of wet rags, fresh garbage bags, and paper towels in her arms, Esther Marie trotted toward them. "I br-br-brought t-t-t-towels to clean up the m-m-m-melted ice cr-cr-cr-eam as we go."

"Maybe you can salvage some of it." Kevin and Jasper dodged Esther Marie's question at the same time. He opened the malfunctioning case and handed her a sagging carton of strawberry ice cream. Liquid that looked like pink milk ran down his fingers and arm and dripped on the floor. "Or maybe not."

"Did you call the electrician?" Jasper stowed three more tubs in the case. When no response came, he looked back. "Isn't that where you went—to call?"

"Nee." She applied elbow grease to the mess in the offending case. With efficient movements, she slid the sopping towels into a trash bag and went back for more. "You said you were in charge."

Not a single stutter. Her emphasis on *in charge* was unmistakable.

"I know, but I—"

"The n-n-n-umber is on the Rolod-d-dex."

Kevin didn't bother to hide his grin. "Checkmate, dude. Guess you better make that call."

Despite the desire to whine "What do I say," Jasper wiped his hands on his pants, nodded, and made his most dignified exit.

A tiny giggle followed him down the aisle—he was almost certain of it.

CHAPTER 5

B eing mean-spirited never felt good. The giggle had escaped on its own. Not admitting to a sin resulted in another sin. Esther Marie scrubbed the freezer even harder, but the ache of her muscles didn't take her mind from the look on Jasper's face as he trudged away to call the electrician. Anxiety and a determination to do what had to be done mingled in a man who everyone said was better suited for farming than running a business.

Fergie and Lucy's other sons were too young. They helped Jasper on the farm when they weren't in school, and they only came to the store for big cleanings or rearranging stock when the entire family got involved. Jasper was the oldest son, but truth be told, Darcie had a better head for business and people liked her. As a wife and mother though, she was needed at home.

How could a smart man be so bad at dealing with people? He didn't say hello to customers or to his father's employees—also his employees. He simply plowed past them without even a nod. People liked to be seen. They liked to be appreciated.

Esther Marie didn't mind if he didn't greet her. It saved her from stuttering a response. She didn't want to be noticed by most people.

She tried to be humble and know her place. But much as she disliked the idea, she wanted to be seen by Jasper.

Maybe she wanted him to recognize that she could run the store. This was her domain, the thing she did well. It wasn't her first choice, but when her friends married and she didn't, the store gave her a reason to get up in the morning. It made her feel useful. She needed it.

And, it seemed, she needed Jasper to notice her. She didn't want to delve into why.

If she couldn't admit the truth to herself, she was in deep trouble. It wasn't about the store. Jasper rarely said much to other people, but when he saw people being ugly to her, he spoke up. He stepped up. He made her feel protected, even when she didn't need it.

"I put the rest of the new stock in with the frozen meals and pizzas." Kevin parked his squeaky four-wheel dolly next to Esther Marie. He glanced at his watch. "I really have to go before customers start calling the boss. People get crazy when they run out of ice cream."

"I b-b-be-lieve it." Esther Marie wiped her hands on a paper towel and took the pen he offered her. A quick signature and their business was finally done. "S-S-S-orry about m-m-m-making you do s-s-s-so much w-w-w-ork."

"What are friends for?" Kevin had a sunny smile and a sunny disposition, yet nothing about him caused Esther Marie to think about him after he disappeared from sight. He came. He went. Right now, he needed to go. "Do you have your next order written out, or do you want to have Mr. Big call me?"

A laugh burbled up in Esther Marie. "Mr. Big. Very good." Four whole words without a stutter. When she relaxed she didn't do badly. Even though the store had a website maintained by an outside company, Fergie drew the line at having the internet in the store. Rather, the Gmay drew the line and Fergie agreed. Esther Marie's opinion didn't count. "We w-w-w-ill c-c-call."

His whistle mingling with the dolly's squeaky wheels, Kevin ambled away.

Esther Marie spent another fifteen minutes moving ice cream sandwiches, Popsicles, Fudgsicles, frozen yogurt, and frozen non-dairy ice cream products into open nooks and crannies in the other freezers. Their new homes had no rhyme or reason. Customers would be up in arms when they couldn't find their favorite cold sweet treat. It couldn't be helped. She glanced at the clock overhead. Almost four. She needed to get those sandwiches made for Mrs. Lowell. The girl working the deli had to focus on the customers in front of her.

She picked up the heavy-duty black trash bag. Her muscles strained. A lot of product had been lost to this small fiasco. Would Fergie want the number of ice cream units counted for sake of the inventory? They sold tons of ice cream in the summer, but not this much. The inventory wouldn't match. She set the bag back down.

Static burst forth from her walkie-talkie. "Esther Marie, come to the office. Esther Marie, come to the office."

Apparently Jasper thought comments over the radio were similar to those done over a loudspeaker. She stifled a giggle. He might want to speak to her in private so he could berate her for making him look bad in front of Kevin. Her lighthearted giggles subsided. Or maybe he wanted to rehash the disagreement with Mrs. Kowalski. Either way, she could hold her own in the discussion—if she didn't stutter so much. "On my w-w-w-way."

"Bring Rachel."

Rachel's red face and frown spoke volumes about her desire to go to the office with Esther Marie. "Why does he want me?"

"I don't know. Let's go find out."

"Did I do something wrong?" Rachel rushed around the wooden counter. She stubbed her toe on the corner, screeched, danced around for a second on one foot, then stumbled alongside Esther Marie. "I've been dusting the displays and straightening the cookbooks between customers. I'm keeping busy."

"It's prob-b-ably nothing." *It's probably all to do with me.* "Don't w-w-w-worry."

"Easy for you to say." Rachel smirked. "Jasper likes you."

"He d-d-d-does n-n-ot." Not in a million years did Jasper like her. He'd never asked her to take a buggy ride with him. To be fair, he never asked any girl to take a ride. He never even made small talk. Which made sense because making conversation with a person who stuttered was no fun for even the most patient person. Jasper had patience for allowing her to finish her sentences, but it was possible he didn't start conversations to avoid all the waiting. "You are d-d-d-d-d-aft-t-t-t."

"He likes you. That's why you make him so nervous. He doesn't know what to say to you."

"I d-d-d-on't b-b-b-elieve you."

"Try talking to him about something besides work sometime." Rachel's worried look had disappeared for a second. Then it reappeared. "Let me know how it goes if I get fired. I'll be at home."

Nothing else needed to be said about this ridiculous topic. Fortunately the later-afternoon lull had started. No customers waited at the registers. This would be true until people started dropping in on their way home from work. Esther Marie took a quick peek at the deli. Martha was busy chopping vegetables for prepackaged salads. It would be nice to compliment her on her industriousness, but Esther Marie didn't have time. Others could throw a quick kind word over their shoulders. For her it would be a laborious, painful process. Instead, she waved and kept going.

Fergie's small, neat office was even tinier with Rachel, Jasper, and Esther Marie crowded around the desk. Jasper stood despite the serviceable office chair. He stared at the Rolodex, which he had pulled forward so it sat directly in the middle of the scarred walnut desk, as if it might uncoil and strike him like a poisonous snake.

"We're here." Rachel scooted closer to Esther Marie. She tucked her hands behind her back like a schoolgirl getting ready to recite her multiplication tables. "Esther Marie said you wanted to see me."

To be able to talk like that, one smooth, pearly word after another strung together. Esther Marie's throat ached with the desire. The speech therapist said it did happen as children matured into adults. Sometimes. Esther Marie had not been one of those blessed with a miraculous clarity of speech.

I know it's not mine to ask why, Gott. But a girl can't help but wonder. The words of a scripture her father often quoted to her when she begged him to explain her plight came to mind. *"Blessed is the man that endureth temptation: for when he is tried, he shall receive the crown of life, which the Lord hath promised to them that love him"* (James 1:12 KJV).

As a child she had no idea what that meant. Mother said it meant she should hang in there and love God just the way she was. So she had and she did. "Jah, w-w-we are here."

Jasper crossed his arms. He had the start of a paunch that would someday look like Fergie's more well-fed belly. He shifted his feet. His gaze moved from the Rolodex to Esther Marie. "I want you to get the number for the electrician and give it to Rachel so she can call him."

At least forty minutes had passed since Jasper strode from the ice cream aisle to the office to make this call. What had he been doing all that time? Esther Marie opened her mouth. She closed it. This was a delicate situation. A Plain woman who never used a phone as a child and rarely as an adult knew how intimidating this instrument of torture could be. Add a stutter to the mix and it was impossible. Esther Marie tried never to be in the office alone. If the phone rang she would have to answer it. She had on more than one occasion, and it had been excruciating. The callers often couldn't understand her, and they couldn't imagine why a place of business would have a person with a speaking disability answer the phone.

Jasper didn't stutter. The phone probably didn't even bother him. The person at the other end of the line did.

Making him feel worse about it served no purpose. Esther Marie picked up the Rolodex and spun it around to the *e*'s. Fergie liked to keep things simple. The cards of his two favorite electricians were missing. "D-D-D-id you c-c-c-c-all?" She pointed to the cards lying next to Fergie's favorite Montana state coffee cup. "Either one is gut-t-t-t."

"One, a voice was talking, but when I tried to answer, it was a recording. I tried to leave a message but it hung up on me." He rubbed the back of his neck and rolled his shoulders. "The other number no one answered."

That was Coop Parker. He was a jack-of-all-trades, but his electrical work was first rate. He figured if people really needed him they would call back.

Esther Marie handed the cards to Rachel. She frowned. "Why don't you call?"

"Because she stutters." Jasper's exasperation crowded the room. He threw his hands up and plopped into the chair. "I'd rather she did it. She knows what she's doing. I don't. But I can't expect her to make a call, can I?"

That had to be the nicest backhanded compliment anyone had ever paid her. He probably didn't even realize what a compliment it was.

Rachel grabbed the cards. "Silly me. I forget sometimes that other people aren't used to the way you talk."

It would be nice if everyone in the world had Rachel and Jasper's attitude. "T-T-ry C-C-C-oop first."

This time the electrician answered. Rachel got to the crux of the situation quickly, and within minutes the store was on his list of stops for the next morning.

"You can go back to work, Rachel." Jasper wore his relief like a sweat-soaked shirt. "Can you wait a minute, Esther Marie?"

With her back to Jasper, Rachel mouthed *good luck* and stuck her tongue out at Esther Marie before she left the office. In the interest of decorum she left the door open. Did the office seem warmer than it had a minute before?

She waited. Jasper shuffled through papers on the desk. He snatched a pencil from a plastic cup and let it hover over a row of numbers on a spreadsheet. It looked like a summary of expenses for the month. Reading upside down was one of Esther Marie's secret talents.

Her armpits were beginning to sweat. Her hair felt wet under her prayer *kapp*. Here she stood alone with a man she couldn't fathom but often thought about right before she went to sleep at night, and he seemed to be ignoring her. "I have to m-m-m-ake M-M-Mrs. Lowell's s-s-s-sandwiches."

He dropped the pencil and leaned back in the chair. "I'm sorry."

Sorry for making her wait? "It's ok-k-k-ay. I still have t-t-t-time."

"Not about that. About Mrs. Kowalski." His deep voice seemed to get lower and lower. "I was wrong. I'm sorry."

Admitting he was wrong probably felt as good as fire ants in his boots. "It's ok-k-k-ay."

What if Rachel was right? Maybe she should try to talk to him. Easy for Rachel to say. Talking never worked out for Esther Marie. She edged toward the door. "I want to help-p-p-p you."

"Danki, but if I need help, I'll let you know."

"Everybody n-n-n-n-eeds help-p-p-p s-s-s-sometimes."

His gaze meandered from the desk to her face to the wall behind her. "If Daed can run a store, so can I. I'm not stupid."

She never, ever thought Jasper was anything but smart. Too smart for his own good. In school he always got his arithmetic problems right, and when he read aloud, he never messed up the English words. "I didn't s-s-s-ay—"

The phone rang. The shrill sound made them both jump.

One ring, two, three. Jasper stared at it as if mesmerized. Esther Marie caught her breath and reached for it. Jasper pushed her hand away. A gentle but firm rebuff.

He picked up the receiver and reeled off the store's name. "Jah. Jah. Gut. Gut. Jah. Ach. I will. *Guder daag.*"

He sat with the receiver in his hands for several seconds. Esther Marie finally took it from him and laid it in the cradle. This time he didn't object.

"Your daed?"

"Jah. He's out of surgery. They did what they had to do." Jasper mopped his face with a faded-blue bandana. He cleared his throat.

"He'll be gut as new, but he has to stay in the hospital for two or three days."

A long time for a man like Fergie to be confined to a bed. He would not like the hospital. If he didn't have Lucy's biscuits and gravy, her fried chicken, her cherry pie, and her fried potatoes, he would be unhappy. He would grouse and grumble and complain to anyone who would listen.

"Gut. He will be back at w-w-w-ork-k-k-k s-s-s-oon."

"Bart says he cannot return to work for at least another two weeks after he gets out."

Jasper sounded the same way Esther Marie felt. Sad. And nervous.

Even a few days was too much.

Jasper stared at her. Esther Marie forced herself not to lower her gaze. The pulse jumped in his jaw. No matter how hard he tried to hide his consternation, his eyes gave him away. Jasper was afraid.

"He'll be fine." A sudden powerful urge to comfort him filled Esther Marie. How did a woman do that for a grown man? Her little brothers only needed a smile and a pat on the back. A hot peanut butter cookie fresh out of the oven and a glass of milk might be necessary if the hurt turned out to be more egregious. When they were younger, she even got away with a hug now and again before they broke loose and ran away, hooting about girl cooties. But a grown man—not a family member—mustn't be touched.

"The doct-t-t-ors in M-M-Missoula are gut-t-t-t." He would be right as rain before they knew it. The words were too hard. If only they would tumble out with no effort the way they did for other people.

The emotions on Jasper's face faded. He fiddled with the pencil. "You're right. He'll be fine, Gott willing." A careful blank look slid into place. "I better get to work. This deposit needs to be to-taled. And you have sandwiches to make."

Esther Marie backpedaled to the door. Words were not the only way to help him. Doing her best work would make his life easier. Keeping the store spic-and-span, the shelves stocked, and the customers happy. She excelled at these tasks. As she would at running the store. If only Jasper could see that. He could go back to the farm and leave her to do what she did best. A default job, true, but the only one open to her when no man stepped forward willing to put up with a bride who stuttered.

"Jah. If you n-e-e-ed anything, c-c-c-call me on the r-r-r-adio."

He didn't look up. "Danki, I won't."

Two weeks stretched before Esther Marie like an eternity.

• • •

CHAPTER 6

• • •

Plain women believed in the healing power of food as the answer for all forms of trauma. The tantalizing aroma of hamburger, onion, and garlic frying greeted Jasper when he tromped through the kitchen door of the only home he'd known in his twenty-five years. Despite the deep-seated desire to have time alone to contemplate all the ways he'd fallen short today—especially when it came to Esther Marie—Jasper managed a smile. The food smelled good. His stomach growled. He hadn't eaten since breakfast.

Aenti Callie stood at the counter chopping tomatoes. With the exception of her still-blonde hair, she could've been Mother's twin. Plump and sweet with a splash of vinegar.

"You're here. I'm making tacos for supper." She waved a knife precariously close to his nose. "Lois brought stuffed shells. Maisie dropped off a tuna-noodle casserole. Cora brought an elk roast. There's a bunch of stuff. I put them in the freezer. Lucy can pull them out as needed."

"Sounds good."

"You're here! I washed towels and hung them on the line." Hannah, Callie's middle daughter, strolled through the kitchen with an empty laundry basket swinging from one hand. Her face was flushed with sun and heat, but her smile widened. "I'll have the pants done in a few minutes."

"Gut. Mudder will appreciate the help." He appreciated it too. "Did Bart call here?"

"Nee, but Darcie came home. She's in the living room." Aunt Callie made shooing motions. Again the knife strayed dangerously close to his body. "Go say hello. She can fill you in. But don't go too far. Supper will be ready in two and a half shakes. If you're good you can have some of the apple pie I made with ice cream."

"My favorite."

"I know." Her sympathetic smile only made her look more like his mother. "After the day you've had, I figured you could use it."

Jasper shuffled into the living room. His whole body screamed with exhaustion. This day had refused to end. He would still be at the store, but Esther Marie had insisted on closing up. She had finished the sandwiches for Mrs. Lowell and said she needed to do a quick inventory in order to prepare a list of items needed for one of their vendors. Leaving while she was still there felt wrong, but she insisted. She practically pushed him out the door.

Darcie was nursing her baby. She cuddled the tiny girl under a lightweight crib quilt. Darcie wore her childbearing well. She'd received all the best attributes of their parents. Father's auburn hair, Mother's blue eyes, average height, but slim as Mother must have been before her years of childbearing. Her peaches-and-cream skin glowed with health. She looked up and smiled Mother's sweet smile. "You made it. How are things at the store?"

"How is Daed?"

"Weak, disoriented, peeved, but he'll be fine." Darcie adjusted something under the blanket and brought little Mary out from under it. The baby's face was pink with heat and exertion. Her lips were bright red. Her forehead furled, and she squawked. "You're okay little piggy. You've had enough. Time for a burp and a diaper change. He wants to come home immediately. The doctor just smiled and shook his head."

Jasper plopped into the rocker on the other side of the huge stone fireplace that dwarfed the room. "And Mudder?"

"A rock as usual. She's worrying about everyone else. She told me to come here to make sure you and the kinner get supper. Of course, the women have taken care of that. Callie even cleaned the bathrooms and swept the whole house."

The men would take care of the chores on the farm too. That's what Plain communities did. "You probably need to get home to make supper for your *mann*."

"Bart is coming here after he stops by the dairy."

Bart was one of several Plain men who worked at an Amish-owned dairy in St. Ignatius.

"No need for that."

"Don't try to hide that you don't like him." Her chuckle held the faintest note of sarcasm. "He means well. He just doesn't know how to take you."

"There's nothing to take."

"Come now, surely you can admit that you're not an easy person to get to know. Bart doesn't usually have that problem. He's a talker, but he expects the other person to talk back."

"He's bossy."

Her chortle startled Mary, who fussed. "Hush, child, it's only your mudder enjoying your *onkel* Jasper's honesty."

"It doesn't bother you?"

"I married him. I don't expect you to like him as much as I do." Her nose wrinkled. "Whew, you need a diaper change. Mary, not you, Jasper. Oh, you mean that he's bossy? Women are used to it. We're taught early on to listen, be respectful, and follow our mann's lead. Unless he's doing something really stupid, then we work to fix it, but behind the scenes."

"Really?"

"Really. Women are wily like that. We know our place." She stood for a second, then knelt on the pieced rug that stretched from one rocking chair to the other. She laid Mary in front of her and reached for the canvas bag next to her chair. "Okay, stinky girl, let's get you changed. What's bothering Onkel Jasper? Do you think he'll tell us?" She cooed at the baby, who gurgled and flailed her arms. "Probably not. He's a crotchety old man before his time."

"Am not."

"Are too."

"Darcie!"

"Come on, *Bruder*, I know something is bugging you. Let your big *schweschder* make it all better."

She was the one person in his life who seemed unfazed by his lack of social graces.

"I don't like working at the store. I'm not gut at it."

"You'll get used to it."

She made quick work of the dirty diaper, but not before Jasper got a whiff of its contents. How could something so noxious come from such a sweet, tiny child? Having sons and daughters of his own was high on his list of goals that seemed far beyond his reach, but the silver lining might be not having to change diapers. Did Father change diapers? No memory of such an event rose to the surface in Jasper's tired brain.

"I don't think so." He told her about the fiasco with Mrs. Kowalski.

"It's okay to rely on Esther Marie's help. She knows everything about everything when it comes to the store."

"That's the problem."

Darcie looked up from the task at hand. Her slim brown eyebrows rose. Her lips turned up in a knowing smile. "Your face is turning red."

"Is not."

"Is too." She tickled Mary's cheek and cooed some more. "Jasper Cotter. You like Esther Marie."

"You're *narrish*."

Darcie scooped up her baby and tucked Mary on her shoulder. She patted her back. "You like her, and knowing you, you don't know what to do about it. You've never asked a girl to take a ride with you ever, have you?"

She thought she was so smart. What he wouldn't give to be able to refute her statement. "So what if I haven't? I've been busy running the farm for Daed. I work hard. I'm tired at the end of the day."

Baby Mary burped and Darcie congratulated her as if she'd won a big race. "How long have you been pining for Esther Marie?"

"Pining? Who said anything about pining? I just . . . think she's a nice person who deserves . . . to be loved."

"And so do you my dear *bruder*." Grinning, Darcie wiped spit-up from the baby's face and her dress. "You do, even though you don't think you do. Inside that crusty exterior lies a mushy heart dying for a soul mate."

"Soul mate?" Jasper clasped his hands to his ears and sang, *"La, la, la, la!"*

"I know you can hear me. You just need a little advice from big sister." She rocked Mary. The baby's head sank to her shoulder. "Stop being *gegisch* and listen to me."

"Grrrrrr!"

"And stop growling like an old grizzly."

He dropped his hands. "I've never been able to talk to girls. My mind goes blank and I sound like a mean, old fart."

She scrambled to her feet with the litheness of a young girl. "Hold Mary."

"I don't know anything about babies."

"You better learn if you're going to be a mann and a daed."

"Who said anything about being—?"

"When you talk to Esther Marie, remind yourself that she is just as *naerfich* as you are. From what I've seen, she has no more experience courting than you do. Start by doing something nice for her."

"Like what?"

"What does she like?"

Jasper searched his memory. Back in school, he'd hung around the swing set and the ballfield, listening to the girls talk. Esther Marie rarely said much. As the years passed he watched her from afar at luncheons after church, the school picnics, and other district events. She smiled a lot, was quick to help, hardly ever sat still, and never said anything mean. Not many people could say that. "She likes jelly beans."

She'd been eating them in the deli today. He'd also seen her eating them at lunchtime one day. She sat on the bench outside the store munching on a peanut butter sandwich and picking through the jelly beans, eating the like colors together. She saved all the pink and purple ones for after she ate her apple. She'd seen him looking at her and turned as pink as the jelly beans.

He probably had too. She probably thought he was spying on her.

"That's perfect. So does Mudder. Did you know she keeps a stash in her sewing basket?"

"How would I know that?"

"We'll wrap some up in a pretty little handkerchief and tie it with a ribbon—"

"Does that really sound like something I would do?"

"Surprise her by doing something out of character. She'll be so bowled over she won't be able to say no when you ask her to take a ride with you."

He shouldn't have told Darcie. His older sister was like a runaway mountain goat. Once she got started up the mountain, there was no stopping her, no matter how steep the terrain. "I'm not asking her to go for a ride."

"Oh yes you are. This evening. After supper."

"I couldn't."

"For a smart man, you are so dumb sometimes."

"Am not."

"Esther Marie is probably just as lonely as you are—"

"Who said I was lonely?"

"Stop interrupting. Anyone with eyes in her head can see you're unhappy. That's why you're so grumpy. And Esther Marie is a sweet woman overlooked by most men because she stutters, and because she stutters, she doesn't talk. Men don't like that. They get nervous if they have to carry the conversation. She never had a chance, really. I don't know why I didn't see it before. You two would be perfect together."

Darcie finally ran out of steam. Thankfully.

"I can't just show up at her house after what happened at work today." He ran through the day's remaining events in short order. "She probably wishes she could get a job anywhere but at the store—at least until Daed comes back."

"That's not Esther Marie. She loves the store. She'll stick it out for Mudder's and Daed's sakes. You still have time to show her you can be nice. You can be nice, Jasper, can't you?"

"I'm nice sometimes."

"Sure you are." She scooted toward the door. "I'll be right back."

His sister had lost her mind. Leaving Jasper with her baby proved it. "Where are you going? Don't you want to take Mary with you?"

"To get the jelly beans."

Jasper should never have let the cat out of the bag. He looked down at Mary. Sound asleep, she had no words of wisdom to offer. Having relieved herself of her noxious load, she smelled pretty good. What would it be like to be a father? To sit in his own rocking chair in his own house and rock his baby while his wife cooked supper?

The aromas floating through the house would be that much more pleasing, no doubt. The knot of loneliness in the center of his chest would dissolve. The sunrise would glow brighter and the stars more brilliantly on a clear, cold Montana night.

He should never have told Darcie. His sister made it seem possible. She made it seem real. When it didn't happen she would be disappointed, but he would collapse back into that perpetual state of aloneness. She had her husband and her three children, with more to come, no doubt. Stymied hope was better than shattered hope.

The dinner bell rang. Mary started and opened her eyes wide. She stared up at him, her tiny pink lips turned down and trembling.

"It's me, Onkel Jasper."

She looked even more worried. "I promise not to drop you. You must promise not to cry."

Her lips puckered. Her tiny fisted hands waved until one of them landed close to her mouth. She sucked on it, and suddenly all was right with her world.

"I found them." Darcie dashed into the room, waving a bag of spicy jelly beans. "And I have a cute little hankie Kimberly embroidered."

"I'm not going."

Darcie patted his head. "Jah, you are, little bruder. Jah, you are."

CHAPTER 7

Most people would consider laughter wafting from the open windows of their home a pleasant sound. In Esther Marie's case it could only mean one thing. A setup. Esther Marie slowed her brisk pace along the sidewalk and up the steps. Her mother's determined chortles sent dread spiraling through her. Laughter usually was a sign her mother or her father or both had invited someone to supper. A man-someone. They meant well.

The result for her generally ranged from severe indigestion to a pounding headache. The desire to please the two sweet people who gave life to her vied with the certain knowledge that she would never find a husband who wanted to permanently yoke himself to a woman who needed five minutes to finish a sentence.

Maybe if she were more pleasing to the eye. Plain men didn't attach as much importance to looks, but they would be lying if they didn't admit that looks played a part in that mysterious attraction called love. She had never experienced it, yet she knew exactly how it would feel. Warm, sweet, all-encompassing, a falling into a place where time had no meaning and the lines between two people blurred until they became one.

The desire of her heart was to encounter that place, but cold, hard reality muttered in her ear daily: God's will might be for her to be alone.

Why? Wasn't it enough that she was scrawny and pock-faced and she mangled two languages? She'd prayed and prayed for her stuttering to be cured. And yet, it persisted. God ignored her prayers for healing.

Why?

Her mother said God's plan was still unfolding. In His time, not hers.

But the facts spoke for themselves.

Most of the men her age in this district were already married. Three older widowers had already been duly invited to the Shrock house and gone on their way, never to return for supper. They knew what Isaiah and Martha Shrock were trying to do and, for the most part, seemed willing to spend an evening trying to make conversation with Esther Marie over Nadine's barbecued ribs, spicy barbecued beans, coleslaw, dill potato salad, and scrumptious lemon bars.

It never went anywhere. The store remained her domain. The one thing she was good at. And now Jasper had taken over that domain. No one expected life to be fair, but sometimes, it rubbed her nose in its determination to be unfair.

Maybe that's why her parents didn't give up. They knew how much she wanted what every Amish woman wanted—a husband and children. They turned a blind eye to the sad fact that this dream had passed their daughter by. They couldn't fix it for her, no matter how hard they tried.

Maybe she still had time to turn around and sprint the other direction. She could go to The Malt Shop and eat a banana split instead. The library on the high school campus had closed for the day. Maybe she could simply walk along the road, enjoying the gorgeous

Mission Mountains until the sun went down and darkness hid her face as she slunk into her bedroom.

"Esther Marie, there you are." Father's jovial voice boomed as he pushed open the screen door. "Get in here and say hello to Nicholas Kauffman."

The name didn't ring a bell. Nicholas didn't live in their district, so he probably didn't know about her stutter. "Daed . . ."

"I know, Dochder." He winked and let the door close behind her. "We bought a saddle from him last year, remember? He lives out by Lewistown, but he's thinking about moving this direction so he can work for the Millers at their leather shop. He handcrafts saddles."

Montanans held this skill in high esteem. Ranchers were willing to pay exorbitant amounts for saddles that stood up against the wear and tear of a working cowboy and his horse. "I'm s-s-s-sorry I'm l-l-l-late." The word didn't want to come out, which underscored what she meant to say. She was too tired to pause, breathe, and imagine the words. "It was a l-l-l-l-ong d-d-d-day."

The look on Nicholas's face said it all. He grabbed his glass of iced tea and slurped down half of it. His expression evolved from a genuine smile coupled with curiosity to barely masked pity. "Don't apologize for working hard. It's a virtue." He had a gruff voice that reminded her of her grandfather.

Nicholas looked to be in his early forties. Silver strands streaked his temples. The glint in his blue eyes hinted at a sense of humor, but the lines around his mouth and eyes suggested hard times weathered. His chin was smooth shaven. He had never married. "I have had days like that."

Did those hard days have something to do with why he remained a bachelor at this stage of his life? It was rare in her community. Men and women were expected to marry, but sometimes circumstances didn't allow for it. Caring for sickly parents. Caring for brothers and sisters after the death of a parent. Or maybe love simply passed him by when he wasn't looking. He didn't have an impediment like she did. Not one that showed, anyway.

"Did something happen?" Mother stood at the door to the living room. Always more attuned to her children's moods, she never missed a sign of trouble. "Is everyone all right at the store?"

"F-F-F-ergie had a heart at-t-t-t-tack." Esther Marie squeezed past Father so she could edge toward the kitchen. "He's in the h-h-h-hospital."

"Ach. The poor man. He's so young." Mother's gaze flew to Father. Fergie and he were the same age. While Fergie's shape resembled a large hard-boiled egg, Father's frame tended toward flat as a screen door. Where Fergie tended toward baldness that would one day make him look like that same egg, Father's iron-gray hair ran wild. His locks stood up and waved at each other. "I'll make a breakfast casserole and run it over to their house. She'll need help with the laundry and cleaning while he's laid up."

"Their dochders will fill in." Father never ceased to be the eternal optimist. "I reckon Jasper has the store under control."

Of course. Esther Marie bowed her head and nodded. "H-H-He's in ch-ch-charge." Never mind the scene with Mrs. Kowalski. Never mind the angst over a phone call to an electrician. Never mind Jasper's sad eyes. Never mind her four years of experience learning every facet of the grocery store business. She could reel off the price of every bulk item. She knew how much inventory they had for all the sewing goods. She could recite every flavor of ice cream served in the deli.

And customers liked her.

Pride went before a fall.

"The lasagna is ready." Mother called over her shoulder as she bustled away. "Lulu set the table. Help us serve. Nicholas must be starving."

Ignoring the urge to flee, Esther Marie did as Mother asked. Supper was a lively affair with the boys arguing over who caught the biggest fish at the pond earlier in the day and her younger sister giving a detailed account of the birth of a foal at her friend Jennie's house. Nicholas ate heartily but said little, despite Father's attempts to draw him out. Esther Marie pushed food around on her plate and calculated how much turkey, chicken, beef, pastrami, and ham she needed to order the next day. To that she added a running total of the ice cream lost in the broken refrigerator case. More needed to be ordered as well.

Finally Mother scooted back her chair and stood. "It's so warm in here. Why don't you and Nicholas go out and sit on the porch, Isaiah. With any luck there will be a breeze. Esther Marie can bring you a piece of her apple pie and some more iced tea. She picked the apples herself from the trees in the backyard."

Mother made it sound as if this was a wonderous feat.

"I'm full to my eyeballs." Nicholas laughed and tossed his napkin on the table. "But I reckon I can find room for a small piece of pie."

In the kitchen Mother slid generous slices of pie onto two plates and handed them to Esther Marie along with forks. "Go."

"Mudder."

"I know you love me and your daed, but I don't think you want to live with us when we're old and cranky. Better to have your own cranky mann than to take care of my grumpy mann."

True, but it had to be the right man for the job, and Nicholas was not that man. Esther Marie trudged out to the porch. Nicholas had chosen a rocking chair instead of the swing. Father was nowhere in sight.

"Isaiah said he forgot to do something in the barn. He'll be right back." Nicholas took the pie with a quick "thank you" and laid the accompanying napkin on his lap. "He also said to tell you he's too full for pie, so you could eat his piece if you want."

Ha. Could Father be more obvious? Esther Marie attempted to hide her consternation. Nicholas's half smile said he knew exactly how she felt. Esther Marie summoned a smile. A person never had an excuse for being rude. "I hop-p-pe you like the p-p-pie. The apples are from t-t-t-trees in our b-b-b-backyard."

Mother had already said that. Embarrassment added to the heat.

He took a quick bite and moaned. "Very gut. It reminds me of my mudder's. She was a gut cook."

"She p-p-p-passed?"

"A few years ago." He settled back into his chair and proceeded to demolish the pie. "Aren't you going to eat yours?"

She eased onto the top porch step and turned so she could lean against the railing. Once settled, she made sure her long skirt touched her dirty white sneakers on all sides. "I'm n-n-n-not hungry."

He cocked his head. His lips crinkled into a smile.

She held out her plate and he took it. For a man who claimed to be full, he'd found plenty of room for dessert.

"I don't get as much home cooking as I'd like." He scraped the plate and shoved the last bit of flaky crust into his mouth. "One of the many downsides of being a bachelor."

"No f-f-family?"

"Back in Kentucky."

He did have a touch of soft drawl in his voice. "M-M-Miss it?"

"Pardon me for sticking my nose where it doesn't belong, but have you always stuttered?"

"Jah."

"It must be frustrating."

"Jah. I p-p-p-pray for Gott to heal me, b-b-b-b-ut He d-d-d-oesn't."

"Like Paul and the thorn in his side."

She hadn't thought about it that way. The apostle Paul planted churches all over the world. He was brave and went to jail for his faith. She was just a girl who stuttered and worked in a grocery store. "His thorn hurt-t-t-t. Mine d-d-d-doesn't."

"Not physically, but it hurts your heart." Nicholas stretched out his legs and clasped his hands on his flat stomach. "You know what Paul said?"

"That Gott w-w-w-as made st-st-strong in his w-w-w-weakness."

"Just something to think about."

That scripture could apply to her personally, the way it did to Paul, which seemed unfathomable. But there it was. "I w-w-w-ill."

Nicholas laid the plate aside. "You weren't happy to see me. Do your parents do this to you often?"

"Jah. Nee. I m-m-m-mean—"

"Don't worry about it. My friends try to fix me up too. I'm old and set in my ways. I'm happy with my dogs and my cats and the quiet."

"R-R-R-eally?"

"Really." He stacked the second plate on top of the first one and wiped his lips with the napkin. "Would you like to take a walk with me?"

Why did he want to take a walk if he wasn't interested in anything more from her? The idea of making conversation on a walk along the dirt road—and all the way back—was daunting. "It's hot-t-t-t."

"There's a breeze." He stood and ambled past her down the steps. There, he stretched his long arms over his head as if reaching for the sky. "It will make your parents happy even though we know there's nothing to it, and it'll give me someone to talk to besides my dogs and cats." He cocked his head, his smile playful. "I don't bite. I promise."

Esther Marie grabbed the railing and pulled herself up. *Gott, would it be wrong for me to smack my mudder and daed upside the head for putting me in this position?*

They walked in silence for several minutes. Esther Marie studied the mountains in the distance. Their beautiful presence steadied her. Blue jays jabbered in the red maples along the edge of the road. An inquisitive squirrel stopped his search for seeds under a spruce long enough to watch them pass by. The longer the silence stretched, the more anxiety tightened its grip around Esther Marie's throat. She halted. "You d-d-d-on't have t-t-t-to d-d-d-do this-s-s-s."

"Do what? Take a walk with a nice girl on a warm but pleasant July evening?" Nicholas slowed. "You like Jasper, don't you?"

Heat more searing than that of a raging bonfire ignited in the center of Esther Marie's chest. She pressed her sweaty hands together and struggled to think. Men and women didn't discuss such topics, did they? Nicholas was a virtual stranger.

"Again, I didn't mean to pry." A light pink crept across his fair skin. "You must think me forward. I saw your expression when your parents talked about him. I recognize that look. I have four schweschders and four bruders. They're all married now. It might help to talk about it."

154

"T-T-T-To you?"

"I suppose not." He picked up his pace. "I've made you uncomfortable. I thought you might need a neutral third party to talk to. You probably have girlfriends and schweschders for that."

Only Lulu and she was ten. Her three brothers were no help. All of Esther Marie's friends were married now and busy raising their children. They sometimes stopped talking when she walked into the room. They had to be discussing their poor friend Esther Marie, destined to be alone. "Why didn't y-y-y-y-you m-m-m-marry when you w-w-w-ere y-y-y-oung?"

"When I was younger, you mean?" Nicholas's amused expression said he found her assessment of his age funny. "I missed my chance. The girl I liked married someone else. I never found another girl I liked as much."

"L-L-L-iked?"

"I guess my lukewarm choice of words says something." He chuckled. "I liked her. Maybe I moved so slow because I wasn't sure I loved her. If you love this Jasper, you should find a way to encourage him. Being the man is hard. You're not sure what the woman is thinking, and it's nerve-racking to try to figure it out. You don't want to be rejected, so sometimes you do nothing."

"Why are y-y-y-you t-t-t-telling me this?"

"Because you seem like you could use a nudge in the right direction." A slinky gray-and-white cat preened under a cottonwood tree. Nicholas held out his fingers and made kissing noises. The cat stopped licking for a moment, meowed, and went back to her bath. "See, she agrees with me. I can tell you from a man's perspective, knowing what to say and when to say it is the hardest part. Is Jasper an easygoing man?"

"N-Nee." She shook her head hard. "N-N-N-ot at all."

"Ah. He's naerfich too." Nicholas made a sudden about-face and headed back toward the house.

"What-t-t-t are you d-d-d-oing?"

"You need to make some more of that apple pie and take it to him."

"We have it-t-t-t at-t-t-t the store."

"The gesture is in the making of the pie."

He tipped his straw hat in her direction. "I should get back. I don't like to drive my buggy in the dark."

"S-S-S-orry my parents w-w-w-wasted your t-t-t-time."

"I ate a delicious meal and took a walk with a nice girl." Nicholas's gaze traveled over her shoulder. The creak of buggy wheels and thud of horses' hooves on the road's packed dirt made Esther Marie turn.

A familiar roan trotted toward them. As it grew closer the driver came into focus as well. Jasper.

The Cotters lived in the opposite direction from the store. The chances of Jasper coming down dead-end Shadowbox Lane were slim and none. Unless he was coming to the Shrock house. Why would he do that?

The buggy rocked in the rutted road. He drew even with Esther Marie and Nicholas.

And kept on going.

Jasper looked her straight in the eye. She waved. He did not wave back.

"Who was that?" Nicholas smoothed his big hand along his mare's back. "Someone you know?"

"That was J-J-J-asper."

"In that case, you may not need the apple pie." Nicholas climbed into the buggy. "A little jealousy may be the spice you need in your recipe."

Jealousy? Esther Marie opened her mouth, but Nicholas shook his head and snapped the reins. "I wish you the best, Esther Marie. Tell your parents I said danki for the food. Gut nacht."

She stood next to the road for a long time, watching him drive away, but Nicholas didn't occupy Esther Marie's thoughts. Instead the look on Jasper's face as he drove past her without stopping played over and over in her head.

She had little skill in reading men's faces, and she might be mistaken, but he seemed disappointed.

Disappointed at what?

CHAPTER 8

A fool's errand. Jasper's hand hovered over the side of the buggy. The handkerchief with its small bounty of sweets swung in the wind. *Let it go. No.* It would be a waste of perfectly good candy and Kimberly's nice handiwork. He tossed the parcel onto the seat and drew a long breath. His blood pressure began to recede. He swallowed against the bitter bile in the back of his throat. The humid night air cooled his burning face.

Darcie meant well, but the idea that he should drive over to Esther Marie's out of the clear blue sky and ask her to take a ride with him had been stupid. He was stupid to think that Esther Marie didn't have a man friend just because he'd never seen her with anyone. A woman as kind and sweet and smart as she was probably had plenty of opportunities to court. Courting was private, and she'd done a good job of keeping hers a secret.

The sight of Esther Marie standing with her man friend in front of her house would be etched on his brain forever. She'd waved as if it were perfectly natural for Jasper to drive past her house after dark on a summer evening. No other farms existed beyond Isaiah's on Shadowbox Lane. The few seconds it took to pass her seemed like hours. Now he could not return by the same road without passing her house again.

He pulled over to the side of the road and stopped. "I'm such an idiot."

Dandy tossed his long neck and whinnied.

"What do you know?" Jasper leaned back on the seat and stared at the moonlit sky. "Gott, I know You're there. What I don't know is what Your plan for me is."

If anyone came by and saw him sitting by the side of the road talking to God aloud, they would think him crazy. Maybe he was. "I like her."

Dandy nickered.

"I'm not talking to you."

Dandy lowered his head and grazed in the weeds.

The man didn't look familiar. He didn't belong to the group of men who grew up in the district and attended school together. They were all married. Except Jasper. Did that mean Esther Marie would move away when she married him?

Who said anything about marriage? Maybe it was early in their courtship. Maybe that explained why he didn't know about it. Darcie didn't know about it, and she knew everything that traveled the grapevine through their tiny Gmay.

How long would he have to sit here to be sure they were no longer huddled together in front of Isaiah's house? Rolling clouds skittered across the sky, blanketing the moon. The night turned darker.

The man had looked like he was leaving. Or maybe he just arrived. Jasper groaned. Dandy's head rose. "It's okay. I'm fine."

Too bad he didn't have a *Budget* newspaper to read. Nothing to do but sit here and contemplate his life. An hour passed. A light drizzle began to fall. Normally the farmer in him delighted in the rain. Tonight he raised his face to the sky and shook his head. "Really?"

He sighed and tossed away the piece of grass he'd been trying to turn into a whistle and forced himself to make the trek back in the other direction.

God was merciful. No one stood outside the Shrock house. No lamp shed light inside the windows. All was dark.

He didn't sleep much that night, which meant dawn came early, and no amount of loitering over breakfast could keep him from finally conceding he would have to go to the store and face her.

At five forty-five, a smile firmly affixed to his face, he jumped from his buggy and strode across the yard to the store. Raindrops spattered his face, but they weren't enough to cool his skin. Humidity thickened the air. Dark clouds hung in the distance, obscuring the mountains to the east. They always needed rain in the summer. Irrigation caught the summer snowmelt and watered the fields, lawns, and gardens, but it was no substitute.

The lights were on and the door unlocked. Esther Marie bent over a box of decorative candles. She looked up, murmured good morning, and went back to arranging them on the shelf next to the Amish cookbooks from Lancaster County.

Cool as snow-fed stream water.

All the speeches he'd rehearsed on the ride over flew out the window. He cleared his throat, scratched his forehead, and kept on walking. "Guder mariye."

"We're r-r-r-r-ready to open as s-s-s-soon as the girls g-g-g-get here."

She still didn't look at him, but something in her tone suggested a question.

What was the question? His head began to throb. "Gut. Six a.m. sharp."

"F-F-F-ine."

Her rendition of a single syllable word followed him to the

office. What did she mean by *fine*? Nothing was fine, as far as he could tell. He tossed the plastic bag that held his lunch on the desk. It fell open and the knotted handkerchief appeared. Maybe he could still give it to her. He could put it on the deli counter when she wasn't looking. Like a secret friend.

She already had a friend.

What a silly idea. He sank into Father's chair and twirled around and around. The chair squeaked under his weight. He thrummed his fingers on the desk. He went through the mail. Advertisements and bills.

The clock on the wall read six a.m. The girls would be at the registers now, ready to serve customers who stopped by on their way to work to grab pastries for their coworkers or older folks who were early birds. It would make sense to walk the store to confirm that everything was in perfect order.

Six a.m. and he was sweating. It had to be the weather. The air pressed on him like a heavy, wet blanket.

He left the jelly beans on his desk and strode through the aisles toward the deli. A stroll by, nothing more.

Esther Marie wasn't behind the deli counter. In fact, she stood in the middle of the bulk aisle with a man who seemed vaguely familiar. Jasper moved closer. The man had the look of a Native American Indian from the tribes that owned and managed much of the reservation on which St. Ignatius sat, including the store. Dark, straight hair parted in the middle almost touched his T-shirt-covered shoulders. He wasn't very tall and was built like a barrel. He said something and Esther Marie giggled. She covered her mouth and shook her head.

The man held out a book. She shook her head again and smiled. He pointed to the book and gestured.

Raymond Old Fox. Now Jasper remembered. The man who pursued his cousin Christine for a few weeks after the Caribou wildfire brought her to St. Ignatius from West Kootenai. Mother and Father had been so worried about Christine's preoccupation with Old Fox, they had forbidden her to see him and made her stop working at the store.

Now here he was again—talking to Esther Marie while a customer stood at the deli counter tapping her fingers and looking around, her expression perplexed.

Jasper moved forward. He slid through the swinging doors and forced a smile. "How can I help you?"

"I need two pounds of garlic bologna, sliced thick, a pound of corned beef, sliced thin, and a couple of pounds of Cajun ham, shredded."

"I'll get right on it." Jasper grabbed rubber gloves from the box next to the scale and struggled to get one on his big hands. They seemed made for tiny fingers. "You said two pounds of bologna?"

Esther Marie turned. Her smile died. "Ach, I'm s-s-s-orry. I just—"

"I see you're busy entertaining a friend." Jasper almost said "just like last night," but managed to corral the words. "I thought I'd jump in and help so this nice lady doesn't have to wait."

Esther Marie darted toward the swinging doors. "I'll g-g-g-get it. You don't know how to use the s-s-s-slicer. You'll c-c-c-cut your f-f-f-fingers off."

"I don't want to interrupt your visit."

The words sounded peevish in his ears. She would think he was jealous, and what business of it was his? Usually employees didn't visit with friends during work hours. That's why it was his business.

But not why it bothered him.

"This is R-R-Raymond Old F-F-F-Fox. He is a f-f-f-friend."

"I know who he is."

"Have we met?" Raymond studied him with eyes so dark they looked like onyx. "I'm bad about faces."

"Nee, but Christine Mast is my cousin."

"Ah." Raymond didn't look the least bit put off by this revelation. "How is she doing?"

"She's doing fine . . ." Jasper let the sentence trail off, hoping Raymond would hear the rest of it: *with you out of the picture.*

"Did she marry Andy?"

"She did." No thanks to Raymond, who got her head all turned around about Native American Indian spiritual practices and ownership of the land.

"Good for her. Tell her I said congratulations, if you think of it."

His words seemed genuine. "It has been good." Jasper tried not to sound begrudging. "I will tell her."

Esther Marie's gaze bounced from Jasper to Raymond and back. Her frown grew. "I'm s-s-s-s-orry. I didn't know a c-c-c-ustomer was w-w-w-aiting."

"I've got it." Jasper pulled a huge chunk of bologna from the cooler.

"I said garlic bologna." The customer shook her head so hard her ponytail bounced. "That's German bologna."

Heat burned Jasper's face. He quickly made the switch. The correct bologna on the counter, he fought with the plastic wrap that encased it. At this rate they'd be here until midnight. Nevertheless, he could do it. "Maybe you want to go have coffee with Raymond."

"N-N-N-ee." Esther Marie's face turned a dull brick red. "I'm-m-m-m w-w-w-working."

"Not so much that a person would notice."

"I'm an archaeology student at Montana U now." Raymond had

a soft, lilting voice, very pleasant to the ear, unlike Jasper's growl. "I like to browse in the used bookstores. When I find one I think might help Esther Marie with her speech impediment, I pick it up so I can bring it by and see how she's doing."

He held up the paperback book: *Stuttering: 25 Most Effective Methods and Techniques to Overcome Stuttering.*

What an extraordinarily nice thing to do. Shame coursed through Jasper. His feelings for Esther Marie were no excuse for being rude to someone who wanted to help her. "That is good of you."

"What are friends for?" Raymond glanced at the black sports watch on his wrist. "I need to get back to Arlee. I'm living in Missoula now, but I came home to visit my grandmother for her birthday. I thought I'd take some cookie dough ice cream to her."

"I'll g-g-g-get it." Esther Marie's tone dared Jasper to argue with her. "T-T-T-ake her s-s-s-ome b-b-b-brow-n-n-n-ies t-t-t-too."

Jasper backed away from the counter and let her have the room. With quick, efficient movements she took care of the lady's trio of meats. She never looked at Jasper.

In fact, she seemed to be pretending he no longer stood in her space. "I'll be in the office," he said to no one in particular.

"Good to meet you," Raymond called after him. "I hope your father gets out of the hospital soon. Esther Marie told me about his health scare."

"Thank you." Jasper hoped so too. Father would get well and everything would go back to normal. He would farm and Esther Marie would be at the store.

And they'd go back to crossing paths only once a week instead of every five minutes.

That's what he wanted.

Wasn't it?

CHAPTER 9

A five-thousand-piece jigsaw puzzle of Niagara Falls would be easier to figure out than one man. Esther Marie gritted her teeth, ducked her head, and cleaned up the counter. She returned the meats to their proper spots in the refrigerated cases. At this rate she would simply take the pie she'd made the night before back home and let the kids eat it after supper. Jasper didn't deserve it. He didn't act like a man interested in anything more than embarrassing her in front of a friend.

As usual Raymond waited with the air of a man who had all day—maybe all summer—to wait. She'd never known anyone with so much patience. His brief appearance in the life of the store had been about Christine and her quest to experience life outside the tight-knit Kootenai community. Esther Marie played a tiny part in their short-lived relationship. She passed notes between them like a girl caught in a schoolyard romance.

Christine had gone back to Kootenai and Raymond moved away. So imagine her surprise when he showed up one day to bring her a sack of books to read. Some were biographies of famous people who stuttered. Others were books about minimizing the speech defect. A few were just for fun. Raymond said everyone needed books as a way to escape their lives, even if only for a few hundred pages.

Esther Marie had never been a big reader, but Raymond's urging had propelled her into worlds she now enjoyed. She forced herself to look up and meet Raymond's gaze. "S-S-S-orry about all that-t-t-t."

"About what?" Raymond handed her the book and smiled. "I'm not in that big of a rush."

"About J-J-J-as-per."

Raymond took the package of double-fudge brownies she offered him. "He seems like he's wound really tight. But it also seems like he really cares."

"Cares?" Esther Marie's voice squeaked in indignation. A person didn't show he cared by being surly and rude. "I d-d-d-on't think s-s-s-so."

"He does care about you." Raymond grinned and pushed his sunglasses farther back on his head. "He seemed jealous, actually. As a guy I recognize jealousy when I see it. I get really jealous when Tonya talks to other guys at parties. Or anywhere, for that matter."

"B-B-B-ut she's your g-g-g-girlfriend."

"Maybe Jasper would like to be your boyfriend."

"F-F-F-Funny way of sh-sh-owing it."

"Guys are like that." Raymond added the carton of ice cream she offered him to the small handheld basket in his other hand. "We don't like mushy stuff and talking about our feelings. It's worse than a root canal."

"No fun for g-g-g-irls either."

"Do you like him?"

"I s-s-s-uppose."

Raymond laughed a deep belly laugh. "You look like you just drank a glass of sour milk."

"He-e-e is h-h-h-ard to underst-st-st-and. He runs ho-t-t-t and c-c-c-old. If he li-li-li-kes me, why d-d-d-oesn't he as-k-k-k me to take a buggy ride?"

"Girls make it sound like that's so easy. It's hard. You never know if you're going to be rejected. It stinks. He just hasn't gotten up the courage yet. Maybe if you started."

"G-G-G-irls don't st-st-st-art-t-t-t."

"Sometimes they do. Tonya did." He saluted and blew her a breezy kiss. "It's always good seeing you, Esther Marie. Take care of yourself. Don't let tradition stand in your way. If you want to know what's on Jasper's mind, ask him. I wasted a whole lot of time not seeing that Tonya is the only woman for me. Life is short. Go for the gusto."

Esther Marie nodded and waved until he turned around and headed for the registers up front. *Go for the gusto.* That didn't sound like something a Plain woman did.

She scrubbed the countertops, washed down the slicers, rinsed the washcloths, and swept the floors. No new customers materialized. She sighed so hard, the wisp of hair loose on her forehead jumped.

"F-F-F-ine." She keyed the radio and asked Rachel to cover the deli for her.

Rachel took no time in speed walking to the deli. If Lucy hadn't made a rule against it, she would've run. "What's up?"

Nothing that could be shared with Miss Diarrhea of the Mouth. Sweet as she was, Rachel could not keep a secret. "I just need a quick break."

"Ah. No problem. Take your time."

167

From her knowing look, Rachel thought this was a potty break. No reason to set her straight.

Before she lost her courage, Esther Marie marched down the hall, rapped on the office door, and proceeded to open it before Jasper had a chance to respond.

"I d-d-d-on't unders-s-s-stand . . ."

The office was empty.

· · ·

First that man in front of her house. Now Raymond Old Fox. Jasper strode to the front of the store. He needed a breath of fresh air. He needed his team of horses and his field of corn. He needed to dig in the dirt and plant something.

Cara looked up from sacking groceries for an elderly couple who yelled at each other about the canned goods' prices. Not because they were angry but because neither appeared to own a hearing aid. "Are you leaving?"

"I'm cleaning up the displays on the porch if anyone needs me."

"I'll tell Esther Marie."

"No need."

He pushed through the door and managed to shut it quietly. No point in taking his frustration out on the building. The porch needed sweeping. A sign trumpeting produce prices was crooked. He straightened it.

He'd been silly to think a smart, tenderhearted girl like Esther Marie would not have suitors.

He grabbed the broom and swept out leaves, dirt, and a variety of bugs into the grass.

His blood pressure returned to normal. His brain refrained

from exploding. He breathed. Raymond Old Fox knew better than to court Esther Marie. He'd learned his lesson with Christine. He was a kind man.

The stranger at Esther Marie's house was an unknown factor. But Jasper still had a chance. Filled with resolve born of the certainty that if he didn't act now he would lose the chance forever, Jasper marched back into the store. Looking neither left nor right, he strode into his office, scooped up the bag of jelly beans, and made his way to the deli.

Rachel stood behind the counter tearing up lettuce for the packaged salads.

"Where's Esther Marie?"

"She needed a break."

"Why, was something wrong?" Or did she go somewhere with Raymond Old Fox?

"I couldn't really say. It was of a personal nature." Her face suddenly red, Rachel wiped her hands on a dish towel. "Could you cover for a minute while I run to the bathroom? It'll only take a few seconds. Too much coffee—"

"Of course. No problem."

She dashed past him before he could push through the deli gate. He waited until she was out of sight to rummage through the items underneath the counter. Esther Marie's canvas bag and lunch cooler sat next to a box of plastic wrap. With a deep breath and a quick prayer, he nestled the jelly beans on top of her bag.

"What are you doing? Where's Rachel?"

Jasper jumped and backed away from the counter at the sound of Esther Marie's inquiry. His calf banged against a huge box of napkins. He teetered and righted himself. "You really need to tidy up around here." He pushed through the swinging gate and swept past her. "Rachel went to the bathroom. I'll let you take it from here."

He could feel her puzzled gaze boring into his back all the way down the aisle.

What happened next would be up to her.

Please, Gott, let one thing lead to another.

Let this be the start of the precious friendship I've always wanted with Esther Marie. Show me what to do next.

Let there be a next.

CHAPTER 10

One step forward, two steps backward. Was it like that with all men or just Jasper? Wiping her forehead with her sleeve, Esther Marie stifled a groan. She stuck the mop she'd been using on the deli floor into a bucket and swished it around. The AC unit in the store couldn't keep up with the humidity in the air. Dark, nasty clouds hid the mountains when she had arrived at work. The only way to get relief would be a good, soaking rain.

And a word face-to-face with Jasper.

Four days had gone by since she found Jasper's lovely gift of jelly beans on her bag in the deli. Finally, a signal, a sign, a move that said Jasper, too, wanted to go for that gusto. He liked her. He'd finally found a way to express it. She waited until he was talking to a farmer in the produce section about buying his corn on the cob to set her offering of apple pie on his desk in return.

The next day the empty, clean pan appeared on top of her lunch cooler with a thank-you note signed "J." The following day an entire bag of jelly beans in every flavor imaginable found its way into her cooler with a note that said "sweets for the sweet." In response she made snickerdoodles and left a package of four on his lunch bag. No note. Instead she waited for him to come looking for her.

But he didn't. Whenever their paths crossed, Jasper smiled,

ducked his head, and squeezed past her with a muttered hello. Like a young boy too shy for his own britches.

There had been no more outbursts, no intruding on her work, and no bossing anyone around. He simply took care of the paperwork, tallied the receipts, and made the deposits. He continued to bring in produce from the farm as his family and friends harvested it. Fresh corn, tomatoes, cucumbers, green peppers, radishes, and leaf lettuce. He smiled at the customers and the employees alike with a hearty "good morning." Esther Marie had to look up to make sure it wasn't Fergie himself, back from his hospital stay.

So why the deflated feeling? The sense of anticipation fizzled. She found herself peering out the window before she went to bed, sure she'd heard horse hooves. Nothing.

Her dream of a buggy ride did not materialize. Not just any buggy ride, but one with Jasper. She should be happy that he obviously recognized that she could run the store on her own. That should make her happy. Instead, the feeling that life had passed her by shrouded the deli while she worked.

Time to get over him and move on. That's what her mother would say if Esther Marie told her, which she did not. It would only lead to more supper guests. What would Raymond say? *Go for the gusto. Time to up your game.* That's what Raymond would say.

How? In this case of two awkward, mismatched Plain people, what would that mean? Esther Marie puzzled over that conundrum as she sprayed the cooler doors with glass cleaner and wiped them down until they sparkled. It had been a busy day, but business was winding down.

"Hey, did you see the sky out there?" Rachel trudged by pushing a bucket on wheels with a mop stuck in it. "It's dark as night. It looks like it's about to rain cats and dogs."

"Ach, nee, B-B-B-art and Darcie are br-r-r-ringing Fergie b-b-b-back to the house this after-r-r-r-n-n-n-oon. They'll be c-c-c-c-caught in it."

"Mr. Daugherty says they're forecasting a gully washer with high winds and hail."

"In that case, we should close up early." A stack of folders and a clipboard in one arm, Jasper strode toward them. He had a pencil behind one ear and a distracted look on his face. "If the weather is that bad, nobody will be shopping for groceries, anyway. We'll put a sign on the door, CLOSED DUE TO WEATHER."

"You sh-sh-should leave n-n-n-ow." No matter how many times Esther Marie reminded herself to breathe, to picture the words, to relax, she still couldn't make them come out smoothly. Raymond's book was full of good ideas, but nothing really changed for her. It was beyond frustrating. To talk to Jasper like a normal woman would be so sweet. Maybe then he would do more than give her jelly beans.

Gott, why? Why can't You take this thorn from my side? "S-S-S-o you c-c-can be there when F-F-F-Fergie g-g-g-gets home."

"That's okay. I should be the one to stay behind and close up." He hugged the files to his chest. "Rachel, tell the other girls to pack up and go. You don't want to be caught in the wind and rain on your bicycles."

"You don't have to tell me twice." Rachel tossed a sympathetic smile at Esther Marie and sped away.

"You go too." Jasper cocked his head toward the back. "I have to finish this paperwork, and then I'll lock up."

"I'm r-r-r-r-running out of the h-h-h-ams. I n-n-n-need to order m-m-m-more." She would leave when he did. She didn't mind getting wet, and folks liked to exaggerate these summer storms. They didn't strike often and they came and went in a flash. Winter snow-storms were far more exciting. "D-D-D-o your paperwork. I'll lock th-th-the d-d-d-oor after the g-g-girls."

He didn't argue. Instead he wandered in the direction of the office. "I'll turn on the radio."

Fergie kept a small battery-operated radio in his office for occasions such as this.

Esther Marie rushed to the front and helped Rachel and Cara close out their registers. She made up the sign as Jasper suggested. By the time she held the door for the girls, she could barely keep it from smacking the outside wall. A menacing layer of roiling black clouds hovered overhead. Rain splattered big fat drops on her face. The girls had to battle the fierce wind to unlock their bikes. None of them tried to ride away but instead began to push them.

"Are you sure you'll be okay?" Esther Marie yelled into the wind. "You could stay until it blows over."

"Nee, we live close." Rachel bent into the wind. "Don't wait too long or you'll be stuck here for hours."

Sally was already across the parking lot. She also lived close by. Much closer than Esther Marie. She wrestled the door shut, locked it, and turned to lean against it. "Whew." Raindrops slapped against the glass in a steady *splat, splat*. She jumped. "Silly girl."

She'd better hurry or she *would* be stuck here. She scurried back to the deli and rustled through the folders she kept on the back counter. She also needed to order more ice cream. The hot weather had customers buying double and triple what they normally would.

She also needed condiments. She scratched her nose and considered the list in front of her. Spicy mustard, Dijon mustard, yellow mustard, and jalapeño mustard.

The lights went out.

Esther Marie froze. Seven o'clock on a summer evening and it was pitch black in the store. "Ach." She closed her eyes for a few seconds to give them a chance to adjust. When she opened them, familiar outlines reappeared.

Moving with care, she edged toward the back drawers. Did she have a flashlight tucked in one of them? Maybe. Plain folks lived without electricity at home, but she had never experienced this darkness in the store. Goose bumps scurried up her arms. She shivered and rubbed them.

"Esther Marie?"

The bright beam of a flashlight danced across the countertops and hit her right in the eyes. She clapped her hands to her face. "Don't sh-sh-sh-ine that in my f-f-f-face."

"Sorry." The light shifted to her chest. "What do we do now? All this frozen food and meat and the produce in the produce room. Everything will spoil!"

Esther Marie slid her hand along the counter, allowing it to guide her closer to Jasper. "We have t-t-t-time. L-L-L-eave the freez-z-z-zer doors shut. The c-c-c-cases will hold their t-t-t-temperature for a f-f-f-f-ew hours."

If the electricity stayed off overnight, they would have problems with spoilage.

"It seems like we should do something." The light bounced up and down as Jasper talked. Esther Marie had the urge to touch his hand, to soothe his shaking. She moved closer. It bounced away. "We could lose a mountain of produce if it gets too warm in the produce room."

"We have k-k-kerosene l-l-l-anterns on the hardw-w-ware aisle." She pushed through the swinging doors. "C-c-c-candles up front by the c-c-c-ook-b-b-b-ooks."

"Gut idea. We can shed light on the situation."

As her eyes adjusted Esther Marie could see the outline of his face but not his expression. He sounded nervous yet pleased somehow.

They were alone in the store. It took a second for that thought to sink in. She and Jasper were alone together for the very first time. In the dark. Heat trailed across her face, down her neck, and finally along her spine. Now her hands shook. "L-L-Lead the w-w-w-way."

He kept the flashlight trained on the floor in front of them. Esther Marie stayed close. She wasn't afraid of the dark, but she had no desire to trip and break her neck either. The hardware aisle proved to be a bust. They were sold out of lanterns.

"I guess people knew this was coming."

People who watched the TV meteorologist's reports and listened to the radio, two things neither of them did. From there, they traipsed to the front. The candle supply had a dent in it, but several remained.

Using her apron as a catchall, Esther Marie collected them. "W-w-w-we can use s-s-s-some j-j-j-ars from the canning section—"

"Look."

She followed Jasper's gaze to the floor-to-ceiling windows that ran along the front of the store on either side of the double glass doors. Rain fell in sheets. Lightning strikes came so close together at times they seemed to light the sky from corner to corner. The continuous rolling thunder sounded like a train coming closer and closer. The trees that lined the far edges of the parking lot bent so low they were in danger of breaking. A *ping-ping-ping* against the glass deepened until it burst into a *bang-bang-bang*. Hail threatened to break the windows.

"I don't think we're going anywhere for a while." Jasper held the flashlight higher. She could make out his face now. Tension mixed with excitement. "We're on our own."

That same excitement ran through Esther Marie. "We can handle it."

Not a single stutter.

CHAPTER 11

Candlelight. In a Plain household candles meant they ran out of propane or kerosene. For some reason Esther Marie couldn't put her finger on, this was different. She'd known Jasper since they played in the mud in her backyard during Sunday afternoon visits. Now they were alone, just the two of them, in a grocery store. One of the least romantic places in the world, except for those people who loved food more than life itself. Esther Marie could take it or leave it most days.

This was different. Together, she and Jasper lit candles in the deli. While he went to try the telephone again to see if his parents had made it home safely, she visited the produce room and decided to leave the door closed and pray the electricity came on before everything started to wilt and soften. She grabbed two Fuji apples on the way out. A snack would be nice if they missed supper.

The freezer doors also needed to stay shut. The cardinal rule paraded through Esther Marie's head in Fergie's booming voice. *"Absolutely do not open the freezer doors until the electricity returns."*

"There's no dial tone on the phone. The lines must be down. I found this blanket in Daed's office. I guess he must use it when he decides to take a nap after lunch." Jasper held up a green-and-blue plaid flannel blanket. His gaze gravitated toward the floor in front of the deli meat cases. "We might as well get comfortable. We'll be here awhile."

Like a picnic? An indoor picnic in the middle of a storm that threatened to wipe the store off the face of the earth?

Why not? There was nothing else to be done. She'd prayed for something to happen with Jasper, and now they were alone. *Gott, this isn't quite what I had in mind.* She accepted the blanket and unfolded it. Could it be possible she was about to sit on a blanket with Jasper? Her hands were sweaty and so were her armpits. Should she go to the bathroom and use a paper towel to wipe them down?

No time. Too dark.

"We're in a grocery store. We might as well eat." He held up the basket in his other hand. "My treat. Don't worry. I made a note so I can pay back what we owe for it."

Always the practical man. "Ok-k-kay."

Was that all she could come up with?

"Like a picnic." He settled the basket at her feet. His gaze bounced from floor to ceiling. "Would you like to have a picnic with me?"

So it was a picnic. He wanted to have a picnic with her.

The faint tremor in his voice revealed just how nervous he was. As nervous as Esther Marie. She breathed and managed a smile. "I w-w-ould like th-th-th-at very m-m-m-uch."

"Gut." He knelt and then looked up. "Have a seat."

She knelt and removed the cellophane from the last big, fat candle. The wrapper said its scent was wedding cake. She smiled to herself and used the matches she'd nabbed from the household goods aisle to light it.

"Hmm, that smells like cake. I like that smell." Jasper removed items from the basket. "No cake in here, but I have bread, swiss cheese, roast beef—"

"D-D-D-Did you op-p-p-pen the c-c-case?"

"I did, but only for a few seconds. I grabbed the smallest pieces. We'll have to eat it all if you don't want to open it again."

For a good cause, Fergie. For your son's first attempt at courting. She assumed it was his first attempt. It certainly was hers.

A nervous giggle burbled up in her throat. "A lot of f-f-f-f-ood."

"A feast."

Together, in companionable silence, they assembled the sandwiches with Esther Marie using plastic utensils to spread the mustard and mayonnaise from small picnic packets sold with the paper plates and napkins. Jasper also had potato chips from the chip aisle, brownies from the bakery, and bottles of warm water from the bottled water aisle. "I didn't want to stumble around in the dark too much or I would have brought a bigger variety. I didn't know if you liked Doritos or Cheetos so I brought both."

"I like b-b-b-oth. I br-r-r-ought these." She held out two apples she'd taken from the produce room before she shut the doors. "You like a-a-a-pples."

When he couldn't have apple pie, he settled for apples. She'd heard him say that once.

"I do. Danki."

He reached for the apple. His fingers brushed against hers. Goose bumps raced up her arms. Heat flared somewhere in the vicinity of her heart. It made it hard to breathe. She grabbed a paper napkin and patted her face. "It's warm in here without the fans."

Jasper wiped his forehead with his sleeve, but his gaze never left her face. "Jah, it is."

She grabbed the sandwich and took a big bite.

"It's okay." His voice didn't shake anymore. "I'm naerfich too."

The words were an invitation to give voice to what was happening. What exactly *was* happening? "Abb-b-b-bout what-t-t?"

He ducked his head. "Us. This."

"W-W-Why me?" The question truly baffled her. No man had looked at her a second time after hearing her talk. The Plain boys in school were always nice to her, but not one asked her to ride home in his buggy after a singing. Jasper never went to a singing. Ever. "I st-st-st-utter."

"I don't care. I don't stutter, and I still have trouble talking to people. You stutter and people like you because you're kind and nice." He took a hurried bite of his sandwich, chewed, and swallowed. "Why did you make pie for me and cookies?"

"I l-l-ike you."

"Nobody likes me." He spoke the words matter-of-factly with no bitterness.

"Th-th-th-at's not true."

He shrugged. "You often seem mad at me."

"I g-g-get f-f-f-rustrated."

"You're frustrated because you know how to run the store and I don't. But women aren't put in charge. The son of the owner is."

"Jah. But also b-b-because you s-s-s-eem m-m-m-mad at me."

"Not at you. I'm never mad at you. I'm mad at me. I want to be like you. I would run the store into the ground without you. The shelves would be empty, all the customers would be going to the big stores in Missoula. We'd have to close."

A huge exaggeration, but Esther Marie appreciated his effort. "Y-Y-You're not-t-t th-th-at bad."

He smiled. The change lit up his face. What a nice gift. She returned the favor.

Their gazes broke. She took a bite of her sandwich and chewed. He did the same. She stared at the candle flames. They danced in an unseen draft. So pretty. *Gott, I hope he knows what to do next because I surely don't.*

Something had to happen next. Of that, she was certain.

Jasper raised his hand. His fingers touched her cheek. "Is it okay if I do that?"

"Jah." Her voice trembled.

His voice dropped to a whisper. "What if I do this?"

His fingers trailed from her cheek to her neck and then to the hair that peeked from her prayer covering. A delicious shiver ran through her, head to toe and back. She couldn't quite catch her breath. "Jah, jah."

"What about this?"

He leaned forward. His face, no longer hidden in the shadows of the flickering light, came into focus. His hands drew her face nearer to his. Jasper's scent of fresh soap enveloped her. Their lips met. Esther Marie closed her eyes. Nothing else existed there in the dark. Just the feel of his soft lips on hers.

She'd waited her whole life for this, and it finally arrived. Perfect. It didn't matter that she stuttered. Nothing else mattered but this moment. She would always have this first, sweet, lovely kiss.

The kiss deepened. Her heart rearranged itself. Life would be different now, no matter what came next.

Jasper leaned back and whispered, "Oh, Esther Marie."

She couldn't look at him. His fingers touched her chin, forcing her to look up. "You are sweet and kind and you deserve better than a grumpy, unlikeable man like me."

"I like you."

No stutter there.

"I'm so glad. I like you too. A lot." He offered her a tentative smile. "Can I kiss you again?"

She nodded.

Kissing proved to be far more satisfying than roast beef sandwiches or Doritos. Finally he drew away, smiled, and handed her the apple. "You'll need your strength."

"Why d-d-d-didn't you say anything about the p-p-p-pie?"

"You didn't say anything about the jelly beans."

"I thought you w-w-w-would t-t-t-ake me for a h-h-h-buggy ride."

"I was afraid." He said the words so simply, so honestly.

"Me too."

"Who was the man in front of your house that night?"

"A f-f-f-riend of Daed's. Why didn't you w-w-w-ave? Why didn't you s-s-s-top?"

"I thought you were courting." Embarrassment made his voice gruff. "Not a friend of yours?"

She shook her head. "H-H-e s-s-s-aid I sh-sh-ould make the p-p-p-ie."

Jasper laughed. "Big of him."

"It was."

"And Raymond Old Fox. What is he to you?"

"F-F-F-riend. A m-m-m-an who is nice to m-m-m-e."

"I'm afraid you won't like me when you get to know me better."

"I d-do know you. Always have kn-kn-kn-own you." She dug deep for the words to make him understand. "I w-w-w-worry you will get t-t-t-tired of my s-st-st-st-utter."

What would it be like to stutter her wedding vows in front of everyone in the district? What a thought. The wedding cake candle had gone to her head.

"I'm bad at talking too, even though I don't stutter." A look of wonder on his face, he took her hand and smoothed his fingers over hers. "Love between two people doesn't need words."

"I p-p-p-rayed Gott would heal me. H-H-H-e didn't."

"I prayed He would bring you to me and He did." Jasper pulled her close for another sweet kiss on her forehead. "He knows I don't care. He knows actions speak louder than words. You are special to Him and to me. Do you understand that?"

"Nee, b-b-b-etter sh-show me again."

He laughed and followed her instructions.

CHAPTER 12

Plain folks loved to talk about the weather. Smiling at the crescendo of chatter, Esther Marie slipped from the bishop's house with a platter of sandwiches to serve to the after-church crowd. The storm had caused plenty of damage, but no one was hurt. Roofs could be replaced. Fences fixed. Sheds rebuilt. Besides, rain was good. After a quick look around she made a beeline for the picnic table where Jasper sat with his younger brothers. He looked sharp in his Sunday suit and black hat.

He always looked sharp to her. A few days had passed since their candlelight picnic, but Jasper had been busy at home. The doctor released Fergie from the hospital with instructions not to drive for a week, to change his diet, to start cardio rehab, and begin an exercise program. All this Lucy shared when she stopped by the store to tell Esther Marie she was in charge.

Jasper was needed on the farm.

No chance to find out if Jasper had changed his mind. Maybe he'd been overcome by the candlelight and the dark. Maybe he regretted those kisses in the bright light of day.

No time like the present to find out. Esther Marie took a long breath, let it out, and approached his table. Jasper held his glass of tea to his lips. His gaze met hers. He coughed and sputtered. "Esther Marie."

"Would you l-l-like another sand-w-w-w-ich?"

"Nee, but danki." He wiped his mouth and face with a paper napkin and threw it on his plate. Ignoring the curious whispers of his younger brothers, he stood and leaned closer. "Can we talk?"

Everyone would see and know. Usually single Plain men and women didn't go off alone—unless they were courting. It didn't matter. Time spent with Jasper would be worth the murmurs and the knowing glances. Her parents would be over the moon to see her talking to a homegrown St. Ignatius man. Especially a hard worker like Jasper. "What did you want to talk about?"

He took the platter of sandwiches from her and laid it on the table. "Boys, have at it. Pass it on when you're through."

They would demolish the sandwiches in no time. Together, yet far enough apart to be seemly, Jasper led Esther Marie toward the road and the line of buggies that stretched along the fence line. The silence grew. What was this about? "How is F-F-F-F-ergie doing?"

"Chomping at the bit to get back to work." Jasper slowed. His hand brushed against hers. A shiver ran through her despite the August heat. Did Jasper feel it too? He ducked his head. "He's thankful for how hard everyone has worked at the store. I'm sure he'll tell you himself when he comes back. I told him you ran the store while he was gone. He's thankful for that."

"You didn't have to do that. We ran the store together. B-B-ut that's n-n-not what you w-w-want to t-t-talk to me a-b-b-bout." Maybe he did regret the candlelight picnic. How could he? Just thinking of his kisses sent sweet ripples through Esther Marie's entire body. She could hardly sleep for thinking of him. "Wh-Wh-Wh-at's wrong?"

"Nothing's wrong. Everything's wonderful." Jasper's smile lit up his face. He took her hand—right there in front of God and everyone. "At least it will be if you want what I want."

The feel of his fingers tight and warm around hers made it hard to think. "What d-d-d-o you w-w-w-ant?"

"I want more kisses. I want to spend time with you. Starting with a buggy ride. Lots of buggy rides."

A buggy ride. Her first kiss and now her first buggy ride. Esther Marie's free hand fluttered and landed on her chest in the vicinity of her heart. A lump swelled in her throat. "You m-m-m-ean you w-w-w-ant to t-t-t-ake a r-r-r-ide with me?"

"Jah, with you. Of course." His smile broadened. "With no one else in the world. Only you. What do you say?"

"I say jah." No stutter. "When?"

"Now."

That everyone would see and know didn't really matter. God's timing was perfect. He had brought Esther Marie her heart's desire. What happened next was up to her. "I w-w-would like th-th-that."

"Jah!" Jasper tossed his church hat into the air and caught it. "You said jah."

"I've been waiting for a long time to say jah."

He tugged her to the other side of the buggy where no one could see them. There, he pulled her close and leaned down. Esther Marie reached for him. She wrapped her arms around his neck. His hands touched her checks and her neck. Pent-up feelings exploded in a kiss that made her toes curl. She might faint or shout for joy or simply never stop kissing him.

He pulled away first. "You're my sweet girl and I love you."

Another first. The biggest and most important one. "I love you too."

"Let's find a better spot to talk . . . and do other things."

"That sounds *wunderbarr.*"

Together they climbed into his buggy and set out for their future together.

DISCUSSION QUESTIONS

1. People treat Esther Marie differently because she has a speech impediment. They make assumptions about her intelligence because of it. Sometimes they're impatient. Other times they're condescending. Why do you think that is? What makes people react badly to people with disabilities? Fergie and Lucy don't let her impediment stand in the way of being an employee. What can we learn from their attitude?

2. In Jesus's lifetime people with disabilities were isolated and shunned. Some suggested their parents had sinned so that they were being punished. What did Jesus say and do about this attitude and misperception? Seek out scripture in which He talks about treatment of the sick and disabled.

3. Jasper doesn't have a physical disability. His disability is in the way he reacts to others. He's socially awkward and has never learned to filter his words. Yet he defends Esther Marie and sees past her speech impediment to who she truly is. Why do you think that is? What can we learn from their relationship?

4. When Fergie is hospitalized with a heart attack, Jasper is placed in charge of the store even though Esther Marie is better equipped to handle it—even with her speech impediment. Jasper is outside his comfort zone. This was necessary for him to learn how to treat others and how to approach Esther Marie with his feelings for her. Has God ever led you to a place outside your comfort zone as a learning opportunity? How did you react? How do we grow spiritually through these experiences?

REELING
IN LOVE

•

KATHLEEN FULLER

To James. I love you.

CHAPTER 1

Nina Stoll loved fishing on Saturday afternoons, but today she felt like she was the one on the hook. And she didn't like that—not at all.

She glanced at Ira Yoder, her best friend since she moved to Birch Creek almost two years ago. As usual, he was quiet, concentrating on catching fish. That was what she should be doing too. And normally she did. Except lately, Ira was all she could focus on.

"They don't seem to be biting today." Ira gave his fishing pole a little yank.

"Huh?" Nina mumbled, his words barely registering. Ira was exceptionally handsome today, wearing a short-sleeved, light-yellow shirt, his brown hair a little on the long side, and his straw hat a tad askew on his head as if he'd just plopped it on and rushed here after finishing his farm chores. She liked the fact that he was always a little mussed. He worked hard on his family's farm . . . and he had the physique to prove it.

"The fish." He looked at her. "They're not biting today."

Everything about Ira appealed to her, but his eyes were especially striking—a mix of green and brown but not quite hazel. Strange that she'd only recently noticed how appealing they were. But

Ira wasn't all muscles and looks. He was kind, loyal, and fun to be around. He was the total package.

"Nina?" He snapped his fingers in front of her face. "Anyone home?"

She blinked but continued to stare at him. She couldn't help it.

He frowned. "Are you all right?"

"*Ya.*" She sighed, never taking her eyes off his. "Everything's . . . perfect."

He lifted his right eyebrow. "O . . . kay," he said, giving her a strange look before reeling in his line. He glanced at her again. "If you say so."

Those last words brought her to her senses. She yanked her gaze away from his, her cheeks heating but not because of the July heat. Life was much simpler when she'd thought of Ira as only her best friend. That had changed at Cevilla Schlabach's wedding a few months ago. She'd been playing volleyball, a game she loved, and as often happened, she was the only female on either side of the net. She and Ira were on the same team, and when they both went to spike the ball, they collided. The impact had knocked the breath out of her, and she'd crumpled to the ground.

Ira, who was as solid as an oak door, had remained on his feet, but he immediately knelt beside her. "Nina! Are you all right?"

She blinked, and when she looked up at him, it hit her. The man gazing at her with concern in his eyes was more than her best friend, more than the one person she could always be herself around without fear of judgment or rejection. And the warm, giddy feeling in her stomach wasn't just because an hour earlier she'd witnessed a lovely wedding ceremony.

Then the unexpected happened. She imagined spending her life with him. Or at the very least giving him a serious kiss.

He grabbed her hand and helped her to her feet, and then he dashed off when he realized she was fine. But she was far from fine. She was in love with Ira Yoder . . . and she had no idea what to do about it.

What she couldn't do was tell him how she felt. As an introverted, stocky woman who loved to fish, she was used to having male friends. But it was a stretch to think Ira would find her wife material. Nina had to keep reminding herself of that. Unfortunately, it was becoming more and more difficult with each passing day—and in today's case, each passing minute. *What is wrong with me?*

They fished in silence. Nina usually enjoyed fishing. No matter how tense she was or how stressful a week she'd had working as a maid at her family's business, Stoll Inn, she was always relaxed with a pole in her hand, the sounds of nature around her, and Ira at her side. She didn't want to ruin all that by acting *seltsam*.

She felt a tug at the end of her line and pulled on her pole. "I think I caught one," she said, distracted from her weird reactions to Ira for a moment.

"About time one of us did." Ira got to his feet and picked up the creel dangling in the water by the bank of the pond on Jalon Chupp's property. Jalon was both Ira's neighbor and related to him by marriage. But anyone Jalon knew had an open invitation to fish there.

Nina reeled in the fish, but she was only halfway there when the line grew taut. "I think it's stuck on something."

Ira dropped the creel back into the water and came up beside her. "You're going to snap the pole."

She relaxed her line and then pulled on it again. "I can feel it give way." She gave it a yank, but the line moved only a few inches.

Ira stepped behind her and put one large hand over hers and the other on the pole. "One, two, three!"

But Nina couldn't move. Ira was closer to her than he'd ever been, and even though she knew he was just helping her reel in the fish—which was probably just a branch instead, considering how stuck the hook was—her breath caught in her throat. He smelled like sunshine, fresh air, and summertime. They weren't actual scents, but she didn't care. He was practically embracing her, and for that moment, she was in heaven.

Then she felt the line give way, and Ira removed his hands. "You can reel it in now," he said, stepping to the side.

"Reel what in?" she said, distracted once more.

"The fish, Nina."

"Oh." She turned the reel's handle and it moved smoothly. When she lifted the line out of the water, a small sunfish dangled from its end.

"All that trouble for this little thing?" Ira took it from the hook and put it in the creel, which they both did when the other person caught a fish. Then he sat down where he'd been sitting before. "Nice catch anyway."

She slowly sat down next to him. Her mouth went dry as she noticed his tan forearms and biceps peeking out from under his shirt sleeves. He was tall, like his brothers. But they were wiry while Ira was broad and at least six inches taller than Nina. They were sitting so close to each other that, if she wanted to, she could lean her head against his strong-looking shoulder. She was sorely tempted.

She sat up straight. Good grief, what was going on with her today? Although she'd accepted that she was in love with Ira, she'd managed to keep a tight rein on her emotions when they were around each other—like when they fished together last Saturday, when she played softball with him and the Bontrager men on Sunday afternoon, and when she took leftover blueberry muffins her *grossmutter* made over to the Yoders' the other day. Granted, she'd taken the treat partly as an excuse to see Ira again, but she'd still managed to act like nothing had changed between them when she handed him the basket of muffins.

For some reason, though, today was different. She just hoped he hadn't noticed.

Ira leaned back and cast his line, appearing to be unaffected by their closeness, for which Nina was both thankful and disappointed. "*Daed's* thinking about hosting a singing soon," he said, glancing at her.

Nina's stomach flipped. "I didn't think you had traditional singings here."

"We haven't in a long time." He shrugged. "Never made much sense when it was all men and only one or two women. Most of us don't care for singing anyway, except during church."

She didn't mind singing, although she wasn't skilled at it. But she had minded going to singings back in Wisconsin. They were awkward for her as she watched all the cute girls capture the young men's attention while she was off to the side. Every once in a while, she would have a conversation with a boy, but it was always about fishing or sports. That didn't bother her too much, because they were topics that interested her. But as she grew older, she realized she would always be just the tomboy buddy to them.

Just like she was to Ira. She sighed.

"You don't like singings?" Ira lifted a brow.

"Oh, they're all right." She tried to keep her tone casual as she brushed her fingertips over the vibrant green grass. "Why does *yer daed* want to hold one after all this time?"

"It's for the younger *kinn*, like Judah's age. Over the past few years more families have moved to Birch Creek, but the *kinner* were

199

young when they arrived. Now a few of them are old enough to attend a singing."

Nina stared at the pond. She still hadn't cast her line, and she wasn't thinking about catching fish. Ira was twenty-two. Would he be interested in someone a bit younger? Or interested in anyone at all? The thought twisted something sharp in her heart. "Are you, uh, going?"

"I might not have a choice since the singing will be at *mei haus*." He tugged on his line again and looked at her. "Why haven't you cast *yer* line? You're not done for the day, are you?"

She looked at the pole in her hand, the empty hook dangling at the end, and then halfheartedly cast it.

"You forgot the bait," Ira said. He frowned. "You've been acting weird today, Nina. Did something happen at the inn?"

She quickly shook her head and reeled in the empty line. Great. He'd noticed her strange behavior. She had to get it together. "Everything's fine at the inn. In fact, we're booked solid for the next month."

"Does that mean you won't get to fish every Saturday?"

She looked at him, wondering if some meaning was hidden behind the question. Would he miss their fishing afternoons? Would he miss her? "*Nee*," she said. "I don't expect that to change."

He nodded, but he didn't say anything else. They were both quiet as they continued to fish, which gave her heart time to settle down. When it was nearly suppertime, the single sunfish Nina had caught was still their only catch of the day.

She set her pole on the ground and picked up the creel. One fish didn't seem worth the trouble, so she let it go and then untied the creel and shook out the excess water. When she turned around, Ira was already on his feet, fishing pole in hand.

"See you next Saturday?" he said.

She nodded, forcing a smile. She'd have to get her wits together before then, or Ira would really think something was wrong with her. "*Ya*, next Saturday at the usual time."

He gave her a smile, making her stomach flip again, this time in a good way. Then he headed for the opening in the copse of trees that surrounded the pond. They almost always parted ways there, one of them leaving before the other. Occasionally, she'd decide to walk to his house with him, so she could say hello to his parents. But mostly they left separately, and that had never bothered her before.

She was plenty bothered now, especially realizing that she was always the one who walked him home. He'd never walked her home, one more piece of evidence that he thought of her as nothing but a friend. Or even worse, like she was his sister. *Ugh.*

Fishing pole in one hand and creel in the other, she realized something else as she made her way back to the inn. Ira had brought up the singing but hadn't invited her to be there. He hadn't even asked if she was interested in going. Her heart sank to her toes. She'd never had so much as a crush on anyone before, and she certainly hadn't known that unrequited feelings could be so painful.

And why did she love Ira when plenty of young, single men lived in Birch Creek? But no, she had to fall for a man who had zero romantic interest in her. "I'm not liking this irony, Lord," she said, scowling as she lifted her gaze to the dusky sky. "Not one bit."

* * *

As Ira made his way home, his thoughts weren't on the fact that he hadn't caught a single fish today—although that pricked his ego a little since he considered himself a good fisherman. He was thinking about Nina. She'd been acting strange today, and he wondered what was going on with her. He didn't believe her when she said everything was fine. He'd seen her staring at him more than once and vacantly out at the pond as if she had something on her mind. She certainly hadn't been focused on fishing. He'd never seen her forget to bait her hook.

But something else gave him pause, enough that he slowed his stride before he reached his house. When he saw her struggling with the fish, his instinct to help had kicked in. That was fine. But when he'd moved behind her to help her reel in the stubborn fish, without thinking, he'd put his arms around her. Then when she leaned back, instantly, fishing was the last thing on his mind.

The top of her head had reached his chin, and he'd breathed in the sweet scent of her shampoo. Nina worked as a maid at her family's inn, but she always showed up for their fishing times wearing a clean dress and smelling nice. Noticing that wasn't a big deal. But he'd paid attention when he realized she fit perfectly in his half embrace.

Nina Stoll was a stocky, athletic girl, a contrast to the women he'd grown up with in his community. She looked nothing like his sister-in-law, Martha, whom he'd had a crush on before she and his brother Seth got together. Nina was different in appearance—and personality—from any woman he'd *ever* met. And the thought of putting his arms completely around her had given him pause. A big pause. Fortunately, she'd been so preoccupied that she hadn't noticed.

He shook his head. What was he doing, thinking about embracing Nina? This wasn't the first time he'd helped her reel in a fish, and she had done the same for him—although he'd helped her more than she'd helped him. Why was this time so different?

Ira shook his head again, pushed the troubling thoughts out of his mind, and quickened his steps. When he reached his family's property, he headed for the shed and put his fishing pole away. He had to take Nina at her word when she said nothing was wrong. They'd been friends long enough—best friends, if he had to put a label on it—that he knew if she wanted to confide in him, she would. He needed to respect her space. Besides, everyone had an off day occasionally. *Seems like today was an off day for both of us.*

He brought the cows back in from the pasture and fed them. The barn still smelled faintly like new wood, even though it had been built a year and a half ago, after the fire that had burned down almost everything on the farm except their house. But they were back in business again, thanks to help from the community—and especially from Nina. She often came and pitched in. He'd been concerned he was taking her away from the inn, but at the time they hadn't yet opened. When they did, Stoll Inn had a slow start, but now business was picking up, and he was glad for the family.

After finishing his chores, Ira went inside the house to wash up for supper. The comforting scent of chicken wafted into the mud-room, making his mouth water. His mother's chicken potpie was the best. After he washed his hands in the kitchen, he leaned against the counter and talked to *Mamm* as she prepared a salad. A minute later, his father walked in, his brother Judah trailing a little behind.

It was hard to believe their family had shrunk so much in the past three years. But with his sisters Ivy and Karen married and Seth marrying Martha last year, it was just Ira and Judah and his parents at home. That made him think about the singing his father had been talking about. One of the main purposes of singings was to give young people the chance to socialize with the opposite sex. That would be nice—if Birch Creek had any single women his age.

Well, there was Nina, but she was a friend. The rest of the girls in their community were way too young for him. Still, the odds of his father allowing him to skip the singing were slim to none.

He sat down as his mother put the salad on the table, already set for supper. When everyone was seated, they bowed their heads for grace. Then after their silent prayer, they passed around the dishes.

"Margaret called me today," *Mamm* said.

"Johnny and Doris's daughter?" *Daed* looked surprised.

"*Ya.* You and *yer bruder* might not keep in touch, but her mother and I do. Margaret wants to come for a visit."

"Just her, or the family too?"

"Just her. She asked if she could stay for a couple of weeks. She wants to visit us, but she's also interested in seeing Birch Creek because she's heard so much about it from *mei* letters to Doris."

"That's nice," *Daed* said. He scooped up a healthy serving of chicken potpie. "She's welcome to stay as long as she wants."

Ira hadn't seen Margaret in years. His family had lived in Birch Creek since before he was born, and they'd visited his uncle Johnny's family in Holmes County only once or twice. His uncle also owned a farm, and while the two brothers got along just fine, they both liked staying close to home. Memories of one of their visits came to Ira's mind. Johnny had four daughters, and Margaret was the youngest, two years younger than Ira. She was also a tomboy, and he remembered how she would always try to keep up with him and Seth.

"She'll be here Friday evening," *Mamm* told them.

Daed frowned. "We'll be in Cleveland on Saturday for the tall ships festival."

Ira had forgotten about that. Every year a festival in Cleveland celebrated the history of tall ships and the maritime industry in the area. Judah and his father were history buffs, and this year was the first time they could go see the several tall ships in the harbor. Ira wasn't interested in going, but he suspected his mother wasn't just going along for the ride.

"I guess we could stay here." Judah stirred the filling of his potpie with his fork but didn't look up.

"I know how much you've been wanting to see the ships," *Mamm* said. "We're definitely going."

Judah grinned and then went back to eating his meal with gusto

"Karen and Ivy will be out of town too." *Mamm* turned to Ira. "I don't want Margaret to spend her first day here alone, so I'd like for you to take her with you when you *geh* fishing on Saturday. I'd also like you to introduce her to Nina."

For some reason the idea of taking Margaret along bothered him. Nothing against her, but Saturday afternoons were his and Nina's time. He realized he didn't want the intrusion. Neither he nor Nina had ever invited anyone else to join them.

"Is that a problem?" *Daed* said, giving Ira a firm look before taking a bite of his potpie.

"*Nee,*" he said. "It's not." He didn't want to be disrespectful.

"I think she and Nina will hit it off well," *Mamm* said.

That was probably true. It was hard not to like Nina once you got to know her. She did like to keep to herself, but that wasn't a bad thing. He also knew she'd struggled a little with Martha marrying Seth because Martha had been her first friend in Birch Creek, and now they didn't see each other as often. Then her brother, Levi, had just married Selah in May, the only other single woman in Birch Creek who'd been around Nina's age. Now that he thought about it, his mother was right. It would be good for Nina to make a female friend, even if it was short-term.

Despite that, he still didn't like the idea of a third person fishing with them. He was used to it being just him and Nina. Fishing with her was comfortable, easy, and relaxing—a time he looked forward to every week. Since the fire, he and his family had been working overtime to get the farm back to what it had been. Ira's father was also the bishop, and he had glaucoma. His condition was controlled with medicine, but the doctor had advised him not to do certain things, which meant more jobs for Ira and his brothers. Ira didn't mind hard work, and he enjoyed farming, but looking forward to his weekly fishing date with Nina helped the week go faster.

Date? Had he really thought of that word when it came to Nina?

"Ira?"

His mother's voice drew him out of his thoughts. He looked at her. *"Ya?"*

"I asked if you wanted more chow chow."

"Oh. Sure." He held out his plate, and she spooned a big helping next to his almost finished potpie.

While Judah and *Daed* discussed going to an auction, Ira stared at the chow chow, still bothered by the direction his thoughts had taken with Nina. Of course their fishing times weren't dates. They were outings. Yes, that was the right word for them. Outings with his best friend, and so what if that best friend happened to be a girl? Not a single thing about Nina made him think of her as anything other than a friend—even if her hair did smell really, *really* good, and her full figure was just the right size to tempt him into an embrace.

"*Yer* food's growing cold on *yer* plate, Ira," *Daed* said with a small grin.

He hadn't heard that phrase since he was a kid. Then again, he never let his food get cold—until now. Ira glanced around. Not only had everyone already finished eating but Judah had left the table. He hadn't even heard his brother get up. He quickly polished off the rest of his meal and then helped *Mamm* clear the table as his father moved into the living room.

"Everything all right?" *Mamm* asked when Ira placed a short stack of plates next to the sink.

"*Ya*. Fine."

She turned to him. "You don't have to take Margaret fishing if you don't want to, despite what *yer daed* said."

"I said I would."

"I know, but you've seemed off-kilter since I asked you." *Mamm* put her hand on his forearm. "I didn't realize *yer* time with Nina was so important to you."

"It's not," he said quickly, but then he regretted the lie. "I mean, it's not a big deal for Margaret to fish with us. I was just surprised you thought she would want to."

"Don't you remember how much she enjoys fishing?" *Mamm* said. "That's one reason I thought she and Nina would hit it off. They're both tomboys."

Ira frowned. "Nina's not a tomboy," he blurted.

Mamm's brow lifted. "Oh," she said, and then she paused before adding, "I see." She turned away from him and started placing dishes into the sink.

Ira frowned, wondering what his mother meant by *I see*. He decided not to question it. But Nina wasn't a tomboy, at least not in his mind. Sure, she liked to fish and play sports, and when she helped out on their farm, she wasn't afraid of getting dirty. But not once had he thought of her as anything but a girl—actually, a woman.

He inwardly groaned. He was thinking far too much about

this, and it was giving him a headache. Nina was Nina. Simple as that.

"I'm going to *geh* feed the horses," Ira said. At his mother's nod, he went outside and put his focus on his chores—and away from Nina Stoll.

* * *

CHAPTER 2

* * *

On Monday morning, Nina went about her job as a maid at the inn, cleaning the four guest rooms, which had all been booked for the weekend. Business had been steady for months now, which not only put her family in a good mood but also confirmed that their move from Wisconsin to Birch Creek hadn't been a mistake. For a while there, they hadn't been sure.

Nina had been homesick as well. Then she'd met Martha, and after that, Ira, and it hadn't taken long for Birch Creek to feel like home.

Her brother, Levi, and his new wife, Selah, who both worked at the inn, made an excellent team, both as business partners and as a married couple. After helping to plan Cevilla's wedding, Selah had switched jobs with Nina, finding her niche as a hostess and event planner. That suited Nina just fine. She didn't want to deal with the guests. They always made her nervous, and when she was nervous, she was clumsy.

She'd spent yesterday and this morning trying not to think about Ira or continuously feel the pinch of pain in her heart because he hadn't asked her to the singing. She hadn't been all that successful. He was still in her mind, but at least he was at the back of it instead of consuming her thoughts. Still, she had a difficult time keeping him there. Being in love, especially a one-sided love, was tougher than she'd ever imagined.

When she finished cleaning all the rooms, she went downstairs and decided to break for a snack. She put away her cleaning supplies in the large cabinet in the mudroom, and then she walked behind the inn to the house she shared with her father, Loren, and her grandmother, Delilah. Selah and Levi lived there, too, but they were in the process of building their own house next door.

In the kitchen, Selah and *Grossmammi* were busy baking muffins for the guests they expected that afternoon. Check in was at three, and they were booked solid until Sunday morning. Sundays had been a concern for a while because most guests left on Sunday morning, and that was when the family attended church services every other week. Then Levi devised a self-checkout system, and his process turned out great. Their guests—many of them there to simply experience Amish Country and enjoy the peace and quiet of Birch Creek on the outskirts of the busier communities in Holmes County—had been honest.

Nina washed her hands and opened the pantry door. She sighed as she searched for the homemade peanut butter and grape jelly. When she found them both, she sighed—again.

"All right, that's it."

Nina spun around at her grandmother's impatient tone. "Huh?"

"You've been sighing and moping since Saturday night." She set her spoon on the spoon rest next to a bowl of batter and marched to the table. "Sit," she said, pointing at a chair.

"*Grossmutter*, I—"

"Nina." She looked at her over silver-rimmed glasses that matched the color of the hair peeking out from under her *kapp*. "We're going to talk."

Nina's shoulders slumped as she dragged herself to the table. Her grandmother was treating her like a five-year-old even though she was twenty-two. She plopped down on the chair and set the jars on the table in front of her. "What do you want to talk about?"

"Selah and I are concerned about you." *Grossmutter* pulled out a chair for herself, across from Nina. "Right, Selah?"

Selah had just put two trays of muffin tins in the oven and closed its door before setting the timer. Now she faced Nina. "Concerned might be too strong a word," she said, wiping her hands on her apron.

"*Nee*, it's not." *Grossmutter* pointed to the empty chair next to Nina, and Selah dutifully sat down. Under the table she gave Nina's hand a squeeze. Both of them knew how *Grossmutter* could be. She'd been haranguing Selah and Levi about having children from the minute they got married.

Grossmammi folded her hands and rested them on the table. "Now, tell us what's wrong. And don't say *nix*, because that would be a lie."

Nina almost sighed again but caught herself. She couldn't lie to her grandmother, especially when she was right. She did have a problem. She stared at the tabletop. "I'm just a little . . . disappointed."

"About what?" Selah said. In contrast to *Grossmutter*'s, her tone was soft and encouraging, her blue eyes filled with understanding.

Nina clasped her hands together. "About . . . about . . ."

"Just spit it out, Nina." *Grossmutter* tapped her plump finger on the table. "How can we help you if you won't tell us what's wrong?"

"Because there's *nee* point," she muttered, looking away. "There's *nix* you—or anyone—can do about it."

"Humph." *Grossmutter* frowned. "I refuse to believe that. *Nee* problem is unsolvable."

Nina looked at her and then at Selah, who gave her a tiny nod of reassurance. Neither one of them seemed ready to drop the subject, which gave her no choice but to tell them . . . something. But how much would she have to say?

"Well, the Yoders are planning to hold a singing soon." She started to sigh again but held it in.

"Really?" *Grossmutter*'s brown eyes lit up like a birthday cake overloaded with candles. "It's about time. There hasn't been a single singing in this community since we moved here."

"Most of the *buwe* here don't like singing," Selah said. "And there hasn't been another reason to have one."

"*Nee* reason?" *Grossmutter* gestured to Nina. "There's a reason right here. The *buwe* around here need to know what *maed* are available."

Nina wanted to sink into the floor. Although she was the only young, single woman in Birch Creek in her twenties, not a single man had shown interest in her. That hadn't been a problem since she hadn't been interested in any of them either . . . until now. But even though she didn't want to date any of the eligible Birch Creek bachelors other than Ira, their lack of attention did bother her. Was she that unattractive and . . . not dateable? Ugh. Now she felt worse than before.

"When is the singing?" *Grossmutter* said, clasping her hands. "Hopefully not before we have time to make you a new dress. Is that it? You were disappointed because you didn't have a new dress and thought no one would have time to help you make one? I do! Other than *yer* two Sunday dresses, all *yer* clothes are full of grass stains."

"I don't know when it is," Nina whispered, dodging the true reason for her disappointment. "Ira didn't say."

"Then we have time. We'll sew this week." *Grossmammi* tapped her chin. "I probably need to take *yer* measurements again. *Yer* dresses have been looking a little tight lately."

Nina pushed the peanut butter and jelly jars away. Her grandmother had made this comment before, more than once. That was ironic since she was more than a little plump herself. Still, Nina didn't need to be reminded that she'd put on a bit of weight recently. *Just a little.* She would never be thin, but she didn't want to burst out of her dresses either.

At least news of the singing had pushed Nina's sighing and moping out of her grandmother's mind. Good. She didn't want to talk about Ira.

"Oh, I just remembered," Selah said, jumping up from her seat. "I promised Levi I would pick up more cleaning supplies from Schrock's Grocery. He wants more of Aden's honey too. The guests can't get enough of it." She looked at *Grossmutter*. "Delilah, would you mind finishing the muffins?"

"*Nee*, but I thought we had plenty of cleaning supplies."

"We're out of a few things, right, Nina?"

Nina looked up at Selah, confused. *Grossmutter* was right. They did have plenty of supplies, enough to get them through the month. Probably through August too. But Selah's eyes grew wide, and she gestured to the mudroom door with a quick nod of her head. "Right," Nina said, not sure what Selah was doing but going along with her anyway.

"How about we *geh* together?" Selah said, walking over to Nina and practically lifting her by the elbow. "You can tell me exactly what we need."

"Uh, sure." Nina stood up before Selah yanked her out of the chair.

"We won't be gone long." Selah snatched her purse from the counter and then guided Nina out of the kitchen before *Grossmutter* could say anything else. Once they were outside and near the barn, Selah let out a breath.

"What's going on?" Nina asked. "You know we don't need more cleaning supplies."

"I'm sorry, but I had to get you out of there. I had to get *me* out of there." Selah looked at her. "I love Delilah, but she can be too much. And Levi did mention we were running out of honey. That part was true."

"*Danki*," Nina said, understanding now. She was relieved she didn't have to listen to her grandmother talk about dresses or singings anymore. "I'll hitch up the buggy."

A short while later, as they were on the way to the grocery store, Selah said, "Nina, you mentioned you're disappointed, but I don't think it's about a dress. Do you think the Yoders will expect you to *geh* when you don't want to? I understand that. I used to dread going to those things, but at least I had Martha there with me. Then Ruby showed up and went to one of them." She paused. "I wasn't very nice to her back then."

Nina couldn't imagine Selah not being nice to anyone, but she knew what her sister-in-law said was true. She didn't know any details other than Selah had trouble with feeling blue and that she saw a counselor. Levi had even gone with her twice. Nina respected that it was Selah and Levi's business, though, and she never asked either one of them about it.

"Anyway," Selah said, "I wonder why Freemont decided to have a singing now. It's not like *anyone* will want to *geh*."

Nina cleared her throat and stared straight ahead.

Selah looked at Nina. "You do?"

214

"It doesn't matter," she said softly. "Ira didn't ask me to *geh*."

"He didn't? Did something happen between you two?"

"Hardly," Nina mumbled, tightening her grip on the reins.

Selah paused for a moment, and then said, "Did you want him to ask you?"

She glanced at Selah. Why deny the truth? Maybe it was time to tell someone she trusted what was going on with her. "*Ya.* I did. But that's me being stupid."

"You're not stupid. And I'm not surprised, honestly."

"You're not?"

"You and Ira spend a lot of time together."

"As friends." Nina guided the buggy to the next road, turning right. "Only *friends*." The disappointing word stuck in her throat.

"Friendship can turn into something else. Look at *mei bruder* and Ruby."

"*Ya*, but Ira and I are different." *I'm different.* She'd known she wasn't like typical Amish girls for years, and not just because her grandmother often pointed it out with a decent dose of chagrin. She wasn't sweet and feminine and pretty like so many girls her age were. She wasn't interested in cooking and sewing, either, although she knew how to do both passably thanks to *Grossmutter*. What would Ira see in her anyway? She was just a tomboy with thick eyebrows and an expanding waistline.

Selah chuckled. "Nina, *nee* two people are more different than Christian and Ruby."

Despite her negative thoughts, Nina had to smile. Christian and Ruby were unusual, not just as a couple but each in their own right. They were their district's schoolteachers, in charge of the two classrooms at the school. But while Ruby was extremely outgoing and lively, Christian was staid and more than a little awkward. Yet they were happy together, which was what mattered in any relationship, along with love.

Nina frowned. Happiness and love. Right now, she didn't have either with Ira.

"Nina," Selah said, fortunately interrupting Nina's train of thought, "if you like Ira, why don't you tell him?"

"It's not that easy." She turned to Selah. "Did you ever tell Levi you liked him?"

"Um, *nee*. Not right away." Selah sighed. "You're right. It's not easy. But *yer bruder* and I had a different situation than you and Ira do. Levi was *mei* boss. You and Ira are already friends and on an even playing field."

"I don't want to ruin that."

"But you're unhappy with the way things are." Selah put her hand on Nina's forearm. "*Ya?*"

She couldn't lie about that either. "*Ya*, I am. I don't know what to do, Selah. I'm confused about everything."

They rode in silence for a few minutes, Nina feeling more miserable than ever. She didn't see a way out of this situation without a terrible ending.

Selah snapped her fingers. "I have an idea."

"Uh-oh." Usually when she heard those words, her grandmother was saying them, and they almost always meant bad news for Nina.

"Don't worry, this is a *gut* idea. Why don't you prepare a picnic for this Saturday?"

"I always do that."

"I don't mean throw a few sandwiches in an old cooler," Selah said. "I'm talking about a proper lunch. A *special* lunch."

"Why would I do that?"

"A picnic can be either friendly or romantic." Selah had a soft look in her eyes. "You can see how it goes, and then if you feel like you can tell Ira about *yer* feelings for him, do. If not, then the two of you are just having a picnic as friends. Ira will be none the wiser."

Nina's face heated. "I can't do that."

"Why not?"

"Because he can't know how I feel. That would mess up everything."

"It didn't mess up things between Levi and me." Selah smiled "I've always wished we would have been more straightforward with each other about how we felt. Looking back, I see how foolish it was not to discuss our feelings. We could have spared ourselves some heartache."

Nina's heart was definitely aching. "I don't know," she said as they neared Schrock's. "What if he doesn't feel the same way?"

"Then you'll learn the truth. Isn't that better than pining for him like this?"

"I wish I didn't pine at all. Things would be so much easier if they went back to the way they were."

"What changed?"

I did.

A car whizzed by, shaking the buggy. Fortunately, their horse wasn't fazed. They bought him from an auction shortly after moving here, and it hadn't taken him long to find his way around Birch Creek. Although Nina didn't appreciate cars speeding past her, she was glad for the distraction, and she ignored Selah's question. She said a quick prayer of thanks when Selah didn't bring it up again.

Nina parked the buggy at Schrock's and looped the reins over the hitching post in front of the building. When she and Selah entered the store, Selah told her she wanted to look around for a few minutes before she picked up the honey. Nina made her way to the back where the cleaning supplies were. If they didn't return home with one or two items, her grandmother would be suspicious. Nina grabbed some toilet cleaner, which they always needed, and a sturdy scrub brush to replace the one that had seen better days.

She'd just started for the check-out counter when she saw Ira come in. *Oh nee.* Of all the times for him to show up. Panicked, she went to the very back of the store and hid in the garden supplies aisle. She was surrounded by tools, peat moss, fertilizer, and seeds as she ducked and peered around the endcap. She had a limited view, but if Ira came back here, she would be able to see him.

Of course, that's exactly what he did. Her heart raced as he came closer, but there was nowhere for her to go. Grasping the toilet cleaner and brush, she made herself as small as possible as she crouched behind the endcap's display of seeds, the hem of one of her oldest dresses grazing the floor.

Nina set the cleaner on the floor and gripped the edge of a shelf, praying Ira wouldn't come any closer. She peeked around the display and watched him as he examined one of the two different hoes the Schrocks carried. He held the handle in his hand and looked at the metal blade. Her legs began to ache. Good grief, how long did it take to choose a hoe?

Finally, he walked away, hoe in hand. She let out a deep breath as she stood with her items, but she was afraid to move until Ira had time to make his purchase up front and leave. She'd wait.

When she saw Selah coming, holding three jars of honey in a Schrock's handbasket, she jumped in front of the display as if she'd been looking at the seeds all along.

"He's gone," Selah said, chuckling. "Apparently he didn't see you hiding from him back here."

Nina didn't see what was so funny, and she was annoyed that Selah had caught her. She could only pray that her sister-in-law was right, because if Ira did know she was hiding from him, she wouldn't be able to face him again. She tucked the scrub brush under one arm and picked up a packet of sunflower seeds. "These would be pretty in the garden, don't you think?"

"*Ya*, but we already have some planted, remember?" Selah took the packet from her and put it back. "Nina, Ira left the store. You don't have to stay here."

Nina stared at her feet, noticing for the first time that her shoelace was untied. "I'm hopeless, aren't I?" she said as she placed the cleaner and brush in Selah's basket before bending down to tie it.

Selah grinned. "*Nee.* You're just a little scared."

"A little?"

"Okay, more than a little. But don't worry. We'll work on that. I'm confident you'll have the best picnic you've ever had on Saturday."

Nina wasn't so sure. "If I do decide to make a special lunch, hopefully you have enough confidence for both of us."

. . .

Ira frowned as he walked home from Schrock's Grocery and Tool. What in the world was going on with Nina? He'd seen her at the back of the store when he entered to pick up a couple of jars of Aden's honey for *Mamm*. He started toward her, but when she ducked behind that display, he hovered over hoes he didn't need just so he could secretly see what she was up to. He knew the aisle she was in had no other exit, so when she didn't come out, he was baffled. But since he couldn't stare at hoes much longer without looking *seltsam*, he finally took one and left. Then he not only had to buy the honey but that hoe.

Surely Nina wasn't hiding from him. But other than Selah and Aden, the store was empty. Why else would she be crouching behind a display of seeds?

He reined in his thoughts. He hadn't done anything that would cause her to avoid him. At least he didn't think so. But as he thought about her behavior on Saturday coupled with how she'd just acted in the store, the combination concerned him. She wasn't acting normally, and whether it was because he'd done something or something else was going on, he didn't like the idea of her being out of sorts. Maybe he should go talk to her. *Or maybe I should mind* mei *own business.* Again, she knew where he was if she wanted to talk to him. But today, it seemed like she didn't even want to be around him.

When Ira arrived home, he was still arguing with himself. He put the jars of honey on the kitchen counter and then went outside to work in the barn, where it was cooler. The walk to and from the store had been pleasant, but once he began cleaning out the stalls, he started working up a sweat.

Before long, his older brother Seth came inside the barn. He opened the side door, where he had pulled up a wagon full of baled hay, the second cut of the season. "Ira," he hollered. "Can you give me a hand?"

Ira closed the door of the cow pen and set the shovel against the barn wall. He brushed off his hands and shimmied up the ladder to where they stored the hay. Seth put the gas-powered conveyor belt against the barn and then turned it on. Ira grabbed the bales as they reached the top of the conveyor and threw them to the side. Once the wagon was unloaded, Seth turned off the belt and then joined Ira upstairs to stack the hay.

Stacks from the first cut of hay were already on one side of the loft, so they stacked the newer hay on the opposite side. After a few minutes, Seth said, "I hear you're going to take Margaret fishing on Saturday."

Ira placed a bale on top of two others and then tilted his hat back to wipe the sweat from his forehead. "Who told you that?"

"Martha. She and *Mamm* and our *schwesters* got together at our *haus* last night to can green beans. I heard *Mamm* say Margaret's arriving on Friday evening."

"Sounds like you're caught up on everything." He grabbed another bale of hay.

"You know how the women like to chatter. Is Nina okay with it?"

Ira swung the bale on the top of the pile, which was nearly above his head now. He looked at Seth. "I don't know. I haven't told her."

Seth paused, beads of sweat rolling down his face. The beard he'd started growing after he and Martha were married was a little past his chin now. "Why not?"

"I don't understand why everyone is so concerned about me and Nina." Ira turned his back on Seth and took a long drink from the water jug his brother had brought up to the loft.

"I didn't say anything about you and Nina." Seth came up behind him. "But if there *is* a you and Nina—"

"There's not."

Seth smirked, an annoying habit of his. "You said that pretty quickly."

Ira spun around. "I didn't get in *yer* and Martha's business when you were dating, did I?"

"Oh, so you and Nina are dating." Seth took a step backward, a sly grin on his face. "*Nee* wonder you're so touchy."

"I'm not touchy, and we're not dating." Ira put his hands on his waist, frustrated that his brother kept twisting his words, not to mention that Seth seemed entertained by it. "Drop it, okay?"

The smile slid from Seth's face. "Okay." He held up his hands, his expression serious. "Consider it dropped."

They worked in silence for the rest of the time it took them to stack the hay. They were both a sweaty mess by the time they finished, but the task was done. The men shimmied down the ladder and into the cooler air of the lower part of the barn.

"Hey, I'm sorry," Seth said. "I was just teasing you a little bit."

Ira shrugged. "It's fine."

"It's just that . . . well, you and Nina do spend a lot of time together. People are bound to wonder, you know?"

No, he didn't know. "How many people are wondering about us?"

"Not too many," Seth said quickly.

"Then those few people should mind their own business." Ira took the shovel and went to the cow pen again. "I've got to finish this before lunch."

Seth nodded, apparently getting the hint. "Talk to you later, then."

After his brother left, Ira leaned against the shovel. It hadn't occurred to him that anyone would be speculating about him and Nina. His friends never said anything. Then again, they'd all vowed not to get involved in any relationship after the Martha fiasco almost two years ago. Ira had been keen on her, as had many of the other men his age in the district. But that had been mostly because she was the only woman available. It had taken him a while to realize that. At the time he'd really believed he liked Martha. Good thing she'd been wise enough to put the brakes on a relationship with him. It hurt at the time, but he knew that had been more about his pride than his heart.

Now she was his sister-in-law, and he couldn't imagine ever dating her much less marrying her. He'd kept his vow not to pursue another romantic involvement even after several available women came into the community. It all came down to trusting his own judgment. He was still a little embarrassed about how he'd made a fool of himself with Martha.

Ira thrust the shovel into the old hay and manure. That was also why he was content with his uncomplicated and comfortable relationship with Nina. He didn't want that to change, not that it ever would. If he had his way, they'd be best friends for the rest of their lives.

He paused mid lift, his shovel filled with debris. Was he being fair? Surely Nina would want to get married one day. The thought of that twisted something inside him, and he flinched. Nina, as someone else's wife. That didn't sit well with him at all.

He shook his head. He was being ridiculous. Thinking about Nina in a romantic way was . . . Well, he didn't know what it was. But he needed to stop listening to people like his brother. They were being gossipy, plain and simple.

Yet as he finished cleaning the cow pen, he couldn't help still being concerned about Nina. Her recent behavior bothered him more than he wanted to admit. Something was going on with her, and he knew it wouldn't leave his mind alone until he found out what it was. He just wasn't sure how to do that.

CHAPTER 3

The rest of the week passed by quickly for Nina. Because the inn was fully booked, she was busy keeping everything clean and tidy. She did enjoy her job, and although she avoided interacting with the guests, she liked to see them happy and enjoying their stay. Between all that work and helping *Grossmammi* with the cooking, both for the inn and for their family, she'd put the idea of a special picnic with Ira mostly out of her mind.

Although she appreciated Selah wanting to help, Nina had to figure this out on her own, and she decided the best way to do that was to stuff her feelings way down, along with an extra slice of pie or two. Actually, she'd had three one night—and then she'd paid for it with a stomachache. She really needed to stop stress eating. That wasn't helping.

On Friday morning, she had cleaned the last empty room upstairs, preparing it for new guests who were checking in later that day, when Selah came upstairs. "When you're finished," she said, "will you meet me in the kitchen at the *haus*?"

"Sure. I just have to finish this bathroom."

Selah left, and Nina cleaned the bathroom until everything in it shone. Her grandmother was picky about that, and she didn't want another lecture on the proper way to clean a bathroom. She had to admit her grandmother was right—the bathrooms did look cleaner and practically sparkled using her method. Satisfied, Nina gathered her supplies. Then she dropped them off in the mudroom before going to the house to see what Selah wanted.

When she arrived, both her grandmother and Selah were seated at the kitchen table. Nina's stomach churned at the sight of a wicker basket in the center. A *picnic* basket. Oh, this didn't bode well at all.

"Nina," *Grossmutter* said, gesturing to the seat next to her. Her brown eyes were bright and full of excitement behind her glasses.

Another bad sign.

"Why didn't you tell me you were planning to have a special picnic with Ira tomorrow?"

Nina glared at Selah, who was staring innocently at the ceiling. How could she have betrayed her like that? Knowing she didn't have much of a choice, Nina sank into the chair just assigned to her. "I hadn't made up *mei* mind about the picnic yet," she mumbled, shooting another dark gaze at Selah, who was finally looking at her with a sheepish expression. At least she had the grace to appear apologetic.

"Of course you must have a picnic with Ira." Her grandmother huffed. "Although at this late notice, you didn't give us much time to plan."

"Plan? *Us?*" Her stomach twisted again, and for once she wasn't craving something to eat. Her nerves were killing her appetite, which normally wouldn't be a bad thing. But that didn't mean she wanted to be a nervous wreck just so she could lose a couple of pounds.

"*Ya.* We have to plan." *Grossmutter* looked at her with a confused frown, as if Nina had suddenly lost her mind. "A picnic like this must be special, and special things must be planned."

This was getting ridiculous. Nina rolled her eyes. "Says who?"

225

"Says me." *Grossmutter* pulled out the pencil stub and small notebook she kept in the pocket of her apron and turned the pages of notes until she came to a blank page. "Now, I think fried chicken would be a good entrée. Not too many spices, and of course *nee* garlic." She gave Nina a crafty grin. "Just in case."

Nina crossed her arms, her face heating. Nothing like hearing her grandmother implying that she and Ira would be kissing. A shiver went down her back at the thought. Not an unpleasant shiver, either, which put another kink in her plan not to entertain any romantic notions about Ira. Not that it mattered. That plan had flown out the window the moment she thought of it. "This isn't a *gut* idea," she said, forcing her attention on the subject at hand and giving Selah another look of irritation.

Selah stared at her hands. "I guess I didn't really think this through when I mentioned the picnic this morning," she said.

"I'm glad you said something," Delilah said. "Otherwise I wouldn't have known about it."

"I was hoping you wouldn't," Nina muttered.

"What?" *Grossmutter* turned her head to the side so her left ear was closer to Nina. "I didn't catch that."

"I believe I said this was going to be a friendly picnic," Selah said, piping up. "Remember, Delilah?"

"Of course, of course. Friendly." *Grossmutter* was practically bursting with glee. "Hopefully, *very* friendly."

Sinking farther in her chair, Nina realized she was fighting a losing battle. This was her fault. She never should have told Selah about her feelings for Ira. She shouldn't have feelings for him in the first place, but she was still annoyed with her sister-in-law. Selah knew better than to get *Grossmutter*'s hopes up when it came to possible romance.

"Fried chicken, potato salad . . ." *Grossmutter* made her list on the small piece of paper. Then she turned to Nina. "What's Ira's favorite dessert?"

"Peach cobbler," she said, the answer automatic.

Grossmutter grinned and wrote that down. "What else does he like to eat?"

"He's not crazy about potato salad," she said, remembering all the times she'd eaten with the Yoders when she helped them after the fire. "He'd rather have coleslaw. Fresh bread would be good, with lots of butter. He especially likes that. I think a few pickles and some apple slices with cheese would be a *gut* way to round out the meal." She paused, *Grossmutter* and Selah's faces coming into view. "What?"

"That was, uh, rather specific," Selah said, her eyebrows raised.

"You seem to know quite a bit about *yer yung mann.*" *Grossmutter* underlined the word *cheese* with a flourish. "All this sounds wonderful. Would he prefer lemonade or tea?"

"Tea," Nina said weakly. "Ira doesn't like lemons."

Grossmutter nodded. "Tea it is, then. I have a lovely old quilt that will be perfect for laying out the food." She turned to Nina and patted her hand. "Don't you worry about any of this. Selah and I will prepare everything. All you have to do is wear *yer* cleanest dress." She frowned a little. "Too bad we didn't get a chance to start making *yer* new dresses this week."

That had been by design. Nina had made sure she was too busy for a measuring session, despite her grandmother pestering her about it. Her self-esteem couldn't take that right now. "I'll be fishing, remember? I don't need a new dress."

"Fishing," *Grossmutter* said with a little chuckle as she got up from the table. "Sure you will."

"Grossmutter!" She shook her head. She had to have the most incorrigible grandmother in the state. *Or on the planet.*

"I'll *geh* get that quilt. I know exactly where it is." She whistled as she walked away.

After she left, Nina turned on Selah. "I can't believe this," she said, lifting her hands in the air. "Why did you tell her about Ira and me? You know how she is!"

"I'm sorry!" Selah said, her contrite expression genuine. "I just casually mentioned the picnic. I promise. Then she started asking more questions, and I couldn't lie to her. Suddenly she was running away with the idea."

Nina rubbed her temples with her fingertips. "Now I have to *geh* through with this."

"It won't be so bad."

"You don't know that."

"I know Ira is a very nice *mann*. And remember, if you don't want to reveal how you feel, you don't have to."

"But he'll wonder why I went to all this trouble."

"Then you tell him the truth." Selah grinned. *"Yer grossmutter* made you do it."

"And *mei schwester*," she said, but at least she was able to smile back. She had to focus on the positive. Selah was right. A picnic might not be so bad, and if it did go south, she could always blame her grandmother.

And if by the slimmest chance something sparked between her and Ira, it could be a wonderful time. Just her and the man she loved, eating delicious fried chicken while enjoying the afternoon breeze. Gazing into each other's eyes, his face moving closer to hers as if he wanted to kiss her . . .

The nerves in her stomach transformed into butterflies. Maybe it wasn't out of the question that Ira might like her. Maybe this Saturday would be the best day of her life. *It couldn't hurt to hope, could it?*

· · ·

When Ira finished working on the farm Friday afternoon, he took a quick shower upstairs before supper. After he dressed, he descended the stairs just at the moment the front door opened. A young woman about his age walked inside, his father coming in behind her. "Just in time," *Daed* said, gesturing with his head to the suitcase he carried. "Ira, you remember Margaret."

He halted, a little dumbstruck. She wasn't the awkward tomboy he remembered. She was petite, slim, and very feminine. "Hello," he said, finding his words. "You've, uh, changed a bit."

"Just a little." She smiled.

Daed chuckled. "You got that right. I almost didn't recognize her at the bus station."

"You've changed since I last saw you too," she said to Ira, looking up at him. "A lot."

"Ira, take Margaret's bag upstairs. She's staying in Ivy and Karen's old room."

He lifted the suitcase and looked at his cousin. "I'll put it at the foot of the bed."

"*Danki.*" She turned to *Daed*. "Where's *Aenti* Mary?"

"Right here." *Mamm* bustled into the living room and gave Margaret a big hug. "I'm so glad you're here." She stepped back and looked Margaret over. "You're the spitting image of *yer mamm.*"

Margaret nodded with a grin. "I've been told that once or a dozen times. A shorter version of her, that is."

That was true. She was small. Not quite as petite as his sister Ivy, who was a little under five feet tall, but she wasn't much taller. Ira realized a gene must run in the Yoder family that affected both women. His sister Karen was a more typical height for a woman, and Ira and all three of his brothers stood over six feet.

"Ivy and Karen went to Millersburg to visit some friends, but they'll be back on Monday," *Mamm* said.

Mamm's and Margaret's voices faded away as Ira climbed the stairs. He put Margaret's bag in his sisters' old bedroom and then joined the rest of the family in the kitchen. Supper was already on the table, and Judah was pouring glasses of iced tea.

"This looks delicious, *Aenti*." Margaret sat down at the table and smiled.

"I remembered you like pork chops." *Mamm's* eyes sparkled.

His cousin looked at the platter of juicy pork chops in the middle of the table. "That I do."

Ira wondered why *Mamm* was so happy to see Margaret and why she'd made one of her favorites. They hadn't visited Margaret's family in years, and while they were close family blood wise, they felt distant to Ira. He was closer to his friends in Birch Creek than to any family in Holmes County.

Then it struck him. Even though his sisters visited quite often, *Mamm* must miss having them living here. He figured it was nice for her to have another female in the house, even for a little while.

After they said a silent prayer and started passing the serving dishes, *Mamm* said, "Again, I'm sorry Freemont, Judah, and I won't be here tomorrow. We planned our trip to Cleveland over a month ago, and it's not an outing we can reschedule."

"That's all right." Margaret looked at Ira. "I'm looking forward to fishing tomorrow. It's been a long time since I last went."

"I thought you liked fishing," Ira said.

"I do. At least I did. I just kind of lost interest in it when I grew up."

That was the end of his conversation with Margaret because his mother took over. She started discussing female things like sewing and cooking, which Margaret seemed more interested in than fishing.

When they finished eating, *Daed* volunteered Judah to clean the kitchen so they could continue their conversation in the living room. Ira knew Judah wasn't thrilled with that. But although his brother would have protested in the past, he'd grown up a lot since the fire had destroyed most of their farm. Ira knew Judah still blamed himself because he was the one who'd decided to burn old wood and leaves on a windy day. Then the flames had burned out of control. But he'd learned a hard lesson, and the family had all forgiven him. He just hoped Judah would eventually forgive himself.

"I'll give you a hand," Ira said, feeling a bit sorry for his little brother. Between the two of them, they made quick work of cleaning the kitchen, and then he and Judah started on the evening chores.

As he fed the horses and Judah checked on the cows, Ira turned his thoughts back to Margaret. She was as nice as he'd remembered, and now that he'd spent a little time with her, he believed she and Nina would get along. He was thankful now that Margaret was going—despite initially seeing her as an intrusion. His last fishing day with Nina had been a little awkward, and maybe having another female to talk to would help her sort out whatever was going on. He wanted whatever it took to get their relationship back on track. Otherwise, he didn't know how he'd shake feeling so off-kilter.

. . .

The next day, Nina arrived at the pond earlier than usual. The sky was overcast, with solid gray clouds obscuring the sun and threatening rain. That worried her. In her daydreams, taking up most of her thoughts since yesterday, rain hadn't been a factor. The weather, like everything else between them, had been magically perfect.

But life wasn't magical or perfect, and now her stomach started churning again as she looked up at the cloudy sky. Actually, she wasn't just worried about the rain. She was worried about everything. She glanced at the picnic basket she'd just set down on the grass, her fishing pole to one side, glad it was Ira's turn to bring bait. While she'd remained positive about the picnic until this moment, now that she was here, she couldn't stem the anxiety pooling inside her. She should have just canceled the picnic and even fishing altogether. Her grandmother would have more than a few words to say about that decision, but Nina could tune her out. She'd done it many times before.

But it was too late to cancel, so she had to make the best of it, along with getting herself together before Ira arrived. She spread out the quilt, which was well worn, very soft, and perfect for a picnic by the pond. Then she tried to straighten the wrinkles the best she could. She didn't know exactly what time it was, but she knew Ira had to be arriving soon. Taking a deep breath, she asked God to make sure everything would go well, and then she opened the picnic basket and peeked inside, trying to keep her hands from trembling.

Once she started pulling out the food, she couldn't help but smile. *Grossmutter* had outdone herself. The fried chicken was covered in thick layers of foil and still warm. She found coleslaw, apple slices, three different kinds of cheese, grapes, fresh bread and butter, a jar of pickles, and of course, peach cobbler for dessert. Her appetite kicked in as she set out the plates and metal utensils and put the cloth napkins under each knife and fork. A breeze swirled around her, and she grabbed the plates before they blew away, although the chance of that was slim since they were made of thin plastic, not paper. Still, she didn't want anything to go wrong. She set the utensils and napkins on the plates, making sure they stayed put.

She sat back, curling her legs under her. Then she sat cross-legged, making sure her skirt covered her knees. Or maybe she should lounge on her side, looking casual. She stretched out her legs and leaned on her elbow. No, that wasn't right either. She moved closer to the edge of the quilt and tried to find another sitting position. Giving up, she decided to stand. Her knee caught on the hem of her dress, and she tumbled right on top of the food.

"Nina?"

Oh nee. Slowly, she lifted her head and saw Ira, fishing pole and creel in his hands, a stunned expression on his handsome face. And he wasn't alone. Standing next to him was a very pretty, petite girl with a perfect figure and a bright complexion even the most devout Amish woman would envy.

"Uh, uh . . ." The words caught in Nina's throat. When she tried to scramble to her feet, she tipped over the jar of pickles, whose lid she'd loosened moments before. The vinegar-scented juice soaked into her dress and, horrifyingly, into her grandmother's precious quilt. She also saw that the foil covering the peach cobbler was half off the casserole dish and that a round-shaped depression sat in the middle of its golden crust. She glanced down at her chest, mortified by the big glob of cobbler covering it.

Ira's gaze darted back and forth between the destroyed picnic and Nina. "What's all this?"

She started to explain, but her voice sounded like she'd choked on a spoonful of peanut butter. She cleared her throat. "I, uh, brought a . . . picnic."

He looked a little confused. "Huh. I wish I'd known. I would have told you to bring extra." He gestured to the woman standing next to him. "Nina, meet Margaret."

"Hi," Nina muttered. She snatched one of the napkins to wipe off her dress, only to flip a fork into the air. It landed tines first in the grass next to the quilt. She should just stop moving altogether.

"You two don't worry about me," Margaret said. "I had a large breakfast this morning, so I'm not very hungry."

Even her voice was perfect—light, sweet, and feminine. Nina glanced up at her. Margaret was smiling, and she also carried a fishing pole. Why hadn't Ira said anything about bringing another girl? And where did he find her? Definitely not in Birch Creek.

Ira crouched beside Nina and handed her another napkin. A swift wind kicked up, ruffling his hair. He wasn't wearing a hat today, and his hair looked so thick and inviting. He was close enough for her to run her fingers through it—

"Ira." Margaret's lilting voice sang out. "What did you do with the bait?"

"It's in the creel." His gaze didn't move from Nina's. Then he glanced at the food she'd laid out. "It looks like you've gone to a lot of trouble."

"*Nee* trouble." Nina tried to laugh, but it came out like a loud bark. *Could this possibly get any worse?* When Ira frowned again, she tried to recover. "*Grossmutter* made everything. In fact, she also *made* me bring the picnic today."

"Why?"

Why? Uh-oh. She hadn't been prepared to answer that. "Because . . . because . . ." She'd never been so embarrassed in her life. Jumping to her feet, she knocked Ira back on his heels. Tears flooded her eyes, and her mind and heart raced. Not only could she not answer a simple question, but she couldn't stop feeling like a fool. Ira had brought another girl. A pretty one. Clearly his type, which Nina clearly was not. And he hadn't told her. Then again, why would he? He didn't owe her an explanation. He had the right to bring someone to their special fishing times. Obviously, though, they weren't that special to him. Not at all.

The surroundings that always made her feel so tranquil, that had been her refuge since she moved from Wisconsin, now closed in on her, as if the pond and trees were mocking her idiocy at thinking she and Ira had something more than friendship between them. She couldn't stay here anymore. She fled toward the woods.

"Nina!" Ira called out.

She ignored him. She should have never listened to *Grossmutter* and Selah. She should have never allowed herself to hope. She should have known Ira would find someone eventually. And she should have known that when he did, it would break her heart.

CHAPTER 4

Ira looked at the wrecked spread of food in front of him. Seeing the pickle juice spilled on the quilt, he grabbed the jar and screwed the lid back on. He could smell the fried chicken, and the coleslaw looked delicious. Although the cobbler had a big dip where Nina had fallen on it, it still looked scrumptious with its brown crust and peach filling bursting through.

But he couldn't concentrate on food, which was unusual for him. He jumped to his feet and, bewildered, looked in the direction where Nina had disappeared. Why had she run off like that? And why had she brought such a fancy picnic—even if her grandmother wanted her to? Usually they each brought a sandwich and maybe an apple or a bag of chips. But this was a full spread, complete with a wicker picnic basket.

"I hope I didn't ruin things with you and *yer maedel*," Margaret said, walking toward him.

"She's not *mei maedel*." He glanced at the woods again. Should he go after her?

"Oh, I didn't realize. I figured with you two having a standing fishing date on Saturdays—"

"They're not dates," he said with a frown, still trying to figure out if he should go find Nina.

236

"Okay." Margaret pressed her lips together and then spread her hands toward the picnic. "Did you forget a special occasion, then? Because this looks like more than a friendly picnic to me."

Ira shot an annoyed look at her. "*Nee*, no special occasion." At least he didn't think so. Had he forgotten something important? He couldn't imagine what they had to celebrate that required delicious-looking food—all his favorites.

Margaret shook her head. "She looked really upset, Ira."

He couldn't deny that. "I know." What he didn't know was why. None of this made sense.

She moved to stand in front of him, craning her neck to look him in the eye. "Why aren't you checking on her?"

Ira rubbed the back of his neck. "I was thinking I'd let her cool off for a little while."

His cousin's eyes widened. "Don't you want to know why she's upset?"

"Of course I do."

"I'm confused." She frowned as she crossed her arms over her chest.

Still bewildered, he said, "You and me both."

Margaret tilted her head as she looked at him for another moment or two. Then she pointed to the woods. "*Geh* find her, Ira. I'll clean up here and take everything back to *yer haus*."

Her words yanked him out of his fog. She was right. He had to find out once and for all what was going on with Nina. "All right," he said, grabbing Nina's fishing pole and then turning to her. He glanced at the picnic again. "Sorry to leave you alone like this."

She smiled. "Hey, I'm a big *maedel*. Well, not that big," she said with a chuckle. "But I can manage alone. I might even do a little fishing after I clean up."

But Ira was already heading for the woods, only half hearing her. "I'll meet you back at the *haus*," he said over his shoulder. "We can *geh* fishing another time."

"Ira."

He turned around but took a few steps backward. *"Ya?"*

"You might think you and Nina are just friends, but friends don't *geh* to this much trouble for a picnic."

He halted. "She said her *grossmutter* made her do it."

"Maybe she's seen how Nina looks at you, the same way I saw her looking at you when we got here."

"Huh?"

Margaret shook her head and chuckled. "Never mind. *Geh* talk to her and make things right."

Ira nodded and left, wondering what Margaret was going on about. Women. They didn't make any sense.

*   *   *

Nina ran all the way back to the inn, and by the time she got there she was gasping for breath. Only when she reached the front porch did she realize she'd left behind not only her fishing pole but the picnic basket, quilt, and food. She groaned. On top of everything else, *Grossmutter* would be upset with her for that. But she couldn't go back there. First, she didn't have the energy. Running all the way from the pond wasn't a great idea, in hindsight. Second, she was too embarrassed to show her face again to Ira and his *freind* Margaret.

She plopped down on the swing and took in gulps of air. How was she going to face Ira after what happened? He had to think she was a complete fool. Then again, maybe his opinion of her didn't matter to him anymore now that he had Margaret. Here she'd been pining away for him when he was already courting another girl. Her jaw clenched.

The front door swung open, and Selah came outside. She raised a surprised brow. "I didn't expect you back so soon. How did it *geh*?"

Nina banged her head against the back of the swing. "It didn't."

"What do you mean?" Selah sat down beside her.

As Nina explained the disaster, the wind continued to pick up, and a low rumble of thunder sounded in the distance. "Of course, I left the basket, food, and quilt at the pond. Even *mei* fishing pole." She squeezed her eyes shut. "Now it's going to rain on it all."

"I'm sure Ira gathered everything and took it to his *haus*."

"If he wasn't too *busy* with Margaret," Nina huffed.

Selah pressed her lips together and put her arm around her shoulders. "I'm sorry," she said. "This is *mei* fault. I should have minded *mei* own business and let you and Ira figure things out for *yerselves*."

Nina leaned her head on Selah's shoulder. It was nice having a sister-in-law, even though she was a tiny bit responsible for the worst moment of her life. "You're not to blame. At least not too much."

"I promise not to interfere anymore."

"I've heard that before." Nina lifted her head and looked at her. "From *Grossmutter*. Although I have to give her credit. She didn't meddle too much. And she made a wonderful lunch." She sighed. "Then I had to mess up everything."

"Sounds like Ira ruined it for you." Selah frowned. "I can't believe he was dating someone and didn't tell you."

"Why would he?"

"Out of courtesy? Because you *are* friends? At least he could have come up with a better way to let you know."

Nina shook her head. "He doesn't owe me anything, Selah. Like you said, we're just . . . friends." A fact that had been driven home like a stake in the ground. *Or in my heart.*

Light rain tapped a soft tempo against the roof of the porch. "I tell you what," Selah said. "After this rain stops, I'll head over to the Yoders' and get everything from Ira." She smiled. "Would that help?"

Nina nodded. That way she could avoid him—and Margaret, too, if she was still there. "I'd appreciate that."

Selah stood and dipped her head out from under the porch roof for a second, glancing at the sky. "Looks like a storm is developing," she said. "I'm going inside. Are you coming?"

"I'll be there in a minute."

After Selah left, Nina stared at the rain now falling steadily. At least she wasn't caught out in this mess at the pond. Although it would have been sort of romantic, her and Ira sitting under the trees, holding the quilt over their heads and huddling together to wait for the storm to pass. He would gaze into her eyes, and she into his, and it would be the perfect time to share a kiss—

Not again. "Stop!" she said, bolting from the swing. Even knowing Ira had a girlfriend didn't keep her from having useless, starry-eyed daydreams about him. She'd imagined kissing him many times, but how could she even think about that after what just happened? "Just stop it!"

"Stop what?"

She turned to see Ira dashing up the porch steps. He was soaking wet. He stood at the end of the top step, water streaming down his face, his clothes plastered against him, her pole in his hands. *Oh boy.* No, not a boy. Definitely a man. She bit the inside of her cheek and tried not to pay attention to that fact. Instead she focused on his expression, a mix of confusion and concern. She was too surprised to flee inside. "What are you doing here?"

He leaned the pole against the porch rail, and then he took a step toward her, water puddling around his black tennis shoes. "Nina," he said, wiping the rainwater off his face, his expression growing stern. "It's time you told me what's going on."

. . .

The deluge had started as Ira neared Stoll Inn. He ran as fast as he could, but he still got drenched. Fortunately, there hadn't been any lightning, but that didn't mean it wasn't coming. His annoyance at the weather disappeared when he saw Nina jump up from the swing. When he heard her say "Stop it!" there was no doubt in his mind that something was seriously wrong, and he wasn't leaving until she explained what it was.

"Ira, I . . ." Her mouth remained open, and then she clamped it shut and looked away from him.

Whatever was bothering her was giving her a lot of trouble, and that made him worry more. He couldn't help but move closer to her. "Nina, we've known each other a long time. We're *gut* friends. You can trust me, whatever it is. I won't break *yer* confidence, and you know I won't judge you."

She didn't look at him. "But you'll probably laugh at me."

He couldn't stand hearing the pain and embarrassment in her voice. "Nina," he said softly. Unable to stop himself, he reached over and touched her chin, gently moving her head so she was looking at him. "I would never laugh at you or make fun of you. You should know that by now."

"I'm sorry," she whispered. "I shouldn't have run off like that. I

241

shouldn't have brought the picnic." She audibly gulped. "I'm sorry I ruined *yer* time with Margaret."

"You didn't. And Margaret said she'd gather everything and take it *mei haus*." He glanced at the water pouring from the eave. "We would have had to cancel our fishing anyway. It's raining too hard."

She looked him up and down and then quickly turned away and headed for the door. "I'll get you a towel before you catch cold."

He lightly grabbed her arm. "I won't catch cold in the middle of summer. Stop dodging me, Nina. I'm not going anywhere until we talk."

Nina whirled around. "Fine. You want to know what's wrong? I like you. That's what's wrong."

He frowned. She was making even less sense than before. "I like you too. I thought that was obvious. If I didn't, we wouldn't be friends."

She shook her head, her hands flapping furiously. "That's not what I'm talking about. Ira, I *like* you. As in romance. As in wanting to *geh* out on a date instead of fishing. As in . . ." Her lower lip trembled. "Anyway, that's what's wrong with me. And I know I'm ruining everything between us, and I didn't know you and Margaret were together, and I don't think we should see each other anymore." She dashed into the inn, the screen door slamming behind her.

Ira couldn't move. He tried to process what she'd just said, the last part of the conversation a whirl in his brain. She liked him . . . like, *liked* him? And what was that about him and Margaret being together? And now she didn't want to see him anymore? Despite his confusion, that last statement hit him like a ton of bricks. Wait, she was ending their friendship too?

He flung the screen door open and stormed inside. Two older English couples were sitting at one of the tables, playing cards in their hands, all their gazes on him. They must have seen Nina run past them, and now he was standing in the lobby, which doubled as a common room, his clothes dripping wet. In his haste to get to Nina, he'd forgotten this was a place of business, and the people gaping at him were the inn's guests. "Sorry," he mumbled, backing out the door.

Ira stood there on the porch, wondering what to do as sheets of rain gushed in front of him. Nina's house was behind the inn. Should he run over there and try to talk to her again? He doubted she would agree to that. But how was he supposed to leave things the way they were?

After deciding he didn't have any real choice, he dashed out into the warm rain and went home. He didn't think it was possible to be more wet, but now he felt like a drowned rat, and he probably looked like one too. He walked into the mudroom, took off his sopping tennis shoes, and left them on the mat. Then he peeled off his shirt and squeezed the water out of it into an old bucket by the door. He'd have to go through the house with wet pants on, but that couldn't be helped.

When he entered the kitchen, Margaret was sitting at the table, looking at a seed catalog. She glanced up, and her eyes widened. "What happened to you?"

He'd forgotten all about her. Clutching his shirt against him, he shook his head and hurried upstairs to dry off and change clothes.

After he dressed, he sat on the edge of his bed. What was he going to do? Nina had romantic feelings for him. Now her behavior made sense. The way she stared at him last Saturday, the elaborate surprise picnic today . . . Even Margaret had seen it, and she didn't even know Nina. He pressed the heel of his hand against his forehead. How could he be such a *dummkopf*?

A soft knock sounded on his door. "Ira?" Margaret said. "Are you okay?"

He hesitated but then got up from the bed and opened the door. "I'm fine."

Her pale-blond eyebrows lifted. "You don't look fine. You also don't sound fine." She gestured to the hallway. "*Mei mamm* always said *kaffee* and company help soothe anyone's troubles."

"Do you believe that?"

"Maybe. Enough that I made *kaffee*. It's fresh and hot. I can dish out some of Nina's peach cobbler too."

Normally he wouldn't turn down food, especially peach cobbler, but he didn't feel right eating Nina's dessert. "I'll take the *kaffee*," he said.

"You might want to brush *yer* hair too." She chuckled. "You look like you got hit by lightning." She paused. "You didn't, did you?"

"*Nee.* At least not the way you think."

They went downstairs, and Ira sat at the kitchen table while Margaret poured the coffee. "Are you sure you don't want the cobbler?"

Ira nodded. He stared at the steam rising from his coffee, but he didn't pick up his mug.

"Did you talk to Nina?" Margaret sat down across from him.

"*Ya.*"

"I guess it didn't turn out well." She took a sip of her coffee. "I'm sorry about that."

He looked at her. She reminded him of Ivy, and not just because they were both petite. Although there was nearly a decade between him and his oldest sister, he could often talk to her about things, and she had always given good advice. And like Ivy, Margaret wasn't pressing him for information. She even picked up the seed catalog and started looking at it again, as if nothing was amiss.

"You were right," he said, placing his hands palms down on the table.

She glanced up at him. "About what?"

"Nina." He sighed. "I have a big problem, Margaret, and I don't know what to do."

CHAPTER 5

"N ina, you need to eat something."

Nina lifted her head from her hand and looked at her grandmother. "*Nee*, I don't. *Mei* dresses are getting too tight, remember?" She put her chin back in her hand and stared at the fried chicken. *Grossmutter* had made extra when she prepared it for the picnic. In fact, the entire supper, except for the peach cobbler, was identical to the picnic lunch. Nina couldn't bring herself to eat one bite.

"Loren, say something." *Grossmutter* gave Nina's father a pointed look.

He turned to Nina. "If you don't feel like eating, you don't have to."

She managed a small smile. "*Danki*. May I be excused?"

He nodded, and as she left, she heard her grandmother sputtering in protest. Selah and Levi had left earlier to have supper at Martha and Seth's. It was quiet for a Saturday night. The two older couples from West Virginia who were staying at the inn had gone to see a play in Holmes County, based on an Amish novel. They wouldn't be back until later tonight.

Nina went to her room and plopped onto the bed. Her insides

were churning with embarrassment and regret. Why was she always saying and doing the wrong things? She thought about a verse in the Bible from the book of Romans. *For that which I do I allow not: for what I would, that do I not; but what I hate, that do I (7:15).* It had taken her a long time to understand that verse, which she'd always thought was a bit convoluted. And although she knew Paul was talking about sinning, she couldn't help but feel this concept somehow applied to her situation. Why had she proceeded with something she initially thought was a bad idea? Why did she tell Ira her feelings when she knew it would ruin their friendship permanently?

But she couldn't stop herself from telling him the truth. He wouldn't leave until she did, and it wasn't fair to leave him confused about her weird behavior. And now their friendship was over. It had to be. She'd ended it by telling him they couldn't see each other anymore. He probably not only thought she was *seltsam* but that she was a jerk too.

She buried her head in her pillow. Birch Creek had so many single men. Why did she have to fall for Ira?

"Nina?"

At the sound of her grandmother's voice, she lifted her head. She wanted to ignore her, but she could tell from *Grossmutter*'s tone that she was worried about her. "I'm okay," she said, not moving from the bed.

"May I come in?"

Knowing that her grandmother was the most stubborn person who ever existed and would never leave until Nina let her inside her room, she replied. *"Ya."*

The door opened, and *Grossmutter* came in with hesitant steps instead of her usual confident stride. Her hands clasped in front of her, she came partway into the room and stopped. "I didn't mean to upset you at supper," she said. "*Yer daed* was right. You're a grown woman, and if you don't want to eat, you don't have to."

"It wouldn't hurt me to skip a few meals," Nina muttered, remembering Margaret's slim figure. So that was Ira's type. Petite, slim, with a pretty face and wonderful skin. Everything Nina didn't have. Nina had never stood a chance.

Grossmutter sat down beside her. She rubbed Nina's back like she had when Nina was a little girl. Her mother died when she was young, and *Grossmutter* had taken care of her and Levi and their father ever since. And while she could be meddlesome, overbearing, and a bit too outspoken, Nina loved her. Tears slipped from her eyes as she felt the comfort of her grandmother's touch.

"Did the picnic really *geh* that badly?"

Nina nodded. "Worse than you can imagine."

Grossmutter patted her back. "I know this is hard on you, but at least you know. Now you can turn *yer* attention to someone else."

Angry, Nina popped up straight. "I can't turn *mei* feelings off like that. I care for Ira. I . . ." She looked at her lap. "I love him."

"Oh, *lieb*." *Grossmutter* took her in her arms. "I was afraid of that. It hurts, and it's going to hurt for a long time. But I promise, God will heal *yer* broken heart."

"You make it sound so simple."

Her grandmother smoothed Nina's brow with her finger. "Did I ever tell you about Cornelius King?"

Nina moved out of her embrace and looked at her. "Cornelius?"

"Not exactly an Amish name, but his father had some sort of distant relative with that name, and Corny was stuck with it."

If she hadn't felt so horrible, Nina would have laughed. "Good grief. Corny is worse."

"I don't know." Her grandmother's eyes turned wistful. "I thought it was cute."

"Was Corny *yer* first love?"

"He was. And much like you and Ira, we were *gut* friends. We didn't *geh* fishing, of course." *Grossmutter* made a sour face. "You know I detest worms. But we both liked to whittle."

"Whittle?" Nina was surprised. "I didn't know you whittled."

"Oh, I haven't for a long time. I enjoyed it when I was younger, but I've never had the urge to pick it up again." She smiled. "Corny and I would sit on my front porch, sometimes his, and spend an afternoon or summer evening whittling away and talking. He was handsome, kind, and a very *gut* whittler. I also thought he was perfect for me."

"But he didn't feel the same way."

"*Nee.* He didn't. And in the end, he was right. We wouldn't have worked out. I met *yer grossvatter* two years later, and we married a year after that."

"What happened to Corny?"

"He left the Amish. He hadn't been baptized yet, and the last I heard he'd married an English woman and moved to Minnesota." She tapped her chin. "Or was it to Montana?" She shrugged. "I can't remember."

Nina looked down at her lap. "That's a *gut* story," she said. "But it doesn't make me feel any better. I can't imagine loving anyone but Ira."

"You can't imagine it"—she took Nina's hand—"but maybe God isn't finished with you and Ira yet. What seems impossible can be possible with God."

"And what if it's truly impossible for me and Ira to be together?

249

What if it's God's will that we *geh* our separate ways?" Just thinking about that made her heart break all over again.

"'He healeth the broken in heart, and bindeth up their wounds.'" Her brown eyes turned soft. "Whatever happens, Nina, God understands *yer* pain, and He's there to heal you."

"Like He did when *Grossvatter* died?" Nina's eyes welled. "And when *Mamm* died?"

Grossmutter's eyes filled too. "*Ya*," she said. "We don't forget the people we loved who died or the ones we loved and didn't love us the same way, but over time, it doesn't hurt as much. The same will happen with you about Ira, the way it did for me about Corny. God has someone in mind for you."

"How can you be so sure? Maybe I'm meant to be single *mei* whole life." Right now, that sounded like a preferable alternative.

"I just know." She tapped her chest. "In here. And if I'm wrong, God will ensure you're contented—whatever the circumstances."

Nina considered her words. She'd always wanted to ask her grandmother a question, and now seemed the right time to pose it. "Did you ever want to marry again?"

Grossmutter paused, running her hands over the quilt on Nina's bed. "Only if God brought the right *mann* into *mei* life, and so far, that hasn't happened. Meanwhile, I've been able to take care of you and our little family. That's been enough for me." She squeezed her hand and then stood. "If you decide you're hungry, let me know. I wrapped a plate for you."

"*Danki*," Nina said. Then she got up and hugged her grandmother tight. "For everything."

"I love you," *Grossmutter* whispered. "You're special. Don't ever forget that."

Nina nodded as her grandmother left. It would be considered

prideful to think she was special, and *Grossmutter* didn't give compliments easily. But Nina had needed to hear those words right now. She wiped her eyes, feeling a little better. Her heart still hurt, but she had hope. Not about Ira. Not even about love. But she knew God would heal her heart eventually. She could count on that.

CHAPTER 6

On Wednesday evening of the following week, Nina was in the living room, working on her new purple dress. When she'd tried it on, she'd noticed the hem was crooked and puckered. She frowned.

Her grandmother had come down with a headache and was lying down, and her father was at the inn with Levi and Selah, who were discussing an upcoming English wedding, their first one booked. Nina was glad they weren't involving her in the preparations. She was content with them telling her what they wanted her to do.

For the past few days, Nina had kept busy helping *Grossmammi* cook and can and making her new dresses. She detested sewing, but it was time she stopped complaining about what she didn't like to do and just do it. She'd made three of them—this mauve-purple one and a dusty-blue one and a light-green one. Her cleaning job at the inn had also kept her busy. They were even booked until September now, which made Levi and her father especially happy.

She hadn't talked to Ira since the ill-fated picnic last Saturday, and she'd avoided him at church on Sunday. That was where she'd learned Margaret was his cousin, making her feel like an even bigger fool.

She'd have to face Ira eventually. She couldn't avoid him in their small district forever. But as long as she could put off that moment, she would.

Yet she was still thinking about him. She believed what her grandmother told her about God healing her heart, but that didn't keep her mind off Ira.

She was halfway finished with the hem when she heard a knock on the door. Frowning again, she stood. They weren't expecting anyone as far as she knew, but then again, none of them minded a little company. *As long as it's not Ira.* Nina grimaced. She was sure she didn't have to worry about that.

"Hello," Margaret said when Nina opened the door.

Nina gaped. Margaret was the last person she'd expected to see on her doorstep. "Uh, hi."

"Do you mind if I come in? I'd like to talk to you."

Dumbfounded, Nina nodded and let Margaret inside. She noticed that even the woman's steps were delicate and graceful, and she felt like an awkward clod next to her. Still, she wouldn't be rude, especially to someone who didn't deserve it. And maybe if she pretended her behavior at the pond hadn't been awkward and strange, Margaret would too.

"May I get you something to drink?"

"*Nee*, I won't be here very long." She sat down on the couch, and a slight frown came over her face.

Forgetting about her insecurity, Nina sat down in the chair across from her. "Is something wrong?"

"Not really." Margaret looked down at her lap. "I feel a little silly talking about this, but I can't help it." Her gaze met Nina's. "You know *mei onkel* is having a singing this Sunday, *ya*?"

Nina nodded, feeling the same pinch in her heart she'd felt

when she'd heard about the singing after last Sunday's church service. *The singing Ira didn't invite her to.* "Ya, but I don't plan on going."

"Oh. I thought you might."

Nina shook her head. "I don't care too much for singings." Which was true, but that wasn't the real reason she wasn't going. She hoped Ira hadn't told Margaret what she'd admitted to him after she ran away from the pond.

"I think they're great fun. But, well, I told *mei aenti* I came to visit Birch Creek to spend time with the family—and that's true—but I also came for another reason, one I haven't shared with anyone. Not even her." She looked a little sheepish. "A few months ago, *Aenti* Mary wrote to *mei mudder* about all the single men in this community."

"Ah," Nina said, understanding dawning. "And you wanted to see that for *yerself.*"

Margaret nodded. "I've known everyone in *mei* district since I was a *kinn*, and I'm not interested in any men there. I thought maybe if I met someone new . . ." She let out a small laugh. "The singing on Sunday is the perfect opportunity."

"It is," Nina said in agreement.

"But now that it's almost here, I'm not so sure. I know girls a few years younger than me will be there, but I really want someone there who's *mei* age." She looked at Nina squarely. "Would you meet me there, so I won't feel so alone?"

Nina paused. Margaret really had no idea what she was asking. Ira would certainly be there, and that would put an end to her plan to avoid him as long as possible. She also wasn't sure she had the energy to witness all the single young men in Birch Creek fawn over Margaret.

"Please?" Margaret said. "I know it's a strange favor to ask, especially since we don't know each other well. But it would mean so much to me if you would."

Great. How could Nina turn Margaret down when she knew how important this was to her? "All right," Nina said, her stomach churning at the idea already.

Margaret grinned. "Oh, *danki*, Nina. I really appreciate it. And if there's ever anything I can do for you, just let me know."

Nina couldn't help but smile back. Margaret did seem like a genuinely sweet girl. Although it wouldn't be easy for Nina to do this, it made her feel better to be helping someone. "What time does it start?"

"At five thirty, but how about coming a bit early? That way we can get ready together."

She nodded but wondered what Margaret meant by "getting ready." For every singing Nina had been to, she just threw on a dress and made sure her *kapp* was clean. "Okay," she said.

Margaret got up from the couch and moved toward the door. "This is going to be so much fun!"

After Nina told her good-bye, she shut the front door and leaned against it. Fun—something she was certain Sunday's singing would never be.

• • •

Ira paced the length of his bedroom as he waited for the singing to start. His mother and sisters had already shooed him from the basement as they were setting up tables with food and drink—twice. They said they had everything under control and didn't need help. It wasn't as if he was going to filch some of the chips and dip

Ivy brought, although he'd done that at past singings. But he'd also been a lot younger. Still, he needed something to do or he would go *ab im kopp*.

He looked in the mirror over his dresser and smoothed down his hair. Margaret had told him about her talk with Nina, which had been her idea. Asking Nina to be here tonight ensured Ira would get a chance to talk to her, and he planned to talk to her alone. That made him a bit nervous, but tonight would be the perfect time to set their relationship back on track. He just wasn't sure how he was going to do that.

Deciding he couldn't stay cooped up in his room, he went downstairs. When his foot landed on the last step, he heard a knock on the door. He opened it to find Nina standing there. For some inexplicable reason, his pulse started to race, and he couldn't take his eyes off her as he swung open the screen door. "Is that a new dress?"

Her cheeks turned red. "Um, *ya*."

"It looks . . . nice."

"Better than *mei* old tight ones, *ya*?" She muttered the words as she looked away. "Is Margaret here?"

"*Ya*," Margaret said from behind Ira.

He turned around. He hadn't heard his cousin arrive. She moved past him and threaded her arm through Nina's. "I'm so glad you're here."

"Sorry I'm late. A water pipe burst in one of the guest rooms this afternoon, and it was a big clean-up job."

"That's all right. Let's *geh* upstairs to *mei* room."

The two women glided by him and started up the stairs before Ira could blink. Too-tight dresses? What did Nina mean by that? He always thought her dresses looked fine. Besides, it wasn't her dress that caught his eye. He said that only because he couldn't say what he'd really noticed—her rosy cheeks, her soft brown eyes with long, thick lashes, and her perfect nose that had a touch of sunburn. She was the same Nina, but for a reason he couldn't fathom, she seemed different to him tonight.

He gave his head a quick shake. He couldn't take his focus off his goal—to get things back to how they'd always been between them. That was what mattered, not how pretty Nina was or how his pulse was still thrumming. Nina would realize their friendship was the important thing, not any romantic thoughts she had about him. She'd get over those. Maybe she already had.

"Why are you standing there with the door open?" Zeke Bontrager—his twin brother, Zeb, trailing behind him—walked past him and into the house. Several of Zeke's brothers followed, each of them telling him hello and heading straight for the basement.

Once they were all inside, he shut the door and glanced at the stairs. What was taking them so long? He waited a few more minutes for the two women to come down so Margaret could leave him and Nina alone. But when they didn't appear, he went to the basement. He would wait for Nina there, and then they would talk.

．　．　．

"You have such pretty eyebrows."

Nina blinked as Margaret took a tiny rounded brush and ran it over one of her eyebrows and then the other. She had always thought they looked like giant caterpillars above her eyes. It was nice to get a compliment on them by someone as pretty as Margaret.

"I know I probably shouldn't have this," she said, slipping the brush back into a tiny black bag. "It's an old mascara brush I cleaned up, left over from *mei rumspringa*. But it comes in handy sometimes." She chuckled. "Sometimes I run it over my eyelashes, just for fun. It reminds me of when I used to wear makeup."

"You wore makeup?"

"Before joining the church." She put the bag on her dresser. "There. We look presentable. Are you ready to *geh* downstairs?"

Nina nodded. She had seen Ira and had survived the encounter. Yes, she was being overly dramatic, but the result was the same—she could be around him without dissolving into a puddle of tears, or anxiety, or whatever. And as long as she stuck to Margaret like a bee on honey, she would continue to survive. That's all she was hoping for—survival.

They went down to the basement, where the group was already singing. Although according to what she'd heard, more females were there than in years past, many of them were barely old enough to attend a singing. That was fine for the younger boys, like Judah and some of the Bontrager brothers, but a problem for the older young men.

She and Margaret took their places with the other women, well away from the men, and Nina started to softly sing. She made sure she could barely be heard, which was best for everyone concerned. She also avoided looking at Ira. When they took a break from singing, she and Margaret made their way to the refreshment table, and several young men followed them. Or at least they were following Margaret, which wasn't surprising.

"Hey, Nina."

She turned around to see Zeb holding two cups of apple cider.

"Hey, Zeb." He was a nice guy, on the quiet side, and different from his twin, Zeke.

"Would you like a drink?" He held out one of the cups. "I've already tried the cider. It's really *gut*. And it's cold."

"*Danki.*" She accepted the cup and took a sip. "You're right. It is delicious."

"Phoebe made it," Zeb said, referring to his sister, who was the oldest and only female among the Bontrager siblings.

"Then I'm not surprised it's *gut*."

Zeb glanced down at his feet, a lock of his sandy-brown hair falling over his forehead. "I, uh, wondered if you have a ride home tonight."

Nina's brow shot up. Zeb was asking to take her home? That usually meant . . . Oh boy. She couldn't believe it. Zeb Bontrager was interested in her.

His cheeks grew red. "If you do, that's fine. I just didn't want you to walk home by *yerself*."

She had to smile. He had a sweet if oafish way about him, and she was flattered. "That's very nice of you, Zeb, but I don't want you to *geh* to any trouble."

"It's *nee* trouble." He smiled back. "I don't mind taking you home."

"You're not taking her home."

Nina and Zeb both looked at Ira, who had appeared out of nowhere. He suddenly took Nina by the arm and practically dragged her away from Zeb and to the basement's back door.

"What do you think you're doing?" Nina said, looking at Ira's hand on her arm.

He let go. "I was about to ask you the same thing. How can you consider going home with Zeb?"

"I never said I was." Nina scowled, wondering why Ira would ever consider Zeb a problem. Did he know something about him she didn't? Or was he just interfering for some reason that made no sense? Either way, how dare he manhandle her?

"But if I do *geh* home with him," she said, "it's not *yer* business."

Ira scoffed. "Oh *ya*, it is."

"Since when?"

"Since . . . since . . ."

Nina lifted her chin. "If you don't mind, I'm going to enjoy the rest of the singing." She turned and went back to Margaret, who held several of the Bontrager boys' rapt attention, even the ones too young for her. Zeb was listening just as attentively when Nina stopped beside him. "I'd like that ride home," she told him, and then she turned and glared at Ira. If she needed a reason to forget about him, he'd just given her one.

• • •

CHAPTER 7

• • •

The next morning, Nina weeded the flower bed in front of the house after she'd worked on the two circling the large trees in the yard. She mounded dirt around a poor little begonia that was wilting even though it was surrounded by healthy plants. "I understand *yer* pain, little flower."

She was still so upset, angry, and hurt. How dare Ira drag her away from everyone like that? Even Margaret had looked shocked at his behavior.

Whatever Ira's problem was with Zeb, it didn't matter. It turned out Zeb was just being a friend. He didn't ask her out on a date or hint at anything other than what he'd told her—he didn't want her walking home alone. That was a relief, because she wouldn't have accepted a date if he'd asked for one.

When she said good-bye to Margaret, who hadn't seemed the least bit wary about being in a room full of attentive men, she made sure not to give Ira a single glance. She didn't want him to know he'd upset her. But that didn't mean she could just shut off her feelings for him.

She was about finished with the flower bed when she heard a buggy pull into the driveway. She turned to see who it was, and her heart both sank and broke into a rapid rhythm. Ira.

He pulled up to the hitching post Levi installed, and then he got out and tied his horse to the post. She couldn't keep her eyes off him. Even after what happened last night, she couldn't help being attracted to him. When he turned, she ducked her head and started yanking at weeds. Only when she looked at the bunch in her hand did she realize she'd pulled up three pink begonias, all healthy. "Oh *nee*," she said before she quickly started replanting them.

"Nina." Ira's strong voice rang out.

She ignored him, her hands shaking as she patted dirt around the crooked blooms.

"Are you going to avoid me forever?"

He sounded annoyed. Almost angry, which made her look up at him. He was tanned from working on the farm, and she had to force her gaze to stay on his face and not drift to his arms, re-membering how they'd felt around her when he helped her reel in the sunfish. *Too late.* She ducked her head and threw a handful of dirt on top of the begonias. "I'm not ignoring you."

"I'm pretty familiar with the way you avoid me by now, so *ya*, you are." He blew out a breath, and when she didn't look at him, he crouched beside her. Very close beside her. "What are you doing to that poor plant?"

"None of *yer* business." She shot up from the ground, tipping over the bucket where she'd been collecting the weeds. He had a lot of nerve showing up here after the way he treated her last night, and she wanted to tell him just that. But cold feet won out, and she dashed off. She couldn't believe she was running away from him again, but she couldn't help herself.

She stalked to the back of the barn and leaned against its wall. Glancing at the patio at the back of the inn, she was glad none of the guests were there. Nina wished Ira would realize that she'd meant what she said about them not seeing each other anymore. When he didn't appear, she thought her wish had been granted.

*   *   *

Ira had followed Nina to the barn but held back when he saw her go around it. Why was she running away from him? How were they going to settle this tension between them if she didn't want to be around him?

Then again, he couldn't exactly blame her. He'd acted like a fool last night, but when he saw Zeb talking to her, something inside turned ugly with envy. And then when Zeb offered her a ride home, he'd lost his senses. He was pretty sure Zeb wasn't romantically interested in her, but just the idea of it propelled him to separate the two of them.

Then he'd been unable to tell Nina what he'd finally realized he felt for her. He still didn't understand his emotions, but he was ready to admit them, and he had to talk to her again. He needed to work things out with her.

He needed *her*.

He slipped around to the back of the barn and saw her there, her head down, her shoulders slumped. She wasn't angry with him as much as she was hurting. He could see that now, and he had to do something to stop it. He approached her slowly, as if she were a scared kitten. "Nina," he said softly.

"Leave me alone," she said, her voice so low that it was almost lost amid the summer breeze fluttering the leaves and tall grasses surrounding the property.

He moved a little closer to her. "Please talk to me."

"There's *nix* to say." She clenched her hands, which were covered with dirt from working in the flower beds.

He paused, waiting for her to look at him. When she didn't, his chest constricted. "Is this how things end between us?" A lump settled in his throat. "Are we never going to speak to each other again?"

She sniffed, her head still tilted away from him. "That's probably for the best."

"It's not, and I'm not going to let that happen." He moved to stand in front of her, placing his palms on either side of her, pressing them against the barn. If she wanted to dash away, she'd have to duck under one of his arms, and he was ready to catch her if she tried. "You're not leaving until we get things straight between us."

"There is *nee us*." She finally looked up at him, her pretty eyes rimmed with tears.

He met her gaze, and his heart moved again. When one tear escaped, he couldn't stop himself from wiping it away with his thumb. He heard her breath catch.

"Wh-what are you doing?"

Ira wasn't sure what he was doing. When he and Margaret talked after Nina revealed her feelings for him, his cousin told him to be honest with himself. That's when he realized the thought of not seeing Nina on a weekly basis made him feel empty inside. But he'd made a mistake with Martha, and he hadn't wanted to make one with anyone else. Yet he hadn't wanted to lose Nina either. Somehow, he'd thought he could convince her they could still make their relationship work—as friends.

That was before the singing. Before he'd seen her with Zeb, before he'd realized that his fear of making another mistake with a woman was getting in the way. His honest assessment of his feelings for Nina hadn't been so honest after all.

He was so close to her that he could see the pain in her eyes, and he wanted to be the one who took that pain away.

She wiped at her tears with the back of her hand, leaving a smudge of dirt on her cheek. "I'm sorry I ruined everything," she said. "I should have kept *mei* mouth shut."

"I'm glad you didn't," he said, his heart pounding harder than it ever had. He was entering uncharted territory, but he knew one thing—he'd never felt like this with another woman. He was attracted to Nina. He wanted to protect her. He wanted to see her smile and laugh again, and he wanted to be the reason she did. "Come fishing tomorrow," he said, the huskiness of his voice surprising him as much as his sudden suggestion.

She shook her head. "I can't—"

"I'm not taking *nee* for an answer." When she didn't respond, he added, "Meet me by the pond at our usual time." Although he didn't want to, he moved away from her. He sensed that if he pushed her anymore, she'd flee. "Don't be late."

"Ira—"

"I'll be waiting for you. All day and night if I have to." He turned and headed for his buggy. He wasn't sure if she would show up, or if he was even doing the right thing. When he got into the buggy, he started praying that he was.

. . .

Nina slowly headed for the pond the next day. More than once she'd turned around to go home. After all, she should be working at the inn on a Tuesday afternoon. Even now, as she approached the woods that surrounded the pond, she was unsure of her decision to come. Having confidence in her own judgment had been a problem lately.

But even though she was tempted to run away again, this time her heart had the final say.

She remembered how Ira had looked at her yesterday, in a way that had made her pulse hum and her mouth feel like cotton. He'd never looked at her that way before, and more than once she thought she'd imagined it. She *must* have imagined it. But had she imagined him wiping away her tears too? Or what he said when he left? *I'll be waiting for you. All day and night if I have to.* No, she hadn't imagined that.

But she'd come for another reason. She couldn't keep their relationship hanging. That wasn't fair to either of them, so she wanted to settle things between them—whatever the outcome.

Nina halted her steps, putting her hand over her heart to steady its beat. She whispered a prayer, asking for the courage not to run away again. She wasn't a little girl, and she was tired of being a coward. Whatever Ira wanted to tell her today, she would handle it—with God's help. She put her trust in that fact.

Taking a deep breath, she went through the copse of trees to the clearing with the pond. When she stepped onto the open grass, her jaw dropped. Ira was already there, with a picnic spread on the ground in front of him. She saw her grandmother's picnic basket, the quilt, the dishes she'd used—everything she'd brought for her own ill-fated picnic. She'd forgotten about leaving them behind. Selah must have also forgotten to get them, and *Grossmutter* must have meant her promise not to interfere—not even by retrieving everything from the Yoder home herself.

Ira was adjusting the quilt when he saw Nina. He stood and gazed at her, not moving. Then he ran his palm over his dark-blue broadfall pants. "You made it."

She nodded and then looked at the picnic spread again. "What is this?"

"A repayment." He gave her a lopsided smile. "Well, not exactly. More like a rain check." He gestured to the food. "I hope you're hungry."

Nina hadn't had an appetite that morning, enough that she'd skipped breakfast. But now that she looked at all the dishes laden with food, she was suddenly starving. She walked toward him and sat down on an empty space on the quilt. He sat down across from her.

"Let's pray," he said.

They bowed their heads, but Nina could barely concentrate on saying grace. When she opened her eyes, she still couldn't believe what was in front of her.

"We have ham sandwiches," he said, pointing to the plate to one side, "and bread and butter pickles, homemade potato chips, some macaroni salad—"

"But you prefer coleslaw," she said softly.

He looked at her. "You remembered that."

"*Ya.*"

"And you knew I like peach cobbler." He unveiled a covered dish and exposed a bowl of pineapple fluff.

She lifted her brow in surprise. "*Mei* favorite."

"I pay attention, too, you know."

She hadn't known, and it touched her. But she was also confused. "Ira, I don't understand."

Instead of responding, he took a plate and filled it with food before handing it to her. "Why don't we eat before we talk. It's a beautiful day. Let's enjoy it." Then he piled food onto his own plate.

Nina took a small bite of the sandwich and somehow managed

to relax a little as she ate. Unlike the day she'd brought her picnic, the sky was cloudless, the sun was bright, and the air was dry and not too hot. Around them birds chirped, the water glistened, and the sun's rays warmed her skin. Ira was right. It was a perfect day, and the tranquility she'd always felt at the pond slowly returned.

When they finished eating, Ira faced her, his legs crossed. "I'm glad you came, Nina."

"I am too." She stared at her dress. She wore the green one today. "I'm sorry," she said, unable to look at him. "I never meant to make things strange between us."

He didn't say anything for a long moment. Then he said, "I didn't mean to upset you the night of the singing."

She lifted her gaze. "I know. There's *nix* between me and Zeb, by the way."

"Just like there's *nix* between me and Margaret." He winked.

Nina laughed. "I should hope not, since she's *yer* cousin." Her smile dimmed. "I jumped to a huge conclusion, didn't I?"

"I understand why you did." He set down his plate and looked directly at her. "For the record, Nina, I'm not seeing anyone. The only woman in *mei* life is you."

For a split second her heart leapt with hope, but then she reined it in. His words could be taken to mean friendship, not romance. Still, she was unsure how to respond, and she grabbed a slice of pickle, crammed it into her mouth . . . and then started to choke.

"Nina?" Ira scrambled across the quilt and started slapping her on the back. "Are you okay?"

She coughed, and a piece of the pickle flew out of her mouth. She gasped for air, and he handed her a glass of lemonade. She gulped it down, and then made a face. Lemonade and pickles did *not* go together. Then she saw the mess in front of her. Ira had barreled through the food, and it was strewn everywhere. When she turned to him, he had pineapple fluff on the front of his light-blue shirt. Unable to help herself, she started to laugh.

He joined her, his hand still on her back. "Whew," he said when he stopped laughing. "I'm glad you're okay. You worried me for a sec."

"I'm fine. But look at the food." She pointed at the fluff. "And look at *yer* shirt."

Ira glanced down, and then he picked up a napkin and wiped off the mess before staring at the wrecked food in front of them. "Picnic number two down the tubes." Then he turned his head and gazed into her eyes. "Guess we'll have to try this again."

She stilled as he took her hand. "What do you mean?"

"Exactly what I said." He looked down at their linked hands. "You threw me for a loop when you told me you liked me."

"I'm sorry I did that." When she started to look down, he took her chin in his hand and tilted her gaze to his.

"Don't be. I'm glad you said something. I was worried about you. You were acting so strangely. Then when you said you, uh, liked me, things started making a little more sense." His cheeks reddened, but he didn't look away. "I value our friendship, Nina. I don't want to lose that."

"I don't either." The spark of hope that Ira might feel for her what she felt for him died. But she realized she'd rather have his friendship than nothing at all. She would deal with her feelings, in time. But she didn't want to push him away again.

"And I don't want to give up our fishing together," he told her.

She nodded. "Agreed."

"So now that we're straight on that, we just have one more thing to discuss."

"What?"

He leaned forward until only inches separated them. "When we're going out on our first date."

Nina froze. "Excuse me?" she blurted, sure she must have heard him wrong.

"A date?" He pointed to her and then to himself. "You. Me. *Nee* fishing poles." He glanced at the food. "And probably *nee* picnics, at least for a little while. We seem to have bad luck with those."

She gaped at him, still trying to comprehend what he was saying. "You want to *geh* out on a date. With me."

Ira smiled. "*Ya*, Nina," he said softly. "With you."

If a heart could do backflips, hers would be flipping out. Happiness soared within her, only to come to a grinding halt when reality set in. "You don't have to do this, Ira," she said. At his questioning look, she added, "You don't have to pretend to like me because I like you. We can still be friends and *geh* fishing together."

"You think that's what this is about?" Ira shook his head. "Nina, I'm not pretending. I admit I'm a little late here, but I realized something at the singing. No, it was before that, when you said you didn't want to see me anymore." His Adam's apple bobbed in his neck. "I don't want to be without you, Nina. And that has nothing to do with fishing or friendship. It has everything to do with this." He leaned forward and kissed her, at first hesitantly but then taking her in his arms.

When he pulled away, she could barely breathe. His arms were at her waist now, and the look in his eyes said her size didn't bother him. *Not one bit.*

"What do you say, Nina? Will you *geh* out on a date with me?"

"Hold on." She gave herself a pinch on the arm.

"What did you do that for?" he asked, looking confused.

"Just making sure I'm not dreaming." She grinned. "*Ya*, Ira. I would love to *geh* out with you."

"Exactly what I was hoping you would say." He took her back in his arms and kissed her again.

I'm definitely not dreaming.

• • •

EPILOGUE

• • •

N ina unpacked the picnic basket she'd brought while Ira set the creel in the water and laid their poles on the bank next to a Styrofoam container with bait. The fall air wasn't too crisp, but it wouldn't be long before cold weather arrived. Then they'd have to put their fishing—and their picnics—on hiatus. But for now, they'd enjoy a nice lunch on their quilt and, hopefully, have a successful afternoon of fishing.

Ira walked over and slipped off his shoes before lowering himself to the quilt. "What are we having today?"

"Sardines."

"What? Ew."

She laughed and pulled out a container of fried chicken. "*Yer* favorite, of course." She handed the container to him.

He opened it and sniffed, and then he grinned. "I knew I married you for a reason. Well, for many reasons."

She smiled back, her heart filled with love. Their first date was followed by several more, turning their friendship into a strong, loving relationship. Three months later Ira proposed, and they'd married last November. His beard, which had grown in fast, was already past his chin but neatly kept. He was still so handsome and kind that sometimes Nina could hardly believe he was hers.

After she finished unpacking the basket—a wedding gift from *Grossmutter*—Ira took her hand, and they silently said grace. Then after they ate, they fished for the rest of the afternoon. A little before suppertime, they packed up everything and headed back to their house, just finished the week before, across the street from his family's farm.

"Just a minute," he said as she started to lift the quilt to fold it. When she turned, he put his strong arms around her waist and kissed her longingly.

As they parted, she smiled. "I'll miss our fishing picnics when it gets too cold."

He brushed the back of his hand across her cheek. "We might not be able to fish, but we can still have picnics. There's plenty of room in front of the woodstove in our living room."

"An indoor picnic?"

"Why not? We can make it just as romantic there as we do here." He drew her close. "Even more so," he whispered.

She leaned into his embrace and put her arms around him. God had healed her heart in the most unexpected way—by making Ira her husband. And she was grateful to them both.

ACKNOWLEDGMENTS

As always, a big thank you to my editors Becky Monds and Jean Bloom for their expertise and encouragement while writing this story. And thank you, dear reader, for coming along on another journey with the residents of Birch Creek.

DISCUSSION QUESTIONS

1. Nina experiences the pain of unrequited love. Has there ever been a time when you or someone you know has gone through the same thing? How did they feel?
2. Do you agree with Selah about Nina being straightforward with Ira about her feelings for him? Why or why not?
3. Do you think Nina and Ira would have gotten together if Delilah and Selah hadn't interfered?
4. Delilah points out that God will heal Nina of her broken heart if she and Ira aren't meant to be together. Was there ever a time when God healed you from disappointment?

PICNICS AND PROSPECTS

.

VANNETTA CHAPMAN

For Dorothy Hollister

I lift up my eyes to the mountains—
where does my help come from?
My help comes from the LORD,
the Maker of heaven and earth.

PSALM 121:1–2

March comes in like a lion,
and goes out like a lamb.

ENGLISH PROVERB

• • •

CHAPTER 1

• • •

Faith craned her head back and stared up at the massive vines that had climbed to a height of at least twenty feet.

"What's holding it up?"

"Hard to know." David stepped closer and inspected the bright green leaves.

"Doesn't look like it belongs here."

"Kudzu usually doesn't grow this far north."

"I've never seen it on the Pumpkinvine Trail before."

Instead of answering, he shrugged. It was one of his habits that irked Faith. When he had nothing to say, he said nothing. David Lapp did not mind uncomfortable pauses.

This resulted in Faith suffering increasing pressure to hold up both ends of the conversation. If only she could be home with her cat and her books and her knitting instead of standing around chaperoning a group of twenty energetic *youngies*. She wasn't an introvert, exactly, but as the age difference grew between her and the young unmarried members of their district, she felt increasingly out

283

of place. Still, they were in sore need of chaperones, and it seemed right to volunteer.

They'd had a tradition in their community for many years to hold outings for the young men and women who had yet to find their special someone. Those dating or even thinking about dating had a chance to spend time with others their age away from family life and farm chores. Being in a group was sometimes less intimidating, especially for the shy among them.

Ages ranged from seventeen to twenty-four. None of the *young-ies* had reached Faith's ripe old age of twenty-five, and David was even older. Which explained why they were chaperones. When had they become the oldest in the group?

Today's excursion was a spring picnic followed by a long walk down the Pumpkinvine Trail. She'd seen a small pup limping along the trail in front of them. Before she could catch up with it, the tiny guy had dashed into the brush lining the trail. Faith stared up at the trees completely covered with kudzu. The mass of green vines towered above them, stretching at least ten feet along the trail, and looked quite thick.

"You're sure you saw a dog run in there?"

"*Ya*, though I don't see how. It looks fairly impenetrable."

"Kudzu can be dense, but there's always a way in or through . . . if you're brave enough to attempt it."

Now he was teasing her. At least Faith thought he was. She found it hard to tell because his tone remained the same and he continued studying the vines quite seriously.

She might have walked away then.

She didn't doubt where the little pup had darted, but more than likely it continued out the other side and was long gone. The poor thing had been limping badly, which was what caught her attention in the first place. Her nature would not allow her to abandon an injured animal.

"Second thoughts?" David was looking at her.

"*Nein*, it's only . . . I'm not sure he's still—"

She was interrupted by a pitiful whine, so quiet she might have imagined it if she hadn't seen the look of surprise on David's face.

"We've found the beast." David poked at the vines until he found a place that parted. Motioning her toward the opening he muttered, "Ladies first," followed even more softly by, "Watch out for snakes."

Faith didn't bother answering that. She had no intention of stepping on a snake, and fortunately they were rare in northern Indiana. Not that she feared them—snakes and spiders didn't cause her to hesitate. That was reserved for the constant worry in the back of her mind that she'd have a panic attack, but the vines couldn't be that thick. And besides . . . the pup needed her.

Ducking, she pushed through the vines. They were dense and scratchy. She sidestepped a long tendril and pretended she was pushing through the darkness of a midnight emergency with Doc England—the veterinarian she worked for. Why calves and foals and even lambs chose the middle of the night to greet the world, she could never understand.

Emergency births, late night calls, animals in need—she'd dealt with those situations often enough. This was no different. She continued to push her way through the kudzu.

Then the vines were behind her, and she was standing in what reminded her of a cave. The kudzu grew up and around the area, muting the afternoon sunlight. Her pulse jumped and her palms began to sweat, but she took a deep breath and reminded herself she was saving an animal. Plus, as she looked around, she noticed the space was actually quite roomy underneath.

David let out a low whistle, causing her to jump and then look back at him accusingly.

"What?" His eyebrows rose and a smile tugged at the corners of his mouth.

David was a nice-looking guy, and he was definitely eligible. He'd never been engaged, which was something Faith couldn't quite figure out. Girls in their community, like in most Amish communities, were always on the lookout for eligible bachelors. It wasn't like they could resort to online dating if they didn't find the right match. Faith could see why the younger girls worked so hard to catch his attention.

He was tall but not too tall.

Dark brown hair that hadn't yet turned gray.

Eyes that reminded her of her morning coffee.

Lean and muscular arms from his work building cabinets and houses. At least, she'd heard he built houses, but maybe they were more like cabins. She hadn't seen one herself, though she'd heard other people talking about them. Yes, David could be considered quite the catch despite his usually somber mood.

Too bad for her the one time she went out with him had been the most embarrassing night of her life.

"Why are you frowning at me like that?"

"You scared a year off my life. I forgot you were here."

"My presence means that much to you?" He raised his eyebrows.

Again with the teasing. She closed her eyes and prayed for patience. She'd known David nearly all her life, though he'd moved away for a few years and had only recently moved back. She was not going to allow herself to be swayed by his charm. The first and only time she'd done that had not ended well.

They both turned in a circle.

"He probably has a hiding spot in here." David pushed at a pile of leaves with his foot.

"But where? I can barely see."

Only the dimmest light pierced through the canopy of vines. It was hard to believe a beautiful spring day in northern Indiana was waiting just outside the kudzu.

David dropped the backpack he'd been carrying, unzipped the outer pocket, and pulled out a small flashlight.

"You're like an Amish Boy Scout."

He held the light under his chin and made a ghoulish face, causing Faith to laugh in spite of herself. He definitely acted more comfortable in one-on-one situations. In a group, he was always the quiet guy standing off to the side.

A dog's whine brought her back to the task at hand.

She straightened her glasses. "Let's find him and get out of here."

They began to search the perimeter as David played the beam of the flashlight along the ground. They'd made a complete circle once and were attempting a second when Faith touched his arm to stop him from moving the light.

"There."

Before he could answer she dashed forward and dropped to her knees. The puppy was curled up on a bed of leaves, its brindle coat blending in almost perfectly.

"Don't let him bite you."

"I've worked with enough animals to know an aggressive one when I see it. This little girl is not a biter."

She scooted closer and slowly held out her hand. The dog was some sort of beagle mix. Her long tan ears brushed the ground. Her coat was short and even. In the dimness of the flashlight's beam, she could see the changes from tan to brown to black. The puppy raised her dark brown eyes to meet Faith's, then tentatively nosed forward and licked her hand.

In that moment, the aggravation of having to spend a Saturday afternoon chaperoning *youngies* with David fell away.

Caring for animals was Faith's calling.

"The poor thing is severely undernourished." She stroked the puppy's head and ears, earning the animal's trust, then felt gently around its paw. "There's a piece of glass in her front left paw."

"Are you going to take it out here?"

"Already done." She stood, holding the offending shard, and dropped it into David's outstretched hand.

"Now what?"

"Now we take her home." Without waiting for him to protest, which she anticipated because David was practical above all else, she untied and removed her apron, scooped up the puppy, and wrapped her in it.

"Is she cold?"

"Bleeding."

"It'll ruin your apron."

"Aprons wash, David."

She turned to push her way back out of the vines but couldn't find the spot where they'd entered. David stood behind her, apparently amused by her confusion.

"There are lots of myths about kudzu," he said. "Some say there are beds of snakes inside."

"Uh-huh."

"Others say it can take over a city in a matter of weeks . . . cover it completely as if the buildings were never there."

"Sounds more like a modern fairy tale to me."

"Kudzu is most prevalent in the southern states. Parents tell children if they're bad, the kudzu vines will come through their windows and wrap them in a cocoon at night."

"What a terrible thing to tell a child." She turned on him then, intent on reprimanding him, but for once, he was smiling broadly. "Can you just . . . get us out of here?"

The puppy's nose was stuck in the crook of her arm. Faith didn't think she was bleeding badly, but she wanted to clean and disinfect the wound and then give her a good meal and some clean water.

David led her across the dirt clearing to the opposite side. How had she become so turned around? He was searching for the way they'd come in when his flashlight landed on a package—a small box wrapped in old butcher paper and covered in tape.

Now how had they missed that before? But then, Faith's attention had been on locating the dog, and it was a relatively small package. The question was—what was it doing hidden beneath the kudzu?

•   •   •

David had been focused on finding the way out. The sooner this afternoon ended the better. It seemed that whenever he volunteered to chaperone, he was inevitably paired with Faith. He couldn't fathom why they kept being thrown together like this. If he didn't know better, he'd think their bishop did it on purpose. Perhaps Bishop Alton was trying his hand at matchmaking. If so, David should tell the man about their terrible first date and how the few times he had tried to apologize, he'd lost his courage.

It didn't help that Faith often seemed prickly, and he reverted to acting like a nineteen-year-old.

Faith Troyer looked exactly as she had five years earlier. She wasn't overly heavy, but neither was she rail thin like many girls sought to be nowadays. Her brown hair had a slight curl. Although she seemed determined to corral it under her *kapp*, strands always broke free, framing her face softly and giving him an irrational urge to reach forward and tug on one to see if it would bounce.

She'd worn glasses since he'd known her, and they gave her a thoughtful look. Today she wore bright blue frames that must be new. Last time he saw her at a church meeting they were black. Why was he thinking about how pretty Faith looked in blue-framed glasses?

David wanted to date, but now wasn't a good time. He spent nearly every waking hour working. He'd been back in Indiana less than a year and was attempting to start a small construction business. His life was going well, and he was finally starting to earn a reputation for himself as a skilled businessman. Now wasn't the time to chase after a woman, especially one who was so obviously not interested in being chased.

Yet here he was. On a picnic.

Each time he volunteered with the group he felt awkward, since he was twenty-seven and most of the *youngies* were between seventeen and twenty. He felt like an old man around them, and he didn't much like that image of himself. After each outing, he promised himself he wasn't going to volunteer next time, but then a month later he'd find himself herding a large group of *youngies* through a park or around an ice rink or on a fishing trip. Most of their activities were outside, even in winter. The cold and snow and wind didn't seem to bother the young folks. But David no longer had an urge to skate around a pond or play volleyball in the park.

Perhaps that had less to do with his age and more to do with his disposition.

Before he could begin to brood over his personality flaws, Faith stepped closer to him and stared down at the package.

"What's in it?"

"I'm not sure."

"Maybe we should leave it."

"Looks like it's been here a long time." He picked up the box and tucked it under his arm. "Maybe we can return it to its rightful owner."

"Maybe the same person is missing a dog." She looked at him then and smiled—the old smile he knew from their school days. It reminded him how comfortable he'd felt around her then, before they tried dating, before he'd done whatever he did to create a chasm between them. Well, he knew what he'd done. What he didn't know was how to fix it.

Looking at her now, he had the sudden urge to kiss her, which made no sense. No two people were more ill-suited than them. Before he did something he would surely regret, the feeling passed.

Faith studied the dog in her arms and said, "We should go."

He found their entry point, and when they stepped out into the sunshine, she took a deep breath. Did the enclosed space inside the vines spark the claustrophobia she'd exhibited several years ago? He hadn't thought of it sooner, but he should have. It was rather obvious—a confined area of any sort would feel the same to Faith. Or perhaps she'd outgrown her fear of enclosed spaces.

They traipsed back toward the group and had barely stepped off the trail when they were surrounded by girls asking where Faith found the dog and boys asking if they'd managed to get lost.

But they weren't boys and girls, he realized.

They were men and women, and they were trying to find their way in a world where it was increasingly difficult to remain Plain.

Or so it seemed to David. He'd spoken to their bishop about it once, and Alton assured him that being separate, being simple, being focused on *Gotte's wille* had always been difficult. It didn't become less so with the advent of computers and smartphones.

"Thought maybe you two had decided to walk home." David hadn't noticed Jacob walk over and stand beside him. He was probably David's best friend, though he was several years younger. They both worked at the RV factory when they were younger. Now Jacob worked his father's farm, and David built custom cabinets and tiny homes for *Englischers.*

"Faith saw the little dog dart into some kudzu vines and was intent on saving it."

"Kudzu? Here?"

"Down the trail about a hundred yards, on the east side."

"Doesn't usually grow this far north."

"I'm aware."

"I've been down this trail dozens of times, and I've never noticed it before." Jacob stuck his thumbs under his suspenders, a sign that he was trying to figure something out.

"I read once that it can grow a foot a day, so maybe it wasn't here last time you walked the trail."

"Another mystery of life."

"I suppose."

"You'll have to show me sometime, but not today. Hey, what's in the package?"

"Don't know. We found it on the ground."

"Too many riddles for one afternoon. We still have ice cream on the agenda, and loading everyone into the buggies will be like . . ."

"Herding cats. *Ya,* I know."

Jacob grinned and walked over to Sarah King. He whispered

something in her ear, she blushed prettily, and then they were walking away toward the buggies.

The rest of the group was moving toward the parking area when he noticed Faith walking off alone toward her buggy. He hurried to catch up with her.

"Don't tell me you're skipping the best part of the afternoon."

"I need to get this little girl fixed up."

He opened the door to her buggy, and she climbed inside, still carefully holding the dog.

After she settled the beagle on the seat next to her, she turned her attention back to David. "What are you going to do about the package?"

"Huh? Oh . . ." He'd forgotten he was holding it. Now that they were out in the daylight, he could see that the handwriting on the outside was long faded. "I'm not sure."

"How long do you think it was in there?"

"A long time, I would guess. Maybe years."

"Are you going to open it?"

"Might have to, if we hope to find out who it belongs to."

"Sounds like you have a mystery on your hands then."

He didn't know what to say to that. If there was one thing he didn't have time for, it was a mystery. And yet, looking at the concerned pout on Faith's face, he found himself offering to help her with the dog.

"If you want to make flyers to look for the dog's owner, I'd be happy to help distribute them."

She looked at him in surprise.

He had to admit, Faith brought out a different side of his personality. Being around her made him want to make things right between them. Or maybe he was simply looking for an excuse to spend more time with her. Could he still be attracted to Faith Troyer?

"*Danki*. More than likely she was dumped, but I'd feel better at least trying to locate an owner. I'll make some flyers at work on Monday."

"I have a job out that way next week. I'll stop by on Monday and pick them up."

"And the box?" She nodded toward the package he was still holding as if it were a snake about to strike.

"I'll bring it with me. We'll open it together."

"Ahh . . . dragging me into your mystery?" She laughed when she said it, though she didn't look directly at him.

The shy Faith was back, but that wasn't quite right. She wasn't shy around their elders or the *youngies*—only around him. She murmured to her mare, and the horse pulled off. David stood there a minute, watching her, and then Jacob called out that he better hurry up, and he realized the rest of the group was still waiting.

At the moment, though, ice cream was the last thing on his mind.

CHAPTER 2

David hurried through his work on Monday so he would be sure to catch Faith at the vet clinic before she left. Doc England catered to the Amish, so his facility tended to hold more horses, donkeys, and cows than cats or dogs. David wasn't surprised when he found Faith caring for the animals in the outdoor pens, the small beagle dogging her every step.

"Someone looks quite attached to you."

"She'll make a *gut* work dog." She continued walking down the aisle of horse stalls, dumping oats into buckets, pausing to speak to each animal.

Faith was in her element here. The tightness was gone from her shoulders, she had a smudge of dirt on her cheek, and pieces of hay clung to her dress. David had always thought she was nice looking, but seeing her here at work, comfortable and relaxed, caused him to study her more closely.

She was more than okay looking. She was actually quite beautiful. The thought popped into his mind, and he nearly tripped over a bucket sitting outside a stall.

"Careful."

"Yup."

"Any luck with the package?"

"I haven't opened it yet. I said I'd wait for you, remember? Since we found it together."

Faith pushed up her glasses. "Yes, but I'm a little surprised you were able to wait. Your curiosity didn't get the better of you?"

"Honestly, I left it in my buggy and forgot about it until I headed over here."

"Men are so different from women."

"In a good way?"

"In some way."

She was watching him closely, and he didn't know if he should cross his arms or let them fall to his sides. Hoping to get her attention off himself, he changed the subject.

"Any word on the dog's owner?"

"I spoke with someone at the Goshen animal shelter, and she said an entire litter of beagle pups was found in a cardboard box not far from where we parked on the Pumpkinvine Trail."

"So she's not lost?"

"Pebbles was dumped, as I feared."

"You've named her?"

"Pets need names."

"Will you take her to the shelter?"

"*Nein*. We could use a dog around here."

Faith had walked into a horse stall with a beautiful roan mare. David crossed his arms over the half-door and watched as she checked a bandage on the horse's front left leg.

The clinic seemed to be doing good business. The parking lot was always full, the waiting room had been expanded recently, and Doc England was in the process of building new pens on the west side of his property.

Pebbles plopped on the ground in the corner of the stall and watched Faith.

"That's the excuse you're telling yourself? You could use a dog around here? Looks to me like you have enough animals to care for."

"Many clinics have a cat or dog . . . or both . . . that are house pets. They serve to calm down visiting animals."

"Uh-huh. In other words, the pup has claimed your heart."

"That too." She glanced at David quickly, then returned her attention to the mare. He felt a strange sensation he didn't quite understand. Before he could puzzle it out, Faith marched on to the next stall.

"I brought the package. It's out in my buggy."

"That really wasn't necessary. I don't mind if you solve the mystery on your own."

"You just admitted that you wouldn't be able to wait to open it, so I know you're curious."

She ducked, her *kapp* strings falling forward, and he wasn't sure if he'd irritated her or made her laugh. When she finally looked his way again, she was shaking her head *no* but smiling *yes*. Why did women do that? Did they even realize how confusing it was? Or was there some secret code he simply didn't understand? Had he fallen asleep in class when they taught *how to understand women and feel comfortable around them*?

"I'm almost done here. If you can wait, I'll meet you out front in fifteen minutes."

"Sounds perfect."

It was her way of dismissing him, but he didn't mind—at least she hadn't sent him on his way. What was it about human nature that made a person interested in someone who didn't seem to return that interest? If she'd been leaving him phone messages at the shack near his place—as several local women had done—then surely he wouldn't have bothered to answer because he wasn't that interested in romance at this point in his life. He had a growing business and a place to stay with his *bruder*. Why mess up a good thing?

But there was something different about Faith. She was like a magnet he couldn't resist. It wasn't simply the challenge of dating someone who was disinterested, it was needing to understand why he had this flurry of feelings when he was around her.

Was he seriously thinking about trying a second time with Faith Troyer?

Or perhaps, since she was clearly not interested in him, he was merely intrigued.

"It wonders me," he muttered to himself, echoing one of his *daddi*'s favorite sayings.

He went to his buggy to fetch the box, then sat on a bench under the clinic's roof overhang. True to her word, Faith showed up at the fifteen-minute mark.

"Can you make out the writing?"

"Only that it seems to say Shipshe . . ."

"Most of the letters have been smudged off." Faith took the package from him and lifted it to her nose, then held it at arm's length.

"Need me to fetch you a new pair of glasses?"

"I do not." She pushed her glasses up with her index finger. "I was just thinking I might be able to make out some of the words if I held it at a different angle."

"Guess we're going to have to open it."

"*Ya*. It seems wrong, though, like we're intruding on someone's privacy."

"But we can't return it until we figure out who it belongs to."

"True enough." She wrinkled her nose, reminding him of a rabbit he'd seen in the field that morning. "Okay. Let's do it."

He began to pick at a corner of the tape that was holding the box together. When he pulled it up, the letters came away with it.

"Wait." Faith jumped up and rushed into the clinic, then returned with a pair of scissors. "Maybe you can just . . . slit the side. That way the words will remain intact."

"*Gut* idea."

Faith scooted down the bench and motioned for him to set the box between them. He pried one end open with the scissors and pulled out a bundle of newspaper.

"Strange to wrap something up and put it in a box." She ran her fingertips over the newsprint.

"Maybe they did so it wouldn't rattle around, and look—we can just make out the date on the newspaper."

"Maybe you can, and maybe I do need a new pair of glasses."

"June 12, 1970."

"That old?"

"I suppose." David peered closer at the newsprint. "This package was sent forty-nine years ago."

"At least forty-nine years. It might have been less. Someone might have kept a stack of newspapers for wrapping things."

"All right. I guess that's possible."

He slowly unwrapped the papers.

Inside was a bundle of letters.

* * *

One of the many details Faith loved about Amish life was that they still wrote letters to one another. Doc England's clinic had both

Englisch and Amish customers, and she'd watched many an *Englisch* person tap away on their phones with their thumbs.

Type, send, and then zip—the other person received the message.

Almost instantaneously.

Was that a good or a bad thing?

The Amish were often portrayed in books and news stories as being hopelessly old-fashioned, and she supposed they were. She sometimes wondered what the point was of living life the old way— usually when she was helping on laundry day. But when she looked down at the letters David was holding, she found herself grateful that they still did some things as their parents and grandparents had. She had to admit, there was nothing quite like receiving a hand-written letter in the mail.

"We're going to have to open one." David had scooted closer so she could read the writing on the top envelope.

It simply said *Mary.*

"This is a man's handwriting," Faith said.

"That's a prejudiced thing to say."

"Is not."

"Just because it's blocky and uneven, you assume it's a man's."

"Want to compare our writing?"

"No thanks. More importantly, there are too many women named Mary to figure out who these were sent to."

"All right." A lightweight twine had been wrapped around the stack of letters. Faith thumbed the corner of the envelopes and counted seven. Seven lost letters. She peeked at David as he pushed the letters into her lap.

"You do it."

"All right." Faith slipped the twine off the end of the bundle and picked up the top envelope. It wasn't sealed, though the flap had been tucked inside. She opened it, pulled out and unfolded the sheet of paper, and began to read, barely aware she was doing so aloud.

June 7, 1970

Dearest Mary,

I hope you are not growing tired of my letters. It helps me immensely to write to you. I hadn't expected to be so homesick. This farm is much like my family's, but Ohio is quite different from Indiana. The people are different as well, and although they follow many of the same customs as our community, they do so in a way that seems unfamiliar and strange.

One thing that remains the same is the work. Today I worked in the back field preparing the soil for planting. I am grateful every day that I am here and not overseas. We had service on Sunday, and Bishop Jeremiah reminded us again that it is best to keep a low profile and limit our trips into town. Though some understand our position as COs, many do not, and there have been instances of harassment and even violence against members of the community.

I don't mind staying on the farm. I have no desire to go to town because there is nothing I need to shop for. The family I'm staying with provides my food and lodging and takes the cost out of my earnings. I send the rest home to my family. I do wish I had more reading material. Perhaps next week I will brave the local library.

I'm pleased to hear you are enjoying my little packages. I will continue to mail you once a week with that week's letters. I like the idea of you sitting under the sycamore tree in your father's backyard, enjoying the glider swing, and reading my words to you. Thank you for the package with the cookies and tea. You can't imagine the joy it brings me each evening as I read over your letters.

Fondly yours,
Peter

David groaned. "Peter and Mary? Do you know how many people in our community have the names Peter and Mary? Might as well add Lapp to the mix so this task can be completely hopeless."

"You're a Lapp."

"I'm aware."

"Do you think Mary or Peter could be a member of your family?"

"*Nein*. I just meant . . . Well, it's going to be hard to figure out who these belong to."

"But there are a lot of clues." Faith felt herself getting caught up in solving the mystery.

"Clues?"

"This person—Peter—was staying in Ohio for some reason."

"Yeah."

"He was working on a farm there . . ."

"Says as much in the first paragraph." David rubbed a hand over his jaw. Then he reached down to scoop up Pebbles, who had been attacking his shoelaces. "And Mary lived here in Shipshe."

Faith read the letter again. Had it really been lost all those years ago? Were the people—Mary and Peter—even still alive? And to think she and David wouldn't have found it if not for Pebbles darting beneath the kudzu vine.

Life was so full of surprises.

A person could wake up in the morning, expecting a perfectly normal day, only to be dropped in the middle of someone else's long-ago mystery before evening.

• • •

CHAPTER 3

• • •

David should have been looking at the letters, but he was having more fun watching the expressions of puzzlement, surprise, and wonder on Faith's face.

She looked up and studied him for a moment as if he might know the answers to the questions twirling through her mind. She finally said, "Mary must have cared for him because she wrote to him as well."

"And she sent him packages."

"This should be easy to solve."

"I'm not so sure."

"The bishop in Ohio was Jeremiah. How many Jeremiahs are there?"

"I can think of four here in Shipshe."

"But they're not all bishops." She said the last word slowly as if he was having trouble keeping up.

"All right, Sherlock . . ."

"Who?"

"Never mind. What other clues do you see?"

Faith scooted even closer so they could both read the pages at the same time. "I don't know what CO means."

"Don't look at me."

"It says here . . ." She allowed her finger to travel down the page and rest on the last paragraph. "Mary has a sycamore tree in the backyard and a glider swing."

"Mary *had* a sycamore tree and a glider swing in the backyard. That solves it!" David bumped his shoulder against hers to show he was only giving her a hard time.

A buggy pulled into the drive-through area. Faith hopped up, slipped the letter back into the envelope, the envelope into the stack, and the stack and newspapers into the tattered box. "That's my *bruder.* I have to go."

"You're leaving?"

"We can figure this out, David."

"We can?"

"Yes. We will solve the mystery of the kudzu letters."

"I'm as intrigued as the next guy, but maybe we should step back for a minute."

Faith had been hurrying to the buggy, Pebbles fast on her heels, but she stopped abruptly and pivoted back toward him.

"What are you saying?"

"That perhaps we should drive over to Goshen and put the package back under those kudzu vines." He couldn't keep a straight face when she looked at him aghast. He started laughing, causing Pebbles to run back toward him and attempt to paw her way up his leg.

"We'll do no such thing," Faith said, slipping her purse strap over her shoulder.

"Ah, I know what's happening now. Your imagination is coming up with some romantic reunion between two people we don't even know."

"I need to go. I don't want to keep Micah waiting."

305

"You want to get home and read the rest of the letters."

Faith motioned to her *bruder* to wait, walked right up to David, and scooped Pebbles in her arms.

"I thought she was going to be a . . . What did you call it . . . companion pet?"

"She is."

"So why are you taking her home?" They were standing so close that David could smell powder and soap and some flowery scent that must have been hand lotion. The combination was intoxicating.

"She's too little to leave alone here now." Faith lowered her voice and kissed the pup on top of the head.

David had nothing against dogs, but this one was claiming all of Faith's attention.

"She'll have to stay with me," Faith added, glancing up at him and then away. "At least for a few weeks."

Pebbles began to squirm in Faith's arms. David took the dog from her, and they walked side by side toward Micah's buggy.

Faith held the tattered box as if it were a priceless treasure. "Wouldn't it be amazing if we could find the people these letters belong to?"

"I'm not sure that's even possible." His common sense was trying to assert itself, though he knew that was probably not what Faith wanted to hear. Still, better that she grasp the reality of the situation now than later. "You're thinking of this as if it's a page torn from a romance novel. Maybe this Mary—whoever she is—is better off never having received these letters."

They reached the buggy, and Faith opened the door.

David leaned past her to greet her *bruder*. "Hey, Micah."

"David. Surprised to see you here."

"Not as surprised as I am to be here."

If he'd hoped Faith had forgotten his comment about romance novels, he was sadly mistaken.

She turned on him now and asked, "What would you know of reading romances?"

"Nothing." He took a step back. That's what he got for teasing her. He should have known better.

"Uh-huh. Maybe you took a peek at one of the books your nieces were reading."

"I don't know what my nieces read."

"Or maybe you have a habit of stopping by the library on your lunch hour."

"Ha! I don't take a lunch hour."

Faith stared down at the box in her hands. "Who should keep it . . . You or me?"

David pretended to be perplexed, tilting his head left and then right. "We could give it to the bishop."

"I heard he's very busy this week."

"Or I could take it home. Keep it safe until I see you at church on Sunday."

"That's a week away."

"Or you could take it . . ." He lowered his voice, though Micah was pretending to be busy cleaning the dirt out from under his fingernails. "You could take it, and we could go to dinner tomorrow night and read the rest of them."

"What?"

"Two people, eating together, at a restaurant."

She pushed up her glasses, looked left, right, and finally into his eyes. "Are you asking me out on a date?" Her voice had dropped to a whisper, and a slight blush colored her cheeks.

"Would you say *yes* if I was?"

Faith rolled her eyes and laughed at the same time. David silently reminded himself that now was not a good time to get involved in a dating relationship, especially not with Faith Troyer. He never quite understood her moods, and he always felt a little off-kilter around her.

Then her eyes met his, a smile still playing on her lips, and his doubts slipped away. They had both found the box, so it made sense to see this through together—might as well do so at dinner.

"All right," she said as if she was agreeing to see the dentist. "But not dinner—I've been wanting ice cream since last Friday."

"I had the hot fudge blizzard. It was so good."

"Don't describe it to me. We don't have any ice cream at home."

"I hope you can wait until Friday."

"Pick me up at six, and I'll bring the box."

"Don't peek at the rest of the letters without me."

She gave him a backhanded wave as she climbed into the buggy. He placed the beagle in her lap and watched them drive away.

Faith Troyer.

Ice cream.

A lost dog.

A mysterious box of letters.

And to think he had been enjoying how calm and predictable his life had become.

⚬   ⚬   ⚬

The day was turning out better than Faith had anticipated. The lethargy she'd been battling had fallen away. The fields looked greener, the spring sunshine brighter, and the days ahead more hopeful.

If she was honest with herself, she would admit that winter had been difficult. She'd turned down invitations from friends, avoided social gatherings, and spent much of her time at home alone. Perhaps she'd been too focused on herself. She could see that now because she was finally looking forward to something—to seeing David on Friday.

It was good to think about someone else for a change. Perhaps the mystery box was just what she needed.

"So . . ." Micah said.

"So?"

"David Lapp?"

"What about him?"

"Looked to me like you two were, you know, interested in each other."

"Ha. Hardly."

"So you're going out with him Friday night because . . ."

Faith explained about the box of letters and how they were trying to figure out who they belonged to. She even pulled the top letter out and started to read it to him, but Micah stopped her with an upheld hand.

"Don't drag me into your mystery."

"Oh, please. As if you have better things to do."

"I do."

"Such as?"

"Taking you home and showering so I can pick up Naomi."

"I like Naomi."

"I do too."

"Is it getting serious?"

Micah was four years younger than Faith, so she always felt strange when she thought of him marrying. It was bound to happen though. Most Amish did marry, and most married before they were her age.

"Define serious."

"Are you going to ask her to be your *fra*?"

Instead of answering, Micah changed the subject. "What's with the mutt?"

Pebbles had immediately fallen asleep on her lap. She made little yipping sounds as if she were chasing a rabbit in her dreams.

"Her name is Pebbles, and she's going to be staying with us awhile."

"*Mamm*'s not big on dogs in the house."

"Which is why she won't be in our house. I made her a bed in the barn. That's where she's slept since Friday."

"You've had her since Friday?"

"*Dat* knew about her."

"Uh-huh, but you haven't mentioned it to *Mamm*. I can't wait to hear her reaction."

"I just worry that Pebbles would get lonely staying at the animal clinic."

"She's a dog."

"Dogs have feelings too, Micah."

"Don't give me another animal lecture. Besides, you're ignoring the subject."

"Which is?"

"David."

Faith sighed and looked out the window. Finally, she said, "My relationship with David—if you can even call it that—is complicated."

"I know you dated him a while back."

"It was one date. Four years ago, maybe four and a half."

"So what happened?"

"He didn't know about my claustrophobia."

"Oh boy."

"His idea of a perfect date was taking me to the fall festival."

"That sounds *gut*."

"And it was at first, until he insisted we go into the House of Mirrors."

"Uh-oh."

"*Ya*." She didn't want to think about that night. The memory still embarrassed her, but maybe it was time to move past it. She'd been working with the bishop for a long time now to learn to accept who she was—both her strengths and her weaknesses.

"To this day I can't tell you exactly what happened, only that I ended up curled in a ball with mirrors all around me. When David found me, he started laughing. I'm still not sure which was worse—being in a complete panic or having someone laugh at my distress."

"I'm sure he didn't know." Micah glanced at her, his eyes full of sympathy and that, more than the memory, caused Faith to tear up.

Pebbles, sensing her distress, whimpered and snuggled closer in her lap.

"Ah, now. Don't cry. You know I have no idea what to do around crying females."

Faith laughed and swiped at her cheeks. "Sorry."

"So what happened next? After he found you curled in a ball in the corner of a fun house."

"He helped me to the buggy. He practically had to carry me because I couldn't make my legs work. Then he took me home. He had no idea what was wrong, though I think someone has clued him in since."

"And after that?"

"He moved. His *bruder* invited him down to Virginia."

311

"I remember him mentioning that. He learned how to do cabinetry work there."

"He lived there a long time. He's only been back since last fall." Faith pulled off her glasses and rubbed her eyes, then slipped them back on. "Now when we're around each other, he treats me as if I might break."

Micah didn't speak again until they were nearly home. As they pulled into the lane, he grinned and tipped his hat back. "You two certainly have an interesting background, but it doesn't mean you can't go forward. After all, think what a funny story it would be to tell your *grandkinner* someday."

The thought of having grandchildren with David made her laugh. She was beginning to fear she was too old to have children, so grandchildren seemed like a distant dream.

"You'll be having *grandkinner* years before me."

"Stop trying to marry me off. I'm just a guy who likes a girl and hopes to have a nice evening with her."

Micah helped her remember to enjoy life. And his girlfriend Naomi? Well, she would be a *gut* addition to the family if her *bruder* did ask her to marry him.

"Let me off at the barn."

"I happen to be going there myself."

As he unhitched Patches and set about caring for the horse, Faith took Pebbles into the stall she'd outfitted with a blanket in a crate, a food bowl, and a water bowl. She scooped some of the food she'd bought on Saturday into one bowl and stayed long enough to make sure Pebbles ate the entire thing. She was underweight, which could make a dog susceptible to all sorts of things. After Pebbles lapped up a good bit of water, she walked to Faith, sat, and cocked her head.

"I have to go."

Pebbles dropped into a crouch and growled, then sat up and yipped.

"You're a hoot."

Spying her tail, the dog proceeded to chase it in circles until she fell over.

"Wear yourself out. I'll see you first thing in the morning."

She thought Pebbles might protest her leaving, but upon seeing Faith walk to the stall door, she tumbled over to her bed and sank onto the blanket.

"There's no place like home," Faith whispered.

Walking back into the main part of the barn, she realized she wasn't ready to go into the house yet. She needed time to process the day's events, so she looked around for something else to do. Micah had finished unharnessing and stabling the horse and had already gone to the house. Faith wasn't ready to go inside. She wasn't ready to face her mother. Her mind darted back to the argument they had the week before about her work. *Mamm* did not understand that circumstances were different for Amish women now than they were during her time.

She also didn't understand that Faith's anxiety practically disappeared when she was around animals. She'd learned to control it when surrounded by friends, but in the back of her mind she always worried she might have another attack. She couldn't remember when her anxiety and claustrophobia had first presented itself. She'd discussed that at length with her counselor, but they'd never managed to pinpoint one traumatic event that might have caused it. Perhaps her condition had developed over time—the first symptoms had probably appeared when she was a young teen.

With animals, she never had to worry about saying or doing the wrong thing. She never felt awkward around a horse. She never wondered what to say to a dog, and cats—well, cats only required a quick scratch behind the ears.

Animals were easy.

People on the other hand, confounded her.

Dating had been especially difficult. She didn't know whether to talk about her condition or not, and she always worried about what they were going to do for the date—if it would trigger another attack. Eventually, she found it easier to just say no, and after a while the young men in their community stopped asking. Which probably explained why she'd stopped dating, which in turn led to her working more hours at the clinic.

That's what the argument with her *mamm* the week before had been about. Her mother thought she should work less and focus on her future—her future as a wife and mother. But she had no future as a wife and mother as far as she could see. Who would want to be married to someone like her?

She'd made the mistake of saying that to her *mamm*, who quickly reminded her that she was fearfully and wonderfully made.

And now she was stepping out with David Lapp.

Oh, her *mamm* would be thrilled. The problem would be explaining that they were simply two friends going out together. *Mamm* would never believe it wasn't a blossoming romance.

Then again, maybe she should let her mother believe what she wanted.

Maybe it was okay if *Mamm* misconstrued the nature of the relationship. Perhaps it would take the pressure off for a little while. And it wasn't lying—not exactly.

"We'll just let her draw her own conclusions," Faith said to Patches, whom she'd stopped to brush. Her *dat* purchased the mare three years ago. She was a lovely black with white patches on her front knees. "It's not our fault if she concludes incorrectly."

Patches actually nodded in agreement, or at least it seemed like she did.

Faith loved her mother dearly. She loved all of her family. It was just that since her twenty-fifth birthday the pressure had increased, and she wasn't responding to it well. With any luck, one of her *schweschders* would announce another pregnancy soon. That always sent her mother into a knitting craze and distracted her from worrying over her youngest daughter.

Faith decided not to fret over her parents' expectations. Instead, she thought of Mary and Peter and wondered if they could be people she knew.

• • •

CHAPTER 4

• • •

David picked up Faith at six o'clock on the dot Friday evening. Her *mamm* waved from a rocker on the front porch.

David had hopped out of the buggy to open the door for her. "Your parents seem nice."

"Uh-huh."

He waited until she'd settled in the buggy and he'd climbed back in on the driver's side, to tease her. "Is there a particular reason for that uh-huh?"

"Nothing I want to talk about."

"Fair enough."

When she looked at him in surprise, he shrugged. "I know how family can be. I'm not married either, remember, and I'm twenty-seven."

"Oh man. That's nearly thirty. Are you sure you can see well enough to drive?"

"Watch it."

"I'm surprised no one has bought you a cane yet."

"They'll probably give me one for Christmas." He chuckled. At least in Faith, he had a friend who understood his dilemma. "Apparently I'm shirking my male duties."

"Ewww. Someone said that to you?"

David scrunched his eyes. "Let's see—my *dat*, my *bruder*, even my bishop down in Virginia when I lived with my other *bruder*."

"Wow. That is a lot of people with their nose in your business."

"Don't I know it." If David had been nervous about this date, which he wasn't willing to admit, the nerves had fled. Riding next to him today was a different Faith—one who acted as if she was enjoying a buggy ride and the prospect of a frozen treat.

"So where would you like to go?" he asked. "There's Blue Gate or . . ."

"Howie's. I love Howie's."

"Same here. Less crowded."

"And we can take our time and go over the letters."

"Ah, yes. The letters." He focused on the road, thinking about putting off what he needed to do. But what was the sense in that? So, he cleared his throat and plunged forward. "You know, there's something I've been wanting to say to you, but it seems we're never alone."

Faith looked at him with such wide eyes, that he nearly laughed . . . but wasn't that what landed him in trouble to begin with? He took her silence as a good sign.

"I want to apologize for what happened when we went to the fall festival."

"The fall festival?"

"I know it was a long time ago."

"Over four years ago."

"You might not even remember—it's not as if I expect our single date to have been so important that you would still be dwelling on it."

"I remember."

"The thing is, I didn't know about your . . . condition."

She pulled in a deep breath, let it out, and then lifted her chin just a tad. "I'm claustrophobic."

"*Ya. Mei bruder* explained it to me when I finally confessed what a disaster our date had been."

"David, that wasn't your fault."

" It kind of was though. I mean, even if I didn't understand why you were so frightened, I shouldn't have laughed. That must have seemed so . . . callous."

Faith stared out the side window. Looking at her profile, he could just make out that she'd pulled in her bottom lip and was worrying it. He was surprised when she turned back toward him with a smile.

"Why now? As you pointed out, it's been a long time."

"Fair question. First of all, I'm reminded of it every time I'm with you, and I feel bad. That guy who laughed at you, well, that's not who I am."

"Okay."

"Look." He shifted in his seat, stared out over the horse and then looked back at her. "I should have done this right after it happened, right after I found out about your condition. I told myself it didn't matter, and then I moved to Virginia. I've tried a couple times since then, but you always seem to hurry away if we're alone together."

"I suppose I was embarrassed about it—even after all this time."

"Really?"

"Mortified, actually."

"It was that bad?"

"I'd had a few panic attacks before then, but never in such a public setting. I didn't . . . I didn't really understand what was wrong with me, what triggered it, or what to do about it."

"But you do now?"

She nodded so hard that a wayward curl popped out of the side of her *kapp*. "I've been seeing a counselor."

"That's *gut*. I guess."

"It is *gut*. I'm aware that it's unusual for an Amish person to see an *Englisch* counselor, but it's helped me."

"Your parents are supportive?"

"They are, and so is Alton. He's a *gut* bishop."

Silence enveloped the buggy, and David realized he needed to hear her say it. He'd come this far with his apology and confession, he might as well step out a little further. "So, you accept my apology?"

"*Ya*. Of course I do."

He picked up his hat and resettled it on his head. "Somehow I thought it would be more difficult."

"You apologized, and I accept your apology. Let's forget about it."

"All right." He ran a thumb under his suspenders. Why hadn't he tried that years ago? "But if you ever want to talk about it or something—anything really, I promise not to laugh."

"That's a relief."

"Now you're making fun of me."

"Perhaps a little."

They drove the rest of the way in silence, which didn't feel as uncomfortable as it might have before he apologized.

Once they arrived and purchased their ice cream—one scoop of vanilla and one of strawberry for her, double chocolate for him—they sat at a table and talked about work.

She hadn't known he was working full-time now in his own business.

He hadn't realized that Dr. England had been loaning her veterinary books to read and study.

They spoke of who was marrying, the new people who had moved in and those who'd left, and their expanding families. When their ice cream was gone and he'd thrown away their napkins and fetched two cups of water, David could tell Faith was ready to get down to business.

"You look like a child at Christmas," he teased.

"It was hard to wait."

"Ha. I knew it. You're like a dog who has caught a scent."

"I'd be offended by that description if I hadn't just acquired a beagle."

She pulled the box from her purse and removed the bundle of letters.

"Ready?" Her eyes were bright, and when she smiled broadly, small dimples formed at the corner of her mouth. Faith Troyer was a pretty young woman, and more importantly she smiled easily and often.

"Ready as I'll ever be."

June 8, 1970

Dear Mary,

Today is Friday. If I were back home in Shipshe I would be glad that the work week was over. I'd probably be thinking about taking you out for dinner or a treat. Do you remember that time we went for hamburgers and you turned away from the picnic table for a moment? Luke's dog swallowed your entire burger before I knew what had happened. You were mad as a red hornet, and I couldn't stop laughing.

Memories like that help me through the hard times.

That and my faith. It warmed my heart when you wrote that you were praying for me.

Yours,

Peter

June 9, 1970

Dear Mary,

Do you understand what this war is about? I don't. I've tried—believe me I have. I know we're pacifists. When I joined the church, I took a vow to follow the Bible and live by our *Ordnung*, and that means we always turn the other cheek.

Today I went to town because one of the other Amish men working here needed personal supplies. We've been told it's best to go places in pairs rather than alone.

After we purchased what he needed and were walking back to the buggy, a young disabled man, no doubt freshly back in the country, was wheeling down the sidewalk toward us. His mother was pushing his wheelchair, and his father was walking beside him. The father was carrying a world of hurt in his heart. His grief and anger were clear from the second I noticed him.

When he saw me and Joshua, his anger erupted like a long-simmering volcano. I won't write the words he threw at us. They're too vile to commit to paper. Suffice to say he blamed us for his son's injury. If we hadn't shirked our duty, if we had served like men instead of cowards . . . He went on and on as Joshua and I stood there, eyes cast down, waiting and praying for it to end. Finally, he spat at us and moved on.

We'd drawn quite a crowd, but not one person in that group

of onlookers spoke a kind word to us. Perhaps they were as shocked as we were. Or perhaps they agreed with the man. I'll never know. When we reached our buggy, we saw that someone had spray-painted the word *COWARD* across the side. The horse was fine and unperturbed by the ruckus.

I'll admit to feeling angry and sad at the same time. Mostly I just felt as if I didn't belong here—like a stranger in a foreign land. I keep wondering when I'll be able to come home.

Peter

June 10, 1970

Dear Mary,

Our Sunday service was real *gut*. How was yours? The weather was nice and we were able to hold the worship service in a member's barn. It is quite large and has big bay doors, which were left open, and we could see out across the rolling hills. Ohio is a beautiful place. I would like to see it with you one day—in the future when this war is behind us.

The bishop reminded us today that *Gotte* is always in control, even when we don't understand what is happening. He quoted from Job, which I will confess to enjoying. Job always seemed like a nice guy to me. Though possibly he had no clue what was happening to him. When he finally confronts *Gotte*, and *Gotte* tells him to brace himself, that always makes me laugh and wonder and appreciate *Gotte*'s patience with us.

After service, we were standing with a group of men, and they wanted to know about what happened in town yesterday. We're not the only ones who have been harassed. The bishop reminded us again only to go to town when necessary and to remember to pray for the *Englisch* as well as the Vietnamese people.

How are your sheep? Do you still have that lazy canine you call a guard dog?

Affectionately,
Peter

June 11, 1970

Dear Mary,

Today I'm so homesick I can barely write. I know my suffering is nothing compared to what others face, but when you're the one going through it . . . Well, it feels bigger than any single thing you can imagine.

Pray for me?

Peter

June 12, 1970

Dearest Mary,

Apologies for my morose mood yesterday. The weather was gloomy and I was missing my family as well as you, but that's no excuse.

I'll tell you something funny to prove that all is not gloom. The farmer's wife keeps a bassett hound. The old dog mostly lies in the sun waiting for someone to drop a scrap of food close to its mouth. His name is Skipper, but I've never seen him skip. He sleeps more than my *onkle* Atlee.

But I digress. Today Mrs. Nicholson was working in her vegetable garden and old Skipper was lying in the sun beside her when a rabbit hopped out from behind a row of lettuce. Skipper howled as if his hind leg was caught in a bear trap. Mrs. Nicholson jumped to her feet and began waving her arms, trying to scare the rabbit away. The rabbit dodged over to where Mrs. Nicholson had left some plastic pots and managed to burrow down underneath one.

By the time Joshua and I ran over to see what all the commotion was about, the pot was moving back and forth on the ground as if of its own accord. Mrs. Nicholson was trying to catch Skipper, and Skipper was lunging back and forth and howling for all he was worth. I suppose he was actually baying, which is such a lonesome sound. Mrs. Nicholson said she'd never heard him do it before and hopes to never hear it again.

I hope that image brings a smile to your face.

Yours,

Peter

June 13, 1970

Dearest Mary,

I received your package today. You can't possibly know how much your kindness means to me. The socks, copies of the almanac, and sweets were much appreciated. But more than that, your letters mean so much to me.

Mary, I know we agreed not to speak of our future together until I return, but dare I ask you to wait for me? Would you consider such a thing? My heart is filled with such affection for you, and I think you must care for me too. At least, after reading your latest letters I have hope that you feel the same.

Yours most affectionately,

Peter

David folded the last letter and handed it to Faith. She slipped it back into the envelope.

"Wow," he said.

"*Ya*, it's like peering into someone's heart."

"And you still think we should get involved?"

"More than ever. They're probably married now, celebrating their . . ." Faith tapped the tip of her finger against her chin.

"Fifty years. These letters were written fifty years ago. A lot can happen in that amount of time."

"It could be their fiftieth anniversary." Faith squeezed his hand, then began carefully refolding the other letters and sliding them back into their envelopes. "Can you imagine how thrilled they'd be to read these words from the past? The letters are so sweet and precious, and . . . Well, they're priceless really. At least, they would be to Mary and Peter."

David wondered if Faith could be right. There was a chance. What she was describing was possible, but it was equally possible that Mary and Peter had never reunited. Life had a way of twisting and turning in unimaginable directions, and fifty years? That was a very long time.

David didn't want to say any of that out loud. How could he? Faith's eyes were shining bright with hope, and her expression said she'd already foreseen a happy ending to the entire situation.

So instead of raining on her happy thoughts, he helped her up from the picnic bench, and they walked toward his buggy in the fading light of a stunning summer afternoon.

• • •

CHAPTER 5

• • •

Faith tried to sleep, but she only succeeded in twisting her covers into a knot. The clock on her nightstand read 2:00 a.m., but it seemed as if it should be closer to dawn. An *Englischer* had once asked her how they managed to sleep without air-conditioning. Her answer was twofold. One, she'd never had air-conditioning, so she couldn't very well miss something she'd never had. Two, though some days could be warm of course, the nights were nearly always pleasant.

Her room was upstairs and looked out over the side garden and the fields beyond. The breeze tonight was enough to require a light quilt, and as she gave up on sleep and pushed her feet into her house slippers, she grabbed her robe.

She didn't exactly plan on going downstairs and rereading the letters, but she couldn't get them out of her mind. What had it been like to be sent away? How had Peter handled living in a completely different environment? Why was he sent there? Why couldn't he go home? His letters seemed to suggest he couldn't. And what about Mary? Had all the men in their community been sent away? What was that like?

And had she waited for Peter?

Faith liked to think so, but she'd seen the doubt in David's eyes.

Okay, so she was a romantic at heart. She could admit that. Just because she wasn't married didn't mean she couldn't enjoy reading about a nice romance—and this one was real.

She snagged the box of letters and made her way downstairs. By the time her mother found her, she'd made a list of information to look into and was on her second cup of coffee. *Dat* said good morning on his way out to the barn to tend the animals. *Mamm* put a breakfast casserole in the oven and asked, "Trouble sleeping, dear?"

"*Ya.*"

"Worried about something?"

"*Nein*, not exactly. It's just that these letters, well, they have my mind spinning."

"Oh, yes. The letters you and David found."

Faith cringed at the way her mother said *David*. If she'd been looking at her, Faith would have seen her eyebrows rise and a smile tug at her lips, so she didn't look. Instead, she reread her list to see if she'd missed anything.

Mamm poured a mug of coffee, sat next to her, and yawned. It wasn't until she'd half-drained her mug that she nodded toward the sheet of paper.

"May I?"

"Sure. Maybe it will jog your memory."

"I doubt it. I'm not that old, Faith."

"But it must have been a smaller community then. Maybe you went to church with Mary or Peter."

"Your *dat* and I didn't move here until after we married."

"Oh, that's right. I forgot. You and *Dat* were married in 1985, right?"

"Correct."

"So the letters were written fifteen years before you got here. But if they married, surely you would have known them."

"There are lots of women named Mary in our church, but I've only known one or two men named Peter, and none who would be the right age."

"Just look over the list. See if anything rings a bell."

Faith scooted her chair closer to her mother, and together they read down the sheet of paper.

Man's name = Peter. Sent to work in Ohio in 1970.

Woman's name = Mary. Stayed in Shipshe.

They were dating?

Ohio Bishop = Jeremiah.

CO?

"I know this one." Her *mamm* tapped the paper where Faith had written CO. "It means conscientious objector."

"Oh. I should have thought of that."

"The Vietnam War was a difficult time for our people and for the country as a whole. The fact that our men refused to fight, well, some people didn't understand that."

"What happened when they refused?"

"Most were sent away to work on farms or in state or national parks. They were expected to serve, though not in a military capacity."

Instead of commenting further, she continued reading down the list.

Mary had sycamore tree and glider swing in backyard.

Luke? Peter's friend. Had a dog.

Joshua worked with Peter in Ohio. Was Peter from Shipshe?

Mary's family had sheep and a dog.

Nicholson family. Owned farm in Ohio where Peter worked.

They also had a bassett hound named Skipper.

Her *mamm* laughed. "Most of these details could describe anyone."

"I know," Faith admitted. "But not *everyone* has sheep. *Dat* won't abide them. He says they eat the grass down to nothing."

"Your *dat* is quite opinionated on some subjects."

Mamm stood and walked over to the stove where she refilled her coffee mug. "Want more?"

"*Nein*. I've already had two cups."

"You know, Faith . . . the devotion described in these letters was quite common in those days."

"What do you mean?"

"Only that people had fewer choices."

"You're saying *women* had fewer choices, right?"

"*Ya*, I suppose I am." *Mamm* sat across from her. "Everyone thinks the Amish life is simple, but truthfully our lives have grown more complicated than they were a generation or two ago—same as everyone else's. It's *gut* that you've found work you love to do, working with animals."

"You're not going to remind me of my duty to marry, are you? Before breakfast?"

"*Nein*. I only wanted to say . . . Well, I guess I wanted to say that I married your *dat* when I was nineteen. Loving him, raising a family, caring for our home—those aren't small things. They're big responsibilities, and I'm grateful for the life I've had."

Faith's defensiveness melted away in light of her *mamm*'s honesty.

"I'm not dismissing what you do at the clinic. I'm only saying that loving someone is also pretty important—it's something you can dedicate yourself to, and in the end, those people are what make your life worth living."

"I know that, *Mamm*. I just don't know if I can envision that life for myself."

Instead of arguing, *Mamm* stood, brushed Faith's *kapp* strings back, and planted a kiss on top of her head. "Your *dat* will be back any minute. We should get breakfast on the table."

Faith set out the plates, cups, and silverware. *Mamm* sliced fresh bread and heated it in the oven, then cut up fruit to go with the egg-and-ham casserole. Faith's brother tromped in with her dad a few minutes later. She'd never even heard him go out.

After they prayed and started eating, Micah began teasing her.

"Your nose was awfully deep in those letters this morning," Micah said. "I could have been a complete stranger traipsing through the kitchen, and you wouldn't have noticed."

Faith didn't bother defending herself. Sometimes her ability to focus solely on one thing was a benefit, and other times it meant she completely missed what was going on around her.

"You know, Faith, we usually try not to interfere in other people's business," her father said.

"Yes, but this is different."

"Could be, or it could be that you're tempted to put your nose where it doesn't belong." *Dat* reached for another piece of bread, spread a thick layer of butter on it, then folded it in half as if it were a hotdog bun.

"So you think we should just . . . throw the letters away?"

"I think you should have left them where they were. It's not your business. Whatever is written there—it doesn't concern you."

Her father was so old-fashioned that sometimes she expected him to suggest they do the laundry at the river with a rock.

Faith breathed a sigh of relief when the conversation turned to crops and weather. As she and her mother were washing the dishes later, she admitted to her *mamm* what she was planning.

"I'm not sure I'd advise getting the bishop involved, but it sounds like you've made up your mind."

"What's wrong with asking Bishop Alton?" When *Mamm* didn't answer, Faith added, "If he says to drop the entire thing, I will."

"Fair enough." *Mamm* reached up and tucked a wayward lock of hair into her *kapp*. "We've spoken of this before."

"Spoken of what?"

"Not being fully involved in today, in our community, with our people."

"I'm involved. I go to work five days a week."

"Where you spend your time with animals." She smiled, which did little to soften her words. "I just . . . I hate to see you living in the past—in someone else's past. There's so much life around you, Faith."

"Maybe I'm meant to be a historian."

"An Amish historian?" Her *mamm* laughed, and the tension between them melted away.

Faith thought it was hard being an adult child in her parents' home. She knew they worried, but why couldn't they just accept her as she was? Instead of tossing that thought around in her mind, she focused on her chores and managed to finish everything before lunch.

She snagged her *mamm*'s shopping list and headed out to the barn. Micah had already harnessed Patches to the buggy. Faith set off in search of answers on what looked like a promising spring day.

•   •   •

David was surprised to look up from his work and see Faith directing her mare onto his *bruder*'s property.

He hurried over to open the gate.

"Didn't expect to see you today."

She looked flushed and out of breath. As he helped her out of the buggy, she studied his worksite, but he didn't think she actually saw what was in front of her. Her mind was definitely somewhere else.

"Spill it."

"I stopped by and saw Alton."

"And?"

"And he's going to help us."

David blew out a big breath. Somewhere in the back of his mind he'd hoped that maybe Alton would tell them to leave it alone. He was worried they might be stirring up history that was best left buried. "You take your Nancy Drew duties very seriously."

"Nancy Drew? Are you referring to the mystery books? How do you even know about those?"

"My nieces check them out from the library—not romances, as you suggested—but they do love a *gut* mystery. Come sit down and tell me what Alton said."

"I'm too excited to sit. Let's walk."

They wandered over to the pasture fence and continued down the path next to it. On the other side of the fence, a half-dozen Hereford cows grazed, their white faces turning occasionally toward their visitors.

"Well, Alton doesn't personally know who Mary or Peter are. He's only fifty, which is somewhat young for a bishop in my opinion."

"Ours in Virginia was closer to seventy," David admitted.

"Anyway, Alton said he would contact some of the older members and ask if anyone knew who Peter and Mary might be."

"That's nice of him."

"He seemed amused by the whole thing."

"Did he now?"

"I was relieved since my parents think we should leave it alone."

"Leave it alone?"

"*Ya*. To quote my *mamm*, 'I hate to see you living in the past.'"

"Ahh."

Faith reached over the fence to rub one of the calves between the ears. She glanced back at him. "I suppose you agree with her."

"Hey, I'm helping. Aren't I?"

Her expression softened. "*Ya*, you are."

When she smiled up at him, David felt the ground tilt. He actually looked down to see if he'd stepped on something or into a hole.

When he saw nothing unusual and looked back up at Faith, he experienced a sudden moment of clarity. He was falling for Faith Troyer. When had that happened? On the day of the picnic when they were under the kudzu vine? When he'd watched her wrap the injured Pebbles in her apron? While they poured over the letters written so many years ago that the pages were brittle?

He supposed the when didn't matter so much as the fact.

David pushed through his meandering thoughts and tried to think of anything to say. "If you have a minute, I'd love to show you what I'm working on."

She turned around and seemed to notice the three tiny buildings for the first time. "What are those?"

"Tiny houses."

"Those are the houses you build?"

"*Ya.* Why do you look so surprised?"

"Because I thought you built cabins."

"They're like cabins, only smaller."

"I'll say. They look like tiny garages, if an *Englisch* car would even fit in them, which I doubt."

"People live in these." He reached for the crook of her arm and guided her toward the closest house.

"What people?"

"People from all over. They're quite the popular thing at the moment."

"I can't imagine someone living in a home so small, and you actually enjoy building them?"

"I do. I still accept custom jobs for cabinetry work, but I don't have to go looking for business anymore. I'm making plenty doing this."

"Building miniature houses?"

"Yup. Sometimes I buy the frame complete, and other times I build it to a customer's specifications. Once the design is right, I finish out the inside. There are a lot of cabinets in them."

The wind had picked up as it was prone to do on March days. Faith held her *kapp* in place with one hand and used the other to keep her apron from flying up in her face. After they walked around all four sides of the house, Faith turned to him and shook her head. "I don't understand."

"What do you mean?"

"It's so small."

"*Ya,* they're tiny. Hence the name."

"Why would anyone want one?"

David tried to think of how to explain it to her. He'd learned long ago that many people didn't understand his work.

"Some *Englischers* are looking for ways to simplify their lives. They don't want to live in a large, three thousand square foot home anymore or pay the expensive utility and mortgage bills that come with a large house."

"I've never understood why *Englischers* live in such large homes when most of them only have two children."

"Exactly, but that has become the average size of new houses. And there are some *Englischers* who have four or five children."

"But not many have ten like we do."

"True. My point is that some are looking for ways to simplify and downsize."

"Downsize?"

"An *Englisch* term."

"Hmm."

"Their solution to overextending their credit is to sell what they're living in and purchase a tiny house." David hooked his thumbs under his suspenders as he looked over the three houses he was working on. The one they were standing next to was nearly finished, the next one was about 50 percent complete, and the third he'd barely started on.

Faith peered up at the structure.

He tried to see it from her perspective. It was small, though he'd become used to that. What he especially liked was the symmetry and the compactness of the projects. "They're very well designed with a lot of storage space, which is how I got started building them. At first, I was adding cabinetry in tiny houses that a company over in Middlebury made. Then I decided to try my hand at constructing my own."

"You build cabinets in there?"

"*Ya.* Storage is super important when you're living in a very small space." He urged her forward. "Take a look inside. They're nicer than you think."

"Oh . . . I don't think I can."

"Sure you can. Just peek inside."

He reached in front of her and opened the screen door. The main door was already open, blocking the light from the window at the end of the room. "Go on in. I'll close the door, and you'll see the nice set of windows I put in."

But as he followed her into the house, he noticed that she began to sway on her feet.

"Faith?"

"I-I can't." She clutched her stomach, her breath came out in quick gasps, and she dropped to her knees.

When David squatted on the floor beside her, he saw that her face was whiter than the bleached pine cabinets surrounding them.

"What's wrong?"

As soon as the words left his mouth, he knew what was wrong, and he knew that once more he'd managed to do exactly the wrong thing.

CHAPTER 6

David confessed the entire situation to his *bruder* later that night as they were completing their final check on the animals. Joseph was four years older and had run the family farm since their parents moved to Ohio to be closer to their *dat*'s parents. Their whole family was rather spread out with David's other brother living in Virginia.

Nathan had been the reason David moved to Virginia. His brother had already established a successful cabinetry business there, and David wanted to learn from the best. His *bruder* was one of the finest craftsmen he'd ever met.

David returned to Indiana because there was a large Amish population, plenty of folks—both *Englisch* and Amish—who would hire him to build cabinets and furniture and even tiny houses. In truth, he liked the area better than Virginia. It felt good to be back on his family's farm, and now his *bruder* was quickly filling their childhood home with *kinner*. They were up to six and had only been married five years.

"Faith passed out?" Joseph stared at him in disbelief.

"Pretty much. I mean, she never lost consciousness, but she wasn't really able to move. I practically had to carry her outside."

"And you think the tiny house caused it?"

"I guess. All she would say was that it felt like the walls were closing in and she couldn't breathe."

"Wow."

"Yeah."

"I wonder if she has trouble riding in buggies."

"Hadn't thought of that, though now that you mention it, hers seems to have extra windows in the back."

"Perhaps Alton allowed it—given that she's dealing with a medical condition and all."

They'd brushed down the horses, put away any tools that had been left out, and walked back outside the barn. David looked up at the stars. The small pinpoints of light calmed his soul. They gave him a feeling of being in a vast open space, but also of being in the palm of *Gotte*'s hand. He wasn't sure why that image popped into his mind.

Did Faith feel better when she was outside?

Did the stars give her a sense of safety?

How long had she been dealing with her condition?

"You care about her," Joseph said, plopping down in a rocker under the barn eave.

"She's a nice girl."

"*Nein.* I mean you care about her as more than a friend."

"I don't know about that."

"She's all you've talked about for the last week."

"Huh."

"*Bruder*, you are a little clueless in regard to girls and dating and your own feelings."

"And you're an expert?" It came out as more of a growl than a statement. He softened it with, "Guess that's what being married does to a man."

"I was never as clueless as you are." Joseph laughed and pushed

the chair to rocking. "You've always been very—what's the word—
focused on your work."

"I like what I do."

"And that's not a bad thing, but sometimes you don't pick up on
hints other people are sending out."

"I definitely didn't see any hints that Faith was going to melt
down, though now that you mention it . . ." He perched on the edge
of the other rocker. "She was a little hesitant to go inside."

"Aha."

"Don't look so pleased. Remember when your oldest lost his
front tooth, and it took you three days to notice?"

"*Ya*, well, this isn't about me."

"I just don't understand how it happens. I mean, if I'm going to
be Faith's . . . friend"—David chose to ignore his *bruder*'s smirk—"I
should probably know a little more about claustrophobia."

Joseph shrugged as he rubbed the palm of his hand up and
down the arm of the rocker. "Go to the library."

"The library?"

"Sure. They have these contraptions called computers."

"I know about computers. How do you think I learned about
tiny houses?"

"So . . . go learn about claustrophobia. That way you can help
your *friend*."

David didn't bother to answer, but Joseph's laughter followed
him as he walked to the main house and clomped up to his room.
Faith was his friend, and he wanted to help rather than hurt her. He
needed to go into town the next day for supplies anyway. It wouldn't
hurt to stop and do a little research at the library.

It didn't mean that what he felt for her was anything more than
a crush.

They were obviously mismatched. A person with claustrophobia dating a man who built tiny houses? Sounded like a plot for one of the romance books she'd mentioned. But his life wasn't anything like a romance book, and Faith . . . Well, he was pretty sure Faith didn't think about him in that way.

He would focus on being a good friend and not worry about where it might or might not lead.

* * *

Faith had just finished helping in the serving line when Bishop Alton walked over and asked if she had a minute to talk. The church service had gone well and the day was sunny. They were meeting at the Shrock's home, which was one of Faith's favorite places. The yard opened out over a lovely view of a pond. Already the children were playing down at the water's edge, closely monitored by older siblings.

She wiped her hands on a dish towel. "Of course." She was a bit alarmed when he turned and motioned for David to join them.

He must want to talk about the letters. She tried to temper her enthusiasm. He might only tell them he'd learned nothing at all. In which case, the letters would probably never be returned to their original owners.

They sat at one of the picnic tables, and her worries melted away. The bishop was smiling, and David looked relaxed. It must be good news.

"I have some answers for you." Bishop Alton wiggled his eyebrows. "I believe I've found the Mary and Peter from your letters."

"You have?" Faith immediately sat up straighter.

"So they're still alive?" David asked.

"Are they married?"

"Are they near here?"

Bishop Alton held up a hand to stop their questions. "Mary Fisher is a widow now. She's here in Shipshe, but in a different church district than ours. Back in 1970, when she was dating Peter Yutzy, her name was Glick."

"Mary Glick and Peter Yutzy." Faith shook her head. "I don't know either of them."

"No reason you would. It's unlikely that your paths would have ever crossed. Peter now lives in Middlebury."

"So they never married?" She tried to keep the disappointment from her voice, but it was difficult. She'd already envisioned them with a house full of *kinner* and *grandkinner*. But their last names were different, so it was obvious they hadn't married each other.

They'd so clearly been in love. What happened? How had it happened? And would they even want the letters now?

Bishop Alton pulled a sheet of paper from his pocket and slid it across the picnic table. "Here are numbers for the phone shacks closest to each of them, if you'd like to contact them."

David studied Faith for a moment, and then looked back at the bishop. "Do you think we should?"

He took his time answering. It was his way, Faith had learned. At times he took so long to reply she wondered if he'd even heard a question. But her *mamm* had explained that he was simply weighing his words, a habit they could all stand to practice more often.

Finally, Bishop Alton crossed his arms on the table and smiled at them. "*Gotte*'s ways are mysterious, yes?"

She and David both nodded.

"That package of letters was hidden beneath the kudzu vines

for a very long time." He studied Faith. "David says a stray dog ran into the vines, and that's why you went in."

"*Ya.*" She thought of the way Pebbles danced around her when she came home, how she already loved to chase after a ball, though she was more likely to fall on top of it than fetch it.

"Going into those vines must have been difficult for you. *Gotte* gave you a compassionate heart, Faith. You cared about that little dog more than your fear."

"It already feels like we've had Pebbles for years instead of weeks."

"You cared enough to go into a situation that might have otherwise scared you."

"It did scare me—a little. But not as much as I would expect." She'd wondered about that. Why hadn't she had a panic attack under the kudzu vines? But then, she'd been so intent on finding the dog.

"*Gotte* directed your paths—both of you." He looked at David and nodded. "I think it would be *gut* to see this through."

And with that, he stood, wished them a fine Sabbath, and went to speak to Mr. Shrock.

"I guess that means we have his blessing," Faith said.

"I guess it does."

"So, do you want to call them?"

"Sure. I can do that." David cleared his throat. "Hey, about what happened at my place—"

"We don't have to talk about that."

"I want to."

Faith thought she might die of embarrassment right then. She'd actually been trying to avoid David before the bishop called him over. Now, the way he was looking at her—waiting for her to say something—she wished she could melt into the ground.

But she couldn't, and perhaps she'd been running from who she was long enough. Instead of making an excuse and running away, she crossed her arms on the table and looked David in the eye.

"I had a panic attack, plain and simple. It was caused by my claustrophobia, which I'm learning to deal with. Certain situations can still bring on an attack though."

"I'm sorry," he said. "I didn't think about how being in a closed space might affect you—again. Call me a slow learner."

"A slow learner?"

"Seems to be that way."

"I think I remember you did well in school."

"School was easy compared to life."

That made her laugh, and then her embarrassment and defensiveness slipped away. David asked if she'd eaten, which she hadn't because she'd been too busy serving the food.

He waited for her to make herself a plate and sat with her while she enjoyed the delicious food.

When she finished, David asked her to walk around the pond.

It was a fine spring Sunday. The strong winds from earlier in the week had died down. All around them trees were budding, the grass was sprouting, and flowers were beginning to bloom. It was almost as if nature were agreeing with her mood. They had a real chance to return the letters to Mary and Peter. She wondered what it must have been like to love someone so much and then see him sent away because of a war.

Glancing at David, she wondered if he'd ever been in love. She'd certainly never felt that way about anyone. Oh, she'd had a crush on a guy before—John Hochstettler in fifth grade came to mind. And she'd been infatuated by a couple different men—most recently her neighbor's cousin who was visiting from Lancaster. But she'd never had the courage to do anything about those feelings. She'd never really wanted to do anything about them.

Had David ever seriously dated a woman?

She didn't ask. It wasn't really any of her business, and they weren't close in that way. She had a sense that they were fast becoming friends, and she was learning that he was a good man, not nearly as somber as she'd thought—perhaps before she'd only noticed him when he was frowning. Now he seemed to wear a smile often, at least when she was around, and the smile accentuated how handsome he was.

Yes, she'd like to be friends with David Lapp, and maybe— well, maybe she could dare to hope that one day they might mean even more to one another. But for now, she'd push those dreams away and focus on their friendship.

That felt good and right.

For now, they needed to put to bed the mystery of the lost letters.

CHAPTER 7

Faith's head was pounding, and the rocking of the buggy only agitated her already nauseous stomach.

"You okay?" David asked.

"*Ya*, just a little . . ." She wiggled her hand back and forth, but closed her eyes, trying to ward off the rising anxiety that threatened to overwhelm her.

"If you're worried about the storm, it isn't predicted to hit until tonight. I checked the forecasts at the library this morning."

Faith nodded, and then realized her bobbing head didn't convey much about how she was feeling. "My counselor says storms are disturbing to claustrophobics for two reasons."

"*Ya?*" David actually seemed interested. When he reached over and squeezed her hand, she jumped. She reminded herself that it was just a spring storm, and David was just a friend, and they were just in a buggy together. She really did need to calm down or she might hyperventilate.

"*Ya*, uh, two-fold. One, the visual aspect of the clouds pressing down."

David leaned forward to scan the sky. "I can see how they might appear that way."

"And two, the barometric pressure dropping might trigger a chemical reaction in my brain. There's a lot that doctors don't know about claustrophobia."

She thought he might not answer, even worried he might think her a child for being afraid of a mere spring storm. Instead, he smiled at her. "I'm glad you shared that with me. I'm sorry you have to deal with it, but if I know what's going on, maybe I can help."

She couldn't look at him. Tears sprang to her eyes, and she was horrified that she might actually cry. What was wrong with her? Why were her emotions pinging all over the place? Her counselor said when her emotions became overwhelming, she should close her eyes and picture something that she enjoyed.

Faith shut her eyes and thought of Pebbles . . . and that, the image of a beagle that was fast becoming a part of her family, calmed her racing heart.

She opened her eyes and looked out the buggy's window. She stared at the sky long enough to understand that the black clouds were still a good distance away. Why could she imagine them pressing up against the buggy? She scooted closer to her door, just in case. In case of what, she didn't really know, but she felt better near an exit.

David turned the horse down a rutted lane, slowing to minimize the rocking of the buggy.

"You're sure this is the place?"

"*Ya*. When I talked to Mary on the phone, she described it quite well."

The *daddi haus* came into view first. David parked near the front porch, set the brake, and jumped out to secure the mare to the hitching post. A woman Faith assumed to be Mary Glick, or rather

Mary Fisher, stood on the porch waiting for them. Faith hopped out of the buggy, her nausea temporarily relieved by the light breeze. She hadn't realized she'd broken into a sweat, but now she shivered slightly as she hurried toward the porch.

"I suppose you're the young man who called me." Mary looked for all the world like the typical Amish grandmother—starched white apron, gray dress, white *kapp* properly pinned in place.

Faith noticed a few wavy white strands peeking from the sides of the *kapp*. Mary was short, somewhat round, and lines stretched out from her eyes testifying to a generally happy disposition. At the moment, however, she looked worried.

"I'm still a little confused why you're here," Mary added.

Was this really the woman Peter had written such heartfelt letters to? It was hard to imagine her young and in love, with her entire life before her. That life was now long in the past. Faith had a moment of doubt, wondering if her parents were right. Perhaps she shouldn't have meddled.

But it was too late for such thoughts.

David was already explaining again about the letters.

"You said as much on the phone." Mary had sat down in one of the rockers, so Faith and David did the same. "I'm old but not senile. I can remember a conversation from earlier this morning. Lots of people named Mary live in the area. Tell me why you think I'm the Mary in the letters."

Faith glanced at David, and he nodded once, smiling, giving her the confidence to proceed.

"Did you once step out with someone named Peter?"

"That was many years ago."

"The letters we found were from a man named Peter to a girl named Mary."

347

"A girl who had a sycamore tree in her backyard," David added. "And a glider swing."

"I spent many an hour in that old swing."

"And Peter was sent to Ohio—"

"Because of the war." Mary clasped her hands in her lap. "*Ya*, perhaps you have found the Mary those letters were addressed to, but that person—that Mary? She doesn't exist anymore. And if I sound bitter, well, I don't mean to be. The war was a very difficult time for all of us. I'm not sure it's a thing your generation could understand."

For the briefest moment, Faith was able to see the young girl who had fallen in love during a tumultuous time. Two bright spots blossomed on Mary's cheeks, and her voice trembled slightly when she tried to speak. She took a moment to compose herself—staring out at the approaching storm. When she raised her eyes to study them, Faith had the sinking feeling that she'd already made up her mind. A hard resolve had come over her features.

"It's true that I once cared for a young man named Peter . . . Peter Yutzy. He broke my heart the summer of 1970." She raised a hand, spotted with age. "*Gotte* is my witness, though, He had another plan for me. I married a *gut* man—one I miss to this day. *Gotte* blessed us with nearly forty years. Together we raised a fine family. My oldest son lives there in the main house. All of the *kinner* are close by, and they take care of me. The *grandkinner* are the joy of my life. I have no desire to step into the long ago."

"We're sorry about the loss of your husband." David's voice was soft, respectful.

"I didn't lose him. He passed." Mary crossed her arms. "I never could abide that term. His life was complete, and I was there when he passed a dozen years ago . . . *Gotte* granted that I could hold his hand as he slipped from this life to the next."

"Mary, we don't mean to upset you in any way." Faith tried to swallow, but her mouth was too dry. She stared at the sky, at the still approaching clouds, and reminded herself it was only a spring storm and nothing to be afraid of. "It's only that we found the letters, and after David contacted you, he was also able to locate Peter."

Mary's head jerked up and her eyes widened. "Peter? He's alive?"

"He is and living over in Middlebury."

"He'd like to see you, Mary." David nodded toward his buggy. "He's home this afternoon. If you want, we'd be happy to take you."

Mary had been brusque since they arrived—a real no-nonsense kind of person. It seemed to Faith that a façade fell away, and she was now looking at a gentler version of the woman—one far less sure of herself. Her hand went to her *kapp*, smoothing it against her head. She stood, turned toward her front door, and Faith could just make out a whispered, "Foolish to care how I look at my age." She turned back toward them, shaking her head as if she couldn't believe what she was agreeing to.

"So you'll go?" Faith asked.

"Let me get my cane. Not that I'm interested in any romantic notions you *youngies* may have cooked up, but . . . My, I never thought Peter might be alive and living in the area. I never . . . I never checked."

Mary fetched her cane and a sweater, then walked to the main house and told her daughter-in-law she was off to see an old friend. Ten minutes later, they were back in the buggy and heading toward Peter Yutzy's home.

As the clouds continued bearing down on them, Faith tried to focus on the calming techniques she'd learned from her counselor—controlled breathing, imagining a bright sunny day, appreciating the solid feel of the leather seat beneath her. She even tried her muscle-relaxing exercises. When that didn't alleviate the knot in her stomach, she prayed and attempted to focus on Mary and Peter and David.

Her counselor had suggested that in these situations she focus on the fact that the frightening feelings would pass. It was true. A part of her mind accepted it was true. This time tomorrow she'd be able to laugh at herself.

But it wasn't funny now, and she certainly didn't feel like laughing.

How long would she have to deal with these attacks?

Why couldn't she be normal?

Why did her mind perceive a threat when there was none?

Thunder rolled and the tightness in her chest increased. If only she could get out of the buggy, she would be all right. She closed her eyes and prayed they would reach Peter's quickly.

. . .

Peter Yutzy stood in the door of his barn staring at David, Faith, and Mary. David had spoken with Peter on the phone, told him about the letters, and even received permission to visit. He supposed hearing a thing and experiencing it were quite different. At the moment, Peter seemed to be struggling to make sense of what Faith said, and David was worried the old guy might have a heart attack right then and there.

He didn't have a heart attack, though, and truth be known, he probably wasn't that old. Seventy, if David had done the math right.

"Mary, is it really you?"

Mary nodded, but didn't answer. She'd been quite stoic on the ride over, but now her armor seemed to have dropped. In its place was a woman staring into her past.

"Peter . . . I didn't know. I didn't know you settled here in Middlebury."

"And you're still in Shipshe?"

"*Ya.* Of course."

They didn't seem to know what else to say to one another. The sky had darkened and made it seem more like night than day. Faith kept glancing up behind her as if something might drop out of the storm and come after them.

"It's only a spring storm," David said, stepping closer to her and lowering his voice. "It's coming in faster than they predicted, but we're going to be just fine."

She nodded, but her posture—she was standing as straight and rigid as an ironing board—told David she was not all right. At that moment, a streak of lightning split the sky and thunder hammered even closer.

"Best get your buggy in my barn. It'll be a tight fit, but you won't want to leave the horse out in this."

David hurried out to retrieve the horse, then guided the buggy into the barn. As Peter had predicted, they barely fit. Peter's horse was in its stall—the only one in the small structure, and his buggy was positioned outside the door. The place was clean, efficient, and compact. Faith was staring at the ceiling, which was remarkably low for a barn, and clutching her arms around her middle.

"This must have been a garage that he converted," David whispered to her. "Are you okay?"

Faith nodded, closing her eyes, and swaying slightly.

"What do you mean I never answered?" Peter's voice rose with each word—troubled and full of emotion. "Of course I answered. I wrote you every day—"

"Until I asked you about marrying, and then you stopped."

"I did not," he stubbornly maintained. "I wrote you every single day until I received your letter telling me there was no point in writing any more, that you'd rather not hear from me."

"I only said that after an entire week of silence . . . the very week following my letter to you speaking of marriage." Mary looked around the barn in confusion, as if wondering how she'd come to be there. "I was a young, strong-willed thing. Why did I think it was my place to bring up marriage? You were so far away, and I was afraid. That's all. For a moment, I let fear rule my better sense. Scared you away, I'm sure."

"You did not."

"It's nothing to be ashamed of, Peter. You changed your mind. That was many years ago, and there's no need to discuss it now. We can't change the past."

"We might not be able to change the past, but we can understand it," David said as he accepted the packet of letters Faith pulled from her bag with trembling hands.

"These are the letters Faith and I found on the Pumpkinvine Trail."

"That's my handwriting." Peter's voice had dropped to a whisper.

"*Ya*, we believe these are letters you wrote. Apparently, the mailman dropped them. I haven't figure out that part for certain. We were on the Pumpkinvine Trail, and Faith's little dog took off into the brush—under some kudzu vines."

"We went in after her and were looking for the dog. The vine had created a cave of sorts." Faith swallowed, licked her lips, and continued. "We rescued Pebbles, and then as we were looking for our way out, we found the box. I suppose it has been there since 1970."

David added, "It took us some time to track down exactly who the letters belonged to."

"The writing is smeared." Mary had stepped closer. She reached out to run her fingers across the address.

"We couldn't make out much. As you can see, it's a real mess. The last name and address—they aren't readable at all." David looked toward Faith for confirmation, but she had backed away and was staring at the ceiling. "So we . . . Well, we had to read the letters. I'm sorry about that, as obviously, they were very personal."

David realized Mary and Peter weren't listening to him at all. They were staring at one another, and he somehow knew they had both stepped back in time to their younger selves and an earlier dream.

"We'll just let you two have a moment alone." David ducked away and turned to look for Faith, but she was gone. She couldn't be gone. The rain was coming down in torrents now, and the noise on the metal roof was deafening. There was no way she had stepped outside.

He found her on her knees at the other end of the barn under a corner window.

She had her arms clutched around her stomach and was curled in a ball, rocking back and forth, her eyes squeezed shut.

Immediately he thought back to the night at the carnival when he found her in a corner of the House of Mirrors. He thought of the afternoon he showed her the tiny house. In that moment, he understood. This was it. This was his chance to correct how he'd acted both of those times.

David thought of all he'd read and how he'd prepared for this moment in case it happened again, and then he petitioned God for guidance.

Squatting beside Faith, he placed a hand on each of her arms, touching her softly but firmly, and hoping she would look at him.

"Faith, you're going to be all right. I know you're scared, but I'm right here with you."

Tiny rivulets of sweat dripped down her face, and when he leaned closer, David realized her teeth were chattering. He waited, giving her time to collect her thoughts, and finally, she opened her eyes. But she only glanced at him a moment, not even seeing him it seemed.

"I need to go." She jumped to her feet, her gaze darting out the window and back, searching—no doubt—for an escape. "I need to get out of here."

"*Nein*. We need to stay put. I'm right here with you, and I'm not going to let anything happen."

She looked in his direction, and then her gaze darted away. Her breathing remained fast and shallow and her skin looked clammy. David had a glimpse of just how hard certain situations were for her, and his heart ached that she was so terrified. He realized he needed to earn her trust.

"I know you're frightened." Once again he put a hand lightly on each of her shoulders, hoping his touch would calm her. "Can you breathe with me? Match your breaths with mine. A little slower now—in, and out. That's *gut*."

The look of panic softened, though her teeth still chattered.

"Do you know what I'd like to do tomorrow?"

She looked at him as if he'd lost his mind.

"I'd like to take you for some more ice cream. We've solved the mystery of the letters. Peter and Mary—they're reading the letters now. I think we've earned a treat. Don't you?"

Faith nodded, as if she understood at least a little of what he was saying.

"Maybe we could try that mint chocolate you were ogling."

A small smile tugged at the corner of her lips—lips he longed to kiss. And then she did something he hadn't dared hope for. With a sigh, she stepped into his arms. She allowed him to hold her. David felt an emotion he hadn't known he could feel swell in his heart. He felt, for the first time in a very long time, that he'd come home.

He understood then that home wasn't a room in his *bruder*'s house. It wasn't a tiny house or a large one. Home was where the people you cared about most stayed.

Faith's breathing had calmed, and her teeth stopped chattering. David offered a prayer of thanksgiving that *Gotte* had put him in the right place at the right time to care for her when she needed it.

Standing there in that little barn with Mary and Peter on the other side, a horse and buggy between them, and a spring storm raging outside, David realized how important this moment was.

He cared deeply for Faith Troyer.

He loved her. He loved Faith Troyer, and he wanted to be by her side through beautiful spring days and stormy ones, through days of mystery and days of hard work, through the trials and the triumphs of life.

Gently holding his arms around her, he felt her trembling gradually lessen. Within fifteen minutes, the sky lightened, and the rain stopped.

Faith pulled back and looked up at him sheepishly. "I'm sorry." She took a step back. "That was . . . embarrassing."

"Please don't say that. Your condition is nothing to be embarrassed about."

"That's kind of you."

He stepped toward her, gently placed his fingers under her chin and raised her head so she was looking at him instead of staring at a spot on his shirt.

"I meant what I said."

"About?"

"Taking you for ice cream."

When she laughed, he did what he'd longed to do for some time now—he kissed her softly, breathing in the smell of powder and shampoo and flowers. He might have stood there another hour, kissing her and reveling in the wave of emotions that had beset him, but they heard laughter from the other side of the barn.

"Mary and Peter?" Faith asked.

"*Ya.*"

"I don't remember . . ."

"They were reading the letters. Let's go see how they're getting on."

• • •

CHAPTER 8

• • •

Faith's emotions felt like popcorn in a hot skillet. On the one hand, she was mortified that she'd had another full-blown panic attack in front of David. On the other hand, she was still tingling from his kiss. And below all of that ran his words, his assurance, that her condition was nothing to be ashamed of. She remembered the look in his eyes, the softness of his voice, and the tender way he'd held her.

Had all of that really happened?

She thought she might have imagined it, but now he reached for her hand, winked at her, and pulled her toward the other side of the barn where Mary and Peter were seated on a bench, the box of letters between them.

The last thing she remembered clearly—before the fog of her panic attack—was Mary fussing in the back seat, saying she certainly hadn't expected upon waking this morning to see Peter Yutzy that day. Mary had grown markedly more perturbed the longer they'd driven, but now her look of grimness had been replaced by something akin to joy.

She smiled up at them shyly and said, "I owe you two an apology. I wasn't very gracious when you came to see me and suggested visiting Peter."

"It must have been very hard," Faith said. "After all these years."

"We weren't sure if we were doing the right thing," David admitted. "We asked our parents, and they said we shouldn't get involved, that we shouldn't meddle in other people's lives."

Peter was shaking his head before David finished. "If you hadn't brought us these, if you hadn't cared enough to pick them up and read them and try to find their owners? Well, Mary and I might not have ever cleared up a misunderstanding that took place long ago."

"During the war," Faith whispered.

"*Ya.*" Mary looked up. "And I suppose we owe you two the whole story."

"Not here though. Let's move to the house now that the storm has stopped. I never married, so I'm an old bachelor who had to learn how to cook or depend on the mercy of widows." Peter laughed at himself. "I made cranberry bars this morning, and I'll fix us some hot tea."

Fifteen minutes later, they were gathered around the small kitchen table. Peter's home was even more plain than most Amish homes—probably owing to his status as a bachelor. Faith noticed a stack of *Budget* newspapers on a plain oak desk under the living room window. "Are you a scribe?"

"I am. Started in 1972, when I moved back to Shipshe. I was devastated to find that the love of my life had wed another—"

"We should start back at the beginning." Mary broke off a piece of the cranberry bar and popped it in her mouth. "These are *wunderbaar.*"

"I told you. I'm a *gut* cook."

"I didn't believe you."

"Probably because I didn't know how to boil water when we were dating."

Mary's smile grew, and it so lightened her expression, making her appear so much younger, that Faith marveled she was the same woman they had picked up just an hour ago.

"You've changed," Mary said to Peter.

"In some ways. In other ways, I'm the same boy who once loved you. I never admitted that in my letters, but I should have. I should have told you how I felt."

She nodded, plainly wanting to comment, but instead she dusted off her fingers and returned her attention to Faith and David.

"Peter and I had been dating a few months when he decided to file as a conscientious objector."

"It was that or go to war, and, well . . . I didn't see how I could go against my faith."

"My heart broke when they sent him away."

"To Ohio." Peter peered out the window. "That seems like so long ago now, and in another way, it seems like yesterday."

"We wrote each other every day but agreed to mail our letters just once a week. That way we'd have an entire week's worth of letters to look forward to."

"I wouldn't have made it through those first few months without Mary's letters. I was more homesick than a child visiting distant relatives for the first time."

"Our letters grew more . . . intimate, and I became quite bold."

"You always did speak your mind, Mary. I loved that about you."

"Finally in one of my letters, the last one of that week in early June, I asked Peter if he thought we might marry one day." She sipped her tea and then continued. "I was afraid he'd meet another woman in Ohio and forget all about Shipshe—and me."

"I never forgot you." Peter's voice was soft, the admission simple and heartfelt.

"When I didn't hear back from him the next week, I feared I'd overstepped."

"Remember, we swapped letters once a week." Peter tapped the bundle beside him on the table. "These letters you found were written at the same time that Mary asked me about marrying, which I had dreamed of but hadn't dared suggest."

"When I didn't receive a package that week, I couldn't imagine what had happened. At first, I thought the mail had been delayed, but then doubt took hold—fear took hold. For several days I worried and fretted. Worked myself up into quite a state. Obviously, I'd revealed my feelings too soon. I was mortified. Finally, after five days and no word, I wrote to him again."

"Uh-oh," David said as he reached for another cranberry bar.

"Exactly. I wasn't thinking straight. I was too embarrassed and too . . . Well, it sounds silly to say, but so heartbroken that my emotions were guiding my actions. You know how it is to be a *youngie*." She cocked her head and looked first at David and then Faith. It seemed she was about to say something, but instead she pinched the bridge of her nose and squeezed her eyes shut. "I wrote a single page, strongly worded letter, ending our relationship and telling Peter I'd rather not hear from him again."

"Because you didn't receive a letter for a week?" Faith was having trouble wrapping her mind around this. It seemed like such a simple misunderstanding. Why would Mary act so rashly if she'd really cared for Peter? "Any number of things could have happened to cause him not to write. Breaking off the relationship seems like an overreaction."

"Have you never overreacted? Had your feelings so sorely bruised that you were all emotion?"

Faith slowly nodded, remembering how she'd felt after her

original date with David. She stole a glance at him as he nodded slightly, and she knew—she was positively certain—he was remembering the same thing.

"It was childish, I admit. But I was certain he no longer cared for me."

"I didn't blame her. It was confusing—to receive the letter confessing her feelings followed so quickly by another saying she'd changed her mind. But I understood that Mary was young, and I was not a very confident young man. Honestly, I didn't know what she saw in me to start with."

"Your goodness, Peter. I saw your goodness."

They stared at each other for a moment, until David finished off his cranberry bar and asked the obvious question. "So what happened when you came back, Peter?"

"I stayed in Ohio for more than a year. That was where I was assigned due to filing as a conscientious objector. Farm work was better than serving overseas. I had no desire to be anywhere near a battlefield. When we were released from our assignment, the family I was staying with—"

"The Nicholsons." Faith could imagine the family and their hound dog barking at a rabbit hidden underneath a pot.

"*Ya*. They were *gut* people—Mennonites. We'd become friends of a sort, and I couldn't see my way to leave them in the middle of harvest season. So I stayed a few extra months. I was in no hurry to come home by that point. My *mamm* had written that Mary had published her intentions to wed Clyde."

"He was a *gut* man too." Mary's chin came up a fraction. "We shared thirty-seven years together. Had seven *kinner* and now thirty-two *grandkinner*."

"I'm glad, Mary." Peter folded his arms on the table and studied the little group in front of him. "Whenever I thought of you over the years, I prayed that you had known a happy life—a full one—and it sounds like you have."

"What about you, Peter? Why did you never marry?" Faith glimpsed light out the window, relieved to see the sun peeking through the clouds. The storm she'd suffered through, the one that had terrified her only minutes ago, had vanished. Like most spring storms, it was there and gone.

"Well, by the time I returned home, my parents had their hands full with the farm and my younger *bruder* . . . He was disabled and could be difficult to handle at times."

"Thomas." Mary pressed her hands to the table. "I'd forgotten about him. He was such a sweet child."

"His teenage years were difficult. He'd become frustrated because he couldn't do certain things. By the time he turned thirty, he had settled down some, but during his teenage years, I couldn't imagine marrying. Afterward it seemed too late. Not that I'm complaining. My life has been full and hard, but also *gut.*"

"What happened to Thomas?" Mary asked.

"Passed a year ago—cancer. He had a *gut* life, though. He was a *gut bruder.*"

They stayed a few more minutes. Then David admitted he needed to get home, and Mary said the *grandkinner* would be wondering about her. Faith was exhausted from the events of the afternoon.

They'd climbed into the buggy when Peter asked them to wait. He went back in the house and returned with a scrap of paper, handed it to Mary and said something too low for Faith to hear. But as David turned the buggy toward Shipshewana, Faith thought she heard Mary humming in the back seat.

* * *

David spent much of the evening thinking about all that had transpired. He wanted to give Faith space, but he didn't want to wait too long. He had no intention of letting her slip through his fingers a second time.

Mary and Peter's story held an important lesson—one he had needed to hear. A person's path in life could turn on the smallest decision. He'd made a mistake when he assumed Faith didn't care for him after the fiasco of their first date. He'd mistaken embarrassment for lack of feelings.

Everything had changed when they stepped beneath those kudzu vines, when they found the box hiding in plain sight.

Had *Gotte* directed their steps that day?

Had He been nudging them back onto the path they'd left several years ago?

The older couple's situation replayed in David's mind over the next few weeks. Peter had known that Mary cared, but he'd been so insecure that he'd readily believed she could stop caring. One phone call could have straightened out the entire thing. Instead, they allowed their fears to drive their actions.

He and Faith were no better.

They had let a misunderstanding build a wall between them, but now they could peek over the wall and see one another. The letters between Peter and Mary had brought them back together. *Gotte* had brought them back together, and now David dared to believe that Faith did care for him.

He hoped she did.

There was only one way to find out.

The next day, he left her a message at the phone shack, and the day after that he stopped by the animal clinic to see if she'd like to go to dinner with him Saturday. He didn't push—didn't rush their relationship. Instead, he thought of the long game. Over the next two months they grew closer, their friendship strengthened, and his feelings for her blossomed more than he could have possibly imagined.

By the time the summer days were at their longest, David knew it was time to step out in faith and act on his feelings.

He arranged to pick up Faith at four on the first Friday afternoon in June. He'd only worked half a day so he'd have time to prepare. He took the old push mower out behind his work area and mowed the grass between the tiny houses and the large elm tree. The shade would be perfect as the sun slanted west.

Joseph and his wife, Betty, had travelled back to Pennsylvania because her *mamm* was having surgery. David's mother had come to help with the children while they were gone. David walked into the kitchen, stared into the refrigerator, and then asked what type of food he should pack.

"Let me take care of that," his *mamm* said.

"That's not what I intended. You have enough work with the *kinner*."

"I do." His *mamm* stood and walked over to the kitchen counter where Betty kept her small but well-used collection of cookbooks. "But this is important. You've never taken a girl on a picnic, have you?"

"Only with the group."

"Group outings are fun, but I suspect you and Faith have moved past that now. In fact, I suspect you've fallen *in lieb*."

David sank into one of the kitchen chairs. "Is it that obvious?"

"To me it is, but then I've known you—"

"My whole life."

"For sure and certain."

"She's special, *Mamm*. I know we had a rocky start, but that was because I was young and foolish. My pride was hurt after she refused to talk to me, after the House of Mirrors." He'd been fiddling with a piece of junk mail—a postcard of sorts announcing a sale at the Fabric Bin. He looked down and saw that he'd torn it into tiny pieces. "Oh, sorry."

"Not a problem, dear."

"I look back on our first date, and I can't believe how naïve I was. And stupid! I never even stopped to wonder why she might react the way she did."

"You were both young then, and you're both older now—more mature."

He ran his fingers through his hair. "I noticed a gray hair or two this morning."

"Well, you know what they say about that . . . It's the beginning of wisdom. Go do whatever you need to, and I'll take care of your picnic dinner."

True to her word, his *mamm* had a full basket waiting when he returned to the house. The thing weighed a ton. Had she packed enough for a family of six?

"Why's this so heavy?"

"I put in two quart jars of tea—one sweetened, one unsweetened. Plus dishes and lots of food."

"*Danki*." He kissed her on top of the head, hoisted the basket in one hand and the faded quilt she'd put on top of it in the other. Faith mentioned once how much she liked flowers, so David picked a few sunflowers and stuck them in an old Coke bottle he'd filled with water. He wedged it between the basket and blanket in the back seat of the buggy, hoping it wouldn't tip over.

Hoping there wouldn't be an emergency at the vet that would cause her to cancel.

Hoping he'd have the courage to tell her how he felt.

CHAPTER 9

Faith wished David had told her where they were going, but he'd only smiled and said he had planned a special outing.

Then he told her not to dress too fancy.

Which could mean any number of things.

Maybe he was taking her fishing or . . . Her mind stalled. She couldn't think why she was supposed to dress plain. Besides, all of her clothes were plain. She was Amish. She picked an older dress that had begun to fade. For some reason, she liked it even better now—the color had started out as a royal blue but was now faded to robin's egg. It reminded her that sometimes age could be a good thing.

Fortunately, her parents had gone to town to run errands, so she didn't have to endure a hundred questions. Not that her *mamm* would have asked that many, but the ones she did ask would have been pointed. She'd been dropping even more hints lately.

Reminding Faith that fall weddings were perfectly acceptable.

Leaving letters lying around from her Ohio cousins—twins who were only twenty-two and had both married recently.

She'd even gone so far as to leave the family Bible open to Corinthians 13. As if Faith needed to be reminded what the Bible said about love and marriage.

Faith respected and admired her parents, but she did not think they understood how it felt to walk in her shoes. How could they? Her parents had married a few months before they turned twenty. At twenty-five, it was no wonder Faith seemed like a spinster to them.

She pulled in a deep breath and let it out slowly.

Tonight wasn't about her parents' expectations. It was about relaxing and having a good time with David, something she now looked forward to at the end of each work week. She often thought about Mary and Peter, about the love they'd denied and then found again. Few people received second chances like that. Faith believed the letters came into their lives to remind them how valuable time is and how opportunities to care for someone, to really connect, should not be squandered.

She was waiting on the porch when David pulled up in his buggy.

As David climbed out of the buggy, Pebbles bounded over to them.

"The beast is growing."

"That she is."

"Is your *mamm* still insisting you keep her outside?"

"She's softening. I smuggled Pebbles into the mudroom during the storm last week. *Mamm* knew, but she didn't say anything."

He walked with her to the barn, where she put Pebbles back in her stall. "I'm afraid she'll follow us if I don't."

Somewhere between the barn and the buggy, David reached for her hand.

"You look pretty today."

"I do?" She realized after she said it that she sounded as if she were fishing for more compliments. Cheeks burning, she added, "I mean, *danki*."

Faith hopped up into the buggy, but instead of closing the door, David leaned in and kissed her softly on the lips.

Whoa! This was new. They'd shared a few parting kisses over the last month, but they'd never kissed at the beginning of a date. The sparkle in David's eyes told her tonight was going to be different.

"Where are we going?" she asked once they were on the road.

"I thought I'd take you on a picnic dinner."

"*Ya?*" She turned and looked into the back seat. "Looks like your *mamm* packed us a basket."

"Now how you do you know I didn't pack that basket?"

"Ummm . . . I don't. It was a guess."

"And a *gut* one. *Mamm* did pack the basket, which means the food should be *wunderbaar*." David reached across the seat and squeezed her hand. "I did pick the flowers myself."

"Did you? They're beautiful. I've never had a picnic with flowers. Mostly we have picnics with my nieces and nephews, which involve a lot of toys."

They fell into an easy rhythm—talking of their week, their families, and even Mary and Peter.

"I heard they told the bishop they plan to marry." Faith noticed the crops in the fields. Soon it would be time for another fall harvest and then winter again. She wasn't sure why that thought sent her mood plummeting.

David's voice brought her back to the present, to the bright and sunny summer day. "It's *gut*, Faith—that they found each other again. That we solved the mystery of the letters. I think in some small way, *Gotte* used us to bring them back together."

And suddenly she wasn't worried about winter anymore.

She was determined to enjoy this evening and get out of her

head. That's what her therapist had said at her last visit. "Sometimes it's good to get out of your own head, stop the thoughts that are circling around, and enjoy the moment."

She'd no sooner made that decision, than David directed the horse to turn into the back of his *bruder*'s property.

"We're going to your workshop?"

"*Ya.*"

"Oh."

If he noticed her disappointment, he didn't respond to it. She'd visited his *bruder*'s house many times, met his *mamm*, and spent several evenings playing games with his nieces and nephews. But the last time she visited his workshop was when she had the panic attack in his tiny house.

Fortunately, he drove toward the far side of the property and stopped the mare near the shade of a giant elm tree. The grass was freshly mowed, and she helped him spread the quilt over the ground.

"This is nice," she admitted, once they were sitting with the basket open, food spread around them, and the yellow sunflowers propped up next to the basket. David's *mamm* had packed freshly sliced ham, homemade bread, potato salad, fruit, and peanut butter cookies.

"I'm glad you like it."

"And the food is *gut*."

"*Mamm* knows how to pack a picnic. I don't know about your parents, but mine are dropping hints left and right."

"Yours too?"

"*Mamm* would have made ten picnic baskets if she thought it would help move our courting along."

Faith wanted to be morbidly embarrassed, but she wasn't.

It was too funny when she stopped to think about it.

David laughed, and then she started laughing, and in that moment she understood what the counselor meant about getting out of her head. Sometimes voicing the thoughts she was struggling with stopped the power they held over her.

She told David about her *mamm* and the talk of fall weddings, the letters from her cousins filled with wedding details, and the family Bible left conspicuously open to Corinthians. By the time she was finished, they were lying on their backs staring up at a clear blue sky and holding hands.

David sat up. "I want to show you something."

"Ya?"

"But you have to stand up." He pulled her to her feet.

When Faith realized they were walking toward the tiny houses he built, her heart sank. She must have pulled back, because David turned and put his hands on her shoulders.

"It's going to be okay. If you start feeling an attack, just squeeze my hand and we'll go back to the blanket. Okay?"

"Okay."

He stepped closer, kissed her lips softly, then turned back toward the small houses.

She was proud of his work, but what if she had another panic attack? She didn't want to ruin their evening together.

Faith felt torn in that moment between the woman she was and the woman she wanted to be. She could accept her condition, and she knew David could too. What was holding her back? Fear that the evening would turn into a disaster? Or fear that she was stepping into a new phase of her life? As they walked toward the tiny houses, she felt like they were walking toward their future.

"I'm working on three different houses right now, but this one at the end is the one I wanted to show you."

"It wasn't here before."

"Nope. It's a new model. I modified the design myself. I think you're going to like it."

They stood outside the small building for a moment. There was something different about this one, but she couldn't put her finger on it. David pulled her toward the steps.

"Let me just get the door first."

He opened the screen and slid the front door into a pocket in the wall.

"That's different."

"The inset makes it easier to leave the door open and lets in more light. I want this to be a surprise, though."

"A surprise?"

"Close your eyes."

"Close them?"

"Just for a minute."

He reached for her hand, his eyes on hers, and Faith understood in that moment that she could either choose to be scared or choose to trust him.

She was tired of being scared.

• • •

David knew Faith was struggling, and he understood when she put her hand in his and stepped up into the tiny house that she was offering him a very precious thing—her trust.

"Just a few more steps. Wait. Okay. This is it. You can open your eyes."

She stood in the middle of the room, blinking and turning in a circle, taking in all the work he'd done.

She walked to the wall of windows, put her fingers against the screen, then looked up at the skylight.

"David, this is . . . It's amazing."

"You like it?"

"It's so roomy and open."

"You gave me the idea. The last time, when you had your attack . . ." He noticed that she winced at the reminder. "Your condition isn't something to be ashamed of, Faith. In this case, it helped me think of a completely different idea from what I've designed before."

"I don't understand."

"There must be other people who struggle with claustrophobia."

"Five to seven percent of people do, according to my counselor."

"Okay, there you go. Five to seven percent. I've been reading up on the subject and coping methods that help alleviate attacks. Just think, five to seven percent of people deal with the same problems you deal with, and some of those people would probably like to live in or at least stay in a tiny house, but they can't because small spaces make them feel . . ."

"Closed in."

"Exactly. So I designed the windows to roll out."

"Which gives the room a much more open feel."

"And I put all the windows on one side, so no matter where you stand in here you still have a good view, an open view. It increases the perception of space."

"There's still enough storage?"

"Sure. I put the drawers and cabinets all on this side." He tapped the kitchen counter. "And by building in a window seat over there, I was able to add storage underneath."

"'Storage is important in a tiny house.'" She quoted his words back to him, smiling as she said them. "The skylight is amazing. David, this entire house is *wunderbaar*."

He twined his fingers with hers and tugged her toward the window seat. They were able to look out over the freshly mowed lawn. The quilt with leftovers of their dinner was right across from them. David could even see the Coke bottle filled with sunflowers—something that seemed silly when he'd done it, but they seemed to lift her spirits immediately. He realized once again what he'd known for a long time. He wanted to spend his life making Faith smile.

He studied her for any signs of panic, but she seemed comfortable. "Do you feel okay?"

"I do. I'm rather surprised, but . . . I'm okay."

"No racing heart?"

"Nein."

He looked down at her hand, rubbing his thumb along her palm. "No sweating palms?"

"No sweating palms."

Then he touched her face. "No tunnel vision?"

She blushed a pretty pink. "My vision is fine. *Danki.*"

"Looking out this window, doesn't it seem like you can see forever? Like we could see our tomorrows?"

Instead of answering, she squeezed his hand.

"Will you marry me, Faith?"

She turned around so quickly she almost bumped into him. "What?"

"Marry me. I want to build a house for you. Not a tiny house, but a house like this—with large windows and plenty of light. A house where you will feel comfortable. A house where our *kinner* can grow up and we can grow old together."

"Wow."

"Is that a yes?"

He waited then, giving her time to gather her thoughts.

"Do you love me, David?"

"More than I thought was possible. More than I've ever loved anyone." Tears clouded his vision, and he wanted to kiss her again. Instead, he studied her and waited.

Touching his face with her fingertips, she whispered. "I love you, too, and yes. Yes, I'll marry you, and I'll have your *boppli*, and I'll live wherever you want to."

He took her in his arms then, and Faith relaxed—truly relaxed— for the first time in a very long time.

"You're sure I won't . . . be too much of a burden?"

"You are no burden at all." He kissed the top of her head and then pulled away enough that he could look her in the eyes. "You do understand that you're perfectly made, right? That *Gotte* didn't make a mistake with you? You're not broken. Faith, you may be different, but there's nothing wrong with you, and in my eyes—the things that make you different also make you special."

Faith realized those were the words she'd needed to hear. David wasn't trying to fix her. He wasn't offering to marry her in spite of her problems. He was simply accepting her as she was. He loved her as she was.

What more could she possibly ask for?

Suddenly a fall wedding didn't sound like such a bad idea.

ACKNOWLEDGMENTS

This book is dedicated to Dorothy Hollister, a member of our fabulous Friday Morning Prayer Group. I mentioned to the group that I had a story to write, and all I knew was that it was Amish and involved a picnic. Dorothy asked if I'd ever heard of kudzu vine . . . and the story flowed from there. Thank you for the help, Dorothy. I'm so glad you're a part of our group.

Thanks also to my pre-readers Kristy and Janet, without whom I have threatened to change careers. I need you both! You ladies are quick, thorough, and relentless in your edits. Thank you. Gratitude also to my agent Steve Laube, my editor Kimberly Carlton, and all the awesome folks at HarperCollins Christian Publishing.

Kudzu vine is prevalent throughout the southeastern United States and has been spotted as far north as Pulaski County, Illinois. Forgive my audacity for introducing it (even fictionally) to northern Indiana. It made for a fun story.

If you happen to be passing through northern Indiana, I encourage you to take a few hours to visit the Amish communities of Shipshewana, Goshen, and Middlebury—located just south of Interstate 90. They are truly a haven of rest in a very busy world.

And finally . . . *"always giving thanks to God the Father for everything, in the name of our Lord Jesus Christ"* (Ephesians 5:20).

DISCUSSION QUESTIONS

1. At the beginning of this story Faith and David find a box of letters. Faith realizes that while she sometimes wishes the Amish weren't so old-fashioned, she's glad they still practice writing to one another. Do you remember receiving letters in the mail? How did it make you feel?
2. Faith admits to herself that she is more comfortable around animals than people. Do you know anyone like this? What do you think is the best way to relate to someone who is inherently shy or introverted?
3. Peter finds comfort in the book of Job. Have you read it lately? Read chapter thirty-eight. How does this scripture make you feel? How does it speak to the omnipotence of God?
4. When David is looking up at the stars, he feels like he is in the palm of God's hand. Does nature bring you closer to God, and if so, how?
5. David reminds Faith that she is perfectly made by God. Sometimes it's hard to wrap our minds around that. What Bible verses can you think of that tell us God has designed us perfectly and wants the very best for us?

CELEBRATE LOVE, JOY, AND THE HOLIDAY SEASON WITH FOUR DELICIOUS STORIES.

ABOUT THE AUTHORS

AMY CLIPSTON

Photo by Dan Davis Photography

Amy Clipston is the award-winning and bestselling author of the Kauffman Amish Bakery, Hearts of Lancaster Grand Hotel, Amish Heirloom, Amish Homestead, and Amish Marketplace series. Her novels have hit multiple bestseller lists including CBD, CBA, and ECPA. Amy holds a degree in communication from Virginia Wesleyan University and works full-time for the City of Charlotte, NC. Amy lives in North Carolina with her husband, two sons, and four spoiled rotten cats.

Visit her online at AmyClipston.com
Facebook: AmyClipstonBooks
Twitter: @AmyClipston
Instagram: @amy_clipston

KELLY IRVIN

Photo by Tim Irvin

Kelly Irvin is the bestselling author of the Every Amish Season and Amish of Bee County series. Her novel *Upon a Spring Breeze* was the Reader's Choice Award for long romances. *The Beekeeper's Son* received a starred review from *Publishers Weekly*, who called it a "beautifully woven masterpiece." The two-time Carol Award finalist is a former newspaper reporter and retired public relations professional. Kelly lives in Texas with her husband, photographer Tim Irvin. They have two children, three grandchildren, and two cats. In her spare time, she likes to read books by her favorite authors.

Visit her online at KellyIrvin.com
Facebook: Kelly.Irvin.Author
Twitter: @Kelly_S_Irvin
Instagram: kelly_irvin

KATHLEEN FULLER

 With over a million copies sold, Kathleen Fuller is the author of several bestselling novels, including the Hearts of Middlefield novels, the Middlefield Family novels, the Amish of Birch Creek series, and the Amish Letters series as well as a middle-grade Amish series, the Mysteries of Middlefield.

Visit her online at KathleenFuller.com
Facebook: WriterKathleenFuller
Twitter: @TheKatJam
Instagram: kf_booksandhooks

VANNETTA CHAPMAN

Vannetta Chapman writes inspirational fiction full of grace. She is the author of thirty-two novels, including the Pebble Creek Amish series, the Shipshewana Amish Mystery series, and *Anna's Healing*, a 2016 Christy Award finalist. Vannetta is a Carol Award winner and has also received more than two dozen awards from Romance Writers of America chapter groups. She was a teacher for fifteen years and currently resides in the Texas hill country.

Visit her online at VannettaChapman.com
Facebook: VannettaChapmanBooks
Twitter: @VannettaChapman